Her Desperate Request

Nora Kensington

Published by Nora Kensington, 2024.

For permission requests, please contact the publisher at: nora.kensington.author@gmail.com

PROLOGUE

KATE

PRESENT DAY

It's still cold. Always cold. Every day. Every night. It's always the same thing. The sun never seems to rise when I need it most, along with its warmth.

And even now, as I watch people walk across the hospital courtyard from my window, I feel a chill, a kind of cold loneliness that consumes me inside and spreads through every cell in my body.

Visitors talk and joke with their relatives: fathers, mothers, siblings, children, nephews, friends. I notice a few hugs exchanged, some smiles of hope. Hope that better days will come.

It's been ten days since I've been here. Or twelve. I'm not exactly sure. I think I lost track of time at some point, as the hours pass. My mother hasn't come to visit me. She almost never does, not even during the other times I've been hospitalized.

I don't think she's ever forgiven me for what happened when I was still very young, and she added that grudge to the decision I made months ago when the world collapsed on my shoulders, and I had to take a stand on something that would change the course of my entire life.

It's a shame that things are this way. I love her so much. I wish she understood and respected my choices, that she would try to leave the past behind and help me move forward without carrying so much guilt in my heart. I was innocent, almost a child. But I carry and nurture this guilt, even though it doesn't belong to me, every time I see the sadness and bitterness in my mother's eyes.

With great effort, I take a deep breath and exhale, trying to push away memories that overwhelm me. Memories that are embedded deep within my chest and etched into my mind.

I close my eyelids for a few moments, overwhelmed by the anguish that takes over me, and step away from the window. Instinctively, I place my hands on my hips. It's been a few hours now that the pain in the area has been constant, along with an annoying cramp that comes and goes at considerable intervals.

I slide my hands over the bulge in my stomach and feel it hard and contracted. I open my eyes again, fear invading me like a cold, dark fog, knowing what's about to happen.

With trembling legs, I lean forward and steady myself against the cold wall, slightly bent. The position alleviates the pain in my lower back, allowing me to release the breath I had been holding. But the relief is as fleeting and quick as smoke dissolving into the air.

"Breathe, Kate. Breathe!"

I try to stay calm, searching for the last bit of strength I have left to bring the baby into the world.

If I let the pain take over and make any noise, the psychiatric hospital nurses will know what's happening. They'll take me to the maternity ward, call my mother, and after the baby is born, he'll be handed over to a social worker, so she can carry out the legal procedures for a possible adoption without me having any time with the child.

I just want a little more time with him, despite all the pain it causes me. Despite all the wounds I carry in my soul and body. I felt him grow inside me, I felt him move in the early mornings while I was alone.

I love him. But I won't be able to keep him.

The contractions increase gradually, and the time between them is lost in minutes, until they become just sixty seconds.

The mucus plug came out a few hours ago. I realized this when I went to the bathroom, just before the cramps got so strong. The moment is approaching. The child is about to be born. Oh God, help me.

I step away from the wall when the contraction subsides, using the brief time to remove the lower part of my hospital gown and squat on the floor. I use the bed to support my back and place my hand between my legs to try to determine how far along the dilation is. The unusual position alleviates the discomfort caused by the contractions, but panic takes over when I feel the vaginal dilation is quite advanced. The time between contractions shortens even more, the pain is intense, my body is exhausted.

Despite the cold outside, sweat runs down my face and neck, soaking the top of my gown. It's a loose green shirt, so long that it covers my entire belly.

A few minutes pass as I inhale and exhale. I feel a thick, warm liquid trickle onto the floor and I'm fully aware that my water has just broken. The floor turns into a mess, becoming slippery and dangerous. The pain intensifies, and the intervals are now almost nonexistent, prompting my body to push harder to expel the baby.

Tears of pain mix with the sweat that covers my skin, but still, I search for strength to hold on until it's over.

The successive contractions take my breath away and I bite my lips to keep from screaming. It feels like I'm going to be split in half at any moment as the pressure in my pelvis grows stronger. Grunts of suffering escape my lips and I place my hand between my legs again. The baby's head is crowning. I can feel the soft hair in my fingers. I can feel the thread of life vibrating from the child to me.

I lose all breath when another strong contraction hits, forcing me to push. And that's what I do, following my body's natural instinct to bring the child into the world. I bite my lower lip and dig my fingers into the bed behind me as I push for the baby to be born. My entire body shakes from the effort, my legs go weak, and sweat mixes with tears of pure desperation and frustration. The contraction eases a bit and I take a breath, feeling so weak that I fear I might lose consciousness.

In a few seconds, the contraction returns, accompanied by an uncontrollable urge to push. The pressure and burning in my birth canal are so intense that I let out an agonized scream. I don't even realize when the door opens and a few people enter the room. Two nurses kneel in front of me. I hear voices around me, firm hands holding my shoulders.

I push again, grunting with pain and anguish, almost out of breath. And then... a sharp cry echoes through the room, and I nearly collapse on the floor when the baby is finally born.

But then, panic brings all my senses to the surface, and I force my body to rise.

The baby... they're going to take him...

I quickly notice one of the nurses cutting the umbilical cord and the other standing up with my baby in her arms.

I extend my hand toward the woman, my limbs trembling and weak.

"The baby... please... give me the baby," I plead desperately, aimless, my chest aching.

The woman nods at me and approaches where I am. Still kneeling on the floor, I hold the baby with the help of the nurse, and more tears rise to the surface.

It's a girl. Oh God. It's a girl. The most full-haired baby I've ever seen in my life. So small... so innocent.

I touch the tiny fingers of her hand, feeling her soft skin, hearing the sharp cry. Everything inside me hurts, especially my heart.

Her nose is so small and turned up, her little mouth rosy, shaped like a heart. Her features so angelic... I try my best to commit every little part of her to memory, the texture of her skin.

"I need to clean the baby and warm her up, Kate. Patty and Julian will take care of you."

I hear the woman, but I can't pull my hands away from the little girl. My shoulders shake with the sobs that take over me, but I try to control myself and lift my head toward the woman.

"Please, bring her back to me," I beg, my vision blurred by tears.

"Your mother and the social worker are on their way, dear..." Her voice sounds sad, regretful. Her gaze meets mine, wary. "It's better if you don't get too attached..."

"Please, Emma... please..."

The woman carefully holds the baby, and slowly removes my hands that are still around the baby's tiny body.

"I'll see what I can do. But I can't promise anything, Kate. You know well your mother's orders."

My shoulders tremble from my sobs as I watch Emma move away with my daughter.

"Emma, please..." I shout her name, completely shaken, my heart filled with anguish. "Emma!"

The door closes behind her, and the two disappear from my sight.

I try to stand, but firm hands grip my arms. Only now do I notice that Julian is also here, along with Patty.

"It's going to be okay, Kate. Stay calm," he says, as he lifts me from the floor with Patty's help and sits me on the bed. "We'll take care of you now."

"My daughter... please..." My voice comes out weak, the words incoherent.

I try to stand at all costs to go after Emma. I struggle as they hold me firmly on the bed.

"Please..." I beg. "I want to see her again..."

"The baby is in good hands, Kate. Don't worry." It's Patty's voice now.

Her gentle hands hold my face, making me look at her, and she moves a strand of hair from my eyes.

"It's going to be okay, dear... Do you trust me?"

Do I trust her? I'm not sure. I don't think I trust anyone in here or anywhere else.

"Will Emma bring the baby?" I cling to the last drop of hope.

"Yes, of course... of course."

In my despair, in my distress, I don't notice what's going on around me. It's too late when I feel the sting in the muscle of my arm.

"Julian... no! Why did you do this? No!"

I turn toward the man who just injected a sedative into my arm. It feels like I've just been stabbed in the back, and the pain is so intense that I can't breathe.

I know the effects well. In a few minutes, I'll be so sleepy that I won't even remember who I am. With a little more time, I'll be completely knocked out.

"You... lied to me."

Another tear slides down my cheek, and the salty drop splashes onto what's left of my bloodstained clothes. I lower my head and stare at my trembling hands, the pale skin of my arms.

"I'm sorry, Kate..."

Julian's voice is whispered.

I don't move when I feel his hands on my shoulders, guiding me to lie down on the cold bed. I don't fight anymore; there's no point in fighting. The battle is lost now.

The next minutes pass slowly as Patty and Julian take care of cleaning my body and changing my bloodstained clothes. And then, everything fades into oblivion, and I fall into a deep, treacherous sleep.

CHAPTER 1

KATE

YEARS AGO

I turn from side to side in bed, hugging the blanket, trying to get more comfortable. I can't fall asleep because I hear the soft sobs coming from the living room, and the sounds torment my heart. It's my mother. She's been crying for some time, but she didn't want to tell me why.

When I asked earlier why she was so sad, mom just replied that when I grew up, I would understand the struggles of adults, and then told me to lie down and sleep.

At some point, I realize she's talking to someone on the phone. The conversation is whispered, so I can't make out the details. When she ends the call a few minutes later, I continue hearing her sobs for a while, and only then do I notice the sound of a car approaching our small house here in San Diego.

I hear my mother's movements on the floor as a horn honks, followed by the sound of the front door opening and then closing. I know I shouldn't care about this and should just stay in bed until I fall asleep, but my curiosity gets the best of me, and I push the comforter aside. I walk carefully to the bedroom window to avoid making noise and wait for my mother to cross the short path from the front yard to the gates that separate our house from the street.

Even with the faint light, I can see a familiar truck parked right in front of the gate, and a man steps out of the vehicle.

I recognize him immediately: it's Garath, a friend of my mother's. I always saw him around here, and my mom used to go out with him at night. However, it's been many days since he's been around, and from the way my mother throws herself into his arms, I can imagine how much she missed him.

I step back from the window as the two talk, and I lie back down in bed. A few minutes later, I hear the sound of the door opening, and their quiet conversation reaches me. This is the first time my mother has allowed Garath to enter our house, and it leaves me momentarily scared.

The minutes pass slowly as they speak in low voices, their movements now coming from the kitchen. Little by little, I begin to relax and eventually fall asleep.

At some point during the night, I wake up to strange noises coming through the wall that separates my room from my mother's. It's like something is banging against the wall. My heart races with fear, but I stay still, only pulling the comforter over my shoulders and neck to cover myself better.

I hear murmurs and confused moans, and only then do I remember that Garath is here with my mom. I just don't understand why there's noise against the wall or why they're moaning so much while whispering things to each other. It's hard to understand adult matters, nothing really makes sense.

After some time, everything becomes silent again. There are no more sounds against the wall, and I no longer hear either of their voices.

I take a quiet breath and fall back to sleep.

KATE

PRESENT DAY

THE DAYS ARE GRAY NOW. Everything seems the same to me when I look at the things around me. The sun doesn't seem to shine at noon, the moon doesn't appear at nightfall. I'm so lost...

I watch my trembling hands as I bring my fingers to the keyboard. I stay still for a few moments, looking at the words I wrote some time ago: *The thousand pieces of a broken heart.* Only then do I start typing again, and little by little, the text fills the screen.

Writing was the best way I found to try to ease the pain in my heart, after everything that happened in the psychiatric hospital. It is through the screen of a computer that I materialize the longing, sadness, and helplessness that I felt and still feel. These are moments of venting between me and the machine, where I recount the anguish of losing a daughter and having to keep waking up every morning.

The book still doesn't have an official title. I just write one chapter after another and that's how I occupy my days.

I spend hours this way, until I feel my legs go numb, and I decide to walk a bit in the backyard to clear my mind and get my blood circulating.

It's almost 4 p.m.; in less than two hours, my mom will be back home after work. Our relationship remains as cold as ever. We barely speak, but we don't mistreat each other either. Despite everything, I understand the reason why my mom decided I shouldn't keep the baby.

I'm still not well mentally. There are nights when I can't close my eyes, my hands sweat, and my heart feels like it's about to leap out of my chest. The panic attacks are constant, and our financial situation is not the best. My mom earns just enough to pay the bills, including the health insurance. Food is sometimes scarce, but we manage as best we can. Honestly, there wasn't much of an alternative for me and that little girl to stay together, no matter how much I wanted it.

Sighing, I get up from the chair and walk away from the worn table that holds the old computer. It is at this moment that I hear the sound of the landline phone ringing, and I stop where I am. My heart races to alarming levels, sweat breaks out on my forehead, and my hands turn cold.

I always feel this way whenever the phone rings or the doorbell is pressed. I can't explain it; it's like my body suffers in advance at the possibility of bad news reaching me. There's also the fear and dread that it might be Angelina, the friend I betrayed when we lived in a convent in the mountains north of New York.

Since everything happened, I haven't been able to talk to her or look her in the eyes. I chose to run away and cowardly hide, just like I've always done: I'm a coward who does everything to avoid facing problems.

I'm not proud of anything. I'm not proud of abandoning Angelina without even attempting to make amends with an apology. I'm not proud of who I am or who I've become, and that's why hearing her voice is so difficult. Talking to her is like reliving everything hundreds of times. It hurts my soul.

Finally, the call ends while I remain frozen in place, my thoughts drifting into a haze.

Without thinking much, I head towards the back door to the yard, and I exhale the air that was trapped in my lungs. I place my hand on my chest and gently massage it, looking at some pots with dry plants abandoned in a corner of the yard.

The cool wind touches my face, bringing the calming scent of the sea breeze to me. The weather is pleasant out here. The beaches are probably packed with tourists now, enjoying the Californian heat.

I walk a little, analyzing the decay of everything. From the neglected backyard to my life, which still has no direction.

More dry plants are piled up in another corner, fallen on top of one another, some with stems already rotting and broken on the ground. I can't even remember the last time I watered any of them. And my mom, well, she never has time.

Tired of everything, I decide to go back inside and start writing again. I pass by the phone on the kitchen counter and notice the little red light blinking, indicating a new unheard voicemail message.

I think about ignoring it, like I always do, but at the same time, I'm so tired of everything. Tired of running away, tired of just surviving instead of at least trying to live. My head is a complete mess.

I approach the counter and lean there for a few minutes. I close my eyes, and yet, I continue seeing the light through my subconscious.

I force my eyelids open and press the button to listen to the message. Her voice sinks into my senses like blood flowing through my veins. Everything inside me destabilizes.

"Kate..." A few seconds of silence, and then she continues: "Kate, it's me, Angel. I... I just wanted to say that I miss you so much. I know you don't want to talk to me, but know that I think about you every day and pray a lot too." — Angelina pauses, but I can hear her labored breathing. "I have so much to say, Kate... So many things have happened since you left. I have a father I didn't even know existed, his name is Andrew. But I imagine you already know that, right?" The silence on the other end tells me Angel is struggling to continue. She sighs deeply, and I know she's holding back tears. "Alex and I are getting married in a few days. I would really love for you to come. I'll leave the chapel address and my phone number. I'll also leave the address of my house in New York." I listen closely, feeling the tension take hold of every muscle in my body. "I love you, Kate, take care." And everything falls silent again.

I'm not sure what I'm thinking when I grab a pen and paper and listen to the message again. I write down Angelina's addresses and phone number, then head over to the computer desk and sit down.

With trembling hands, I reread everything I wrote, even though I know it doesn't matter to have her address in my hands. Angelina is in New York. I'm in California. We're more than 4,000 km apart. Besides, I don't know if I have the courage to speak to her again. All this time, I've rejected her calls and any other way she tried to reconnect. It was too shameful to admit that my brain had suffered a breakdown, and I spent months of my life alternating between a psychiatric clinic and the house I swore I would never return to.

After rereading my notes for the fifth time, I fold the paper and tuck it inside a little notebook I use to jot down random ideas, wondering if I'll ever see her again or if the friendship we nurtured for so many years is destroyed.

Angelina's words don't leave my head, and I repeat them silently countless times: "I have a father I didn't know existed. His name is Andrew."

I vaguely remember my mother talking about it some time after I discovered I was pregnant. Angelina called frequently, but I never spoke directly with her. The few pieces of information I had were what my mother decided to share.

CHAPTER 2

KATE

YEARS AGO

I wake up a bit disoriented as I hear voices coming from the kitchen. In a jolt, I sit up in bed and rub my eyes, fearing I'm late for school.

Fully awake, I rush to the window and notice that the sun is already high in the sky, so I hurry to get ready and look presentable for another day of school.

When I approach the kitchen, now dressed with my hair tied in a low ponytail, I find my mother and Garath talking very closely to each other. He's eating a piece of pancake that she puts into his mouth, and they both smile at each other, not noticing I'm standing at the kitchen entrance, watching them.

"Good morning?" I say quietly, a little uncertain and nervous about interrupting their conversation.

My mother doesn't move away from the man when she notices my presence in the kitchen, she just smiles broadly at me.

"Good morning, Kate."

I force a smile too, and the tension in my shoulders is replaced by a mix of surprise when I see the table set up.

The wooden surface is piled high with delicious-looking food. My stomach growls from hunger as I see the golden pancakes with syrup, scrambled eggs with lots of bacon and sausages, rolls, bagels, cereals, and even muffins.

There's also coffee and milk on the table. The sight of all this food is mouth-watering and eye-catching.

I look back at my mother, and she smiles again, her eyes sparkling with happiness as she gazes at the table full of treats.

"Go ahead, dear, eat as much as you want. Garath bought all this for us."

I glance shyly at the man, who is also watching me closely, and I see the shadow of a smile form on his lips.

"Enjoy, little one, and don't be shy. All this is for you."

He winks at me and wraps his arms around my mother's waist.

I avert my gaze from the two of them, despite the discomfort I feel from being the target of such kindness in the morning, and focus back on the food. I don't even remember having such a hearty breakfast before. My stomach growls again.

Garath and my mother sit down at the table and invite me to join them. Garath whispers something in my mother's ear, and she laughs, the smile stretching from ear to ear, her eyes sparkling as she looks at the man.

While they enjoy themselves, I bite into a muffin, and the explosion of flavors in my mouth is wonderful. I devour everything in the blink of an eye, getting a little messy with the chocolate drops.

After trying the bacon and eggs, I drink some milk and grab another muffin, then stand up to go to school.

My mother bids me goodbye with a huge smile on her face and stands up to plant a kiss on my forehead.

"You look so beautiful, Kate. Have a good day at school, darling."

Her firm hand caresses my hair and slides down to my cheeks.

"From today on, I don't want you worrying about anything. Everything will be fine, okay?"

I nod and lower my gaze as she steps away, a little stunned by the sudden change in my mother's behavior. Acts of affection and care were never part of her persona, even when I was little. I end up not knowing what to do, so I just turn my back on her and follow the same path I take every day.

KATE

PRESENT DAY

A FEW DAYS HAVE PASSED since I received Angelina's call, and I've been working diligently on the book I committed to finishing. During this time, I researched some publishing options and discovered a digital platform that monetizes authors through sales royalties. I thought it might be a good opportunity, so I decided to go ahead with the plan. I created a pen name and finally settled on the official title for the book: *When Everything Ends.*

I'm so focused on drafting the final chapters that I jump back in my chair when I hear the shrill ring of the doorbell.

My mom left a few hours ago for her shift at work, and as far as I know, she hasn't made any arrangements with anyone or left any messages or items for me to deliver or receive on her behalf.

My heart starts racing as I take a breath and try to stay calm to open the door. It's always like this when I have to deal with people I don't know. My hands sweat, I can't keep my breathing coherent, and I turn into a walking disaster.

Taking a deep breath, I get up and walk slowly to the door. The doorbell rings insistently, and whoever is on the other side seems to be in a hurry with whatever they came to do.

Slowly, I turn the doorknob and begin to open the door. I take another breath and look toward the yard, toward the iron gate. At first, I don't recognize the person standing in front of the house, maybe because I imagine it's someone unlikely to be here, and my mind prefers to believe the sight is a mirage. But then the woman moves and calls my name: "Kate? Hi..."

Emma? What is she doing here?

Memories of the day my daughter was born strike me, as it was the last time I saw Emma before leaving the psychiatric hospital. It was also the only moment I saw the baby.

"Can we talk?"

I pause for a moment, still shaken by the unexpected and turbulent visit. Emma's presence makes my heart beat against my chest so hard that I can almost feel the organ marking my chest with its frantic thumps.

Slowly and silently, I walk toward the gate and open it so Emma can enter. I don't say anything to her, staying quiet without being able to look directly into her eyes.

"Can I come in for a moment? I'll be quick."

I step aside so Emma can enter, and once she does, I close the gate and walk back into the house.

The woman follows me into the tiny living room, and I motion to the couch for her to sit. I settle into an old armchair and wait to hear what she has to say.

"Kate, I won't take long, I just want to give you something, I'm sure you'll like it."

I remain silent, hurt. I look in every direction except at her. It's something I can't avoid, and it's the only way I've found to protect myself from situations that cause pain.

Realizing I won't say anything, Emma sighs tiredly and continues.

"Oh, Kate, I'm so sorry. So sorry. You don't know how hard it was for me to see you suffer over the absence of that little baby. But I had orders not to let you see her, otherwise, the separation would've been even harder."

I completely understand what Emma is saying, as it was the same speech my mother gave me when I begged her to bring my daughter. I understand all this overprotectiveness around me, but it's something I just can't accept.

Out of the corner of my eye, I see the woman open the bag in her lap and pull out a brown envelope. She runs her hand over the opening a few times, takes a deep breath, and hands the object to me: "These are pictures of her, Kate. Take them!"

For the first time since the woman arrived, I finally gather the courage to lift my head and look directly at her face. Emma's eyes are watery. Unspilled tears darken her thick lashes, highlighting a deep sense of remorse.

My body trembles as I raise my arm and take the envelope from her hands. I look at the paper and then at her several times before breaking the seal that keeps it closed. My fingers work quickly to open the envelope, and I plunge my hand inside, rushing to reach the contents with all the urgency within me.

I place the paper on my lap and cover my mouth with my hand as I see the first image. A mixture of emotions floods me from head to toe, and my vision blurs from the tears that form and insist on falling down my face.

There are three pictures of her. In the first image, the baby is dressed in a green onesie, her little eyes closed as if she were peacefully sleeping. I recognize the silver locket I inherited from my grandmother, pinned with a brooch on the collar of the onesie. It's a piece of great sentimental value to me, I would recognize it anywhere because of the turquoise stone, greenish-blue, carved in the center of the pendant.

I run my fingers over the old locket and trace up to her rosy little face. A painful moan escapes my lips, and I need to forcefully inhale and exhale to keep my breath steady.

"This photo was taken right after she was born, Kate. Your mother took the locket and said it was a family heirloom."

I sniffle softly, watching how perfect the baby is. Her dark hair covers her ears, her tiny pink mouth resembling a delicate heart.

Everything inside me hurts so much. The distance, the longing to have her with me, the little scent I felt for such a brief time. It hurts to remember every second since her conception.

I move on to the other pictures, and in them, she's a little bigger, I imagine she's about three months old.

Her toothless smile warms my heart, her cheeks are so chubby that my fingers ache to pinch them. And her little eyes... her eyes are as blue as mine. She looks like a little doll in a red onesie with white collars.

"She's so perfect..." I whisper, unable to take my eyes off the images. "This locket was a gift from my grandmother. It was here at home when the baby was born at the psychiatric hospital. I'm glad my mother remembered to place the pendant with the baby's things. Somehow, this brings me peace, because I feel like a little piece of me is with her."

I lift my gaze to Emma and notice her compassionate expression. She moves closer, leans in front of me, and holds my hands firmly.

"She's doing well, Kate. Your daughter is being well cared for and loved very much. And I hope from the bottom of my heart that these photos can ease some of your pain."

Moved, I squeeze Emma's hands back.

"What name did they give her?" I have a genuine hope of learning just a little more about the baby who shares my blood.

Emma sighs but doesn't deny me this precious information.

"Hannah. Her first name is Hannah. I'm sorry I can't provide more information about her, Kate, it's confidential."

I nod and return to looking at the photographs, my heart leaping in my chest.

"I need to go now. To be honest, I shouldn't have come here, but I thought you deserved to see her and at least know her first name."

Emma steps back, and I get up to accompany her to the gate. As we approach the exit, I call to her, and Emma turns back toward me.

"Thank you so much, Emma. You have no idea how moved and happy I am with the gift you've given me today."

The woman nods and gives me a small smile.

"I'll see you around." She says her goodbyes and leaves.

I remain standing by the gate as I watch Emma walk down the street until she disappears from my view. Despite the loneliness surrounding me, I no longer feel so alone. Now I at least have a name I can whisper softly. And I have the photos. I have an angelic face to look at.

My heart smiles, and everything inside me is reinvigorated.

Since I'm already outside, I decide to go to the mailbox to see if there's any mail. To my surprise, there are some papers for my mom and another addressed to me.

The sender's address is in Angelina's name.

Hastily, I close the gate and run back inside. I leave my mom's papers on the table and rush to the desk to open the envelope, feeling the tension take over my limbs.

Trembling, I open the envelope and take out its contents. There are two plane tickets to New York for two days from now. One in my name, and the other in my mom's name. Along with the tickets is a short note from Angelina.

You don't have to come if you don't want to, Kate. I'll understand, and the last thing I want is to pressure you into doing something you're not ready for. I miss you.

Angelina.

I sigh a few times and sit down with the tickets in my hand. The truth is, I'm not sure if I'll ever be ready to face the world again, but maybe trying to start over could be the little nudge I need to pull myself out of this abyss I've fallen into and never intended to leave.

CHAPTER 3

KATE

PRESENT DAY

"In two days?" My mom asks, shaking her head as I hand her the envelope with the tickets and explain what's going on.

I sigh and step back a little, my head lowered.

"Yes. It's for her wedding." My voice is quiet, almost a whisper.

I hear her grumble, and she takes the cigarette from her mouth, shifting in her chair. I raise my gaze and look at the woman I call mom, noticing the signs of time on her face and hair. The fine wrinkles around her eyes and mouth are a clear warning of how relentless time is. Her hair has gray roots, with the rest of the tips dyed brown, giving her a careless air, although she's still a beautiful woman. However, even beauty has its price to pay.

"I don't know. I don't like this friend of yours. She's too nosy," she comments, looking away from my face. "You know, when you were having problems and needed to be hospitalized, and she kept calling to gossip. I felt bad having to pass on information about you, especially with everything that happened."

"She was just worried. We were like sisters."

"Still, I don't like her."

I nod to my mother as the acidity of her words churns in my stomach.

"Fine. I'll go alone then," I whisper.

I hear the sound of the chair scraping against the floor as she moves. My mother walks around the table and heads to the counter, her steps heavy and dragging.

"You're not well enough to go alone. You know that, you're not 'thinking clearly,' Kate. You shouldn't be worried about going to a friend's wedding."

I place two fingers on my temples and close my eyes, feeling the area pulse. Sadness washes over me, and discouragement and uncertainty embrace me tightly, and I feel the urge to scream. Even though I know how limited I am, hearing this from her feels like a knife being shoved into my chest. It hurts so much.

"I need to apologize to her..." I whisper softly, not allowing my mother to hear what I'm saying. Memories that I need to forget come flooding into my head, and I squeeze my eyelids shut harder.

Forgive me, Angel. Forgive me... Forgive me.

I left my best friend behind at the moment she needed me the most, and thinking about it takes my breath away, as if a hand is choking me, squeezing my throat until I suffocate.

"I'm going to see her!" I say, challenging my mom, even though I'm afraid of her reaction.

I stand up as well and look in her direction. Her gaze is alert, but she remains silent.

Something inside me screams for me to go, to tell Angelina how sorry I am for being weak and running away. Staying here where I am, watching time pass and take my life with it, is making me even sicker.

"Fine..." My mom takes another drag from the cigarette and exhales the smoke through her mouth. "If that's what you want, then let's travel to your friend's wedding. But after you torment yourself seeing that she moved on while you stayed stuck in time, don't say I didn't warn you, Kate."

I breathe a sigh of relief for having convinced her and nod in agreement.

"I'll pack my things," I announce, and I look at her one last time before heading out.

I walk to my room and stand in the doorway for a few seconds, observing the disorganization before me. The faint sunlight of the late afternoon peeks through the half-open curtains, casting a play of light and shadow on the unmade bed. I sigh deeply, knowing exactly what I need to do. I need to react and take control of my life, and I begin by fixing everything that's out of place.

A great knot tightens in my throat as I finish tidying up and grab the suitcase to pack my clothes and everything I'll need. Angelina's wedding is just a few days away, and it makes my heart race with intensity. I think about the years we shared so many moments together, from when we were novices to now, when our paths have taken us to different destinations. She's preparing to take a big step in her life, while I've stagnated in time.

I place a change of simple clothes in the suitcase, a skirt and blouse set that my mother bought for me after my daughter was born. I've never worn it, so I consider it the only suitable outfit for the occasion.

I feel nervous, my heart tight. Fear and doubt continue to torment me.

As I pick up a long-sleeved shirt, my eyes fixate on a medium-sized box resting on the highest shelf of the wardrobe. The worn wooden box is a testament to my journey with Angelina. Slowly, I reach for it, touch its rough surface, and pull it down.

I place it on the freshly made bed and sigh quietly. I open the lid of the box and reveal its contents. Old photos, crumpled notes, and small objects are meticulously arranged. Each one is a reminder of our friendship and our commitment to faith.

Carefully, I pick up a framed photo of the two of us smiling in the convent's garden. Our habits envelop us, but our eyes convey joy.

I find a small prayer book we used to share, the pages worn from the hours we spent together in silence, seeking inner peace.

A tear escapes my eye and rolls down my face, clouding my vision. Gently and slowly, I begin selecting a few mementos to take with me. A handwritten note, a simple necklace she gave me, and a small dried flower that symbolizes our friendship. I add the baby's photo I gave birth to, along with a letter where I explain to Angelina how things happened after the massacre at the convent. I organize everything into another box and carefully close the suitcase.

THE SMELL OF COFFEE and the constant chatter of travelers fill the air at Los Angeles airport, while my mom and I wait for our flight to New York.

The flight is already more than two hours delayed when the loudspeaker announces the boarding. My heart starts racing, and the anxiety that's already high intensifies. A mix of fear and apprehension takes over me from head to toe, but I try to remain as calm as possible.

Inside the plane, the tension only rises as we fly eastward, crossing the country. I feel my hands sweating, my stomach in knots, my forehead cold, and the air feels hard to breathe. My mom watches me without saying a word. We've been in complete silence since we left home. I can feel her judgment with every glance in my direction.

But it doesn't matter, my thoughts are solely focused on Angelina and the fact that we will soon see each other, and I will face her after everything.

When we descend from the plane, the warm climate embraces my body, contrasting with the cold air conditioning. I walk down the narrow corridor toward the baggage claim area, beside my mom, and

I feel the palms of my hands sweat, my breath becoming short. Deep down, I know exactly what this means: anxiety is coming, and there's nothing I can do to stop it.

I take a deep breath, trying to stay calm. I inhale and exhale repeatedly.

As soon as I step into the bustling terminal, the voices and hum of conversations fill my ears, making everything deafening. The whirlwind of unfamiliar faces makes my heart race, leaving me restless and anxious. I feel my mom's presence beside me, and she holds my shoulder, trying to keep me calm. She says something, but I can't absorb it coherently. Her voice seems distant, almost a whisper.

I shake my head, trying to control my thoughts, but the oppressive feeling only increases. My vision blurs, my breath shortens, and I panic, knowing I need to find a place to regroup. I pull away from my mom as quickly as I can, and start following the signs pointing to the bathroom, completely ignoring her voice calling for me.

The hallways seem endless as I fight against the anxiety wrapping around me like a cold shadow, pushing me into a deep abyss, difficult to escape.

Finally, I find what I'm looking for and enter, closing the door behind me. Tears start to flow down my face as I try to regain control. It's always like this when I find myself surrounded by many people or unfamiliar places. My fears take shape, and the panic attacks don't fail.

I breathe deeply, focusing on each inhale and exhale, until my breath normalizes and my heart stops pounding erratically. After minutes that feel like an eternity, I wash my face and look at my reflection in the mirror. The guilt corrodes me when I realize I'm not well enough to be presentable for Angelina's wedding. Either way, I'll be content just to see her from a distance.

I leave the bathroom and find my mom waiting for me. Her expression is neutral and a little tired, but she doesn't say anything. She maintains a firm, impassive stance.

A little calmer, we pick up our luggage from the conveyor belt and head toward the arrivals area, following the highlighted signs. As we approach, I notice a well-dressed man holding a sign with my name written in all caps. I stop in my tracks, feeling nervous, but my mom steps forward and walks toward him. They talk for a few brief seconds, and then they turn in my direction. The man approaches where I am and introduces himself:

"Hello, Miss Kate, I'm Alfred, the driver Mrs. Angelina sent to pick you up from the airport."

"Hello..." I reply, looking from him to my mom.

"Shall we? I fear we're already late for the ceremony, but I'll do my best to get there on time," he emphasizes the flight delay by a few hours.

I nod and ask for a few minutes to change clothes in the airport bathroom before we head to the church where Angelina and her fiancé will get married.

I sigh softly, grab my suitcase, and head toward the bathroom to do what I need to do.

AN HOUR LATER, THE driver announces that we are almost at the wedding venue, a small chapel located in Staten Island. I am sitting in the back seat next to my mom, far from the center of New York. The towering buildings are behind us, replaced by residential neighborhoods with white houses and a family atmosphere.

I feel my skin sweat, my hands cold. My body feels like a trembling mass as we approach the final destination.

I spot the chapel in the distance. It's a very old building, but in perfect condition. Its beauty is stunning, in Gothic style with sculpted reliefs on the brick and stone façade. But what impresses me the most is the immense tower with a cross at the top and the huge bell.

I take a deep breath and divert my attention to the entrance. It is at this moment that I notice the movement of people at the chapel's door. I clearly see when Angelina steps out of the church beside her husband, and they embrace each other tightly. They look happy, surrounded by friends.

My heart races, and my throat tightens as I feel an immense joy for her, but I shudder inside as I realize it's too late. I've arrived late for the ceremony and missed everything, once again disappointing her. I close my eyes for a moment, taking in a breath and asking the driver to park the car some distance away.

"This is good for me," I say, not looking at him.

I can't take my eyes off the scene unfolding before me. Angelina smiling, in the arms of her husband, surrounded by children and other wedding guests. I notice when she pulls away from Alex, and the two talk, smiling for a few moments. Then, one by one, people approach and congratulate the couple on their union.

"Wait here. I won't take long," I say to my mom and open the car door to step out.

I walk slowly, holding the box of mementos covered in brown paper. My heart beats so fast I can almost hear it. Each step closer to my best friend feels like reliving that night. It hurts the soul, it corrodes, everything inside me breaks, again and again.

Angelina looks so beautiful, in a delicate white dress, a fine veil covering her hair. Her smile is wide, her movements light. She is radiant.

I stop halfway when I see an older man approaching her. I feel a tingling in my chest, a kind of chill that momentarily disorients me.

He is tall, with fair skin, full brown hair, and graying temples. I've never seen him before, but I feel like I already know him. I realize this when I glance back at Angelina and notice a subtle resemblance between the two.

They talk, exchanging hugs and pleasantries. I notice when he smiles at her and holds Angelina's shoulders, making her turn to face him. And then, after saying something, his gaze shifts in my direction, and I clearly see the greenish gleam in his irises.

Angelina's husband also notices my presence and approaches his wife. Within seconds, Angelina turns her body, facing me.

Her wide eyes show the surprise at seeing me here, on this grand day. She doesn't wait a single second before lifting the hem of her dress and hurrying down the steps of the beautiful chapel, coming in my direction.

Emotions overflow from my body in the form of tears, and I let them fall uncontrollably, completely overcome by the happiness and anguish that Angelina's presence brings me. When she gets close enough, I hug her tightly, feeling my body tremble, my breath shallow.

"Kate," she whispers my name, her voice choked, hugging me back.

"Forgive me, Angel. Forgive me for leaving you alone that night. I didn't..." I try to speak through my sobs, trying to make her forgive me for everything, but Angelina interrupts me: "Stop, Kate." The tightness of her arms around me intensifies. "Forget that, my friend. I'm the one who should apologize for everything that happened. It was my fault."

"I'm so sorry, Angel. So sorry," a sharp pain takes over my insides. "It was so hard to come here, but I needed to see you. To congratulate you on this very special day."

"I'm so glad you came." She pulls back and looks at me more calmly, observing my faded glow, the deep dark circles of my suffering, my chaotic state that embarrasses me so much.

"I love you so much, Angel. I hope you can forgive me sometime..." I insist on apologizing, but Angelina doesn't allow it.

"Kate, don't worry anymore, it's in the past. The important thing is that we're here now, together." She wipes away a tear that's rolling down her face and looks at me. "I love you so much too, my friend."

I try to force a smile, but the attempt fails.

"Angel, I'm leaving now." I feel unable to approach the rest of the guests. "I came here just to see you and give you something."

Angelina's eyes widen, clearly disappointed by my rush to leave. However, I feel the anxiety attack knocking on my door again, and the last thing I need right now is to have a meltdown in front of everyone.

I take a step back, taking a breath.

"Aren't you staying for the dinner?" she asks anxiously.

I look at Angelina and then at the guests watching us from the church door with curious eyes. I shake my head, turning my head to the side, trying to avoid her noticing how agitated I am.

"No. I can't..." A tear rolls down my face, and I wipe it with the palm of my hand.

"Are you okay?" I feel my heart race when I hear a man's voice behind her. I watch him now up close, and once again, the hairs on my body stand on end.

His eyes are even greener up close, and I notice his attention is focused on me. There's a mixture of confusion and curiosity on his face.

His deep voice penetrates my ears and echoes, completely destabilizing me from the closeness. I can't control the fear that overwhelms me and lower my head, taking a step back. I do everything I can to hide from his intense gaze.

"It's okay, dad..."

Dad?

I blink a few times, surprised, and glance at him again.

So he's Andrew? Angelina's father?

"Can you help me with the others, please? I'm already going." She asks him, and the man nods. Andrew looks at me one last time before stepping away and returning to the chapel.

"Angel, I'm leaving... I shouldn't have come and... I'm not feeling well." I move forward and justify the reason for my departure.

"Don't leave like this, Kate, please. Don't go."

My heart tightens as I notice how hurt she is, but I simply can't stay. I can't...

"I'm so sorry" I shake my head and extend the box in her direction. "There's something for you in here, but I ask that you don't open it now. Open it after your honeymoon, after you've fully enjoyed this moment in your life. Can you do that for me?"

With no other option, Angelina agrees and takes the package. Then, I hug her one last time with all my strength, not knowing for sure if this will be our only meeting or the first of many. Only time will tell.

CHAPTER 4

KATE

PRESENT DAY

"Garath is going to live with us now, Kate." I hear my mom's announcement about him, and I nod in agreement, although I can't really say if I'm happy about it. It's always been just me and her at home, no man has ever lived here, and I never knew my father.

"Okay," I say quietly.

They're both standing, holding each other in the kitchen, while I sit at the table, eager to eat. My mom smiles at me and turns all her attention back to him.

"I want you to be a good girl and respect him. Garath will be your dad now. Right, darling?"

The man smiles at her, showing some wrinkles at the corners of his dark eyes.

"Of course." He holds my mom's hand and gently pulls her to sit at the table. "What do you think of the idea, Kate?"

I don't know what to respond immediately. The truth is, Garath scares me a little, but I try not to let that show. He's big and strong. His arms are enormous, and he has a horrible breath of alcohol coming from his mouth. I keep wondering how mom can be so close to him like that.

"It's... nice."

"Oh, come on, little girl, cheer up." He says, opening his arms.

I try to smile at both of them, and that seems to make them happy, as Garath's lips curve, and my mom follows suit. She kisses his cheek and sits next to him.

"Well, then let's celebrate, shall we, darling? It's time for dinner. Your first dinner as the head of this family."

I remain silent as I listen to my mom's words. I've never seen her so full of life, smiling. Most of the time, her expression is serious, her lips pressed into a thin line of concern. Now, the problems seem to no longer exist.

The smell of food makes my stomach growl when she begins serving a plate for Garath. Mashed potatoes with gravy and chicken steak is what we have for today, and it looks very appetizing.

I can hardly believe it when mom does the same for me, adding plenty of gravy to my plate as I like. I thank her softly and begin eating slowly to savor each bite.

After dinner, I leave them in the kitchen and head to my room. It doesn't take long before I notice that Garath and my mom leave the house. She works as a waitress at a bar all night, and as for him, I have no idea what he usually does besides drink a lot.

ANDREW

PRESENT DAY

I LEAVE MY OFFICE AT the FBI department and take the elevator straight to the underground parking lot. It's Friday, and all I need now is a relaxing bath and a good meal to end the night. I walk through the parking lot towards the luxury black sedan parked there, get in the car, adjust the seat, and start the engine.

As I drive through the busy streets of New York, I reflect on the day's tasks and ongoing investigations, especially the new lead in the child trafficking case in the district. It's a real snowball that will likely put a lot of important heads on the chopping block.

The traffic is chaotic, but my skills in navigating the busy streets of New York are legendary. I owe it to the many years I've dedicated to investigations. I know every street and alley in this city like the back of my hand.

I arrive home a while later, a stylish Tudor Revival house with a steep wooden roof and exposed red bricks, located in the Forest Hills neighborhood of Queens. The area is fully wooded, and the houses are spaced far apart, which is great because it guarantees me more privacy.

I park the car under a tree and get out, looking around carefully, a habit I've had since I became an FBI agent years ago.

My daughter's house is next, down the same street. Everything is calm and quiet there, since Angelina and Alexander decided to travel again with the kids after their brief honeymoon in Brazil.

I enter the house and head straight to my office. I put my belongings in their proper places. The clock on the desk, along with the file containing important information that I decided to bring from the investigation department.

I sigh deeply, carefully analyzing all the baggage I carry on my shoulders as the director of the FBI New York Field Office, one of the FBI field offices in the United States. It's a tough and even painful job, but one I do successfully and enjoy.

I leave the office and return to the living room. I take off my black suit and leave it on the back of the couch while rolling up the sleeves of my dress shirt and heading to the bar to pour myself a strong drink. I sit back in a relaxed chair, lean my head back, and let my mind wander.

Memories of a recent scene appear in my mind. It's been about three months since Angelina got married, the same amount of time since I saw her friend Kate for the first time right after the ceremony at the church. At first, I was struck by the deep blue color of the girl's eyes. But her gaze had no life, it didn't shine, it seemed dead. That left me completely intrigued for a while, until I had the chance to talk to Angelina about her.

What I learned about Kate's life was enough for me to want to keep the girl in a protective bubble. I was completely tormented by everything she went through. I couldn't reconcile that young, sweet girl with all the terror she faced at the convent.

Even now, as I sit here alone with a glass of whiskey in my hand, her image materializes in my head. Her sapphire-like eyes, completely terrified by my approach, her dark, straight hair falling over skin as pale as porcelain, the shape of her slender body, hidden under clothes too big for her. Something was born inside me at that moment. Something I couldn't explain and still don't understand. I just had the impulse to protect her from everything, from the world, from people.

Kate...

I say her name in my thoughts, the image of the girl coming strongly into my mind. I can almost see her eyes blinking in front of me, that angelic gaze surrounded by long, dark lashes, hard to forget.

Restless, I decide to get out of the bubble I've trapped myself in. I finish my whiskey and hurry to take a relaxing bath. I do everything on autopilot. I allow the water to carry away the fatigue of the day and wrap a towel around my waist, feeling a little more relaxed.

I return to the bedroom, grab my phone, and decide to end the night with a delightful fuck. In a few seconds, the person on the other end picks up my call.

"Andrew?" Her voice is soft and hoarse, making my cock hard just imagining everything I'm about to do.

"Safira? Are you available to have some fun today?" I get straight to the point, no games or beating around the bush. She knows exactly what I mean.

Safira and I have known each other for a while, since before my divorce. We've been friends since then, but I never cheated on my ex-wife. Safira and I started having sex after Katrina signed the papers and left. Safira became a kind of reliable comfort. We became each other's anchor. She understood me, I understood her, and us in bed was a pleasurable consequence. However, it never went beyond that. She knows I'm closed off to relationships, and what we have is enough for both of us.

"I'm waiting for you at my apartment." I can hear her low, dirty giggle from the other end. "You know I'm always waiting for you, Andrew."

"I'll see you soon." I curve my lips into a silent smile.

I hang up the call and quickly get dressed, opting for a long-sleeve shirt and jeans. I spray some Sauvage cologne from Dior, which is basically my signature scent and I know Safira loves it. I grab the keys and walk to the door, combing my hair with my fingers.

Soon, I'm at the lobby of the building she lives in, carrying some bags of food and a bottle of excellent French wine.

Safira is waiting for me when I ring the doorbell, and she opens the apartment door in an instant. As soon as I step in, she jumps into my arms, smiling. "Andrew, it's so good to see you."

"Hello, my dear" I feel my skin burn with desire, especially when she pulls away and nibbles her lips, her dark eyes shining with ecstasy, letting me see the whole look she put together while waiting for me.

The woman in her early thirties is wearing a small red nightgown that accentuates her beautiful breasts. I can see the shadow of her tiny panties through the thin fabric, as well as the shape of her well-defined and enticing body.

She is very beautiful and knows it. She uses all her beauty tricks to her advantage. Her face is slender and oval-shaped, her lips are small and well-defined, her eyebrows arched. Her upturned nose perfectly complements her large eyes.

"I'll put all this in the kitchen. I'm looking forward to doing something else," I wink at a smiling Safira, and she helps me with the bags.

We place everything on the kitchen counter, and I pull Safira to me, wrapping my arms around her waist.

"Come here," I murmur, burying my face in the curve of her neck. "You look stunning."

I enjoy complimenting her when we're together. Despite the great sex we have, her friendship is important to me.

"And you smell so good. You know I love catching that scent on your neck."

"Oh, really? And what else do you love?"

Safira laughs, throwing her head back, her blonde hair cascading down her back, her slender neck entirely exposed to me. I press a kiss below her chin and trail down her warm skin until I reach her ear.

"You know exactly what I love. A big, thick cock in my mouth, Andrew," she says, all coquettish.

My body shudders instantly, longing for the promise of a blowjob. My cock twitches inside my pants, as hard as steel.

"Then take what you like, hmm?" I suggest.

I capture her small mouth, trapping her lower lip with my teeth as I slide my tongue into the moist opening.

Safira throws herself at me, running her hands once again along my neck. She deepens the kiss, fully giving herself to the desire and pleasure, taking my tongue completely into her mouth.

The kiss is brief. She's an expert at teasing me and knowing exactly how I like it. She pulls away, biting her lips without breaking eye contact. Dropping to her knees in front of me, she massages my cock over my jeans.

"I love sucking you, did you know that?" I slide a finger along her chin and neck, reaching her nape and grabbing a good handful of her hair.

"And I love it when you open that little mouth to take me all in, Safira."

Her dark eyes spark with desire, and she quickly works to unzip my clothes. Within seconds, my pants and underwear are on the floor, and my rock-hard cock points at her, large and thick just the way she likes, pre-cum glistening on the swollen head.

"Suck, Safira..." I command, hoarsely.

She obeys. Opening her mouth, she takes my entire cock in while massaging my heavy balls. I throw my head back, overwhelmed by waves of exquisite pleasure, a visceral craving to devour a pussy.

Everything between us is intense and enjoyable, but our relationship is light, free from demands or obligations. She satisfies me, and I satisfy her. We end up breathless in her bed, sweat covering our bodies, lust abated, smiles on our faces. Safira curls up against me, playing with some of the hair on my abdomen.

"This just keeps getting better, Andrew," she says with satisfaction. "I hope this doesn't end anytime soon."

She sits up in bed, letting me admire her completely naked body. Her small breasts pointing towards my face are a tempting invitation to start all over again.

"I don't see why it would end, Safira. We're friends, we get along well, and the sex is amazing." I sit up to face her, reaching out to cup both her breasts with my hands. I give them a light squeeze. "Isn't this great?" The woman leans in, kissing my mouth, her hand roaming over my back.

"Yes, it's very good," she confirms with that seductive air only she possesses.

Satisfied from the sex but hungry and exhausted, I pull away and get out of bed.

"Let's eat, then. I'm starving." She nods, and I quickly wash up in her bedroom's bathroom. I put on my underwear but don't bother with the rest of my clothes. I like staying relaxed during my downtime.

Safira does the same. She takes a quick shower and puts on a cheeky little pair of shorts. We share another passionate kiss in the bedroom before heading to the kitchen, but it doesn't go beyond that.

"Wow, this pasta is incredible." She comments, referring to the Italian spaghetti with red sauce I brought for our dinner. "And this wine..." She takes a generous sip and places the glass back on the table. "Exquisite. As always, you don't disappoint, Andrew."

"Are you talking about the wine or the sex?" I joke, taking another bite of food.

Safira laughs heartily, her eyes gleaming as she looks at me. "Both."

She wipes her lips with a napkin after finishing her meal, takes another sip of wine, and gazes at me intently as I continue eating.

"Changing the subject. How's Angel? When will we finally meet?" she asks, bringing up the fact that I have a daughter I hadn't known about until a little over a year ago.

I sigh softly, a bit impatient with how insistent Safira has been on this matter. Ever since I told her about Angelina and how I discovered, at forty-four, that I was the father of a twenty-three-year-old woman, she's been pushing me to introduce them. However, introducing my fuck buddy to my daughter would make it seem like my relationship with Safira is far more serious than it is, and I don't want that. Things are good as they are; there's no need to complicate them.

"We've talked about this before," I remind her. I've always been honest about what we have, and she agreed.

The woman pouts and rolls her eyes. Finally, she speaks again: "You and your habit of keeping things separate. But alright, Andrew. In due time, I'll meet her—that's a promise."

She smiles and gets up to clear the table. She takes the dishes to the sink while I lean back in my chair, lost in thought. I think about my daughter, who just married a former mercenary, and wonder when my life turned into a ticking time bomb. After all, Alexander was an assassin, and now he's married to the daughter of the New York FBI president, occasionally doing specific jobs for me.

I run a hand over the back of my neck, feeling the tension there. I look at Safira, washing the dishes and occasionally glancing my way with a slight smile. And then I realize I can't keep involving her in my life this way. It's not fair to her.

I need to put an end to this friends-with-benefits arrangement before she ends up more hurt than she deserves.

CHAPTER 5

KATE

YEARS BEFORE

It's strange having a man living in the same house as me. It's completely embarrassing to see my mom's boyfriend get out of the shower in just a towel and wander around the house. She seems to think it's amazing, but for me, it's confusing and uncomfortable. However, I can't do anything about it, so I settle for staying in my room and leaving them alone. It's also disgusting to witness the kissing scenes whenever they're together, especially during meals, but mom seems happier than ever. So I keep quiet and try to be happy for her.

Things remain the same here. My mom works at night, and Garath goes out with her. Sometimes he comes back early and stays in the living room watching TV until she gets home in the early hours of the morning. At other times, I hear the noise of the two of them arriving home. Most of the time, they spend the rest of the night drinking in the kitchen and laughing loudly. Over time, I'm getting used to this routine change. I'm a person who adapts easily, and now I understand that I need to follow my own path, ignoring the noise they make and trying to sleep as best as I can to have the strength to go to school in the morning.

That's how the days go by. There are times when I'm completely ignored at home, and other times they talk to me at dinner.

Every now and then, Garath and my mom fight, but I don't know why. A few nights ago, he didn't come back with her, and he also didn't show up in the morning. Mom spent hours crying in the kitchen.

The next night he returned. His eyes were red, his clothes dirty. I heard my mom shouting through the house. She was saying something about his shirt being stained with lipstick and that he smelled like cheap perfume. I didn't quite understand what she meant, actually, I tried to distance myself from them as much as possible.

Little by little, the arguments became more frequent, until one day Garath slapped my mom across the face. That night I was scared, very scared. I'd never seen him that angry before. But the next morning, the two of them were calm and happy in the kitchen, as if nothing had happened.

KATE

PRESENT DAYS

I FINALLY MANAGED TO earn some money through writing. Something I didn't think would work out, but fortunately, it's surprising me. The book I completed a few months ago, which I managed to publish on a reading platform after much research, pays monthly royalties, and the return has been satisfactory. Nothing too grand, but enough for me not to feel so useless and like a burden on my mom. Now I can contribute something to our livelihood and even buy some clothes for myself, as well as start an emergency savings fund.

I check the balance in my bank account, hardly believing what my eyes are seeing. I'm so grateful, so happy, something I haven't felt in so long. Then, several ideas begin to pop into my head, and I start putting them into practice. I rush to the Instagram page I created using a pen name and post a story with a mysterious excerpt from the next book that came to my mind.

In no time, I receive messages from eager readers who have read my recently released book and connected with the story. This is like seeing the sun come out after a week of rain. My smile spreads easily, my heart warms, and I begin to understand that I can finally make a difference in my life from now on.

I turn off the computer and head to the kitchen to prepare a quick snack. I decide to make two bacon sandwiches with pickles, lettuce, tomato, and mayonnaise. One for me and the other for my mom, who's about to come home from work.

She still doesn't know the news; in fact, she has no idea that I write. The last time I tried to tell her, I couldn't express myself very well, and she didn't pay any attention to what I tried to say. So, I couldn't get any information across, and I decided to wait until I made my first dollars before telling her.

I finish preparing the sandwiches on the counter, wrap hers in plastic film, and carry mine on a plate to the kitchen table.

I take the first bite and only then realize that some orange juice would go perfectly with the snack. I get up and start making exactly what I had planned. I'm almost done when I hear the door open. Soon after, I hear my mom's footsteps echoing through the room, shadowed by the twilight.

I can see from her expression that something is wrong. Her head is down, and her gaze carries a sense of guilt or apprehension, I can't quite identify it. I just know that my mom is looking at me with that look of someone about to tell something bad. She sets her bag down on the table and doesn't say anything at first. She stands still, watching me, her mouth locked in a thin line.

"What happened? Something bad at work?"

She shakes her head in denial and makes a move to leave. She turns her back to me but stays rooted in place, like a motionless statue.

My chest begins to tighten, and something inside me screams loudly that there's something different in the air. As if dark clouds were hanging over our heads, bringing an omen of bad days ahead.

"Mom?" I call her as I stand up from my chair, my heart racing.

"Kate..." She begins, her voice hesitant.

It's as if I knew, just by feeling the tension that now fills the kitchen. My throat goes dry, the air feels heavy, hard to breathe. I close my eyes and wait for her to say everything at once.

"He's back. Garath is back in San Diego."

The weight of her words hangs in the air, and my stomach clenches instantly. I breathe deeply, bracing myself to face this topic that eats away at me like acid, a conversation that no matter how much time passes, reignites wounds that never heal.

"To what extent?" The fear of her answer is like having the air cut off, as I don't know for sure if he's only back in San Diego or if he's back in her life. When it comes to my mom and this man, the latter possibility seems very likely.

"I don't know yet." That's all she says. I feel like I'm losing my footing with every passing second.

What does this mean? That there's a chance they might see each other again like before?

No... she wouldn't do that...

I dig my fingers into the table, hardly caring about the sharp pain shooting from under my nails due to the force with which I make this movement. I take another breath, my thoughts confused, my brain refusing to relive it all.

"You need to understand, Kate. Things aren't that simple."

It's an answer I've heard so many times before. An answer that always leaves a bitter taste in my mouth, a flavor of powerlessness. Her words accumulate inside me, a storm of resentment and painful memories rises to the surface.

"You know what he's like. Things haven't changed..." I argue, almost out of breath, seeking validation and understanding for my pain.

"Maybe it's different now. I think I deserve a chance to be happy."

The conversation quickly turns into a heated exchange. It's been so long since I felt like this, like a child who discovered paradise and suddenly had to return to a colorless world. A few moments ago, I was reclaiming my life, now I just want to die, the same way I've wished for so many times in my existence.

"How can you... say that... after everything?" My voice falters, the anguish taking its toll.

Emotions spill over like water from a dam about to break. I begin to unearth painful memories, spilling out years and years of accumulated frustrations. Tears mix with anger as I relive moments I would give anything in the world to forget.

My mom responds with an unrelenting defense, a protective shield around a destructive relationship that I never understood.

"You're so selfish," she shoots back, her words as sharp as knives. "Hasn't everything he's done to me been enough, Kate?"

It's the final blow. It hurts. It cuts deep. I feel completely abandoned, struggling to express the magnitude of what I'm feeling. The magnitude of everything Garath represents in my life, no matter how many years have passed.

And as she turns her back to leave the kitchen, I allow my shoulders to slump in pure despair and hopelessness. I let the tears roll down my cheeks and fall to the floor. I let everything good I've built little by little inside of me crumble once again.

CHAPTER 6

KATE

YEARS BEFORE

I cover my ears with the pillow as I lie on my stomach on the bed. I can feel my heart pounding, my body trembling. The screams downstairs are deafening and pierce my eardrums with such force that tears of pure terror stream down my face.

It's been a while now that Garath and my mom have been fighting. He came home drunk in the morning, so drunk that I could smell the alcohol from quite a distance. My mom was restless and nervous, sitting at the table waiting for him, while I was making scrambled eggs for breakfast. Then he staggered in, his eyes bloodshot like he hadn't slept in weeks, and his clothes were stained with something sticky that looked like vomit.

"You're filthy, like a pig, Garath," my mom yelled and pushed him when he tried to grab her.

I felt my heart race in that moment, because I already knew how this was going to end. I just didn't understand why she didn't do anything about it. Why did she allow herself to be treated like this by Garath?

Were all men like this? Drunk, filthy, and violent?

I didn't even stop to eat. I turned off the stove and leaned back against the wall, watching them.

"Youuu slut..." Garath's voice was slurred as he staggered backward but steadied himself on the table. Then he lunged at my mom. "Bitchhh. I want to fuck you, bitchhh. Stay quiet."

"You pig. Don't touch me with that rotten breath, Garath. Son of a bitch."

The insults came one after the other as Garath tried to hold my mom, and she pushed him away with rage. I had never seen her this angry before, and this was the first time I saw Garath so out of control. He was getting worse every day, more violent.

Then the sound of a punch echoed through the kitchen, and my mom staggered backward, screaming. It felt like my heart was about to leap out of my mouth. I looked around, searching for something to hit him with before he did something worse, and I saw the still-hot frying pan with the scrambled eggs.

"Get out of here, Kate," my mom shouted as she got up from the floor, one hand on her cheek. Her hair was covering her face, hiding the bruise Garath had caused.

"Mom..." My voice was a whisper, but I was so scared I couldn't move.

"Get out of here, you stupid girl!"

Her eyes weren't focused on me. She didn't take her attention off Garath. The man was glaring at her with his fists clenched and his breath quickening.

"Leave!" His shrill voice hit me like a punch.

Then fear took over, and I ran straight to my room. The only place that gives me a false sense of safety. The shouting continued, the insults. I heard glass breaking, furniture crashing to the ground. Nothing new under the sun.

I sniffle quietly and stay in the same position, my heart pounding so hard that I fear it will burst from my chest any second. Then, a few minutes later, silence takes over. I don't hear any more screams or objects being thrown. I take the pillow from my ears and sharpen my senses to listen more closely. Pure silence, cold and terrifying. Exactly like the other times.

They fight, and then they make up like nothing ever happened. But they don't know that with every outburst, they take away a piece of my soul. My heart hurts so much. I'm so scared.

KATE

PRESENT DAYS

I AM STILL SHAKEN BY the recent events of the day. The argument I had with my mom about Garath is fresh in my mind, as if no time has passed. She simply locked herself in her room since we ended the conversation, and we haven't had any contact since.

Despite my heated mind, I continue to jot down some scenes for the next book. The cold night wind that comes through the window calms me, and I take the opportunity to put everything that comes to my head on the computer screen.

I write and rewrite sentences. I repeat the process countless times until I finally give up and surrender to mental exhaustion.

I turn off the computer and get ready for bed. I head to my room and snuggle under the blankets. My thoughts won't stop, and every moment, flashes of the past haunt me, reminding me of everything. Of all the harm Garath caused my mom and... me.

I take a deep breath and roll over on the mattress. I feel exhausted, but sleep won't come. It's already late at night, I hear the sounds from the street, cars speeding by, sirens blaring. And then, something I haven't heard in a long time happens. Someone parks a vehicle in front of our house.

My heart races, breathing becomes difficult. I feel a cold sweat running down my forehead, anticipating what I know is coming.

Slowly, I get up and walk to the window, keeping the blanket wrapped around my body to stay warm. And then I see him. Garath is standing in front of the gate, looking directly at the front door. He looks older, much older than I remembered, his skin marked by the passage of time, his hair gray and thin. But his sinister gaze is the same, cold and frightening as before.

A huge lump forms in my throat, making it almost impossible to swallow. I feel like I'm petrified in place because I can't move. Everything inside me turns into a dark mass of dread and fear. It's like I've been transported back in time, as if I'm reliving the first night Garath was here at our house.

The man moves, walks to the gate, and rings the doorbell. As he waits, I notice the moment his attention shifts toward the window of my room, and I jump back. I cover my mouth to prevent myself from screaming, my body trembling uncontrollably.

I slowly move away until I reach the wall. One step at a time.

I hear my mom's footsteps downstairs, the front door opening. Voices and murmurs.

I feel the air leaving my lungs and close my eyes. I clench my fists tightly. I try to control myself, but the panic sets in hard, my legs lose balance, and I slide straight to the floor, tears streaming down my face like a waterfall.

"No... please... no..." I breathe in and out. Inhale, exhale. Over and over.

Seconds pass, then minutes, hours. I don't know how long I stay huddled on the floor trying to breathe. My mind seems lost in a cloud of smoke. All I can feel is the cold, sharp fear tearing at my soul.

Then I remember her, Angelina. My thoughts begin to make sense again. I see her, beautiful, leaving the Church in a white dress, and I remember her plea for me not to leave.

I sniffle quietly but force myself to stay calm, pushing my body to react. I refuse to go through this again.

Still shaking, I get up from the floor, steady myself against the wall, and walk disoriented to the wardrobe. I throw my documents and debit card into a small bag, along with a change of clothes and the notes I made with Angelina's number and address. I don't pay attention to anything in particular, I just do what I need to do as quickly as I can. I put on jeans and a loose t-shirt, and on my feet, I slip into worn but comfortable sneakers. My trembling body and dazed mind don't allow me to think of many details, so I follow my instincts and pack only the essentials.

I walk slowly, as quietly as possible to avoid making noise. I hear some noises and soft voices coming from my mom's room, but I walk right past, not caring about the conversation or whatever they're doing. I open the door and come face to face with the dimly lit street waiting for me.

The night is dark and a bit cold. I clutch the bag with my few belongings and walk quickly without looking back. I try to keep my thoughts neutral while quickening my pace. I try not to think about the hell I've lived through, I try not to think that now Garath is back. The only thing I focus on is Angelina and the hope that I can get her help to start over.

I wander the streets of San Diego, being careful not to walk through the too dark and empty areas, until I reach the train station. The panic is coming, I feel it, but I keep moving forward, pulling in and releasing my breath to try to stay calm.

I grip the bag tightly as if my life depends on it. The circulating crowd at the station frightens me, I feel my breath leaving me, the world spinning around me. I lean against the wall, close my eyes, and take a deep breath again.

I think of my daughter, how beautiful she was, such a beautiful baby. My heart aches, but it's a good kind of pain, as it distracts me from the imminent panic. Little by little, my breath steadies, but I keep thinking of everything, of the day my baby was born and taken from my arms. I recall every detail of her little face, her dark hair. She was mine, only mine. And they took her from me.

I swallow hard, just now realizing that thick tears are sliding down my cheeks. The sound of the train approaching is like a clock ringing, pulling me out of the trance I'm in.

I dry my wet skin with the backs of my hands and move to board the train. I bump into a few people along the way and clutch my bag even tighter, a mumbled apology caught in my throat.

"Watch where you're going, girl!" I hear an irritated voice from a man.

"Pay attention, miss!" says another.

Dazed by my own mess, I board the train and sit by the window. My body trembles, my heart is racing, but I turn my attention to the crowd of people moving around the station.

Some time later, I'm entering the airport. I head straight to the check-in counter to buy a ticket.

"Hello, how can I help you?" The friendly attendant looks at me. Her gaze is discreet, but I notice her briefly analyzing me, probably wondering if I'm some kind of crazy girl.

"I'd like a ticket to New York for the next flight, please," I reply without hesitation.

I run my hand through my hair and try to keep it as neat as possible.

"May I have your documents, please?"

I fumble a bit to grab what I need from my bag, but finally hand my documentation to the woman. I wait for a few moments, and then she gives me some information.

"The next flight to New York departs at 4:00 AM. Can we proceed?"

I sigh quietly, realizing that I'll have to stay at the airport until the early morning to board. I nod to her and answer a few questions.

With the ticket in hand, I look for a place to sit and wait. I mentally calculate how much money I probably still have on the card. Likely enough to take a taxi when I reach my destination, but not much more than that.

Time passes slowly as I remain quiet. It's cold, and my skin tingles. At some point during the night, I doze off in the waiting seat, but I wake up shortly after.

Just after 4 AM, I board the plane. Despite everything, I thank God I didn't lose control and take advantage of the long flight to get some rest.

THE TAXI STOPS IN A beautiful neighborhood, right in front of a house with a steep roof and a wooden and brick façade. I pay the driver and get out of the car with my bag, while looking around at everything around me.

The streets are well aligned and peaceful, with rows of houses in a style I can't identify, but it reminds me of an 18th-century English movie set, right in the heart of New York. The landscape is unique. The gardens are well-kept, the sidewalks are neatly laid out and straight.

At first, I observe everything in awe, before turning my attention to the solid oak door right in front of me. The wooden boards creak under my feet as I climb the stairs leading to the entrance of the house.

When I reach the top, I feel my heart pounding hard. I raise my hand and knock on the door, but the knock echoes through the silence of the neighborhood. I anxiously wait, hoping to hear footsteps approaching. Nothing. Absolutely nothing.

I approach the window next to the door and try to peek inside, but the curtains are tightly closed. I only see the reflection of my tired face in the glass.

I take out the notes I had left in my pants pocket with Angelina's address and confirm everything once again for the thousandth time. No doubt, I'm at the right place, but apparently at the wrong time.

I return to the door and knock again, harder this time. I wait, clinging to a shred of hope. Nothing. Once again, nothing. The minutes pass, and nothing happens. Only silence. No one is home.

I tuck the paper back into my pocket and walk back to the street. I approach a tree in front of another house and sit down on the sidewalk, placing my bag beside me. I see no other option but to wait until Angelina comes back home.

And so time passes. I watch the few people moving around the street as the day progresses. The sun peeks shyly through the sky in the morning, but by the time I realize it's past noon, I notice that the temperature is dropping, and the light is growing dimmer.

Tired of waiting, I decide to walk around the neighborhood in search of a more comfortable place. A few blocks later, I come across a small park. The orange and yellow leaves of early autumn begin to fall, painting the ground with colors. I notice a few children playing there under the supervision of a woman. There are two boys and a girl. I end up smiling as I watch them from a distance and take the opportunity to sit on a bench under the trees.

A cold wind begins to blow, and I huddle in place, hugging the tree trunk with my arms. My stomach growls, and it's only now that I realize I ate just the day before. I do the mental math on how much money I still have left on my card. I believe it's enough for a snack, but I need to save as much as I can until Angelina returns home.

I turn my attention back to the children and feel my heart tighten when I see the smiling little girl, about five years old. Her hair is long, dark, and slightly wavy, and her cheek is red from running back and forth.

Once again, I think of my daughter. I imagine each phase of her life. Will she be like this little girl when she's the same age? I believe so.

Soon, the adult woman calls the children, and they all leave. Only a few young people remain, talking and smiling amongst themselves, and an elderly couple walks together. I close and open my eyes, still there, waiting.

The day fades again, and the entire park is consumed by the shadows of the night. The cold is intense now, and only a few people wander the area.

I decide to return to Angelina's house in hopes that she's come back. As I approach, fear overwhelms me when I realize the lights are off, and there's no movement around. Still, I knock on the door a few times and wait. Nothing!

It's at this moment that I hear the sound of a car on the street, and I turn around to see the vehicle slowing down as it approaches the house. My heart leaps with the expectation of seeing Angelina again, but I feel as though I've been slapped in the face when a large man steps out of the vehicle that has just been parked and walks toward me.

I don't need to think much to recognize that face. He looks serious, dressed in a dark suit and expensive shoes. His gaze examines me carefully, but I notice a shadow of tiredness on his face.

It's Angelina's father!

"Can I help you with something? My daughter isn't home."

I swallow hard, feeling the air leave my lungs.

"I... I need to speak with her... Angelina. Do you know if she will be long?"

The man moves closer. His presence is imposing. I use all my self-control to stay quiet in the place I'm standing. His eyes are even more intense up close, reflecting the glow of the streetlights.

"It's Kate, right?" I shrink, imagining that Angelina may have mentioned me to her family.

"Yes!" I reply.

"Nice to meet you, Kate. I'm Andrew, Angelina's father." He extends his hand to greet me, but I can't move. The direct proximity of a man leaves me completely paralyzed.

Noticing that I won't shake his hand, Andrew clears his throat and lowers his hand. His inquisitive gaze moves from me to the bag in my hands, then returns to my face.

"My daughter is traveling with her husband and the kids, they'll probably return in a few days." I am completely speechless, only feeling that desperate sensation taking over me from the inside out.

In a few days? God, what am I going to do?

Andrew seems to notice my chaotic state, as he takes a deep breath without taking his eyes off my face.

"I imagine you're tired. It was a long trip here. Well, my house is right there." He gestures toward another house on the same street, just as beautiful and large as this one. "We can go there, you can settle into one of the rooms, and I'll call Angelina. I'm sure she'll rush back as soon as she knows you're here."

I feel a pang of guilt in my chest for interrupting Angelina's trip, but I force myself to respond to him.

"I would really appreciate it if you could speak to her for me." Despite the fear, I feel relief wash over me, knowing he'll be able to contact her.

"Well, shall we go? Either way, she won't be able to come back today. So, you can stay at my place, Kate."

I look at him and then at the direction of the house he just pointed to. The place is dark, which means no one is waiting for Andrew there. It also means we'll be alone... for the night.

Feeling my body tremble, I take a step back.

"It won't be necessary... I... I'm staying at a hotel nearby," I lie as a wave of panic overwhelms me just thinking about being alone with him.

I notice Andrew raising an eyebrow and scanning my bag again. "Are you sure?" he insists.

"Yes. I'm sure. Thank you, Andrew," I say with conviction, not giving him a chance to respond.

I take a few more steps back, feeling lost, tired, and hungry. I have the urge to cry, but I need to be strong, I need to hold on until Angelina returns.

Andrew nods, before analyzing me one last time and turning to head back to his car. As he drives away, I let my shoulders slump in defeat, and I almost lose the battle against the persistent tears.

I feel my stomach growl again as I think about what I will do. Where will I spend the night? Everything inside me is unstable. Going back home isn't an option, even if I wanted to, I've used up the last of my royalties to get here.

Completely helpless, I begin to wander aimlessly down the street, then I remember the park nearby. It might not be the most comfortable place to spend the night, but I think it will do. I just need to stay unnoticed by the people who pass by.

I arrive at the location a few minutes later. Everything is quiet and empty, there's no one here.

I feel a chill run through my body, knowing this could be dangerous. But what choice do I have? Spending the night alone with a man is out of the question. So, I follow through with my plan. I look for a bench in a more discreet corner shaded by the trees and sit down. I feel the cold wrap around me and hug my trembling body.

I arrange my bag on the bench and lie down, using the bag as an improvised pillow.

Only then do I allow the sobs to escape my throat, and warm tears wash down my face as the darkness of the night surrounds me like a cold blanket, and I prepare to spend the night on the street, completely alone.

CHAPTER 7

ANDREW

There are no hotels around here.

That's the first thought that crosses my mind when I notice the lie slip from Kate's lips, saying she's staying at a hotel in the area.

The girl looks like a cornered animal as she looks at me, her extremely blue irises standing out. Her expression is tired, her face pale. The dark circles under her eyes are visible, as if she hadn't slept well in days. I feel the fear radiating from her body, as if she might run at any moment the moment I take another step forward.

Angelina had told me that her friend had been hurt when they lived in the convent, but she didn't go into detail. I only know the basics, or what Angelina felt comfortable sharing. Kate had been hurt, needed to spend some time in the hospital, and the two of them lost contact. I suspected the situation was much worse than that, but I decided not to press the issue.

But now, seeing Kate in front of me, I notice how deeply she hides her wounds. A visceral fear is etched in her sapphire eyes. An almost palpable distrust. She analyzes everything moving around her as if she has the same reflexes of a war veteran.

The girl takes a few steps back, firmly rejecting my offer to stay at my house for the night. So I don't press further. I nod to her and analyze her small, very thin frame inside the oversized clothes before heading to the car.

In less than a minute, I'm climbing the stairs that lead to my house. I stop before opening the door, still able to see the moment Kate turns her back and walks down the empty street, clutching her bag tightly, practically dragging herself with every step.

I continue to watch her steps from a distance. She doesn't turn to look in my direction, seems to have a goal set in her mind. A few meters later, she turns onto the street that leads to a wooded park nearby, and what crosses my mind makes my blood boil in my veins.

"She wouldn't... would she?" I murmur to myself.

Would the girl be stupid enough to spend the night in a park, alone?

I shake my head, trying to think that she wouldn't be that naive at this point. New York is dangerously extreme, even in neighborhoods that seem as calm as this one. Clenching my jaw, I open the door and step inside, forcing my thoughts to shift as I go through my daily ritual. I try to convince myself that Kate is an adult and knows what she's doing.

I take off my suit and the gun from the holster, leave my briefcase in the office, and head to the kitchen to cool off with a glass of cold water. Then, I grab my phone and make a call to my daughter, but the call goes straight to voicemail. The same happens with her husband's and eldest son's numbers.

"Hello, darling. How's the trip? Are the kids okay? I'm waiting to hear from you. Your friend Kate is in town, she came looking for you, but since you're not here, she left. Please call me back as soon as you can." I leave the message on Angelina's voicemail and slide the phone into my pocket.

Restless, I roll up my shirt sleeves and unbutton it down to my chest. I take a deep breath, feeling the exhaustion take hold of me.

The day has been full, the incidents relentless. I feel like chaos is taking over this city, and the impact will be imminent.

I decide to have a drink to relax a little, so that's what I do. I walk upstairs to the living room, fill a glass with whiskey and ice from my little personal bar. I sit in an armchair and take the first sip, savoring the unique taste on my tongue. I lose track of time as I enjoy the drink down to the last drop. I hear the voice of silence, missing the noise of the children, Angelina's kids. The loneliness hits me hard, that familiar anguish that tightens the chest. The anguish typical of a man alone. I grab the bottle and pour another glass. As the amber liquid flows into the glass, I find myself drowning in my own thoughts.

The feeling of emptiness, the lack of connection with something I can't define, weighs on me like an unwanted anchor. Maybe it's the price of my independence, or maybe just the inevitable consequence of my choices. I'm a divorced man, and until recently, I didn't even know I had a daughter. Although nothing makes me happier than meeting Angelina, she has her life, her husband, her kids, and her career. And I have my job and my solitude.

As I raise the glass to my lips, my phone vibrates softly. A message. I know who it's from even before I pick up the device. It's her. Safira. The woman who insists on inserting herself into my life, despite my clear disinterest in having anything beyond an affair.

With a sigh, I slide my finger across the phone screen, reading the message that flashes in front of me. Seductive words, empty promises of pleasure and passion. I can almost smell her perfume, hear her soft voice in my ear. But my body doesn't react. Nothing.

"I miss you, Andrew, it's been so many days since we've seen each other. I didn't think you were serious when you said you were going to end our affair. I miss you, darling, your smell, feeling your cock in my mouth... inside me."

"Take care, Safira."

There's no spark in my reply as I type back. No heat in my words. I'm not interested in continuing what we had, not anymore. We were a distraction for each other, until she tried to cross the line when

I decided to end everything. Now Safira has turned into a fleeting shadow.

I set the phone aside, returning my attention to the golden liquid in my glass. As I drink, I let the gentle burn of the whiskey push away the unwanted thoughts and all the stress of the day.

The last drop of whiskey slides down my throat, burning like a small flame before it fades. I place the empty glass aside with a sigh, feeling more clear-headed than I have in a long time.

A sudden sense of restlessness overtakes me, a need to escape the silent oppression of the walls of the house. I rise from the armchair, leaving my phone forgotten on the coffee table. I walk to the window and open it, letting the cold night air enter and caress my face. A flash of lightning splits the sky, a storm seems to be on its way. I look beyond the grass, at the empty street bathed in the dim light of the street lamps. Then the memory of the girl comes strong into my mind. *Kate*. Her face appears in my thoughts like a sudden wave, flooding my mind with images of her scared eyes, as blue as a gemstone, *a sapphire*. What an irony fate holds.

Without thinking twice, I run down the stairs and grab the car keys. I head in the direction where I know I'll find her, I head towards the park. The road is silent, only the distant sound of cars echoing in the night air. As I approach, my heart beats faster, that protective instinct rising fiercely. I link it to the fact that the girl is Angelina's friend, and despite my initial objections, I know I wouldn't be able to sleep if I didn't go after her, and that's just crap.

I park the car and my eyes search frantically for her among the shadows of the trees. I walk slowly, scanning the benches, the hidden spots. The darkest corner from there. And then, there she is. Lying on a bench, completely still, apparently asleep.

I move toward her, careful not to make a sound. I don't want to scare her, especially not in a situation that leaves her so vulnerable. I get close enough to hear her soft sobs. My heart tightens in my chest seeing her like this. Her hair is spread out on the bench, as dark as the night, her eyes closed. Thick tears glisten in the light flashes. I lower myself slowly, watching her for a moment, a little mesmerized by her almost surreal beauty. She looks so fragile, so vulnerable there, alone. So lonely.

Carefully, I place my hand over hers, feeling her cold skin against my warm one. I sense her shiver, and she slightly opens her eyes, surprise overtaking her expression.

"Andrew?" she murmurs, disoriented, her alarmed gaze meeting mine. She forces her body to sit up and brings her hand to her wet face. "I... well... What are you doing here?"

Kate averts her gaze, visibly embarrassed, and takes a deep breath, uncomfortable with my presence and the fact that I caught her in this situation, but I don't care about that right now.

"There are no hotels around here, Kate," I reply softly, although I'm still irritated that she lied and put herself at risk like this.

"I know... I just... I have nowhere to stay." Her words are evasive, and she doesn't meet my eyes as she answers.

I narrow my eyes, studying her face, seeing how scared she looks, like a little fox, I can feel her trembling from where I stand.

"I spoke to Angelina, she'll be here soon," I lie, knowing that if I reveal the truth—that I couldn't get in touch with my daughter—Kate would become even more suspicious and fearful.

Her eyes light up when she hears my daughter's name on my lips. I stand and sit on the bench to speak with her calmly.

"Really? What did she say?" Her attention is fully back on me.

"She'll be back as soon as she can. In the meantime, she asked me to take good care of you."

I clench my fists, bothered by my own lie, even though I know it would be exactly what Angelina would have asked if I had been able to speak with her.

I notice how uncomfortable she is with my closeness. She becomes even more defensive and cornered when I make it clear that she will have to come home with me. But damn it, I won't let this girl spend the night out on the streets unprotected, even if I have to carry her home in my arms and force her.

"I'm not sure it's a good idea." She pulls away to a corner of the bench, clutching her bag in her lap.

At that exact moment, I feel a few raindrops fall on my face, and within seconds, the drops turn into thick sheets of rain.

Another flash of lightning cuts through the air, illuminating Kate's face as she looks at me, disoriented. The cold intensifies, and with it, the rain comes.

"I think we don't have much choice, Kate. I'm not leaving you here alone, and unless you decide to come with me, we'll both be soaked to the bone," I practically yell so she can hear my voice over the intensifying downpour.

I rise from the bench and extend my hand to her.

"Come on, you'll be fine. You can trust me."

The water streams down my face, and my clothes stick to my body. I'm soaked in seconds, watching Kate.

She looks at my hand and then at my face. She seems undecided, but Kate knows that staying here in the rain, not only is it dangerous but also foolish. She could catch a serious cold or pneumonia that would leave her hospitalized.

Slowly, she extends her hand toward mine. It's trembling and cold when I touch her fingers and help her stand.

"I don't want to be a bother, Andrew..."

"You'll be a bother if you stay here. It'll be a very unpleasant night for both of us in this rain and cold."

She takes a deep breath and nods in defeat, lowering her head.

Not letting go of Kate's hand, I lead her toward the car I parked on the other side of the park.

I open the passenger door for her and walk around to settle in the driver's seat. As I drive back home, Kate remains completely silent, her attention fixed on the street as she hugs her bag. The object is as wet as our clothes.

Minutes later, I open the door to the house for her to enter. The girl remains defensive as she walks through the hallway. She carefully observes everything around her, then turns her attention back to me, as if waiting for a command.

"I'll show you the room you'll be staying in," I say without delay, doing my best to avoid making her uncomfortable. "This way."

I climb the stairs, hearing her soft steps behind me. Once in the hallway, I show her the TV room and point to the corridor leading to the bedrooms. I indicate the guest room, which is just past mine.

"You can stay here. It has a bathroom and a big bed. It's comfortable." I open the door, turn on the light, and step aside to let her enter.

Kate walks slowly into the room. She looks at the white walls and the neutral space with minimal decoration and turns to me again.

"Thanks. This is way better than any hotel room... or that bench." She's still distant, but I keep my distance to avoid frightening her more. I watch carefully every detail of her movements. Kate clutches the soaked bag, just like it is, inhales deeply, and brushes a wet lock of hair from her face.

From where I stand, I hear her stomach growl and realize that, besides being alone and cold, she's also hungry.

"How long has it been since you ate?" I ask without hesitation, being careful not to let my frustration with the situation show.

Her cheeks turn red with embarrassment, and she looks away before responding:

"It's been a while!" She's not being direct, but that doesn't matter now.

"Feel free to take a shower. I'll get you something dry to wear and start dinner. You can come down when you're ready."

I leave the guest room without waiting for a response and rush to my room to change clothes and grab one of my shirts for her. When I return to the room, I knock on the door, but Kate doesn't answer. I open it quickly and enter to leave the shirt on the bed while I hear the sound of the shower running.

As quickly as I entered, I exit the room and head to the kitchen to check which frozen food I'll heat up in the microwave. I end up not choosing any pre-made meals. I grab some steaks and decide to grill them. As a side, I prepare some potatoes.

Twenty minutes later, I hear Kate's footsteps coming down the stairs. She appears at the kitchen door in seconds.

"You can sit down, dinner will be ready in a minute." I point to the stools by the kitchen island and briefly observe her.

Kate has her hair loose and still wet. The dark strands form a dense mass around her angelic face, making her even more beautiful. Her intense eyes stare back at me, but she quickly looks away. She's not wearing the shirt I left for her in the room. She's dressed in a loose top and pants, slightly damp and wrinkled from the rain we got caught in.

"I'll put your other clothes in the dryer later," I comment and turn my attention back to the steaks, which are nearly done.

"I appreciate it. I was lucky these didn't get too soaked in my bag."

Silence returns to the kitchen. Kate doesn't say anything else, and I stay focused until everything is ready. The air feels dense, almost palpable. I can hear the girl's breath so close to me. Glancing at her again, I'm momentarily stunned when I realize how soft her skin looks. Every detail of her forms a combination unlike anything I've ever seen.

I feel my blood boil when I think of her alone in that park, completely at the mercy of some lunatic.

What happened to you, Kate? What brings you here?

Unanswered questions pile up in the recesses of my mind.

I feel anger, but I can't explain exactly why it affects me. It just bothers me that she seems so helpless.

"Dinner's ready." I clear my throat and grab plates, forks, and knives from the cabinet. I serve both of us and place Kate's plate in front of her.

I sit next to her and begin cutting my steak without raising my gaze.

"Thank you..." Her thanks comes out so softly, almost as a murmur.

She waits a few seconds before beginning to eat. Then she devours everything with alarming speed, as if she hadn't eaten in days and was at her limit.

I get up and head to the freezer, grab two cans of soda, and hand one to her. I sit back down and finish my meal, although the last bites of meat get stuck in my throat.

I sit for a moment, thinking about everything, bothered by the unanswered questions, but I don't make a move to ask anything. I don't have that right, and apparently, Kate isn't willing to open up.

In silence, the girl picks up the dishes from the island and takes them to the dishwasher. When she's done, she turns toward me and says goodbye: "Thank you for everything, I'm going... I'll go to bed."

I nod without turning toward her.

A few minutes later, silence reigns throughout the house, except for the sound of the torrential rain outside.

I drink another shot of whiskey before heading to my room. I take a quick shower and put on a pair of light pants to sleep in. I fall asleep in minutes, but wake in the middle of the night to the sound of screams.

Immediately, I sit up in bed, still disoriented, feeling like I just woke from a nightmare. But the screams coming from the guest room are very real.

I don't even bother putting on a shirt. I leave my room as I am, barefoot and shirtless. I slam open the door to Kate's room, and the scene I see leaves me completely paralyzed.

The girl is writhing on the bed, her eyes closed, tears streaming down her face.

"No, please! No! No!"

I approach Kate at an alarming speed and touch her shoulder, trying to wake her up. Despite the cold, I notice that she is warm, sweating, and gasping. The sheet is bunched at her feet, and she's wearing my shirt to sleep. The fabric is tangled above her hips, leaving her slim legs and underwear fully exposed.

"Kate! Kate!" I call her name and shake her shoulders to wake her up. "Come on, Kate, wake up. You're having a nightmare."

"No! Don't do this!" She screams, kicking her legs as if fighting with all her strength.

"Kate! Wake up!"

"No, Garath!" Then one last scream echoes through the room, and she sits up in bed, completely in shock, her breath ragged.

"Calm down, Kate, it's me, Andrew. You're safe. Calm down."

She stares at me with a terrified look, brings her hands to her face, and deep sobs echo through the room. I don't think coherently when all I want to do is protect the girl from everything. From the world, from people, from any bastard who might have hurt her. I approach her, and without hesitation, I kneel on the bed and pull Kate into my arms. I hold her tightly, resting her head on my chest as she cries almost uncontrollably. I feel the temperature of her skin against mine, and I close my eyes. I can almost feel the anger radiating through my body, along with the visceral desire to protect her.

"It's going to be okay, little fox. It's going to be okay..." I say through clenched teeth, even though I realize the pain she carries is greater than I can imagine.

CHAPTER 8

KATE

YEARS BEFORE

I'm alone at home tonight. Mom just left for work, and as for Garath, I haven't seen him in three days.

So I make my dinner. Mac and cheese with a bit of bacon. I put everything on a plate and walk to the kitchen table.

I'm starting to eat when the front door opens, and I jump in my chair. I hear footsteps in the living room, my heart pounding in my chest, and fear overwhelms me. I stay quiet while the sound of footsteps echoes through the house, until his face appears in the kitchen. Garath seems sober. Despite his red eyes, he doesn't stumble as he walks and sits at the table with me.

"Did your whore of a mother go to work?" His eyes are fixed on my face.

Despite the discomfort I feel hearing him speak about my mom, I don't dare respond, I just nod with a slight shake of my head.

"Great... How about you give me some of that you're eating?"

I glance at Garath and push the plate toward him. I won't argue, as I know it's dangerous. Even though I'm starving and there's not much left in the cupboards or the fridge. I've seen up close how violent he can be. So I avoid him as much as I can.

"You can eat it all, I'm already full," I lie, though I can feel my stomach growling.

I stand up to leave and go to my room, but Garath calls me, stopping me from going any further.

"Don't go, Kate. I like your company. Sit down, little girl."

"No..., I need to..."

"Sit down, girl, don't be silly!" His hands slam the table forcefully, and I jump, startled. My body trembles, my sixth sense screams at me to get away from this bad man, but fear prevents me from following through with my thoughts.

With my body shaking, I return to the table and sit where I was. I stay still, hands in my lap. I clutch the fabric of my dress.

"So tell me. How was your day?" He chews and fills his fork with pasta, bringing the food to his mouth again.

I look at Garath, completely incredulous, since he's never cared about my day or what I do. When the man focuses his attention on my face, waiting for an answer, I realize that I've been holding my breath, the tension taking over my body. My hands are trembling, I feel my heart racing. I'm scared of him.

"It was fine," I murmur.

"And school? Do you have many little friends at school?"

"Just... just one," I stutter involuntarily, pressing the fabric of my dress tighter.

"Really? What's her name?"

Garath shovels two forkfuls of pasta into his mouth, chewing while looking at me. It's disgusting to see him eat, but still, I feel my stomach growl with hunger.

"Melissa. Her name's Melissa."

"And the boyfriends? Have you kissed anyone, Kate?"

My cheeks flush with his invasive question, but I shake my head in denial. I remember a boy in my class, the most handsome I've ever seen in my life, but the closest we've been was exchanging a few words when we did a science group project.

"You know, Kate, I don't believe you, little girl." He examines my face and stands up. "You're a pretty little girl. And you've got a very attractive body. You're growing a nice pair of tits."

He smiles at me, and I shrink back in the chair, feeling naked under his evaluation. The discomfort in my stomach hits hard, and I stand up to leave his presence.

"Don't let any boy touch those tits, you hear me, Kate?"

I run as fast as I can to my room. I can still hear Garath's laughter behind me, and it makes me hurry my steps.

I lie on my bed, feeling breathless, my heart pounding.

After I calm down, I go to the door and lock it. I try to listen for any noise Garath might be making, but everything is silent. So the only alternative I have is to go to bed while my insides churn with hunger.

I curl up under the covers, trembling, calling my mom's name softly while I try to calculate how much time is left before she comes back.

A long time. It's going to be a long time before she returns. I conclude in my thoughts, and it terrifies me.

Garath's gaze, that gaze was bad, I could feel it.

KATE

PRESENT DAYS

CONTROL COMPLETELY escapes me as I feel Andrew's strong arms around my body. I seem to be lost in an endless nightmare. I hear the sound of the rain outside, feel my tears wetting my face, and my sobs are constant. I have the urge to scream in desperation as I recall every detail of everything.

I can almost feel Garath's grip on my arm, the punch he threw at my face. The nightmare was so real that even his smell seemed to be present, lingering in my nostrils.

"It's going to be okay, little fox, it's going to be okay." The voice and the proximity of a man, 99% of the time, leave me trembling and on high alert, but I don't understand why I don't feel such great fear now, even after waking up screaming. Maybe because Andrew has been respectful this whole time, maybe because he's Angelina's father and my friend trusts him. Or maybe... I really can't explain it.

I just close my eyes and allow myself to be comforted for the first time, without feeling the weight on my chest or the obligation to say anything. I let myself feel human warmth without having to give anything in return, I allow myself to be protected. When my trembling stops, I pull away from his arms and dry my cheeks with the palms of my hands. I look at Andrew and feel my skin burn with embarrassment for seeing him there without a shirt, his abdomen exposed, probably disoriented from being woken up in the middle of the night.

"I'm sorry... I... had a horrible nightmare..."

I can't look at him any longer. I simply can't face his questioning eyes. I don't want to talk about it, I don't want to talk about anything.

"Don't apologize." Andrew's voice invades my eardrums. It's calm, deep, penetrating the very core of my being.

I feel his fingers on my face, and Andrew turns my face to him, forcing me to look at him.

"You're safe here, Kate. Do you understand that?" His eyes seem like sparks as he looks at me. There's a mix of indignation and distress on his face that leaves me momentarily confused.

"Yes, I understand," I murmur softly, my voice barely escaping. "Sorry for making you upset, I..."

I try to apologize for all the discomfort I'm causing him, but Andrew interrupts me before I can finish my sentence.

"Don't say that, Kate." He takes a deep breath and slides his fingers along my chin, his green eyes locked on mine. "You haven't done anything. I'm just upset about this whole situation, not with you."

I blink, still more confused than before. "I don't understand."

Andrew pulls his hands away from my face and stands up from the bed. He seems tense, as if he's about to explode. In a quick motion, the man turns his back on me.

It's impossible not to notice how imposing he is. His shoulders are broad, his arms muscular, and his back as well. Everything about him is big, a huge contrast to my small stature. And I'm completely at his mercy here alone. Andrew wouldn't have any trouble overpowering me. It would be too easy to hurt me, force me to do disgusting things. And I wouldn't have any chance against him. Yet, he doesn't show anything that scares me. He doesn't look at me as if I were a piece of juicy meat, he doesn't even seem to notice that I'm a woman.

"You were alone on a bench in the park at night. You ran away from me as if I were the devil himself, and then this nightmare." Andrew stares at me again with that inquisitive expression. "I know you're going through something really bad, Kate, and it's throwing me off. However, I don't have the right to interfere in your life. You're welcome in my house whenever you need, and I'm not the one who will pressure you to say anything."

I feel my heart race as I observe this practically unknown man, yet at the same time, so human and right. Or is that how he wants me to think? He walks to the bedroom window and watches the rain pouring outside. He closes the curtains and returns to the center of the room. Andrew watches me closely for a few seconds, and I feel like I'm almost an open book under his analysis.

"Take care, Kate. Good night."

"Good night, Andrew..." I respond almost in a whisper.

Then he heads to the door and leaves, leaving me there, lost with my own thoughts and the demons from my past.

CHAPTER 9

KATE

After Andrew leaves, I stay awake for a few minutes, recalling everything. The threats from the nightmare are still deep in my soul, but I'm no longer afraid. My racing heart slowly starts to calm, my trembling body steadies. I focus on the peace I felt when he held me. I felt protected, safe. But for how long? When will he demand the price for me sleeping in his house and eating his food? Isn't that what men do? They feed you, protect you, and then enslave you. Well, at least that's what I've known for most of my life. That's what Garath did to my mom.

I close my eyes again and fall asleep while the heavy rain falls outside. There are no dreams or nightmares. It's a silent sleep, almost like a prelude to death.

I wake up disoriented and completely lost. The room is fully lit and the temperature slightly warmer. Flashbacks of the previous night come back to my mind, and I remember everything. The park, the fear I felt while being alone on that bench, the cold rain falling on my face. And then Andrew rescuing me from that nightmare.

I bring my hand to my face and rub my eyes. I recall every second of what happened last night, how much I cried in his arms *there*.

I take a deep breath, shivering, feeling my cheeks warm, my head spinning. I can almost feel the warmth of Andrew's body when he held me tightly. I can almost smell his scent.

I shake my head from side to side, feeling confused, and decide to get out of bed. I look at the window, noticing the bright sunshine, and conclude that it's too late to wake up in someone's house who is hosting you out of pity. What will Andrew think of me? That I'm a freeloader, for sure.

I pull the sheets off my body and stand up. To my complete surprise, I find the clothes that were wet from the rain, now dry and folded at the foot of the bed. I carefully take the shirt and feel the scent of flowers and the softness of the freshly washed fabric.

I simply stand still, unable to move, completely touched by Andrew's care in every detail. I look at the shirt I wore to sleep and then realize that even the clothes I'm wearing belong to him. This disorients me more with each second, as it makes me wonder what the price of all this will be?

Quickly, I pull the shirt over my head and put on my loose clothes again. I use the bathroom, brush my teeth, tie my hair into a ponytail, and decide to go downstairs to ask Andrew for some information about Angelina's return.

As soon as I go downstairs, I hear voices coming from the kitchen. I approach slowly to avoid interrupting the conversation. I see Andrew with his back to me, dressed in a black suit, talking to someone on a laptop screen, and I quickly recognize Angelina's voice.

My heart races with happiness and surprise, and I quicken my pace. I completely forget that I should be quiet and end up drawing Andrew's attention, who turns toward me. His scrutinizing gaze meets mine, and seeing him so imposing in those expensive clothes makes my breath quicken a little.

"Hello, Kate." He smiles and waves his hand for me to come closer. "Come here. Someone wants to talk to you."

The fine wrinkles around his eyes match the few gray strands at his temples. He gives off an air of an experienced and insightful man. He is a handsome, mature man, someone I can't decipher. He doesn't fit my expectations, as I keep waiting for the moment he'll demand something in return for his kindness.

Andrew turns his attention back to the laptop, and I approach, little by little, calculating my steps. When I'm close enough to see the screen, my eyes light up when I see Angelina on the other side, smiling, holding a beautiful little boy in her arms.

"Kate, oh Kate, I'm so happy to see you." She says and shakes the baby's little hand. "Say hi to her, my love, this is Kate."

The baby smiles at his mother's antics, and I feel my heart leap so hard it hurts. It hurts in my chest, in my soul. It hurts deeply. I'm enchanted by the sweet smile, everything inside me overflows. He looks almost the same age as my daughter.

"Hi, baby," I take a few more steps toward the screen, feeling my body tremble. "How beautiful you are." I take a deep breath and raise my eyes to Angelina. "Hi, Angel."

An agonizing lump forms in my throat as I watch the interaction between mother and child. The baby is chubby, with folds around his neck, and when he smiles, I can see his adorable little teeth in his mouth.

Andrew moves beside me and pushes the laptop toward me, allowing me to sit on one of the stools and rest my elbow on the counter to get comfortable.

"I'll be back in a minute, Kate. Feel free." He stands up and leaves the kitchen, giving me privacy to talk to her.

His perfume lingers in the air. It's strong, distinctive, a bit rustic. It fills my nostrils and steals my breath for a few seconds.

"I'm so glad you came to New York. Sorry I didn't reach out sooner, we've been in Africa on a volunteer mission, and yesterday we spent the day in a remote area, away from civilization." Angelina snuggles the baby more closely and plants a kiss on his little head. "So you know, no internet, no cell service, no running water."

Her smile widens, and it's clear how happy she is with the life she's chosen for herself.

"Everything's fine. The important thing is that we're talking now," I respond, and for the first time in a long while, a sincere smile graces my lips.

"But tell me, are you okay? How was the trip? I want to hear everything when you get back home."

"I'm fine. Your father has been very kind in hosting me." I try to sound as natural as possible, but I confess, the fear of an uncertain future looms like a shadowy threat. How long will his kindness last? What will he demand in return?

The image on the screen begins to glitch, and Angelina's voice cuts out, making it impossible to understand what she's saying.

"Angel? Angel?"

Within seconds, the transmission resumes.

"The internet signal here is terrible." The signal falters again, and her voice breaks up before returning. "Kate, don't worry, I'll be back home in a few days. In the meantime, you can stay at my father's house. He'll take good care of you." The image freezes, and the sound cuts out, making me clench my fists in frustration.

I wait a few seconds, which quickly turn into minutes. I'm about to step away when the connection resumes, and her voice echoes through the kitchen.

"Kate, can you hear me?"

"Angel? Yes, I can."

"I'll try to talk to you later—" the transmission falters. "It's impossible to communicate properly right now. Talk later, Kate."

I can still see my friend waving goodbye before the image freezes again. Then, the connection is cut off.

I take a deep breath, staring at the black screen in front of me, my heart aching with longing for her. The mixture of missing her and the joy of seeing her well and happy stirs within me. At the same time, the baby's smile seems etched into my memory like a tattoo. I think of my daughter, wondering if her smile is now the joy of someone else's life. Someone else, not mine.

I stand still for a moment, staring at nothing, and jump in surprise when I hear Andrew's voice behind me.

"Kate? Did Angelina hang up? I imagine the connection wasn't great."

His voice is casual and relaxed, but I still feel a chill run through me.

"The connection was bad, but I'm glad I managed to talk to her."

I turn to look at him and see him placing a few bags on the island.

"I hope you're hungry. I brought food for lunch." He checks the time on his wristwatch and then walks to the cabinets to grab plates and utensils. "Do you like pasta?"

I honestly don't know how to look at him without revealing my embarrassment. It's already lunchtime, and here I am, standing like a statue in Andrew's kitchen after waking up so late.

"Thank you, you didn't have to go to the trouble. And yes, I love pasta."

"No need to thank me, Kate. Just eat and be well." He turns toward me with the plates in hand, and I notice his green eyes shining.

Lunch passes in silence. The food is appetizing and very flavorful. I devour everything on my plate in a matter of minutes. When I finish, I move to stand and begin clearing the plates from the table. I sense Andrew watching me carefully, his eyes fixed on my movements, making my blood freeze in my veins. I stop what I'm doing, trembling, and leave the plates on the counter, waiting for the moment he asks for something—payment for everything he's done for me.

I lift my gaze to look at him and swallow hard. I can't decipher his expression. Andrew is serious, seeming thoughtful, but there isn't that strange look Garath used to give me whenever he found me alone in the house.

"Did you sleep well?" he finally breaks the anguishing silence.

"Yes," I say firmly, despite the strong beats of my heart.

"I'm sorry for everything, Kate." I blink, completely confused, and keep staring at the man. "I have no idea what you must have gone through, but I know it wasn't easy, and it isn't easy now. I hope that one day you can leave it all behind."

What does he want? To earn my trust only to make his move later?

I clench my fists as I feel anger rising within me, coursing through my body. I look at this man—so powerful and imposing, someone who can have whatever he desires and who certainly wouldn't hesitate to make me bend to his will—because I am nothing compared to him.

"I'll be fine!" I say curtly. Though I am grateful for everything he's done, my survival instincts tell me to keep my distance before it's too late. I need to get out of here before Angelina returns.

"Alright. I hope so." He sighs and checks the time on his wristwatch again. "Look, I need to leave now. But you can make yourself at home. Feel free to use the laptop I left on the counter if you'd like."

I remain silent, listening to his words, feeling my world spinning.

I lower my head and close my eyes for a few seconds, recalling Angelina's words: *"You can stay at my father's house. He'll take good care of you."*

Angel is wrong. No man is trustworthy. Not even her father.

"Will you be okay here alone for a while?" Andrew asks, and I turn to face him. His expression is serious as he waits for an answer.

"Yes!" I murmur through clenched teeth, already calculating my next steps.

To my utter surprise, I watch as he reaches into his pocket and pulls out a wallet. He takes out a credit card and hands it to me. "Buy yourself some clothes and anything you need. I won't be gone long. You can also use the card to call a cab."

I hold the card in my trembling hands, feeling the air leave my lungs, afraid I might explode at any moment. First his house, his clothes, his food. Now his money. What will be his next demand? My naked body in his bed as payment?

A lump forms in my throat, and I fight back the tears threatening to fall.

"What do you want from me?" I ask in almost a whisper, letting the card slip from my hands and fall to the floor at my feet.

Andrew watches me with an unwavering expression. Not a single muscle in his face moves, and nothing in his gaze shifts. It's as if he knows exactly what I'm feeling, as if he can read my thoughts with just a look.

He remains silent, his eyes fixed on me, but I refuse to back down. I won't fall into his nice-guy trap.

"I have nothing, Andrew. I can't give you anything in return for what you're giving me. And I..." A tear escapes and runs down my face, but I quickly wipe it away. "And I won't sleep with you as some form of payment."

Only then do I notice his pupils dilate, and his jaw tightens. A furious fire ignites in his eyes, making fear prickle across my skin.

"No one will lay a single finger on you, Kate." His voice is deep, menacing, making me want to get as far away from him as possible. "No one will ever hurt you again. Do you hear me?"

I widen my eyes, utterly alarmed and confused by his reaction—completely opposite to what I had imagined. "What are you saying?"

"I'm saying exactly what you heard. I wasn't born yesterday, girl, and I have a pretty good idea of what you've been through. So I'll say it again: no one will ever touch you again. Not ever. That's a promise, Kate. I understand why you're afraid of men, why you're afraid of me, and why your defenses are up. But believe me, I see you the way I see my daughter. I will protect you the same way I would protect Angelina. And I will take care of you as if you were her."

My heart races even more with everything I hear. Everything inside me feels destabilized, and conflicting thoughts make my temples throb. I swallow a sob, and Andrew crouches to pick up the card I dropped. He places it back in my hand and closes my palm around it.

"Use it. Buy whatever you need. You don't owe me anything, little fox. I'll never ask you for anything in return."

With blurry eyes, I focus on his serious face and murmur:

"Thank you."

"I won't be long." He winks softly and gives me a subtle smile, coaxing me into doing the same.

I feel my face flush with shame over everything I said, but I decide to let it go as he walks toward the exit until he's out of sight.

CHAPTER 10

KATE

YEARS EARLIER

It's so cold here, the air feels like it's freezing around me as I try to huddle further under the thick comforter.

I squeeze my eyes shut tightly, trying not to think about how dark the room is.

I'm so scared...

Mom is working tonight at the bar, as usual. She said she'd be home sometime in the early hours of the morning. She's been so tired and irritable lately that I didn't have the courage to ask her to take me with her. A few days ago, when I tried convincing her, I ended up grounded for a week.

So I do my best to manage. I had instant noodles for dinner, made them myself, and washed the dishes before heading upstairs to my room. I rushed through everything so I could get to bed and try to fall asleep before *he* comes back from his nightly outings. I hope I didn't leave anything out of place in the kitchen.

I have no idea what Garath does out on the streets until late, but every time he comes back, there's a strong smell of alcohol, and his strange gaze falls on me. His presence makes me uncomfortable in a way I can't explain, which is why I try to avoid him at all costs.

Even now, as I struggle to steady my breathing and calm my fears, I hear noises downstairs in the living room. I know he's back.

I don't understand why Mom allows this strange man to live with us. They argue all the time, shouting through the house. Not to mention the bruises he's left on her face. It's terrifying.

I squeeze my eyes shut even tighter as I hear Garath's footsteps on the stairs. I pull the comforter over my head and curl up on the mattress, wishing I could disappear and wake up somewhere far away. Just me and Mom.

His steps approach the room he shares with my mom. He pauses for a moment, and everything goes silent again.

I can almost hear the pounding of my heart.

Seconds drag on, and then it starts again. His slow, deliberate steps head toward my room. I hear the creak of the door opening, and the light from the hallway seeps through the comforter covering me.

I stay quiet where I am, whispering a prayer to God that Garath will go away. I don't like him; I never have. Since he came to live with us, something in my young heart has been screaming for me to keep my distance.

Trembling, I feel Garath's presence as he stops just a few steps away from my bed.

Minutes pass, and I can picture his gaze on me, even though my body is completely hidden under the covers.

"I know you're awake, little girl," his low, menacing voice breaks the silence in the air.

I feel the mattress dip beside me as he moves closer and sits down.

I curl into a tighter fetal position, hugging my body. The cold air raises goosebumps on my neck as Garath pulls the comforter away, and a wave of helplessness washes over me.

"Look at me, little girl," he says softly, but there's something deeply wrong in his tone—I can feel it.

I don't want to open my eyes. I don't want to look at Garath.

I shake my head and bury my face in the pillow, sniffling quietly so he won't hear. I clamp my eyelids shut as tightly as I can, as if that might make him vanish into thin air.

I hear the click of his tongue, and the mattress sinks further as Garath shifts closer to me.

His rough fingers touch the nape of my neck, gripping it firmly. I shudder at the intrusive touch.

"Mom should be home soon," I say, my voice trembling with the terror coursing through me.

Maybe, with the mention of Mom returning soon, Garath will go to his room and leave me alone.

But against all my silent pleas, Garath leans closer to me. I can smell the strong stench of alcohol mixed with cigarettes. His breath on my face is so foul it's unbearable to breathe.

"Tonight, I'm going to teach you something. Something I've always wanted to do, but I had to wait for the right time. So, be a good girl for Daddy. Don't scream, don't fight, and nothing will happen to you or your mom."

Tears well up in my eyes, and panic overtakes me as I try to comprehend what he's planning to do. I whisper prayers under my breath, begging for my mom to come back soon. She has to come back soon.

KATE

PRESENT DAY

I FINISH CLEARING THE plates from the table and load them into the dishwasher. Then, I tidy up the kitchen and wipe down the counters with a damp cloth.

I glance at the credit card I left on the counter, debating whether to use it or not. My eyes shift to my worn-out clothes, knowing they won't last forever. What if I treat the card as a loan? I could pay Andrew back as soon as next month's royalties hit my account.

I deliberate for a while and decide to do just that. It's still early, and I won't take long. I'll be back before Andrew even thinks about returning home, especially since I've also decided to make dinner tonight.

I dash to the guest room I'm staying in and fix my hair in the bathroom mirror. I tie my hair into a ponytail and head back downstairs.

Walking through the quiet neighborhood streets, I soon find a main avenue. A few minutes later, I catch a cab and ask the driver to take me to the nearest shopping mall. For now, I'll stick to alternative transport until I figure out how to navigate the subway system on my own.

I pay the fare when the cab stops in front of a massive building and step out. My body trembles slightly as anxiety hits me, but I take a deep breath and try to steady myself. This might be the first time I've gone shopping without someone supervising me, and it feels both amazing and terrifying.

I mentally create a basic list and begin searching for what I need. At first, I feel completely lost amidst the crowds of people. My breathing becomes shallow, and sweat forms on my forehead. Everything inside me feels off-balance. I stop and take a moment to observe my surroundings. I see a smiling couple walking hand-in-hand. Across the way, a blonde woman pushes a stroller. I peek inside and feel my heart melt at the sight of a little girl sleeping with a pacifier in her mouth.

Life moves on. People chat, interact, shop, smile, and have fun. For some reason, I feel more alive, less terrified. I feel like myself again.

With newfound courage, I take a few more steps. A brave smile forms on my lips as I enter the first clothing store.

"May I help you?" A friendly saleswoman approaches. Her brown hair is loose, and she wears casual clothes, unlike the standard uniforms I noticed on other employees in other stores.

"I think so," I reply, forcing a smile. "I need some basic pieces for everyday wear and... maybe a nice dress."

The last part comes out uncertainly. I'm not sure if I'll have the courage to wear a dress or anything outside of my usual style, but I also don't want to look sloppy. It's always good to have something more refined, especially now that I'm in New York, far from Mom and Garath. I don't want Angelina or Andrew to be embarrassed by me at any special occasion.

She nods and asks me to follow her. Some time later, I leave the store carrying bags with basic clothes, a long-sleeved black dress, a comfortable sleep set, underwear, and a pair of low-heeled sandals. I stop by another store to pick up personal hygiene items and a lightly scented moisturizer. After gathering everything I need, I treat myself to an ice cream and find a cab to take me back to Andrew's house. Within an hour, I'm back at Angelina's father's house.

I put everything away in the guest room and head downstairs to the kitchen. Glancing at the wall clock, I start the task I set out to do—making dinner. I begin by rummaging through the pantry and fridge to see what's available.

My shoulders slump in disappointment as I realize I should've asked Andrew what he likes to eat. The available options aren't great either, as I've noticed in the short time we've been living under the same roof—he either reheats something frozen, eats out, or picks up meals from a restaurant.

I find frozen chicken in the freezer and some nearly overripe potatoes in the fridge. I defrost the chicken in the microwave and prepare the marinade. With some improvisation, I gather everything I need to bread the chicken thighs and breasts.

While the seasoned chicken rests, I cook the potatoes and whip up a salad using the only cabbage I could find. I season everything and bread the chicken for frying.

I smile proudly when everything is ready. The chicken is crispy and golden, the salad is well-seasoned, and the mashed potatoes are as smooth as a cloud. The delicious aroma filling the kitchen makes my stomach growl. I'm setting the table when I hear footsteps coming from the living room, drawing closer to the kitchen. Andrew steps into view, and I lift my head to look at him. Despite his tired expression, I notice his face softens as he takes a deep breath, savoring the scent of fresh homemade food in the air.

Andrew smiles as he takes off his jacket and steps further into the kitchen.

"Did I die and go to heaven? Is that it?" he jokes while rolling up his sleeves.

I feel my face heat up, but I can't deny that his excitement makes my heart leap with joy, knowing I finally did something right.

"I hope you like fried chicken and mashed potatoes." I walk around the island, placing plates, cutlery, and serving dishes on the table. I try to suppress a smile, but it doesn't last long.

"Does anyone not like fried chicken, Kate? If they do, I've never met them."

Andrew leans against the wall, continuing to watch me as I finish setting up. I realize it's been a long time since I've felt like this—useful, alive, like I've finally found a place where I belong.

"I don't know anyone either. But since I didn't know what you liked and fried chicken seemed like a safe bet, that's what I decided to make."

"You're going to spoil me like this." His smile widens, and I find myself analyzing his expression. A deep feeling stirs within me—a kind of pride, knowing that something I did has made him happy.

In the mix of aromas and smiles, our eyes lock for what feels like too long. My smile fades as I realize my heartbeat is spiraling out of control. Andrew seems to notice the same, clearing his throat and stepping away from the wall, as if shaking off a momentary trance.

"I brought something for you, Kate," he says, breaking the strange, confusing atmosphere that had enveloped us.

I blink a few times, unable to guess what he might have brought.

"What? Andrew, you didn't have to go out of your way. I—" I start to protest that I've already bought everything I need, but he interrupts me.

"Come with me. I'm sure you'll like it."

I leave everything as it is on the counter and take a few steps toward Andrew. I follow him through the house at a brisk pace until we reach the living room. Near the entry hall, I see the most adorable little thing in the world. Andrew walks to a small carrier and pulls out a Golden Retriever puppy. The little one whines in his arms but quickly wags its tail, as if sensing he's a trustworthy man. I stand frozen, unable to believe what I'm seeing—a man holding a puppy and handing it to me.

"I've always wanted one of these," he begins, extending the puppy toward me. "But work doesn't allow it, and I didn't want him to be alone. Now that you're here, I think we can fix that."

I take the puppy in my hands, feeling the softness of its fur. But I can't quite grasp what he means by "now that you're here to take care of him."

"I don't understand. The puppy... he's beautiful. But I'm not staying here forever."

Andrew laughs and slides his hand into his pocket, watching me intently.

"But while you are here, you can take care of him, can't you?" he asks, his lips still curved into a smile.

I look down at the puppy, who starts barking and wriggling to get my attention, then back at Andrew. "Alright! But what about when I leave?"

He steps closer and strokes the puppy's fur.

"Don't think about that right now. I'm far too hungry at the moment. How about we dig into that amazing feast you've prepared?"

I nod at Andrew, smiling as I hold the puppy close to my chest, my heart leaping with happiness. The little one starts licking my hand, and I stroke its soft ears.

We walk back to the kitchen, and I set the puppy on the floor. I grab a temporary bowl from the cabinets, fill it with water, and place it on the ground for him. After washing my hands, I sit at the counter with Andrew and watch as he serves himself. He eats heartily, taking generous forkfuls of food. I smile to myself, a shiver running down my spine. I start eating too and surprise myself with how good everything turned out. The chicken is perfectly cooked and flavorful, and the mashed potatoes are delicious.

We eat in silence, but the comforting feeling lingers in the air.

I take a bite of the breaded chicken and glance up at Andrew. I watch how his mouth moves as he chews and swallows the food, as though he's savoring a heavenly feast. When he finishes, he uses a napkin to wipe his mouth and sighs deeply, clearly satisfied.

"I think a good wine would be perfect right now." He places his hands on the table, the tension in his arm muscles visible through the fabric of his white shirt.

I feel my throat go dry as I take in every detail of his face, his shoulders, his arms, and his strong hands. He stands, but it feels as though his presence fills the entire kitchen. I sense him in every inch of the walls and air. I smell his cologne, feel the strength of his body. I feel safe in his presence.

CHAPTER 11

KATE

YEARS EARLIER

I hear the sound of Garath's zipper being undone, and the grip of his hand on my neck tightens.

"Please... let me go..." I plead softly, feeling the strength of his hands bruising my skin. Thick tears stream down my face; I feel cold, breathless, my entire body trembling.

"I've always wanted to touch you like this. And I've always wanted to feel you touch me too." A disgusting laugh escapes his mouth.

"No... I don't want to do this..." I say, choking on a sorrowful sob.

Garath takes a deep breath and starts sliding his hand over my shoulders and down my back.

"You'll like it, little girl. You'll beg me for more, I know you will. Relax a bit, hmm?"

His vile hands move down my ribs, sending a wave of revulsion through me. The invasive touches intensify as he reaches the front of my body, caressing and squeezing my small, budding breasts. Instinctively, I recoil.

I hear Garath's laughter, reveling in my fear. Tears well up in my eyes with even greater force.

"I told you to look at me, Kate!" I shudder at his threatening tone and force myself to open my eyelids.

My vision is blurred, but I can still make out the curve of a smile on Garath's face.

"Please, Garath. I need to sleep."

I try to push him away as Garath pulls my pajama pants down.

"No, Garath... No, Garath... No, Garath..."

I lean forward and bring my small hands to stop him from continuing what he's doing. But I don't have enough strength to fight Garath. I don't have the strength to stop him from removing my pants and my underwear in the process. I thrash around. I beg him to leave me alone. His touch on my skin makes me feel a terrible nausea, and shame washes over me from head to toe.

Why is Garath doing this to me? I don't understand. He says I'll like it, but why does it feel so wrong?

One of his hands covers my mouth to muffle my sobs and pleas, while the other holds my hips, forcing me to lie on my back on the bed.

"You're not being a good little girl, Kate. Do you want the neighbors to hear you? If they hear, you'll never see Mommy again. Do you want that, little girl?"

I become even more distressed at the thought that he might hurt Mommy. That I won't see her again when the sun rises in the sky.

I shake my head, pure panic streaming from my eyes, soaking my face and hair, blurring my vision. I try my best to stay still despite the trembling.

"That's it, stay quiet. Daddy's proud when you obey like that."

You're not my dad. It's what I think of saying, but I don't have the strength to speak, and Garath still keeps his hand clamped over my mouth.

The man adjusts himself on the mattress, sitting near my head.

Unable to face him, I turn my head to the side as I feel his grip on my mouth loosen.

I swallow the sob forming in my throat, feeling the terrified pounding of my heart, and squeeze my eyes shut. I try to transport myself to another dimension, another space, another place. A place where I don't have to endure Garath's hand sliding between my thighs, touching the most private part of my body.

ANDREW

PRESENT DAY

KATE LOOKS AT ME AS if she can see every compartment of my mind. Her eyes scan my face, shoulders, and chest, but she doesn't seem to realize it. Her pale skin takes on a pinkish hue that makes her even more beautiful. She's such a gorgeous girl, so young and shy, or at least that's how she appears to be behind all the trauma she carries.

Kate has created a hard protective shell around herself. She's aloof, suspicious.

But in moments like this, when she's not scared, I can feel her essence and how life pulses through her veins. It's not hard to understand her fascination as she watches me. I notice it in the way she analyzes the details and how nervous she gets when I get closer, her face flushed, her breathing quickening. She's just a girl, too young and too confused. She knows I wouldn't hurt her, but the trauma doesn't allow her to see it clearly. She knows I'm the father of her friend, but she also knows I'm a man, and that desire pulses through my body every second our gazes remain locked.

Shit!

I feel danger lurking, my skin heats up, and an agonizing spark starts to form in my groin. I notice that her lips are even redder than they seemed a few minutes ago. The blue of her gaze grows more vivid, and her slender body takes on a form that's too tempting for my liking.

I swallow hard, feeling the blood heat up and concentrate where it shouldn't, and I shift my attention to the puppy running through the kitchen. The little animal starts barking at Kate's feet, and she gets distracted.

She laughs when he raises his front paws, jumping at her calves.

"Hey, little guy, what do you want?" She crouches down and picks him up, speaking soothingly to him. "We need to come up with a name for you. What do you think of Spot?"

I inhale deeply, regaining control of my body, and clench my fists, completely irritated with myself. I cross my arms over my chest and watch their interaction.

"What do you think of that name, Andrew?" she asks with a smile, petting the puppy's belly.

"I think it's a good name. It suits him."

I end up smiling when I realize that the name Spot would fit any breed of dog. It seems like it was created for furry creatures, even if the reference comes from the movie *The Good Dinosaur*, an animated film that Angelina's children love to watch, where Spot is actually the human pet of the Dinosaur.

"I think it suits him too. So it's settled, you'll be called Spot."

I simply forget about the wine. I lose track of time as I watch Kate laughing while playing with Spot and putting him back on the floor. The puppy whimpers, wanting her lap again, but what captivates me most is the shine in the girl's eyes.

Obviously, I was rude when I brought the animal for Kate to take care of without asking her first. But the years of experience in the FBI have given me some advantages: I know enough about traumatized people to understand that they feel more confident when they are useful. Living under my roof, Kate is protected, but she feels out of place. However, from the moment I ask her for her help, she starts to feel necessary and no longer a burden.

"I brought some food for him. I'll go get it from the car. But tomorrow, you can buy other things for the dog's well-being, what do you think?"

She nods and walks over to the counter. She grabs the credit card I gave her earlier and walks toward me.

"Your card, Andrew. I used a little to buy some clothes and personal items, but I promise I'll pay you back as soon as possible." She extends her hand to give it back to me, and I hold it for a moment before returning it to her.

"Use it to buy Spot's things tomorrow."

Kate takes the card uncertainly, I see confusion in her expression.

"Andrew, I can't spend any more..."

"Don't worry, Kate. After all, the dog is mine too, right? Spend it on whatever you need, you'll be doing me a huge favor. Go ahead and buy some food and drinks, okay?"

I don't tell her that I won't accept the money she spent on the clothes back. I don't want her to feel bad about it. Slowly, she'll get used to the way I handle things, and over time, she'll understand that I don't want anything in return for helping her.

"Alright," her lips curl slightly, and she takes a step back.

"I'll do the dishes while you grab the food."

I nod in agreement and step out of her line of sight. I rush to the car, grab the food, and return quickly. When I enter the kitchen, I see Kate finishing loading the dishes into the dishwasher while speaking softly to the puppy. I feel her scent, I sense her presence strongly. It's as if the house has gained a little more life and color since she's been here.

I leave Spot's food on the counter and leave without her noticing. I head to the bedroom and take a quick shower to relax. The tension of the day, and the fact that my body responded to Kate's gaze that way, left me on edge.

When I finish, I put on some comfortable black pants and a short-sleeved shirt of the same color. I head to the minibar upstairs to grab a bottle of wine, but I only find some cans of beer, so I decide to go downstairs to get the drink I want from the lower floor. Everything is quiet. When I enter the kitchen, I find the little puppy cozy on the rug near the back door. There's a bowl of food beside him and another with water.

I grab what I need, the wine and two glasses. I head back upstairs and knock on Kate's door. She answers a few minutes later, wrapped in a red towel around her body and another around her hair. I notice a few strands falling from the towel, contrasting with the tone of her skin, revealing her shoulders, still wet from the shower.

"Andrew?" She looks at me, surprised, and then shifts her attention to the bottle and the glasses in my hand. "Do you want something?"

I stare at the skin of her neck, as pale as porcelain, and swallow hard. I shouldn't be paying attention to this, but it's hard to control the intrusive thoughts when my hands start to tremble with the urge to feel the softness of her skin under my fingers. What kind of lunatic am I?

"I thought we could take a minute to have some wine. I'll wait for you to get dressed while I wait in the living room."

I quickly shift the focus of my thoughts and scold myself internally for looking at her in such a raw way, even if just for a few seconds. I step to the side, so that the image of the girl in just a towel isn't so clearly in my view.

"Alright, give me just a minute."

Kate closes the door, and I breathe deeply, feeling like an idiot. I'm a mature man, far too experienced to be swayed by any fleeting desire. But there's something about her that I can't explain.

Something that stirs my deepest instincts, something that makes me want to pull her close and keep her in my arms so no one else can get near.

With my muscles tight, I walk to the living room and place the glasses and the bottle on the coffee table. I sit on the leather sofa and turn on the TV almost automatically. I look for something interesting to watch on the streaming platforms, but everything seems meaningless, and nothing grabs my attention, so I leave it as it is.

I open the wine and pour some for myself. As I savor the drink, I hear Kate's footsteps approaching and turn to look at her. I thank God to see her wearing a loose pajama pant and a yellow SpongeBob T-shirt. The seemingly comfortable set is the epitome of tackiness, and it makes her look incredibly funny. Her hair is loose and still damp, and her face is slightly flushed from the warm shower.

"What are you watching?" Kate points toward the TV and sits beside me.

"Nothing yet. What do you like?"

I grab the bottle of wine and fill the other glass. I hand it to her.

"I don't know..." She smiles softly and brings the glass to her lips. "I can't remember the last time I watched a movie."

"You can pick something if you want."

She looks back at the TV just as an image of a couple embracing appears, facing each other in the sunset, dressed in period clothing. It's a romance movie called *Love's Redemption*. Kate's eyes sparkle as she watches the screen.

"Can we watch this? It looks so romantic."

I raise an eyebrow, a bit surprised by her enthusiasm for a romance film.

"Are you sure? Don't you prefer something less fictional?"

I'm not really into romance movies because they're totally unrealistic, but I don't say that to Kate.

"How about making a deal?" She suggests and takes another sip of wine. "We'll watch this one, and then you pick another one you like, okay?"

I shrug but agree with her proposal. I hit play to start the movie, and Kate turns her full attention to the screen, leaving her half-empty wine glass on the coffee table.

I take the last sip of mine and do the same as she did.

The image of a young, very beautiful blonde woman appears on the screen. She's looking out the window of what seems to be a building, focusing on the pedestrian traffic below. The clothes, the setting, and the people indicate that the movie takes place during the California Gold Rush, around 1850. Everything is going well until the image expands on the screen and shows a skinny, dirty man dressing poorly behind her. Soon after, the man places a significant amount of gold dust on the table and leaves the room, indicating that the place is nothing less than a brothel, and the woman in question is a prostitute.

I shift my attention to Kate and notice how intently she's watching each scene. She seems fascinated by the costumes and the whole setting.

The minutes pass, things unfold, and the story begins to make sense. When I finally understand why all of this is happening, my heart races with anguish. Once again, my attention is drawn to Kate. I see the girl tense up, her face looks pale, her fingers digging into the thigh of her pajama pants.

I raise my hand and gently touch her shoulder to make sure she's okay. Kate jumps in fright, and her body shudders.

"Are you alright?" I ask.

She turns her face toward me and searches for my gaze. I see affiliation in her eyes, fear, terror. It's all laid bare right there.

"What did they do to that poor girl, Andrew?" Her question seems to refer more to herself than to the character in the film, and that realization makes my blood boil.

A tear slips from Kate's eyes, and she sobs quietly, bringing her hand to her eyes to wipe them, her emotions coming on strong like a storm.

I pause the movie and hold her trembling hand, pulling Kate closer to me, trying my best to calm her.

"Hey, sweetheart, it's okay," I whisper, continuing to massage her hands, her wrists. "Do you want me to turn off the movie? We can watch something lighter."

She shakes her head in refusal and tries to compose herself once again. The tears keep flowing, her gaze seems distant, as if she's remembering something.

"No, Andrew, I want to watch it until the end."

I inhale deeply and agree, but I don't let go of her hands. I feel like I'm dying inside just thinking about all the shit going through Kate's head right now, everything she's lived through. Hatred consumes me from the inside out, and I curse myself for having met her too late.

"Okay. But promise me that if it gets too much for you, you'll let me know."

She nods, her eyes shining from the tears.

Involuntarily, I bring my fingers to her face and wipe away a tear that has slid down her cheek. She closes her eyes and takes a deep breath, trying to control her fears.

"What happened to you, I'm so sorry," I say softly, almost in a whisper, but it's enough for her to hear.

"Nothing! Nothing happened to me." She stirs, overwhelmed by shame, perhaps a little guilt. And that's what drives me mad.

"I'm here, Kate. Trust me," I plead, almost begging. My whole body screams the word protection. I will protect her from everything, from everyone, even if my life depends on it. A little less agitated, she nods and I pull Kate into my arms. I press her face to my chest and wrap my arms around her, holding her close and safe in my embrace.

"I'll be here to listen if you need to vent."

I wait for a response, but the girl remains silent, so I continue:

"I'm going to unpause it now."

CHAPTER 12

ANDREW

The movie resumes, and she focuses on every scene while still nestled against me. I feel her breath on my chest, the heat of her hands on my skin over the shirt. My body stirs, the blood heating in my veins. I feel every little piece of her against me, every movement, the smell. The scent of her hair fills my nostrils, and I have to breathe deeply as I try to maintain control. I stay completely still, just surviving the moment, worried about moving and her noticing how restless I am.

Minutes pass, hours. After all, it's a two-hour movie. The credits appear on the screen, and the silence in the room is broken only by the closing music. I must admit, I'm a little impressed, as the story has nothing to do with what I expected. I was pleasantly surprised in the few moments I managed to pay attention, without imagining how it would feel to touch the girl's skin, naked.

Kate moves and pulls away from my arms, fixing her hair. I let out a pained sigh and adjust myself on the couch, searching for a comfortable position. I see a satisfied smile curve on the girl's lips, and she brings her hand to her mouth. The frightened girl from earlier has been replaced by a woman with a dreamy smile.

"Oh my God, that was amazing. It was so... so emotional and... deep... and beautiful. How can a movie be so beautiful and sad at the same time?"

She laughs, still overwhelmed by everything she saw and felt.

I return the smile to Kate and get up from the sofa, feeling lighter seeing a happy expression on her face.

"Well, now it's time to watch something less fictional, as we agreed." I express, relieved to be able to get up and step away from her for a moment to breathe. "I'll grab another bottle of wine because this one is warm."

Kate also gets up, full of energy. Although her eyes are red and her hair messy, she's still the most beautiful girl I've ever seen in my life.

"Alright, you get the wine, and I'll make us some sandwiches. All this emotional mix made me hungry."

"Okay." Despite the sudden hunger in my stomach, I allow a frustrated sigh to escape my lips, as leaving the room and going to the kitchen with her wasn't part of my plan to relax for a few minutes without the scent of her skin tormenting me every second.

Her lips curve again, and she takes a few steps to leave. Reluctantly, I follow Kate to the kitchen and grab another bottle of the drink I enjoy so much.

She stops for a moment to play with the puppy, and I lean against the door for a few moments, watching the girl. Her smile is contagious as she pets Spot's fur. Soon after, she washes her hands and prepares two quick sandwiches with slices of bread and melted cheese. Once ready, she puts them on separate plates, and we head to the living room to the sound of barking.

"This night is going to be long. It will take a while for him to get used to being alone in the kitchen," I comment.

"I'll come back later and bring him to sleep with me. I want to see the movie soon; I'm excited to know if it will be as good as the other one."

She's frantic, smiling, but I confess that imagining her sleeping with the puppy is at least curious. I catch myself thinking about her small hands petting the puppy's fur as he sleeps, and suddenly, I find myself in the puppy's place, feeling her warmth under the covers.

Annoyed with my lack of sense, I narrow my eyes and try to change the course of my thoughts before it becomes unbearable.

We both sit on the sofa, and she places the plates on the coffee table. I pour the wine into the glasses and take the first sip. She does the same, taking a generous amount of the purple liquid.

"Wow, this is delicious. It's even better than the other one."

A little of the wine spills from her mouth, and she reaches up to wipe it, ending up sucking her finger in the process. Something inside me ignites, and I feel a fiery heat begin to burn in my gut. It's strange, sensual, too strong to ignore. I feel my erection harden as I look at her, and I need to put my hand in my pants pocket to disguise it. The way my body reacts to her is almost ridiculous. It shouldn't be like this; it can't be like this.

I clear my throat and divert my attention from Kate. I take two more glasses of wine, one after the other. I fill her glass and grab one of the sandwiches from the table. I quickly eat everything on the plate, trying my best to change the focus of my thoughts.

"You were hungrier than I thought," she jokes, and begins to eat as well.

She takes a sip of wine between bites, and we sit there on the sofa. No movie, no conversation, just the purest silence, broken only by the sound of Kate's bites and my wine sips. My attention is focused on every little movement she makes, from the movement of her mouth to the small hands holding the glass and bringing it to her lips.

I feel my body sweating, I'm agitated in a way I've never felt before. And no matter how much I try to tell myself that Kate is like a second daughter to me, we both know that's nothing but a lie. I've only just met the girl, and we definitely haven't formed any familial bond—there hasn't been enough time or space for that. I see her as a woman, a beautiful and seductive woman, and even though she subtly sees me as a man.

When she finishes, I put on the first movie from *The Godfather* trilogy. It's a comfort film, I watch it whenever I need to distract myself from the world.

The scenes I know well begin to play on the screen, and I watch every second with the utmost attention, and for a moment, I forget that Kate is sitting next to me and how tempting her natural scent is.

The movie is halfway through when I decide to look to the side and ask Kate what she thinks, but to my complete surprise, the girl is asleep with her head resting on the back of the sofa. I pause it and raise my hand to wake her, but I think better of it. There's no reason to wake her now; she's probably tired.

I get up, and without thinking twice, I lift her fragile, slender body in my arms. One hand goes behind her back, and the other behind her knees, and I carefully carry Kate to her room and place her gently in the center of the bed.

Strands of hair fall across her face, and I gently brush them away. I notice that her expression is tense, her eyebrows furrowed, too tight for someone who should be sleeping peacefully. I step back a little, and she shifts on the bed, opening and closing her mouth as if trying to say something in her sleep.

"No... please... no."

Shit, she's dreaming. And it doesn't seem like a pleasant dream.

Her body twists on the bed as Kate starts moving from side to side.

I move closer again and hold her hand gently with mine.

"Kate... Kate..." I whisper her name, trying not to startle her, but I confess that all the anguish I see on her face torments me.

"Don't touch me... no..."

She keeps squirming, and I notice her forehead starting to sweat. Things are starting to slip out of control.

"For God's sake, Kate. Wake up, you're having another nightmare." I touch her shoulder and try to wake her with subtle movements.

"Garath!" Kate calls out the name of a man as she makes agitated movements with her arms and legs, as if trying to push someone away. I etch everything she says into my memory, my blood boiling as I imagine the meaning of it all.

"Kate, it's me, Andrew!" I try to calm her in her restless sleep. "You're dreaming, sweetheart."

Then slowly, the ripples in her body begin to dissipate, and she opens her eyes slowly. Her frightened irises analyze me carefully, and she sits up on the bed in a quick movement.

"Andrew..." Her name comes out whispered from her lips, and Kate throws herself into my arms, wrapping her hands around my neck.

Her painful sobs are like a knife being driven into my chest.

"Please don't leave me." She pleads, distressed, her body trembling. "Don't leave me alone!"

"I won't leave you alone!" I respond, stunned, as I pull her body tighter against mine.

"Every time I close my eyes..." She tries to speak, but her words are cut off by her sobs.

"I see him, I don't want to see him, Andrew."

"Who, Kate? Garath?"

Silence. The room is filled with pure silence, she doesn't say anything else.

"Don't leave me here alone," she asks again after a few moments.

I close my eyes and breathe deeply, filled with anger, anxiety. An insane desire to kill someone.

"I need you to tell me what happened so I can help you. Who is Garath, Kate?"

"Another day, Andrew, not today, please, I'm not ready."

Despite all the rage inside me, I try my best to control myself so she doesn't notice my state of mind and get even more nervous. Carefully, I gently push her body back and lay her on the bed.

I bring a hand to her face and caress her soft skin, wiping away the tears in the process.

"Try to rest, okay?"

I move to get up to grab a blanket, but she places her hand on my shoulder, stopping me from pulling away.

"I'm just going to get a blanket and turn off the light, alright?"

She nods with a small gesture and slowly removes her hand from my shoulder.

I get up from the bed without taking my eyes off her face, grab the blanket, turn on the room heater, and turn off the main light. I leave the lamp by Kate's side on, with the light set to a minimum, so the room isn't completely dark but also not too bright.

I lie down facing Kate and pull the comforter over us both. I bring the girl close to me, placing her head on my arm, close to my chest, and resume gently stroking her dark hair.

"Sleep well, Kate. I won't leave you."

She doesn't respond, but I feel her warm breath on my skin, and that activates all my senses. In a few minutes, I hear her soft, deep breathing—a strong sign that she's fallen asleep. Time drags on as I remain still, looking at the shadow of her body under the blanket, wondering what kind of trouble I've gotten myself into.

Her sleep is peaceful, and in a way, that calms me as well. Despite the closeness and all the mixed feelings the girl is awakening in me, I end up falling asleep, with my daughter's friend in my arms.

CHAPTER 13

KATE

I slowly open my eyes as I wake from a deep sleep. I feel my skin warm, my body cozy and revitalized, as if I had slept for days. I move slowly as my mind processes everything that happened the night before. I vaguely remember falling asleep while watching a movie with Andrew on the couch and...

Then I turn my face to the side and find him asleep. My heart races as I try to understand what he is doing here, in bed with me. Andrew is sleeping on his back, his body slightly angled toward me. His breathing is heavy, indicating that he's in a deep sleep.

I lift the blanket slightly and realize that I'm still wearing my clothes and nothing seems out of place. The same goes for him. Andrew is fully dressed, despite us sharing the same blanket. I watch his chest rise and fall with the rhythm of his breathing, and I'm mortified when I realize that I was curled up against him.

Confused flashes come to my mind, and I vaguely remember waking up in the middle of the night with my heart racing after a bad dream. I remember begging Andrew not to leave me alone. I couldn't be alone, or I'd lose it, and apparently, he kept his promise and stayed the night with me in bed.

I check my clothes again to make sure nothing abnormal happened. I slowly get out of bed and go to the bathroom to check further. And nothing, absolutely nothing happened between me and

Andrew. We simply slept, and I didn't have any more nightmares. I fell asleep like a carefree child in his arms.

It's still not fully clear when I return to the room and peek through the curtain. Then I decide to brush my teeth, change clothes, and go downstairs to prepare breakfast. I do everything in complete silence so I don't wake Andrew, as I also don't have the maturity to have his eyes on me right now. I'd die of embarrassment.

I tiptoe downstairs and find Spot, all perky, waiting for me. The puppy starts barking, wagging his tail, and I hurry to pick him up to quiet him.

"Hey, little guy, be quiet. We don't want to wake Andrew," I say softly and snuggle Spot against my chest as I head to the kitchen. And as if he understands everything I say, he starts licking my neck and wagging his tail even more, all happy. "Little rascal," I laugh at his antics and grab his food to put in his bowl.

I place the puppy on the floor to eat, clean my hands, and begin preparing breakfast. I make scrambled eggs, bacon, and some toast. I leave the pancakes for the next day because I couldn't find any syrup in the cabinets to put on the counter.

When everything is ready, and I place the plates and utensils on the counter, I see Andrew enter the kitchen, already showered, dressed in a suit and tie. Now, seeing him in these expensive clothes while finishing fastening his watch, I realize that he doesn't look at all like the man who watched the movie with me last night on the couch, and then hugged me to sleep.

Now he exudes power from every pore. His expression is imposing, his features set hard, his forehead furrowed. He looks worried: "Good morning, Kate. Woke up early."

He walks to the counter and opens the laptop that had been there since the previous day.

"Good morning, Andrew," my voice almost doesn't come out as I respond to him. "I made breakfast."

At the same time that I can barely look at him after we slept together, he doesn't seem fazed at all. He keeps messing with the laptop, his shoulders stiff and his expression focused, his body bent over the counter.

"Thank you. I usually only have black coffee when I get to the office."

He doesn't look in my direction when he answers. He checks the time on his wristwatch and stands up. Only then do I notice his inquisitive gaze briefly studying my face.

"I left the laptop set up to receive Angelina's calls. She should call at any time today. But you can use the device for whatever you want."

I feel a little frustrated by his coldness, but at the same time, I know that Andrew is acting correctly. What could I expect? That he would hug me just because we slept together out of pity? No, my confused thoughts are making me too dizzy. He isn't like other men. Andrew doesn't even seem to notice that I'm a woman, and that makes me sigh in relief. I am safe with him. I know that.

"I appreciate it, I really needed it."

He nods at me and walks over to the table. I watch as Andrew grabs a piece of toast and pours some coffee. He doesn't eat much, constantly checking the time on his wristwatch, looking in a hurry.

His phone rings, and he slips his hand into his pants pocket to answer it.

"I'm on my way, I won't be long. You can go ahead without me," I hear him say to someone on the other end of the line. "Go ahead without me."

Then he hangs up and stands, putting his phone back in his pocket. It's at this moment that I see a gun strapped to his waist. And only now do I realize that I know absolutely nothing about Andrew's life. I vaguely remember Angelina mentioning in one of the messages she left for me that her father worked in something related to the FBI.

Noticing that my attention is on the gun, Andrew adjusts his suit jacket and looks at my face carefully.

"Does this bother you? I didn't mean to scare you, but as a Federal agent, I'm always prepared for combat, even at home."

I swallow hard as he justifies himself to me, constantly worried about what I will think. Does Andrew think that I will run away in any situation where I feel even the slightest bit threatened?

"It's okay. I didn't know for sure that you were an FBI agent. But the fact that you carry a weapon doesn't terrify me, if that's what you're thinking."

Not being you. I don't finish this last part of my thoughts, obviously.

I realize my mistake when his lips curve into a smile that I could define as proud.

"Not exactly an agent. But 'director' suits what I am better."

I blink as my brain processes this information, but I remain silent.

"Would you like to have dinner out tonight? Be ready by 8:00 p.m., alright?" He states and simply leaves, giving me no chance to refuse the invitation.

With my heart racing, I quickly walk to the laptop and use the search program to learn more about Andrew's life.

And there it is. Andrew Thompson, 44 years old, Director of the FBI New York Field Office, responsible for one of the largest and most important FBI offices in the United States, where he plays a crucial role in investigating a wide range of criminal activities, including terrorism, cybercrime, organized crime, and human trafficking.

"Wow!" I let out, feeling completely in shock. I had suspected he was an important man, but I had no idea just how much.

Since the laptop is on, I quickly log into my account to download all the cloud files. I reread some things I had drafted while in

California, and I end up having more fun than I expected during the process. An hour later, I'm finishing another chapter of my next book. The ideas are flowing easily, which makes me incredibly happy.

In the meantime, I'm interrupted by Spot's barking and whining. I set the writing aside and play a little with the puppy.

After satisfying the little spoiled pup's desires, I quickly tidy up the kitchen and return to the laptop. I reread everything I've done with care, a smile on my face, as I feel extremely proud of myself. Around noon, I receive a video call from Angelina. My heart leaps with joy when I see my friend on the other side of the screen. This time, the connection is a little better, and the news is good.

"Kate, it's so wonderful to help people. I feel like I'm part of something really big every time I can make a difference in someone's life." Angelina briefly talks about the work she, her husband, and the kids are doing in Africa. It's incredible to see how fulfilled she is with the life she's chosen, and I end up laughing when she tells me everything she had to do to convince her husband to go.

"I'm so happy for you, really," I inhale deeply while we chat.

"You're smiling today. Looks like everything's alright over there, huh?" She asks, her eyes full of expectation.

My lips curve into a quick smile, and I lower my head for a moment, thinking about everything I've experienced in the past few days. It's like the Kate from a few days ago is disappearing. It's both scary and unbelievable to come to the realization that living in that house with my mother was killing me.

"Yes, I'm really good. Your dad is very kind, and he treats me like... like a daughter." My voice falters when I say the last part, maybe because I don't see him as a father, and what I just said sounds like a lie.

Angelina's smile widens even more: "Yes, he's wonderful. One of the best people I've ever met. I feel more at ease knowing everything is fine."

"Don't worry, Angel."

We talk a bit more about our days, and I tell her about Spot. Angel obviously thinks it's great that I now have a dog to distract me. I decide not to tell her about my writing just yet, I'll talk about it when she returns.

While we're talking, I hear the door to Angelina's room open, and an Alex with his chest bare, wearing a towel around his waist, enters my view. In his arms, I see a smiling little boy holding a rubber duck.

Angel turns toward her husband, and the detailed look with which she watches him makes my hair stand on end in embarrassment. She holds the baby in her arms, and her husband gives her an unabashed kiss on the lips before stepping away from the screen. She then returns her attention to me.

"Look at Auntie, love."

The sound of laughter resonates from the other side.

Angelina also smiles and showers the little boy with kisses.

"I'm going to change this little guy now. Can I call you back in a bit?" she asks, and I nod, still fascinated by their interaction.

After Angelina hangs up, I sit for a few moments, thinking about everything. The baby's laughter lingers in my mind, and when I close my eyes, it's as if I see my daughter. That emptiness in my chest returns with force, that pain that tightens my heart so strongly it hurts.

Hot tears stubbornly threaten to fall, but I stop them. Taking a deep breath, I return to working on my book, and the day passes as if by magic.

I only stop to eat a quick sandwich and give Spot a little pet. Angelina calls back, and we talk a bit about the kids. She tells me that she will be returning to New York as soon as possible, but I reassure her, telling her there's no reason to interrupt such an important trip for me, besides, I'm safe here. In the late afternoon, I remember that

Andrew had left the credit card for me to stock up the fridge and buy a few things for Spot. So, I go to the nearest supermarket and buy everything in the most generic way possible to avoid mistakes.

I return to Andrew's house and put everything in its proper place. Only then do I go upstairs to take a shower and get ready.

I admit, the idea of going out to dinner makes me a little insecure. But I don't want to disappoint Andrew. He's been so kind to me, and most likely, he's eager to eat something different. I should be grateful that he thought of me, he could very well go out alone or with a colleague from work. Or a female colleague.

I shake my head in denial when I realize that my thoughts are taking unexpected turns.

After the shower, I put on the dress I had bought and slip into the low-heeled sandals. I look at myself in the mirror and for a moment, I hesitate whether I should wear this or not. I'm not sure if I look presentable, I seem so "on display." But then I close my eyes and sigh, remembering why I bought this dress. I don't want to look sloppy.

My hair is wet, I comb through it and leave it loose to dry naturally. I apply a light moisturizer and head downstairs to wait for Andrew.

Anxiety consumes me as I wait for him. I place my hands in my lap and barely manage to play with Spot. The puppy barks and runs around me, but I'm so tense, so nervous. I keep imagining what Andrew will think when he sees me dressed like this. *Will he find me beautiful or not care at all?*

I end up realizing that I'm more concerned with this than the fact that I'm going out to an entirely unknown place. I simply don't understand what's happening to me, I don't get why there's such a mix of thoughts and conflicting feelings.

When I hear the sound at the door, I feel my hands sweat and my heart race to extreme levels. I hold my breath as I wait for him to appear in my line of sight. And without any explanation, everything inside me stirs, my throat goes dry, my hands tremble.

CHAPTER 14

ANDREW

The events of the day were hard to swallow.

Two women were found dead and missing their organs in the basement of an abandoned house in the Bronx. The bodies had already started decomposing when they were found, naked, with their hands bound behind their backs. Two weeks ago, another woman was found in the same condition just a few blocks away, which suggested we were dealing with the shit of a *serial killer*, the type that carefully chooses the profile of his victims: young women, long hair, fair skin, and a big mystery. What did he do with the organs he removed?

Dozens of questions need answers, and we only have the tip of the iceberg. As I analyze the information, I check the time and realize I should have already gone home. It's almost 8:00 p.m., and I promised to take Kate to dinner. I leave my office and say goodbye to a few agents still on duty. I drive home with a hot head and heavy thoughts. A whirlwind of heavy emotions leaves my nerves tight, but I don't let it interfere with my plans. I just want to relax a little and help the girl unwind. Kate needs to get out a bit to clear her mind, and so do I.

I park the car in front of the house and get out of the vehicle. I walk quickly, intending to take a quick shower so we can head out. As soon as I enter, I pass through the hall and walk toward the living room. I come across her sitting on the sofa. Kate watches me anxiously and stands up, crossing her hands in front of her body. But what intrigues me the most is seeing her for the first time in a dress. I feel all the air leave my lungs, and I have no idea why this is happening.

She's wearing a modest black dress, but it shows a good portion of her legs and outlines her small body. Despite her slim build, her legs look soft and far too inviting for my liking. She looks stunning. She isn't wearing makeup or accessories. She's adorned only by her loose hair and the anxious gleam in her sapphire eyes, and she's perfect just like that.

"Ready?" It's when I realize I've spent more time observing her than I intended.

"Yes, I was waiting for you." I notice the anxiety in her voice.

"I'll take a quick shower and be right back. I won't take long."

Kate nods, and I practically rush to leave. I feel out of place in her presence, as if I'm doing something I shouldn't, something that feels wrong and outside moral standards.

I take a quick shower and dress in jeans and a white long-sleeve shirt. I grab a blazer and throw it over my clothes, just in case it gets colder later and Kate might need a jacket, as I noticed that the fabric of the dress she's wearing is too light for a night like this. The cold is setting in strong.

A few minutes later, I'm coming down the stairs. The girl is talking softly to the puppy when I return, and she jumps back when I call out: "Shall we?"

She nods, looking at me with that charming yet scared look, then follows me outside. I get in the car and open the passenger door for Kate. I try not to focus too much on her steps, but I can feel every movement of her body as she sits beside me.

"Thank you for the invitation, Andrew." I look at her for a few seconds.

Her eyes reflect gratitude, and I wonder how much this girl has been neglected or overlooked throughout her life.

"It's going to be fun, Kate," I say casually, but inside, I'm restless. "I made a reservation at an Italian restaurant I like, but we can go somewhere else if you prefer."

"No, no need. The Italian restaurant is great."

I nod affirmatively and start the car. The place isn't too far, and in less than half an hour, we're entering the establishment.

It's an iconic restaurant that offers a luxurious take on Italian-American cuisine, with an atmosphere inspired by the Italian restaurants of the 20th century.

It's not easy to get a last-minute reservation here, but being "friends" with the owner has its perks.

As we're greeted and led to our table, I watch how impressed Kate is with the place. She examines every detail with clear admiration while seeming to feel out of place.

"Is everything okay?" I pull out a chair for her to sit. "You seem tense."

Kate settles in, and I sit across from her, always attentive to her movements.

"I'm fine, it's just... this place. It's a bit too much for me." Her cheeks flush.

I smile slightly, noticing how this nervous air makes her even more beautiful, with a touch of innocence.

"You don't like it? We can go somewhere else if you prefer."

Her eyes widen, and she looks around briefly before responding:

"No, of course not!"

Choosing this place wasn't by chance. It's a sophisticated and expensive setting, and I brought Kate here so she can realize that she deserves everything good life has to offer, and if I'm the one tasked with showing her that, so be it. I admit it's been an interesting experience, and seeing the sparkle in her eyes makes me feel satisfied.

"Great, then let's order. Do you want anything?" She glances at the menu quickly, furrowing her brows, then looks back at me.

"I don't recognize anything on here."

"I'll choose then, and you can tell me if you like it or not."

The little sideways smile that appears on her lips stirs something inside me, an unsettled feeling in my chest.

"Deal."

I ask the waiter to bring the house's recommended appetizer, tortellini as the main course, and a bottle of the best wine. The wine is served in a few minutes, and Kate tastes it. She smiles after the first sip, showing how much she enjoyed the drink.

"This is wonderful," she says with that surprised and satisfied look that only she knows how to show. "I would drink this forever."

"Maybe it's not a good idea. Beautiful girls and excessive wine may not be a great combination."

She smiles softly and touches the bottom of her lips to wipe away a drop of the drink that slipped down.

"So you think I'm beautiful?" She asks innocently, as if it's such an insignificant detail, when in fact, she's one of the most beautiful women I've ever known.

"Let's just say yes. You're very beautiful," I respond honestly, looking at her.

Kate looks back at me, and I see the sparkle in her eyes intensify a little. Her expression is playful, while she also seems fascinated.

"Tell me about yourself, Andrew."

I finish my wine and refill our glasses without taking my eyes off her face. Every moment analyzing her curiosity about me.

"I'm a bit of a loner, as you may have noticed. I divorced a few years ago, and I thought I didn't have any children, until I met Angelina. Now I have a daughter and several grandchildren." The last sentence makes me sound like a seventy-year-old, but Kate just lets out a little amused smile.

"I can't imagine you being a grandfather. You're still so young."

I narrow my eyes as I look at her. She seems sincere in what she's saying.

"Appearances are deceiving, Kate. I'm over forty. The only thing is, when Angelina was born, I was too young. But nothing changes the fact that I'm already a doting grandfather."

She laughs again and puts her hand over her lips to stifle the delightful sounds coming from her mouth.

I try to speak casually, but the truth is, I feel a lump choking me from the inside, especially when I analyze the girl's face—so young, so innocent, the complete opposite of me.

"But what about you?" I shift the focus of the conversation. "Tell me a little about you, Kate."

I notice her expression change, but she takes a deep breath and nods, shaking her head slightly.

"There's not much to say about me." She pauses, as if thinking carefully about the next words. "I'm 20 years old, and I spent a big part of my life... in a convent." Kate lowers her eyes when she talks about the convent, and I notice her breathing quickening slightly.

"You're very young," I murmur, feeling suffocated. It feels like I'm chewing on glass. And it's not the first time I've felt something like this since she arrived.

Knowing that Kate is simply twenty-four years younger than me makes the agitation in my body increase uncomfortably. That feeling of making a huge fucking mistake returns with force, even though I haven't even touched her. But only I know the obscene thoughts that have been crossing my mind since she started living with me.

"Maybe..." She looks back at me after a few seconds. "Angelina and I were inseparable. We did everything together and shared the same room." She smiles again, a smile so wide that her eyes sparkle. "I was the friend who got into trouble, and she was the good girl who followed all the rules."

"I'm glad she had you."

Kate lets out a little laugh, reminiscing about the good times, and I'm even surprised to learn that she was the rule breaker.

"I used to break the big silence all the time, a period when the nuns and novices were forced to remain silent without saying a word. Angelina would go crazy with me. I also didn't like doing my chores much, and I'd always read romance books, hidden."

I smile at Kate, completely incredulous at her behavior.

The image of the two girls, dressed as novices and walking through the corridors of an old monastery, flashes in my mind, but it bears no resemblance to the woman I see in front of me now.

"I'm impressed," I admit, still laughing. "In my head, you've always been the well-behaved one."

Kate's eyes briefly study me, and her lips remain curled in a smile.

"You might be surprised by me, Andrew," she teases in a provocative tone.

She takes a deep breath and places both hands on the table, thoughtful.

"I have a sister. Or I did, I don't know. She left a long, long time ago."

The smile fades from her face, and the serious, withdrawn Kate comes back to life.

"I'm sorry, Kate."

I move my hand toward hers on the table and touch it lightly. I feel her skin warm and delicate, and I try to comfort her a bit with the subtle caress.

Kate shudders under my touch but doesn't pull away. Her sapphire eyes meet mine again, and she turns her palm up to close her fingers around mine.

"She was much older than me. I was at the convent when I heard from her for the last time. My mom said my sister just called, saying she was moving to another country, and that was it."

Her grip on my fingers tightens, our gazes locking as if drawn by a magnet, in a pull so intense it's hard to explain. The moment is interrupted by the waiter, who arrives with our orders, and Kate quickly pulls her hand away.

Dinner proceeds in silence. She seems lost in her thoughts, as if the wall around her has been rebuilt.

When she finishes, she stands up and says she's going to the bathroom. I follow her movements from a distance, from when she asks the hostess where the women's restroom is, to the moment she disappears from my line of sight.

A few minutes later, Kate returns, but before she reaches the table, she accidentally bumps into some guy. They exchange a few words, and although she seems tense at first, I see the curve of a smile emerge on her lips when he says something that seems to please her. This swift movement is enough to make my blood boil with jealousy. A totally ridiculous and senseless jealousy.

I clench my fists on the table and wait for her. Kate returns to the table and sits down, still smiling from the encounter, despite her trembling hands.

"I think I've gotten out of practice communicating with people," she says, but quickly realizes she said more than she intended.

With a cough, she shifts her attention back to me: "Thank you for bringing me, Andrew, the dinner was wonderful. The wine, perfect."

I nod at her and call the waiter to order another bottle of the wine Kate loved. Though I'm still agitated from seeing her smile at another man, I don't let it show. She takes a sip, her eyes closed, and I almost groan quietly as I watch the pleasure etched on her face.

Everything inside me heats up, and I hate myself for it. I need to remind myself constantly that she's only twenty and my daughter's friend. A convent friend to make everything even more complicated.

What does that make Kate? An ex-novice? And what if she plans to return to religious life?

Shaking those thoughts off, I try a little of the wine and listen to everything Kate says about the convent and Angelina. The minutes fly by in our conversation. The girl is uninhibited now, no longer the shy little fox who arrived at my house looking lost. She smiles as she recalls the memories, and before I know it, another bottle of wine is gone.

"I think it's better if we go home, don't you?" I ask as she finishes the last sip and places her glass on the table.

Kate agrees with a nod while wiping her mouth with a napkin. She places both hands on the table and takes a deep breath before looking at me.

"I think the world is spinning, Andrew." Then she smiles again. "Oh my God, I really have no sense."

Kate smiles again when she realizes she's a little drunk, but the only thing I notice is how beautiful she looks like this, with her lips curved and smiling.

"It'll pass soon, it's nothing too serious," I tell her, and that intense look stares back at me.

"How can you be so sure? Have you ever been drunk before?" She asks with an amused expression.

I also smile and gesture to the waiter.

"A few times," I wink.

"So the powerful Andrew Thompson has his moments of fun too?"

I shake my head from side to side, also smiling: "Powerful, huh?"

Kate's eyes shine as she looks back at me. I feel her meticulous analysis of me, on my face, my shoulders, and chest, and then her cheeks take on a rosy hue.

The waiter approaches with the check, and I decide it's time to go. I pay the bill and tip, then help Kate to stand. The girl clings to my arm as if her life depends on it, but I walk slowly with her to the exit to wait for the valet with the car. I take off my blazer and place it over her shoulders.

Some time later, I park the car in front of my house and get out of the vehicle. Kate stays in the passenger seat, as if analyzing how to proceed. I turn around and walk to her, opening the door.

"I think the world is spinning, and I feel like I'll hit the ground if I move from here."

She lets out a nervous giggle and looks at me, biting her lip. The way she moves her mouth isn't sexual, but my dick doesn't seem to get the memo as I feel it fill with blood. With tense muscles, I shift my focus away from her face, trying to look at anything but Kate, anything but her.

"Let me help you. Come on." I extend my arms for her to grab onto so she can get out of the car, but I stay silent, my body rigid, irritated at my own weakness.

Kate moves and takes my hand. At first, everything goes smoothly—she stands, leaning to place one foot on the ground, then the other. But then she stumbles, her small hands reaching for my body. In a swift motion, I grab her by the waist and pull her toward me. It's almost cruel how the universe conspires to put me in such a precarious position. Her arms instinctively wrap around my neck as I lean in to steady her. Kate's eyes meet mine, her breathing heavy, her body trembling.

"I'm so sorry. I shouldn't have had so much wine."

"Don't apologize," I say, unable to tear my eyes away from her lips. Every sense in me is on high alert.

Her scent invades my nostrils, and I take a deep breath. Everything stops as our gazes lock, our faces far too close. Internally, I scream for Kate to move away, to yell at me, to feel fear. But she seems as paralyzed as I am, trapped under the same venom that has left me completely ravenous.

Her lips part slightly, and she runs her tongue over her reddened lips, igniting chaos inside my pants. I practically salivate at the thought of tasting her mouth. Her irises, as deep as the ocean, stay fixed on my face, and I lose myself in their pull. The closeness takes my breath away, erasing my reason. I do what I should never even consider doing, but the pull I feel toward her is too strong to resist. Without waiting another second, I slide a hand to the back of her neck and draw Kate closer.

She gasps in my arms but doesn't move. It's all the invitation I need to tilt my head and bring my lips closer to hers. I feel her breath, warm and laced with the scent of wine—the best wine I've ever tasted. I graze her lips softly with mine and feel her fingers dig into my shoulder.

Her lips are as soft as a feather, and I crave more. It's nearly impossible to control myself. I kiss her lips gently, careful not to scare her with my hunger. When I realize Kate is frozen in my arms, even though I'm desperate to slip my tongue into her mouth, I pull back briefly and hold her face in one hand while the other remains steady on her waist.

She looks into my eyes, her expression a mix of curiosity and fear.

"I... I've never done this before," she says softly, her shaky voice breaking the spell I'm under. It finally dawns on me how insane this all is.

I pull away, helping her regain her composure, my entire body trembling with unfulfilled desire and guilt for having kissed her. Without wasting another second, I grip Kate by the waist again and lean down to lift her off the ground.

I carry her into the house to ensure she doesn't stumble again. I need her to be safe before I can step away, take a cold shower, and put some distance between us—quickly.

She sighs deeply as I carry her inside. Neither of us speaks; the only sound is the deafening silence of our thoughts.

CHAPTER 15

KATE

YEARS AGO

I feel Garath's fingers sliding over my private parts, and I cry softly, terrified of making noise and being hurt by him.

"Please, Garath, no," I plead through desperate tears, my voice weak with terror, my body paralyzed in shock.

"Quiet, little girl. Don't you like Daddy's caresses? This is just the beginning of what I'll do to you."

I sniffle softly and swallow with difficulty, feeling the air escape me. Then he stops what he's doing and grips my hand tightly, pulling my arm closer to him. I clamp my eyes shut, but Garath's demanding voice forces me to face him.

"Don't close your eyes, Kate. Look at me, little girl. Now!"

I open my eyes, feeling fear invade me from the inside out, and Garath places something hard and sticky in my hand. I shudder in disgust as I realize what he's doing. I'm not so innocent as to not know that it's his male parts he's forcing me to hold. My stomach churns, my body turns cold, and a strange, nauseating smell fills the air.

"That's it, good girl."

The man groans, and I sob, utterly terrified, at his mercy, at the mercy of his desires...

"Such a beautiful child, so innocent." His fingers reach my face, wiping away the thick tears streaming down my cheeks—tears I hadn't even realized were falling.

With his other hand, Garath forces me to keep holding that revolting thing, forcing my fingers to touch its slimy tip. The disgust makes my stomach turn, and I fight the urge to vomit in front of him. Otherwise, I know Garath will hit me like he does my mom.

"You're a little whore, Kate. A little whore." I hear his groans, feel his breath reeking of alcohol mixed with his body's nauseating odors. I want to scream for help. I want to scream for my mom.

He lets out a strange snort, almost like a grunt, and then my entire hand is coated with a sticky, disgusting liquid, leaving me horrified. Garath stands up from the bed and steps away. I see that thing hanging out of his pants as he adjusts himself to leave. His threatening gaze is fixed on my face.

"Don't tell anyone about this. Tomorrow you won't go to school, do you hear me? You'll stay in your room until you learn to behave. Then we'll see."

I can't move. I keep trembling, paralyzed by sobs and terror. All the emotions are taking their toll. Garath finishes adjusting his pants and gives me a disgusting smile, his eyes scanning my bare skin. And then he leaves the room.

Thick tears streak my face as I get out of bed, my legs failing me. Still, I manage to open the door and run to the bathroom. The vomit comes violently as I kneel before the toilet. The force of the contractions makes my stomach ache, and I throw up everything I ate during the day. I crawl to the bathtub, turn on the faucet, and climb into the hot water. I sit there hugging my knees, staying for hours, frightened and alone.

Downstairs, everything is silent. I don't know if Garath has left, but I'm afraid to move in case he hears me. So I stay quiet, waiting for my mom to come home. After some time, I grab a towel from the small bathroom cabinet and make my way back to my room slowly, taking care not to make a sound.

I lock the door, put on pajama pants and a loose shirt, and lie on the bed in a fetal position, my mind replaying every second of what happened here.

I can't sleep. I'm afraid to close my eyes and wake up with Garath on top of me. So I wait, praying softly that my mom won't take long.

Soon, I hear noises downstairs. Voices, whispers. My heart calms when I recognize my mom's voice. She and Garath are talking in the kitchen. They seem happy, exchanging affectionate words that make my stomach churn again. Then they head to their room, and I hear the bed creak and their moans. The fear returns, even stronger this time, and I cover my ears with a pillow.

I WAKE UP THE NEXT day feeling suffocated, as though my entire body has been assaulted. I get up to brush my teeth, and that's when I notice a purple mark on my wrist where Garath had gripped me tightly. Trembling, I shake my head, refusing to keep remembering everything, feeling so weak. I brush my teeth as quickly as I can, use the toilet, and return to my room.

Minutes and hours pass as I remain quiet, unable to move. I jump on the bed when I hear a knock, and soon the door opens. My heart races desperately, and I almost cry in relief when I see it's my mom.

"Good morning, Kate. Aren't you going to eat, sweetheart?" She approaches me.

I look at her face, surprised by her affectionate and gentle tone. She rarely acts like this with me, which makes me think that things between her and Garath must be good now, because when they fight, my mom becomes a nervous wreck.

"I'm not hungry," I respond softly, averting my eyes, feeling anger at my mom for liking him so much, for allowing him to stay with us.

"Don't be silly, Kate. Come eat." She insists, but I stay quiet.

"Leave the girl alone, love." Garath's voice echoes through the room, and my heart starts pounding with fear again. Every part of me goes on high alert. "She'll eat when she's hungry. Now come here, I'm eager to show you something."

I hear my mom let out a small laugh, and then the two of them leave. Only after they're gone do I realize I was holding my breath, and how much my body is trembling.

I don't get up to eat or drink anything. I stay in my room, pretending to be sick for the rest of the day. My mom doesn't come back to check if I'm okay, and Garath doesn't show up either. The house is silent; there are no fights, and I don't hear any yelling between them like I usually do.

When night comes, I check the time to see if it's time for my mom to leave for work. Only then do I change my clothes. I put on jeans and a T-shirt and fix my hair, deciding that I'll go to the bar with her. I'll help with anything, just to get away from here.

I walk slowly through the house until I find my mom in the living room, looking at herself in the mirror, or rather, at something on her neck. She's still so beautiful, but her face looks so tired. Yet she's smiling and seems happy.

There's no sign of Garath, and that makes me sigh in relief.

When she sees me, her smile widens, and she comes closer to where I am, her hand touching her neck.

"Look, darling. Isn't the necklace Garath gave me beautiful?" She smiles softly and doesn't even wait for an answer. She goes back to looking at herself in the mirror, caressing the golden necklace.

"Yes," I murmur. "It's beautiful."

Then she removes the necklace and places it in a small box, as if it were the most precious thing in the universe. She puts the necklace in her bag and adjusts her hair.

"I have to go to work now, Kate. Make sure you eat something," she says without looking at me.

"Mom, I..." My voice falters, but I gather courage and continue. "I want to go too. I can help if you need, and..."

"No, Kate, you're not going. That's no place for little girls like you."

My heart starts racing desperately, but I keep insisting, fear consuming me from the inside out: "Please, Mom, I'll behave, please."

My voice comes out desperate, but she doesn't seem to notice the torment consuming me.

"I said no, girl. Go wash up and get that tired look off your face. You look terrible, Kate."

Her eyes scan me briefly with a mix of anger and disdain, making my heart ache. Even so, the fear of staying here with Garath is greater than anything else.

So I run after her as soon as she turns her back and heads toward the door.

"Mom, please. I don't want to stay here!" I grab her wrist, trying to get her attention, trying to make her understand that something's wrong, that I'm suffering. "Garath, I..."

"Enough, Kate!" Her shout echoes through the room, and I feel my ears ringing when she slaps my face.

I spin to the side, almost losing my balance, and bring my hand to my face, trembling. My skin burns, and tears sting my eyes.

"Look at what you made me do, you stupid girl! Don't you see I'm late? I don't have time for your silly complaints."

And then my entire world collapses when the door opens and Garath walks in. Through the tears, I see him assess the situation, looking from my mom to me.

"Did something happen?" he asks seriously.

I see my mom shrug and pull herself together, the anger still gleaming in her eyes.

"Nothing happened, dear. It's just Kate giving me trouble, as always."

She approaches Garath and kisses him on the lips, making my stomach churn, and then she leaves the room as if nothing happened.

Trembling, I feel his gaze fall on me, and a malicious smile curves on his lips. I don't wait another second to return to my room and lock the door, because I know Garath won't let me leave the house. The only alternative I have is to try to keep him outside and hope he doesn't try to do what happened last night again.

I don't turn off the lights; I don't have the strength to stay in the dark. The brightness from the lamp gives me a small sense of safety and pushes away a tiny bit of the fear I feel. I don't know how much time passes after I lock the door and lean against it. My heart is racing and aching, and I wonder why Mom didn't take me with her. Why doesn't she realize she brought a monster into our home? I raise my hand to my eyes to wipe the tears and go to bed. At every little noise I hear outside, my body jumps in fear.

My stomach growls with hunger, and my throat feels dry, but I can't even think about leaving this room. Time passes, and I know it's late when I catch myself dozing off, overwhelmed by exhaustion. My eyes slowly close, and I start losing awareness of my surroundings until I am completely consumed by sleep.

And then my worst nightmare happens. I wake up with a start, completely alarmed after hearing a bang on the door. I'm dazed, unable to understand anything. My head is so confused.

It feels like my heart will leap out of my chest at any moment.

Panicked, I get up to try to understand what's happening, and that's when I hear another crash, and the door bursts open. Garath storms into the room, his face enraged, advancing toward me.

I let out a scream of fright and try to slip past him to get through the broken door, but his hand finds my hair, yanking me back.

"Garath! Help!" I try to scream and fight to free myself from him, but his strength is too much for me.

The pulling on my hair intensifies, and Garath covers my mouth with his other hand.

"Shut up, you little bitch." His alcohol-laden breath hits my face. "Did you really think you could escape from me?"

He drags me by my hair across the room and throws me onto the bed. Despair consumes me, and I begin screaming for help, begging for someone to save me.

"Help, Mom!" Garath slaps me hard across the face, and the taste of blood explodes in my mouth.

"Shut up, damn it! If anyone hears your screams, I'll kill you and your mother. Do you hear me, you little bitch?"

I whimper softly on the bed, curling up breathless, trying to find the strength to breathe again. I feel lost, confused, unable to comprehend why this is happening. Does God not like me either, like Mom?

I feel the bed sink under Garath's weight, and I try to move away, but it's too late. His rough hands grip me tightly as he climbs on top of me, crushing me with his weight while he covers my mouth again.

"You're going to stay quiet. Not a word, do you hear me?" Alarmed, I nod at him, still dizzy from the slap, terror consuming all my senses.

"Good girl."

Then he slowly removes his hand from my lips and starts unbuttoning his pants. That hard thing springs out when Garath pulls his clothes down, and my stomach churns.

"No, Garath, I don't want to... I..." I beg him not to force me to hold that thing again, but he responds by slapping me on the other side of my face.

A coughing fit overtakes me as I bring my hand to my mouth, feeling the small cut on my lip.

"Quiet, little girl. Quiet, or I'll hurt you badly."

I see in his eyes that Garath is dead serious.

Trembling, I fall silent, sobbing quietly as I stay still.

He steps back just enough to slip his fingers into the waistband of my pants and pull them down my legs, leaving me exposed from the waist down. I try to fight back, kicking him and landing a blow on his hip, but he just grabs my leg tightly enough to hurt me.

"I'll punch you again, Kate, and it won't be pretty this time."

I choke back my tears and let despair consume me, too scared to make another move.

Garath climbs back on top of me, and I turn my face away as he spreads my legs and positions himself between them. I feel his finger enter me, and the tears come in desperate, cutting sobs. I gasp and struggle, but he's strong, and he covers my mouth with his free hand.

In one swift motion, he pushes that thing inside me, and I groan in pain as though being torn apart from the inside. My sobs are lost amidst Garath's moans, and I can no longer fight him. I close my eyes, willing myself to disappear, as anguish overwhelms me. He hurts me with every movement, like he's slicing me open from the inside out. The pain is so intense that my screams get caught in my throat, and I can't breathe. I can't breathe.

Garath doesn't last long. Soon he gets off me, and I feel something trickling down my legs.

I can't move. I'm groggy, weak, my eyelids heavy. I feel like something is wrong with me. I confirm this when I hear Garath curse, but I no longer understand anything. It's as if I'm drifting into another dimension, and his voice grows distant.

"Damn it! Damn it! Damn it!"

And then I see nothing more.

CHAPTER 16

KATE

YEARS AGO

I slowly open my eyes, feeling as if a huge weight is pressing down on my body. I have no strength, barely able to move in bed. Everything hurts, especially between my legs.

I feel weak, but I still try to move. My thoughts are confused, everything seems unreal.

"Mom..." I call for her, but my voice barely comes out.

With difficulty, I manage to sit up and lift my body while the throbbing pain between my legs intensifies. That's when I see the bloodstained sheets, and the flashes of everything that happened explode in my mind. I remember Garath on top of me, taking off my clothes. I remember the slaps he gave me, I remember the pain.

I try to get up, but as I feel warm liquid running down my legs, I sense my strength fading again, and I need to hold onto the bed to avoid falling. I can only realize it's blood before I lose consciousness again.

I can't quite understand what happens next. At some point, I hear what sounds like altered voices. I feel fast hands holding me, lifting me from the bed. My world turns into a whirlwind of confused and strange sensations. And everything fades away again.

When I regain consciousness, I hear the voice of someone nearby, and I realize it's a woman. I slowly open my eyes, the brightness making my eyes hurt. Little by little, I get used to the light in the place and see my mother talking to a woman dressed in pants and a white shirt.

"Mom?" My voice comes out weak. I feel so limp, sore.

They both turn toward me, and my mother hurries, walking in my direction.

"Kate, how are you?" She takes my hand. I notice her worried expression, as if she's nervous.

"Where am I, Mom?" I look around, only now realizing there's an IV in my arm.

"You're in a hospital, sweetheart. You had a hemorrhage."

I notice when my mother looks from me to the nurse, and the woman approaches.

The distressing memories return forcefully, and the fear of seeing Garath again makes my breathing accelerate.

"Mom... Garath... he..." I try to ask about the man who hurt me, wanting to know where he is because I don't want to see him again, but my voice falters, and no matter how hard I try to speak, I can't.

"Don't talk about him, sweetheart. It's over." I notice that, although my mother's voice comes out softly, it has a harsh and dry tone.

The nurse approaches where I am and places her hand on my forehead, her expression concerned: "Kate, I'm Nurse Christine. How do you feel?"

"I'm fine, but I'm scared." My voice catches, and tears begin to blur my vision. "Garath, he... where is he?"

"Kate, sweetheart, forget about it." I hear my mother's voice, but she's soon interrupted by the nurse, who ignores her protest about not mentioning Garath's name.

"Don't worry, Kate. You're a strong little girl. The police are handling everything now!" Christine says with such conviction that my eyes widen. "I want you to rest for a while because in a few hours, you'll have some visitors and have to answer some difficult questions, so you need to save your energy, alright?"

I nod at her and look back at my mother. I notice tears in her eyes, her expression showing concern, but she quickly regains composure and runs her hand through my hair.

"Sleep, Kate, you'll be alright!"

KATE

PRESENT DAY

THE DAYS PASS IN SUCH a calmness that it's almost frightening to feel so good. I don't think I've ever felt this way, to be honest.

Since the night Andrew kissed me, our interactions have become a bit distant, though he's always kind. Neither of us brought it up the next morning. It's as if that kiss never happened, but the truth is, I can't forget. The closeness, his scent taking over my brain, that soft touch on my lips. I should've been scared, I should've pulled away from him, left, but that's not what I wanted to do. I wasn't afraid of Andrew. His lips on mine was something unexpected that left me utterly confused simply because I wanted more. I wanted more from him, and that torments me every day. It feels so wrong.

Taking a deep breath, I close my laptop and decide to play with Spot for a while. I look at the device in front of me and smile, thinking about how much I've written over the past few days and how I'll finish the book soon.

It's almost time for Andrew to arrive, and maybe, just maybe, he'll invite me to run with him again, like we did yesterday. Just imagining it, I already feel the pain returning to my body, yet I've never felt freer.

I leave the kitchen, my favorite place to write, and search for Spot in the garden. I find the little dog digging in the grass and nearly faint when I see the damage he's caused. I rush over to him, my heart racing, but as I approach, I can't stay mad at the little guy, who starts barking and wagging his tail in my direction.

Spot jumps up at me so happily that I burst into laughter and scoop him up into my arms.

"You're such a naughty little thing, Spot. Now, how are we going to fix the mess you made before Andrew gets back?"

I analyze the situation carefully before kneeling on the ground and starting to fill in the holes he made, being careful to make the clumps of grass as presentable as possible. As soon as I finish, I hear the sound of Andrew's car approaching, and I rush to enter through the back door, carrying Spot with me. I laugh when I reach the kitchen, with my hands and clothes dirty from the dirt, and my forehead sweaty from the effort of fixing Spot's mischief.

Andrew enters the kitchen right behind me, looks from me to Spot, raising an eyebrow.

"Is there something I need to know?" He shifts all his attention to me, observing the dirt residue on my clothes.

"Nothing at all, Andrew, everything's fine here," I lie shamelessly, but I can't hide my smile.

His eyes light up as he looks at me, and it makes the blood in my veins rush. Then his attention shifts to Spot in my arms.

"Funny, Spot's fur is full of grass."

Caught in the act.

I lift the little dog in the air, smiling again when I realize I failed miserably at trying to hide Spot's antics.

"Okay, fine. You caught us. But I'll just say he made a tiny hole in the garden."

"A tiny hole, huh?"

Andrew is smiling when I look at him again, but he quickly moves, placing a large black bag on the counter.

"You should use this for our run today," he points to the contents of the bag. "I'll be back in a minute."

Andrew turns around and leaves the room, taking off his jacket as he walks. Once he's out of sight, I rush over to the counter and grab the bag he left. Inside, I find some sportswear, including a pair of sneakers with socks and everything.

Well! He really thought of everything.

I gather everything up and rush to the room I'm using. I remove the traces of grass and dirt from my body and choose black leggings and a long-sleeve top in the same color. I tie my hair into a ponytail, put on the sneakers, and head downstairs. I find Andrew waiting for me, checking the time on his watch. Not even the running shorts and white shirt highlighting his biceps take away from his imposing, powerful man presence.

He watches me for a few moments, and for a moment, I feel exposed in his eyes, wearing something so out of the ordinary that it emphasizes every curve of my body. However, I take a deep breath and decide not to care about that right now.

"The clothes look good on you," he comments casually, but I notice the intense gleam in his eyes.

My face warms when I hear what he says, while my heart races, pleased to have pleased him. A smile forms on my lips.

We don't say anything else to each other, I simply follow Andrew out the door, and we begin our run. The day is coming to an end, the twilight shadows the streets, and the cold whips across my face. But it feels so good, so liberating, that soon the temperature becomes just a small detail.

As we pass by the busy park, I feel my lungs burn, as if I've run a marathon. Andrew continues without breaking stride, but when he notices I'm slowing down, he stops and runs toward me. I stop, placing my hands on my knees, breathing deeply.

"Are you okay, Kate?" he asks as he approaches.

"I'm fine, just catching my breath a little."

"Come on. I'll help you." Andrew extends his hand to me, and I place my palm over his. "Soon you'll get used to it and won't feel so tired."

I straighten up and look at him, feeling my skin tingle at the contact with his.

"Ready?" he asks, and I nod.

However, before we continue, I see the silhouette of a man pass through the trees, and a strange chill runs down my spine. Everything inside me freezes when I realize that the man looks very much like Garath. As he walks, he looks in my direction, but I don't have the chance to observe closely because Andrew pulls me out of my daze.

"Kate?"

I look at him, completely tormented, my chest hurting, my breathing erratic. I turn my attention back to the shaded trees where I had seen the man. There's nothing there. Everything is empty, it's as if the guy had evaporated into the air.

Andrew looks in the same direction where my eyes were fixed, and then places his hand on my face, drawing my attention back to him.

"What did you see?" He's direct. Andrew knows I keep deep, destructive secrets to myself.

I shake my head, pretending everything is fine, though I'm trembling from head to toe.

"It's nothing. I thought I saw someone I knew, but it was just my mind playing tricks."

Andrew looks back toward the trees and then back at me. He holds both my hands in his.

"You're shaking, Kate. Whatever you thought you saw, it really shook you. I'm taking you home."

I nod at him, and Andrew continues holding one of my hands as we head back.

"I'm sorry about this," I say softly, feeling like a burden.

"Don't apologize. I was already dying to go home, it's so cold here," he jokes.

I force my lips into a smile, but the truth is, everything feels automatic now.

When we arrive at Andrew's house, I pull away from him to take a shower, and at dinner, I can barely touch the food he brought from a nearby restaurant. Soon after, I retreat to bed, feeling weak and anxious. The images of the man play in my head like a movie, and I end up concluding that I'm going crazy.

Garath doesn't know where I am. Not even my mother knows. There's no reason for him to come to New York. The trauma from the past is confusing my mind, and I can't allow the past to destroy my present. Everything had been so perfect.

It takes me a while to fall asleep, my anxious mind won't stop. Everything feels off. But when exhaustion finally takes over, and I drift off, images so real of Garath on top of me make me twist, scream, and cry. It's as if I've gone back in time, as if I'm that little girl again, going through everything once more. All the abuse and pain.

I wake up crying and sit up in bed with a start, completely trembling. The door opens the next moment, and I see Andrew rushing toward me, his concerned gaze scanning me from head to toe.

"Kate!" He kneels on the bed in front of me and holds my face in both hands. "I'm so sorry about this."

Thick tears flood my eyes, but when I feel him so close, it's as if the terror I felt in the dream turns into smoke, and I only see Andrew, the man who protects me and understands me, the man who makes my body crave things I never imagined were possible. The man who makes me long to be kissed, so that I forget the touch of Garath's hands on me and remember only him.

"Another nightmare. I..."

"Shh, you don't need to say anything." His fingers on my lips stop me from speaking, and I nod.

His hands pull me into him, and I snuggle into his strong arms. The warmth of his bare torso from the waist up heats my skin, and a shiver runs down my spine. Everything in me seems to awaken with his touch, his masculine scent triggers my senses, and everything around us seems to lose meaning.

I run my hands around his neck, and involuntarily, I caress his face with mine. I feel Andrew's breath quicken, his heart against mine starts beating faster, it's as if we're living in the same rhythm, in perfect sync.

My hands caress his neck, his shoulder, my instincts long for him, I don't understand it, I just do it. Andrew's hands hold me tightly at the waist, and I'm practically crushed against his strong, warm body, to the point that I almost feel like I can't breathe.

There's no more Garath, no more fear. There's only him and me. And in this mix of feelings, our faces slowly meet. Andrew tilts his head slightly, and I do the same until we're face to face, so close that I feel his warm breath. Our eyes lock, and I feel the magic happen. All his attention focuses on my lips, and I moisten my lips with my tongue, longing to be kissed again.

Then I wait, and Andrew doesn't disappoint. He lowers his head, and his experienced mouth meets mine. At first, he's calm, tender, but then I feel his hard tongue penetrating my mouth, and a low groan escapes his throat. Andrew's hand grips the back of my neck while the other keeps holding me by the waist. Everything is strange and confusing, but at the same time so captivating that I let myself get carried away.

His mouth tastes like whiskey, the kiss is urgent, Andrew demands more. He nibbles my lower lip, thrusts his tongue into my mouth, and sucks all my air. I feel weak in his arms, my movements clumsy from a lack of experience in kissing, but I try to keep up with him.

He pulls back slightly, letting me breathe, and I gasp, pulling air desperately into my lungs. Our foreheads remain pressed together, our frantic breaths mingling, everything inside me feeling like a whirlwind. Then the kiss begins again, slower this time, but no less delicious. Andrew tilts his head from side to side, both arms crushing me against him. His heat intoxicates me, and I feel dizzy with a pleasure I've never experienced before.

I reach for his hair, threading my fingers through the short strands, surrendering my lips to him, slowly getting used to the movements of his mouth, trying to mimic what he does. I'm driven by instinct and desire, allowing Andrew to suck my tongue into his mouth. I let out a soft moan, feeling strange sensations deep in my belly. My intimacy pulses, and I feel my panties damp, slippery, everything happening so fast that I feel dazed.

His lips leave my mouth, and Andrew finds the curve of my neck, planting kisses and gentle bites.

"Andrew..." I try to say something, but my head is clouded, nothing coherent comes out.

"Hey..." His voice floods my ears for just a second before our mouths are fused again, our bodies so tightly pressed together that I can almost feel the blood rushing through his veins.

Placing a hand on the nape of my neck, Andrew leans forward and pushes my body back until my head rests on the pillow. I'm completely at his mercy, trapped between his body and the bed. As he covers me, my heart races faster, and a pang of anguish grips me.

Though tension begins to take hold of me, Andrew doesn't seem to notice, continuing to kiss me ardently. I suck in air again, refusing to think about Garath now. No. This isn't Garath. This is Andrew.

I open my eyes and see his face completely transformed by desire, his brows knitted, eyelids tight, breaths erratic. Andrew's mouth devours mine hungrily, and I place a hand on his chest, feeling the hot, smooth skin beneath my palms. Somehow, this calms me a little.

His large hands begin to roam my body, gripping my thighs firmly, spreading my legs, and positioning himself between them. I feel all of him—the bulge in the front of his pants, the strength in his hands. This blend of sensations triggers a warning signal in my brain. I feel fear, desire, a mixture of panic and excitement. I want Andrew away from me, yet I also want him inside me.

Before I know it, I'm squeezing my eyes shut again, struggling against him, turning my face away to refuse a kiss, even as my hands pull him closer.

"Kate..." His voice echoes through the room, and everything suddenly becomes calm. No kisses, no touches.

I open my eyes slowly and meet his distressed gaze. The face, once transformed by desire, now seems burdened with guilt.

"Damn!" He shuts his eyes tightly, his expression anguished, as if in pain. "I can't do this to you, little fox."

He studies me intently, his gaze lowering to the space between my legs, where our sexes are separated only by fabric. I see the prominent bulge at the front of his pants and swallow hard, imagining the size, the thickness. My body feels weak, tense. Even so, I can't utter a single word. My mind is so confused, everything so different, and the worst part is that I want him, but I also can't.

Andrew pulls away, and I feel as if a void has replaced him. I feel cold where he touched me, guilty for being so broken. The urge to cry comes strong, but I hold it back as much as I can.

I notice him trying to adjust his erection within his sleep pants, but it's futile. Andrew doesn't say a single word before leaving the room and locking the door behind him.

Breathing unevenly, I can still feel the dampness in my panties. I inhale and exhale deeply to calm myself, though I'm far too agitated. After a few minutes to collect myself, I get up from the bed and decide: I won't be a coward. I need to apologize for letting things get out of hand. He didn't do this alone. I was just as much a part of it, and I'm just as guilty as he is.

I leave the room and walk down the corridor toward Andrew's quarters. Still nervous, I don't wait for him to be gentlemanly enough to receive me. I simply turn the knob and open the door without asking for permission, rehearsing an apology in my mind as I step into his private space.

"Fuck!" He curses the moment he notices my presence, and I freeze in the middle of the room when I see him lying on the bed completely naked, his hand moving rhythmically over his hard cock. "Kate... hell..."

Andrew lets out a rough moan and throws his head back. I notice the tremor in his body and the moment the first jet of semen hits his abdomen. One after another.

I feel a warm liquid trickling through my core, and I have to summon all my strength to keep from collapsing as my legs threaten to give way. My throat feels dry, my body trembling too much, a whirlwind of sensations taking over from the inside out.

When Andrew finishes, his anxious gaze searches for mine, and I can almost see the pain radiating from his expression. Guilt? Unfulfilled desire? I can't tell.

I gather strength from deep within my soul and force my legs to obey my brain's commands. I leave Andrew's room as quickly as I can, nearly breathless, my face aflame, my heart pounding so hard I fear it will burst through my ribcage.

CHAPTER 17

ANDREW

"Fuck!"

I can still feel my body trembling after coming like a teenager in puberty. I should have stopped when Kate entered the room, but the crazy desire was stronger, and knowing she was there, seeing everything, made me lose total control over my body.

I came like a maniac, calling her name. I hated my weakness, but damn, I was at my limit. Kate had pushed me to my limit even with her innocent delicacy. And like the asshole I am, I couldn't control my most primal instincts.

Now she ran out of the room, probably terrified, thinking of some way to leave. While I feel the weight of guilt gnawing at me, after practically corrupting her in bed, and if that wasn't enough, I came in front of her like an animal in heat with zero control over my instincts.

Feeling my temples throbbing, I get out of bed and walk to the bathroom to wash myself and get rid of all the filth I've caused. I turn on the hot water and step under the shower, placing both hands on the shower stall. I close my eyes for a few moments, and my thoughts are fixed on her. I can almost feel the girl in my arms, completely surrendered to me, offering me her full lips.

It's like falling into an abyss, knowing you're going to crash, but not giving a damn about it.

I let out a groan when I feel my dick hardening again, as if I hadn't just come a few minutes ago. I think about Kate's hands pulling my hair, how soft and fragrant her skin is. I was dying to strip her completely naked, dying to taste her pussy, and then shove my cock inside her. I had to use every bit of self-control to avoid doing something crazy and crossing the line.

It was only when Kate rejected my kiss that I realized the torment in her body. It hit me then. I realized she's the fucking forbidden girl. She's my daughter's best friend, and she's shattered into little pieces. I couldn't be such an asshole.

I feel my balls aching with arousal, but I refuse to masturbate again thinking about her. I finish the shower and return to the bedroom, exhausted. Dying to fuck. I feel the nerves flaring, but I ignore my physical reactions and put on a pair of sleep pants. My cock is visibly outlined in the fabric, as hard as steel, and that pisses me off even more.

I sit on the bed, thoughtful, replaying all the shit I did. Fuck! I can't stop thinking about how delicious it would be to suck her small breasts and shove my tongue in Kate's pussy, feel the taste of sex all sticky, make her come moaning my name. I realize I'm sweating when I'm awakened by the sound of my phone. I answer without looking at the screen and immediately regret it.

"Love?" It's Safira. "Oh darling, you finally picked up."

"Hi Safira. How are you?" I glance down at the middle of my legs. Damn, maybe it wasn't such a bad idea for her to call me now.

"I've missed you, you disappeared."

"I'm sorry. You know I'm busy."

I can almost imagine her pouting on the other side of the line.

"I can't stop thinking about you since you decided to end our relationship. I miss you so much, Andrew."

I take a deep breath, already regretting answering the phone. Even though I'm dying to fuck and Safira is beautiful, the fact that

I ended things wasn't accidental. The woman was getting everything confused when I had made it clear that I didn't want a relationship. What we had was strictly and only sex.

"I need to hang up now"—I feel uncomfortable. That's an understatement.

"Why don't you come over to my place?" She's direct, and my cock twitches. The woman is experienced, knows how to play and get involved, and she caught me at an opportune moment.

"Safira..."

"I'll be waiting for you, Andrew."

And then she hangs up, practically leaving me with no way out.

I throw the phone on the bed, giving in to my body's impulses, but before going to Safira, I decide to check on Kate. My sense of responsibility is still strong, and I need to make sure the girl is okay.

KATE

HE PREFERRED TO JERK off rather than move forward with me, and that left me even more stunned. I feel angry at myself for being so broken, but at the same time, I feel irritated and confused with Andrew. He doesn't want me? Am I really that strange to him? My head has turned into a real whirlwind, and I don't know what to think anymore.

I pull the sheets over my body and try to sleep, but sleep doesn't come. I can't stop thinking about him, about his strong arms holding me, about the demanding mouth on mine. I can't stop thinking about how terrifying and yet fascinating it was to see Andrew Thompson touching himself and coming.

His face was completely transformed by pleasure, his body trembling all over, the moans escaping his mouth embedded themselves in my ears and made my core pulse. I almost felt jealous of his hand.

I feel mortified every second I think about how big, thick, and veiny his cock is. A monument to destruction. I also don't understand why I don't feel disgusted by Andrew. I should be terrified, wanting to leave here, but I find myself thinking about his mouth again, and again.

My skin burns when my mind screams at me to slip my hand down to the center of my legs. I've never done this before, but it's as if my body knows what it needs and the instinct is so loud that I take a deep breath. Slowly, I begin to slide my hand down my stomach until I reach the waistband of my sleep pants. I pull the waistband of my panties aside with my fingers and slide my hand inside the fabric. I caress my inner thigh slowly, feeling the strange and intense sensations.

Little by little, I continue my self-exploration until I reach the opening of my sex. I moan softly when I notice how much wetter I am than I imagined. When my fingers gently touch the little hood covering my clitoris, my body reacts with a spasm that makes me jump. The area is sensitive, swollen, painful.

Andrew's name slips from my mouth in a silent murmur.

I withdraw my hand from the area, feeling trembling and anxious, and it's at that moment I hear a knock on the door. My heart races, my skin warms. I quickly adjust my clothes as best as I can and get up to answer. I can barely take a step, my legs feel like they're failing me.

Andrew is on the other side when I open the door, wearing a long-sleeve shirt and jeans. I blink, looking at him closely, a little confused.

"Kate..." he murmurs my name, seeming uncomfortable, and we both know why. "Is everything okay in here?"

I nod with a small movement of my head and step aside so he can enter, wondering if Andrew has any idea what he just interrupted.

"Yes..., everything's fine." My voice is almost inaudible. It feels like something is trying to rip my vocal cords out.

Andrew takes a few steps forward, but stops before fully entering the room.

"Kate, about what happened between us... what you saw. I'm sorry, I shouldn't have touched you like that."

For a few seconds, I feel like I've just been hit with a bucket of cold water. His gaze is fixed on me, his expression showing conviction, his face unreadable.

"Andrew..., I... I'm sorry too. That was what I intended to do when I entered the... " I can't control myself in front of the images I witnessed and glance down briefly at the most private part of his body. "Your room."

I raise my eyes and find his jaw clenched, his brow furrowed.

"I'm just as guilty as you. I'm sorry," I conclude.

He nods and runs a hand through his slightly graying hair. Every movement of his body makes my breath intensify.

"I need to take a walk, do you mind being alone for a while?"

I don't know exactly how to respond when the first thing that comes to mind is that he's probably going to meet someone, a woman. And no matter how much I try to deny it, the fact that I'll be alone bothers me much less than imagining him with someone else. I can't explain it, I just feel a tightness in my chest. So I react the best way I can.

"Can I go with you?" I go straight to the point, even though I'm anxious. "It's just... it's late and I..." I try to justify myself, but my voice won't come out.

Andrew looks at me with a surprised expression, indicating he didn't expect me to offer to go with him. And it's most likely that I've really overstepped the boundaries, but I couldn't control my impulses.

There's a mix of agitation and disbelief in his face. Andrew seems embarrassed, and that only makes me more certain that he's going to meet a woman. Everything in me tightens, my chest aches deeply, my heart races uncontrollably, and a painful lump forms in my throat. A kind of anguish that leaves me breathless, and I have to fight hard to keep it from showing.

"I... I'll wait downstairs." He says and then looks me up and down again before leaving.

When I close the door, I exhale the breath I hadn't realized I was holding. When did I become so out of control and jealous? And worse, by someone who could be my father's age and who is nothing to me. He's just my best friend's father, and that's why he's giving me shelter out of pity. Either way, I need to stick to the plan or everything will get even more awkward.

I rush to the bathroom and quickly wash my face, inhaling and exhaling deeply. I look at myself in the mirror and find a somewhat tired, distressed expression, my face showing everything my heart is feeling.

I change clothes, opting for pants, a shirt, and a warm jacket. I don't know how things will go from here, but I try not to think too much about it.

I find Andrew waiting for me in the living room. He looks uneasy, and the silence between us is palpable. I follow him to the car, feeling like an idiot, a spoiled child who can't stand being contradicted.

Andrew drives through the streets of New York with such precision that it seems like he has a map in his brain. After a while, he parks the car in front of a huge building, which I soon recognize as the Empire State Building, an old and touristy skyscraper, quite popular for its observatory at night.

"Have you been here before?" He finally asks.

"No," I answer, impressed by the height of the monument.

"Come on, let's go up."

We get out of the car, and Andrew takes my hand, guiding me to the entrance hall. After we buy the tickets, we enter the elevator heading for the 86th floor, where the observatory is.

He doesn't let go of my hand as the elevator moves. I'm trembling a bit, and I know it's because of the closeness, the touch, but I still don't want to pull away.

When the doors open, it's like a whole new world is revealed in front of me. New York is beautiful, and I can see all four corners of the city lit up from here.

I let out a sigh of admiration, my eyes shining as I walk along the deck. There are hardly any people here due to the time, and that makes everything even more fascinating.

Andrew takes me to the safety railing, and the cold wind blows my hair from side to side, sending shivers down my body. But nothing can dull my fascination.

"It's beautiful here," I say, mesmerized, and look at Andrew.

He smiles slightly and tightens his grip on my hand a little more, drawing my attention to the gesture. My cheeks flush from the way we're standing, looking so intimate, holding hands in the night as if we were a couple. Andrew doesn't seem to care.

"Thank you for bringing me here," I say again.

"I like to come here sometimes. It's a good place to be alone and think."

His hand slides to my left temple, and Andrew strokes the spot. He tucks a few strands of hair behind my ear.

"You're special, Kate," he murmurs. His words hit my chest.

"You are too," I respond without thinking. "I...," my voice falters, but I continue. "Thank you for everything, Andrew."

His caress continues, his gaze turning to my mouth. My throat goes dry, anxiety takes over me from the inside out, and I long for him to kiss me. But that's not what Andrew does when he pulls me closer.

His lips kiss the top of my head, and then he pulls away.

"I won't let what happened today repeat itself, I promise you. I don't want you to be scared or afraid. I want you to trust me, I want you to see me as someone who will always take care of you, like family."

All I should do is smile and be grateful to him. I should sigh with relief, knowing that Andrew respects me and sees me as family. But in reality, what I feel is more like disappointment, and that's so frustrating. Because while I want him close, I can't give him what he needs.

I'm not stupid enough to think we could live as a couple without having sex. Besides, everything is so strange that it's almost scary.

"You're right," I use all my self-control.

And then his phone starts ringing. Andrew steps back, takes his phone out of his pocket, takes a deep breath, and ends the call.

I don't need much to know that it's probably the woman he was going to meet.

Embarrassed, I watch him end the call again and turn off the phone, putting it back in his pocket.

"I'm sorry about that," he looks up, confused.

"About what?" I ask.

I point to the pocket of his pants and exhale, feeling deflated.

"About that. You were going out with someone, weren't you? And I ruined everything."

His expression doesn't change. He keeps looking at me seriously, making the unspoken truth clear. Finally, the words that come out of his mouth confirm my suspicions.

"Yes, I was going out with someone."

I feel a pang in my chest, but I remain steady.

"I think we should go home."

CHAPTER 18

ANDREW

Another dead girl. The body was found on the top floor of an apartment in Brooklyn after an anonymous tip. The same characteristics as the previous murders, the same physical traits as the other victims.

I glance at the clock and resume analyzing the body lying on the floor. She's face down and completely naked, her hands bound behind her back. Her hair is dark, and her skin is very pale. It follows the same pattern the department has been investigating for some time.

Coagulated blood spreads around the body. The medical examiner begins his work and shifts the victim's position, turning her onto her back. The body is completely opened, from the chest down to the vagina. The deep cut exposes the entire thoracic cavity.

"The organs have been removed," he informs as he examines.

Her eyes are open and cloudy, her skin marked by bruises, as if the girl had been tortured before she was killed.

"What was the cause of death?" I'm still shocked by the brutality of the scene, even though I've seen it all in this world.

Maybe because the girl reminded me a bit of Kate, or even my daughter Angelina. The fair skin, dark hair, small body. And the fact that we're dealing with a serial killer makes everything even more challenging.

"Everything points to her dying while the organs were being removed. It was a brutal death."

I take a deep breath, but stay focused, observing every detail, swearing to myself that my team will find the bastard.

I exchange a few words with the local police chief, then decide to leave. I get in the car and make my way back to the investigation department. As I drive, I recall the images of the completely disfigured girl on the floor, bathed in her own blood. Her expression blends with Kate's, and I feel my blood boiling in my veins. The anger surges intensely. A sense of anguish that I've never felt overtakes my chest, and right then, I'm absolutely certain I would do anything to keep Kate safe, no matter if someone has to die in the process.

KATE

I END THE CALL I JUST had with Angelina and inhale softly, feeling completely renewed. I'm becoming more and more enchanted by the babies. Caleb is adopted, and Kaleo is Alex and Angelina's biological child. Two little eccentric and very smiling creatures that make my heart melt every time I see them on a video call.

After stepping away from the counter, I play with Spot for a bit and change his water. Then I prepare a simple meat and cheese sandwich for my lunch, since Andrew usually doesn't eat lunch at home.

As I eat, it's hard not to think of my daughter. The blue eyes I saw in the photo are like crystal-clear pools, identical to mine. She must be much bigger now, while another family gets her smiles every morning. I eat half of the sandwich and leave the rest on the plate, feeling a lump in my throat.

Spot barks at me, wagging his tail, so I give him a small piece of meat. I'm no longer hungry, so I take the plate to the sink to be washed, and it's at that moment I hear the doorbell. I dry my hands and walk toward the living room. I head to the door and open it, thinking it's a neighbor or one of Andrew's colleagues.

The mistake people often make is being so sure of their own safety that they hardly realize that a simple opening of a door can be the start of a nightmare. And that's exactly what happens to me. I feel like I'm reliving a nightmare, everything inside me stirs, everything inside me crumbles.

"Mom?" My voice hardly comes out, and I need to hold onto the door tightly to keep my balance.

The woman removes her sunglasses and looks me up and down, squinting her eyes.

"Hello, Kate?"

"What are you doing here?" I regain my composure and start to watch her with the same coldness with which my mother addresses me. "How did you find me?"

"What do you mean, what am I doing here? I came after my daughter." Her tone is soft, and that's what worries me the most. "It wasn't hard to figure out where you would be. After all, your friend Angelina had left several messages on the voicemail with her address. I just put two and two together. What surprised me was coming here and finding out you're living with a man, not with your friend."

My mother walks past me and enters Andrew's house without asking for permission, much less being invited. Her eyes scan every detail of the walls and the furniture that decorates the place.

"You know very well why I left!" I say firmly, despite my trembling. I make it clear to my mother why I left.

She continues to examine everything minutely. She runs her hand over the coffee table in the living room, observes the pictures on the walls.

"Everything's so fancy, isn't it? So the man you're living with is rich."

A lump forms in my throat, and the anger rises inside me.

"Leave, mom, please. Don't make things harder."

And then she looks at me, and now I can clearly see the contempt and anger in her eyes.

"Now you're kicking me out of your luxury hideaway, Kate? How ungrateful you are, you little bitch." She curses, and my nerves flare even more, the resentment coming on strong.

"You know why I left. How do you expect me to live under the same roof as Garath after everything he did?" I ask, unfazed. One of two things: either she's lost her mind, or...?

"You ungrateful bitch! It's your fault Garath had to run away. It's your fault I spent years and years struggling to put food on the table. And now that he's back, you want me to be unhappy? I sacrificed my life for you, Kate."

Tears of pure resentment fall down my face, but I won't accept being treated like a burden again, not when everything is going so well now. I take a deep breath and look my mother squarely in the eyes, making it clear that I've changed, I've risen, and I won't fall again, and the truth needs to be shouted until it's understood.

"Garath raped me, I was just a child, or have you forgotten? That monster violated me, I had to undergo surgery after suffering a laceration and hemorrhaging. I almost died, because of him."

She shows no reaction when I bring it up. Nothing seems to faze her damaged character, not even when I remind her of all the harm and terror that man put me through. Then she takes a step toward me, coldly, her face coming just a few inches from mine.

"And what's changed now, Kate? You're still giving your pussy in exchange for a roof!"

The weight of her words hits me so intensely that I lose control, and I end up retaliating in the worst imaginable way: I slap my mother across the face. It's not hard, but it's enough to make her head turn to the side.

Her reaction is completely different from what I imagined. She brings her hand to her face and glares back at me, her skin turning a shade of red. Then she laughs, and her mocking laughter leaves me even more stunned. I feel ashamed of what I just did, because I've never been violent, I've always just accepted everything silently.

"So the dead fly finally learned to fight back."

My mother returns the slap with all the strength in her body, and I stumble backward, feeling a ringing in my ear. I place my hand on my cheek, my skin throbbing hard, the world around me spinning as if I'm about to lose my balance and fall at any moment. Everything blends together—the physical pain, the heartache, the memories I fight to forget.

"Leave! Leave me alone!" I scream and take a deep breath, my vision blurred, anxiety consuming me from the inside out.

"Of course I'm leaving, and you're coming with me, Kate. Garath misses you, and this time you'll do what needs to be done."

She grabs my hand, and I push her away, freeing myself in the process.

I watch her again, and at the same time, a click awakens in my mind and fear hits me: "What do you mean?"

And then everything starts to make sense. I remember everything. The beatings she took from Garath, the insults, the abuse. But when he left, she would go crazy, she would panic, she became someone else. And suddenly everything changed. Garath came back home, and she became happy again. He started treating her with affection, buying food again, paying the bills. He started giving her crumbs of love, and she was content with that.

She doesn't need to say a word for me to understand that nothing was accidental, it was all premeditated: "You knew, didn't you? You... knew he was molesting me?"

I want to scream and disappear, I want to forget that this woman in front of me is my mother. But the only thing I do is keep staring at her, waiting for her to finish stabbing the knife in my chest. Maybe it's better this way.

"We needed to eat, Kate. We needed a good health plan. I don't remember seeing you complain when your belly was full. It was just a small price to pay."

Her coldness in confessing everything is what scares me the most.

"You're a monster. Worse than him!" I spit the words, moved by pain and anger. "Leave, I don't want to ever look at your face again."

I point my finger toward the door, but my mother doesn't even move to leave. On the contrary. She comes closer again, her expression determined.

"If you don't come with me, Kate, I'll call the police. Does the guy you're living with know you're crazy? That you were committed to a psychiatric hospital?"

I can't speak. My voice is caught in my throat.

"He doesn't know, does he? Poor guy. And as for you, if you don't want to be committed again, you'll obey me and come back to California. You don't have a choice, Kate."

And then she moves forward, grabbing my arm in the process.

"No..." I try to pull away and distance myself from her, but I receive several blows to the face, accompanied by low, cruel insults. "I'll report you... you..."

And then, the woman who brought me into this world grabs my hair and delivers another slap to my face: "You crazy bitch. No one will believe a crazy person like you, Kate. So shut your mouth and let's get out of here!"

"What's going on here?" Andrew's voice echoes through the room, and she releases me, startled at being caught in the act of assaulting me. "Who are you?"

Andrew walks quickly toward me, and I practically throw myself into his arms, trembling, crying, completely disoriented.

"She's my daughter. I came to get her." My mother advances toward me, but he turns my body to the side, blocking her from reaching me.

"Stay away, ma'am!"

"She's my daughter. And I'll call the police if you stop me."

I can't say anything else, I just sob quietly, clinging to him, my face pressed against his strong chest, my heart pounding with pain and fear of what might happen.

Then Andrew reaches inside his jacket and pulls out something that resembles a badge: "Andrew Thompson, FBI Director New York. I'm the authority here."

I glance at her, noticing her mortified expression and the paleness that has overtaken her skin.

"You can't do this, Mr. Andrew..."

"I ask you to leave and not come back. Kate will not go with you. And after what I've witnessed, I advise you to be quick, or things will get very difficult here. And I'll make sure they do."

Her expression changes from disbelief to shock in a matter of seconds. My mother's gaze falls on me threateningly, but she doesn't say anything more. There's nothing left to say or try.

She simply turns her back and walks out the door without looking back.

CHAPTER 19

ANDREW

Kate is trembling in my arms as the woman leaves the room and disappears from sight. My whole body feels like it's about to combust seeing her like this, completely disoriented, anxious. As if she had just seen a demon.

"What happened, sweetheart? What did that woman want?" I know something very serious happened for the girl to react this way.

"She knew everything, Andrew... my mom knew everything and allowed it." Her voice is shaky, dragged out, Kate is not making any coherent sense.

"What did she know?"

She sobs quietly against my chest, and I can almost feel her pain, the anguish that has taken over her body.

"When I..." She tries to speak, but her voice falters.

"Come, you need to sit down, Kate. When you calm down, you can tell me everything that happened."

I guide Kate to the living room couch and sit with her. The girl clings to me as if I'm her safe haven, her face resting on my chest, and the tears soaking her face wetting the fabric of my jacket.

I tighten her body in my arms and we sit in silence for a few minutes until I feel her breathing calm down and Kate starts to speak on her own.

"I was ten or eleven, I don't really remember." I close and open my eyes, feeling the weight of her words, wondering what's coming next.

"My stepfather, Garath, he raped me." It feels like a knife is being shoved into my chest, rage tears me apart from the inside, revolt. Everything inside me boils over, and all I can think about is killing this bastard with my own hands.

"Damn!" I whisper, completely overwhelmed by the agony of thinking about everything she went through at the hands of that man. I squeeze the girl tighter, almost suffocating her, but I refuse to let her go.

"Today I found out my mom knew everything." She sobs quietly, and I close my eyes again, feeling inadequate, restless. Blood boiling, everything in me losing control. "She did nothing to stop it, Andrew."

Minutes pass as Kate sobs quietly, trying to recover from the pain.

"I didn't want to have so much hatred, but I do. I'm sorry, sweetheart, I'm sorry for everything you've been through."

Kate stays silent for a few seconds, I feel the strong beat of her heart. I feel on her skin how much disappointment and betrayal hurt.

"My mom was never really present or affectionate. But she was my mom. She fed me, took me to the doctor when I was sick, played her part. But then this man showed up, and because of him, she forgot about me and who I was. She sold me, exchanged me for food, jewelry, and attention..."

"You are precious, Kate. You're an amazing and brilliant girl. Never think you're undeserving of love. Your mom was a criminal, and she deserves to pay."

I feel a knot in my throat, and it's hard to keep breathing. I try my best to control myself, but it's almost impossible to stay quiet when all I want is to end the lives of those bastards.

"I'm going to assign an FBI agent to keep an eye on you when I'm not home, alright?"

Kate pulls her head back, and her bright blue eyes meet mine. She nods, and I feel like I'm going to explode just thinking about her still being a child, abused by a criminal, without even having her mother fight for her safety.

"Thank you... I'll feel better that way."

I bring a hand to her face and wipe the wetness from her cheek with my fingers. Kate closes her eyes and sighs quietly, for the first time letting down the walls that surround her, revealing just how fragile, hurt, and broken she is like an abandoned puppy.

"Everything will be okay, sweetheart. Don't think about it. Try to forget." I say, and she looks at me again, her expression more relaxed.

"Andrew..." Her tone is softer now.

"Hi..." I remove my hand from her face.

"What are you doing here, at this hour?"

I pause for a few moments, a bit surprised by being caught off guard. The truth is, the only reason I'm home is simply to check on Kate after witnessing the brutal death of that girl in Brooklyn. However, I don't tell her that New York is being targeted by a serial killer.

"I forgot some papers and took advantage of my lunch break to grab them."

She nods and steps back a little: "Did you have lunch? I can..."

"No, Kate." I interrupt her just as she offers to do something for me. I wonder how much a mother's neglect has affected a young girl's psychology to the point where she's always trying to be helpful, even when she's completely destroyed. "I'm fine. I need to get back to work."

"Okay." Despite everything, I feel like my refusal has disappointed her.

"Will you be okay?"

"Yes. I'll be okay."

Still heavy-hearted, I head to my office to grab some papers and return to the investigation department. The first thing I do is assign a trusted agent to ensure Kate's safety.

I return to work, but nothing can remove from my mind the terror and panic I saw in her eyes. I can't forget the tone of her voice as she told me everything she lived through, the anguish she suffered, I could feel her pain. So, I decide to quickly look up some information on Garath, the girl's mother, and Kate herself.

It doesn't take long, and I find what I need. Garath Murphy, forty-eight years old, received eleven years in prison for the rape of his stepdaughter in California. I skim through the details about the man, and all my rage consumes me when I realize he's free, which is probably why Kate ran away. I quickly go through the details of Nellie Smith, the girl's mother, and start reading about Kate.

I feel my blood freeze and my heart nearly stop when my brain processes the information in front of me. Kate spent several months in a psychiatric hospital, and during that time, she had a child. The words blur in front of me as my brain processes the information. I wonder what happened for her life to have taken such a tragic turn since the incident at the convent.

Angelina had told me about the murder of the nuns, she said that her friend Kate had been hurt on that fateful day, but she didn't go into detail. I didn't insist either, because my daughter was too hurt to relive this subject. The most I got involved back then was using my influence and position to erase any trace of Alexander Russell, Angelina's husband, being involved with the American mafia.

I set the information aside and take a deep breath, trying to understand how a mother could become this cold with her own daughter. I then decide to do a more thorough investigation and send an email to the FBI department in California, requesting updated data on Garath.

I shift my attention to other matters, though I am too restless. I bring my hand to my neck and massage the area, feeling tense, anxious. The questions are endless in my head. I come to the conclusion that the more I get to know Kate, the more my thirst for knowledge increases, and I feel a desperate need to know everything about her, each of her steps.

Although I have some sense of the mess that happened at the convent, I need her to trust me and tell me the truth. I need her to tell me about the child and free herself from everything on her own. Kate is like a solitary bird, trapped in the cage of her own heart, held captive by the traumas that destroyed her soul.

Restless, I step away from my desk and stand up. I walk to the glass window of the building, watching the cars circling below. Her images don't leave my mind. That watchful gaze, that withdrawn expression. A frightened little fox ready to flee at the first sign of danger.

"Damn, Kate..." I whisper to myself. "What did they do to you?"

I return to work some time later, the afternoon passes quickly, and I try my best to focus on what I need to do. At the end of the day, I receive the response I needed, and it drives me insane with anger.

Garath is living under the same roof as Nellie, in the same house where he abused the girl. And the bitch took him back as if nothing happened.

I feel a strong discomfort in my chest when I think of Kate having to run away, needing help. Now everything makes sense. All the pieces of the puzzle fall into place, from the moment she ran away from me that first day, preferring to spend the night on a park bench alone. She preferred getting sick in the rain to being near a man.

KATE

YEARS BEFORE

A FEW DAYS AFTER I left the hospital, life didn't go the way it should have. Everything around me terrified me. The shadows, the night, the sounds. Sometimes, I woke up at night crying, shouting for my mother. Most of the time, she didn't come to me, and with that, I got used to being alone, to overcoming my fears on my own.

I noticed her becoming more distant, her expression always empty, her eyes filled with dark circles as if she had cried all night. I understood that she missed Garath, and I felt guilty for it. Maybe if I didn't exist, my mom wouldn't have to be without him.

In a way, it was eating me up. The whole situation I had been put in. I didn't like seeing my mom sad, I felt sad too, my heart ached so much, my chest was always tight. It was like I was losing my mom in some way.

I learned from my mom that it was she who called the emergency service when she found me unconscious on the bed and bleeding. She said I kept waking up and passing out all the time, asking for help and screaming for Garath to stop. That's how the police located him so quickly, and the suspicions were confirmed.

Garath was arrested, she said. *He won't hurt you anymore*, she kept repeating.

Garath had been arrested. I was safe. I just didn't feel that way.

The days passed, I went back to school, and it felt like I was the center of attention. People looked at me with pity, the news had spread. My mom grew more and more distant, colder, crueler, spending days away from home. I had to fend for myself, but that wasn't a problem; I was used to taking care of myself.

Months passed, then years. Nothing changed between us. I started helping her at the bar to earn some tips, but it didn't last long, because according to my mom, I was nothing but a slut and attracted too much attention from men.

Five years passed, I was sixteen when my mom told me I was going to New York, going to a convent, and my sister Klara would take care of everything. I didn't contest it, just nodded to her, and in a way, I felt happy. I hadn't seen or heard from her in a long time. I didn't even remember her face until now.

I take a deep breath as reality hits me again, and I let the memories of the past fade into the air.

I look to the side and watch Klara at the wheel of the car, driving down a dirt road toward the monastery. There's an orphanage there that belongs to the congregation, and it's there I'll stay until I finish my studies and turn eighteen to dedicate myself to the novitiate. I'll have a bed, food, and education in exchange for helping the sisters care for the children. It will be a test, a way for me to adapt to the new life waiting for me. And to be honest, I don't care if I become a nun. I just try to forget the past and pretend I had a normal childhood, that nothing bad happened, and that it was all just a terrible nightmare. I try to think of myself as a regular teenager, living a regular life.

Klara looks like my mom, with curly hair, a thin face, fair skin. She's several years older than me, and we were never close. In fact, I saw her very little throughout my life, and our contact was practically zero.

"We're almost there, Kate." She says, not taking her focus off the road ahead.

"Alright..." I reply, and that's the end of the conversation.

The conversation doesn't go anywhere, there's nothing to say. Klara seems nice, but our little contact creates a big distance between the two of us. So I stay quiet, waiting for the moment we'll reach my new home.

After a while, the car turns around a bend, and the massive gates of a monastery appear before me. The entrance is huge, and the gate is made of old iron, with carved details at the top.

I take a deep breath and get out of the car when Klara parks. I feel the morning aroma filled with the soft scent of white rose bushes intertwined in the gate's ironwork. The wind blows hard against my face, swaying my long hair from side to side, and I look ahead, to the destination that awaits me in this place, completely isolated from the world.

CHAPTER 20

KATE

I close the laptop as soon as I hear the sound of the doorbell. My heart is pounding with anxiety, and I quickly adjust my hair to look at least somewhat presentable. Spot stays alert by my side, already wagging his tail, eager to greet our visitors.

I take a few deep breaths, put a big smile on my face, and run to the door, knowing exactly who's on the other side.

As soon as I open it, three beautiful pairs of eyes are staring back at me. The little boys look serious while watching me, but Angelina is all smiles and very elegant, wearing a red long-sleeve dress and her hair pulled into a ponytail. She steps forward, and we embrace tightly while Kaleo, in her arms, protests for being squeezed in the process.

"Angel, finally," I say, overwhelmed with emotion seeing her again.

"Kate, my God..., it's so amazing to have you here."

I smile at her as we pull apart, and I turn my attention to the boys, who are now watching Spot and his playful barks.

Little Kaleo watches me closely and gives a beautiful smile when I hold his chin. He's so cute, a bit like Angelina, but at the same time, his features aren't as delicate as hers. His expression is striking, just like his father's.

I look at the other child, who is also watching me a bit shyly but quickly kneels down to pat Spot on the head. My heart nearly melts. Caleb has subtler features and is just as chubby as Kaleo. His hair is thick, and his eyes shine. I'm completely smitten watching the children.

"Your kids are so beautiful." I'm so enchanted that I only now realize I'm blocking the doorway.

I step aside, and Angelina takes Caleb's little hand to lead him into her father's house. "Yes, they're little sweethearts. You need to meet John, you can't imagine what a treasure that boy is."

I nod at her, imagining how lucky she is to have such a family.

She places Kaleo on the floor, and he quickly starts playing with his brother and Spot. We sit on the living room couch, and Angelina sighs, turning to face me.

"Kate, you look beautiful," she says, and I smile as she takes my hands, squeezing them tightly in hers.

"The days I've spent here have done me good," I nod in agreement.

"I hope my father has taken good care of you."

My cheeks heat up as I remember my moments with Andrew. The movies we watched together, the runs in the park, our kisses. Everything inside me stirs, but I maintain composure in front of Angelina. Despite everything, Andrew respects me so much, and he has never crossed the line. Everything that happened between us, I allowed, and I'm not too proud of it.

"He's very kind."

My friend smiles and raises an eyebrow with a mischievous look.

"Very kind, and very handsome," she comments, winking in my direction, watching my reaction.

I don't know what to say in response to her suggestion, my voice catches. So, I stay quiet, completely mute, my heart almost jumping out of my chest.

Angelina laughs and lets go of my hand, crossing her legs in the process.

"I'm just teasing you, Kate. I had to see your face when I suggested you might find my dad handsome."

I try to smile, but the truth is, she's absolutely right, and it's just too unsettling. Andrew is very handsome, and it leaves me extremely confused because he makes me desire things I never thought I would want in my life.

"You seem pretty excited." I change the subject, because just thinking about Andrew while I'm with Angelina makes me feel like I've betrayed her trust. "When we were at the convent, you were usually the more reserved one, and I was the energetic friend."

Angelina broadens her smile, reminiscing about our schemes back then, but soon her smile fades, and I know exactly why. I lower my gaze, feeling ashamed, and she reaches for my hand again: "Hey, Kate, look at me."

I lift my head to look at her, still carrying the weight of guilt for having run away that day, consumed by fear.

"Angel..., I... It's hard to forgive myself."

She nods, her gaze indicating how difficult this subject is for both of us.

"You were scared and..." She tries to justify my cowardice, but I know exactly what I must say. As Andrew now knows, Angel also deserves to know. It's part of my healing process. I don't think much when I open my mouth to express what I should have said a long time ago. I take a deep breath and go straight to the point, no detours, no mysteries.

"I was abused, Angel, by my stepfather. I was just a little girl at the time, but I still carry the trauma of the past." She widens her eyes, completely alarmed by my confession. "When that thing happened at the convent..." I stop for a few seconds, taking a breath, gathering courage to continue: "When those men attacked us, I felt like I was going back in time. I just kept thinking about Garath hurting me. And that's why I couldn't stop and help you. I wanted to run away from Garath, from the ghost of his memories." Her eyes are overflowing with tears now, and Angel sobs, staring at me with sympathy.

"Oh Kate. I'm so sorry..., so sorry."

I feel my vision cloud over too, but I promise myself that the past will no longer be part of my life. I will move on, no matter how painful it is. It will be like cutting through heavy chains, but now I have someone who can help me do that.

"When I entered the convent, I tried to be a different person. I tried to live like a normal teenager, pretending I had been a happy child. None of what I pretended to be was true, I was just a girl with a smile on her face, full of tricks, with an empty heart. But I loved you, Angel, so much. You've always been, and always will be, my best friend. My refuge. Thank you for being part of my life."

I finish saying those words and feel as if I've just lifted a huge weight off my shoulders and heart.

Angel approaches again, and we embrace, tears falling from our faces, forgiveness rising to the surface as it should. Our friendship being rekindled in a strong bond once more.

Then we pull apart, drying our faces. Angel looks around for the children and finds them smiling and playing with Spot. Then she turns her attention back to me.

"I want you to stay with me, at my house. Since I just got back from the trip, I need to sort a few things out, but it'll be enough time for you to organize your things here. Is that okay?"

I nod in agreement to Angel and look around. The details of the room, the pictures on the walls, everything exactly the same as when I arrived. I place my hand on my chest when I feel something tighten deep inside, knowing I won't be as present in Andrew's life anymore. I can't explain what's happening, I just feel something pressing on my heart with force.

"I'll pack my things," I say to her, though my voice falters.

Angel stands up and adjusts her dress.

"I'll see you in a bit then."

I nod to my friend, and she heads over to the boys. She picks up Kaleo in her arms and holds Caleb's little hand.

I say goodbye to the three of them, completely enchanted by the children, happy with the direction my life is taking, and at the same time, heavy-hearted to be distancing myself from Andrew. I need to keep repeating to myself that this will be better, that the kisses we shared didn't mean anything.

After Angel leaves, I go to my room and start packing my things. I begin by taking everything off the nightstand, then grab the clothes in the wardrobe. I find Andrew's shirt that I wore when I first arrived here, still among my belongings. I hold the fabric carefully, feeling the strong beats of my heart, and bring the shirt to my face to smell it. Maybe it's just an illusion in my head, but I'm sure Andrew's scent is still on the fabric.

I feel my breath quicken and put the shirt aside, realizing the effect it's having on me. It's at this moment I hear a knock at the door, and I jump, startled.

"Kate? Are you in there?" It's his voice.

Agitated, I glance at the shirt, wondering whether I should return it or not, but I end up choosing the second option: "Andrew? Just a minute."

I put the shirt in my bag and throw some clothes over it. I quickly fix my hair and try to control my breathing. When I feel calmer, I walk to the door and open it for him.

Andrew stares back at me with that imposing look that destabilizes me. He smiles, but his smile fades within seconds. His expression is neutral, but his gaze seeks mine with such intensity that I hold my breath.

"Want to come in?" I invite, stepping aside.

Andrew doesn't say anything, continues to look at me intensely, as if trying to read my thoughts, as if he wants to memorize every detail of my face.

"Andrew?" I call his attention, and it's like pulling him out of a trance.

"Angelina... She told me you were moving to her house today." I nod, though I'm trembling for no reason.

"Yes, I'm packing my things." I gesture toward the clothes on the bed and turn my attention back to him.

"I have something for you." Andrew is direct. He extends his hand and gives me a small white bag. "It's a gift."

I look at him completely surprised and take the item from his hands. I pull out a small box with the Apple logo on it and am astonished when I find a state-of-the-art phone inside.

"Andrew... no... I can't accept this!"

He takes the phone out of the box and places it in my hand.

"Yes, you can. Accept it." His voice is almost pleading.

I look at the phone in my hand again, knowing that I won't be able to afford something like this anytime soon.

"Please, Andrew, I owe you so much, and there's still the stuff from the card I bought and..."

"You don't owe me anything. Absolutely nothing."

"But..."

"Kate..." He interrupts me. "You were my guest here. You're my daughter's friend, so..."

"So you also see me as a daughter." I finish his sentence, even though that's not exactly how I feel. And even less how he feels.

"Yes. That's it!" He confirms, but I notice the exact moment when Andrew clenches his jaw, and his posture changes from relaxed to rigid. Even the veins in the back of his hand seem to scream: lie!

"Alright. Thank you for the gift." I try to appear as mature as possible and hold the phone tightly.

"I saved my number for you. You can message me if you need anything."

"Okay."

Andrew looks at me one last time and turns his back to leave. I open my mouth to say something, maybe thank him again, say goodbye with a hug, but I don't know exactly what to say, I just don't have the courage to move forward. I feel a lump in my throat, chills on my skin. I feel his scent in every part of the room. But I allow him to leave, to disappear from my sight.

I need a few minutes to compose myself when I close the door again. I place my hand on my neck, feeling tense, so strange. I take a deep breath and return to what I was doing. After I finish packing my things, I pick up the phone Andrew gave me and start exploring the available apps. I log into Instagram and check my account. Time passes as I enjoy responding to some messages and comments. The readers are eager for the next book, and so am I. It's almost here.

After everything, I check my contacts and there it is, his name. Andrew. I type a message and send it to him.

I'm very grateful for everything.

I wait a few minutes, but he doesn't reply. Then I gather my things and go downstairs, making sure I don't leave anything behind.

It doesn't take long before Angelina returns to her father's house. When I open the door to greet her, I come face to face with her and the walking wardrobe that my friend calls her husband. Alex is simply huge and very strong. His expression is a little terrifying, I must admit, especially because of the scar he carries on his eyebrow.

"Hello," I say to both of them.

Alex responds with a nod, and Angelina frees herself from him to enter.

"I brought my husband to help with your things," she announces.

I look at the huge man in front of me, dressed in jeans and a black leather jacket, a true contrast to Angelina's small stature. I find myself wondering internally how she manages all of this, and I swallow hard, a little frightened by his presence.

I vaguely remember Alexander from the night of that tragedy at the convent. He saved my life when I thought it was all over. He was God's messenger when I prayed for the last time since then. His hair is shorter now, but I would recognize him anywhere.

"There's no need, Angel. I have only a few things. I brought just the essentials."

I point to the small suitcase on the couch, containing my documents, mementos, and the few clothes I bought here.

Ignoring my protests, Angelina grabs the suitcase and hands it to her husband. He watches her, curving his lips into a subtle smile, but I can't help but notice the way Alex inspects his wife's body. There's a kind of fire in both their gazes when they look at each other.

Then he turns his back and walks away.

"Shall we? My father is right there, playing with the kids and the puppy. By the way, he's a cutie, the boys are in love with him."

I smile at her, thinking of Spot's tricks. He's becoming an important part of my new life, something I can no longer imagine living without.

I follow Angelina toward her house, and I soon spot Andrew playing with Kaleo and Caleb in the garden. He lifts both boys in his arms, spinning them around, and Spot barks behind. It's one of the most beautiful sights I've ever seen in my life.

That older man, with his mysterious air, his expensive and imposing clothes, completely surrendered to the charms of the boys. Andrew smiles and puts Caleb on the ground, playfully messing with Kaleo. He repeats the same process with the other and also with Spot. The four of them create a true party of laughter and barking.

I should smile, I should feel happy witnessing something so charming, but the only thing I feel is a tightness in my chest when I think about my daughter. And I long so much, so much, for a baby.

A baby of my own, so I can care for it and nurse it from my breast. So I can love without limits or fear.

When he spots us, Andrew holds both children and walks toward us with a big smile on his face. When his gaze locks on mine, the image that comes to my mind frightens me and clouds my thoughts, but I can't stop imagining what it would be like to have a baby with Andrew. Would it look like him? Would it have his features? Would it be gentle?

When I return to reality, I'm trembling from head to toe, my eyes fixed on him, my heart filled with pain for something I can't have.

CHAPTER 21

KATE

A month has passed since I started living with Angelina, and now we're in the freezing winter of New York. Our routine is well defined, and it's been a fun experience. We take turns caring for the kids, as I make sure to help with whatever I can. I divide my time between writing and some housework, in addition to helping with the boys. At first, my friend was firm in not accepting my help, but I insisted until she understood that I would feel much better being useful.

From what I understand, Alexander works with Andrew on classified and very dangerous assignments for the FBI, so he's harder to see. When he's home, they spend most of their time together, so those are the moments when I get closest to the boys. However, despite loving all these people, despite Angelina being my best friend and us getting along really well, I still feel uncomfortable, like I'm intruding on the couple's privacy. So in the meantime, between chapters, I look for houses in the neighborhood to rent.

One, in particular, caught my attention. It's a small white house with a small rose garden in front. It's a few blocks away from here. I'm planning to rent it as soon as I finish the book. I've been saving every penny from the royalties I made this month.

I hear the sound of messages, and the screen of my phone lights up on the bed. I feel my heart leap, knowing it's Andrew. He's the only person I keep in contact with daily, besides Angelina. I handle work matters through email.

Since I moved in, we've kept our contact distant. I see him little, most of the time from afar. It's become a routine for me to peek out the window when his usual time to return home is near, and that's exactly what I'm doing now for the thousandth time, since Andrew hasn't returned home at his usual time.

I put Angelina's laptop aside and grab the phone to check the time. It's already past 10:00 PM.

I rush to the window of the room I'm staying in, which, ironically, gives me a privileged view of Andrew's house, and pull back the curtain.

I see the car parked in what was supposed to be the garden, now covered in snow, and I notice his bedroom light is on. I try not to think about what Andrew is doing, but it's hard to control my thoughts. My imagination runs wild, especially that night when I saw him pleasuring himself, his naked body and erect penis ejaculating.

I look back at the screen of my phone, feeling something strange in my groin. I feel my skin heat up, and my panties get damp. It's such an intense feeling that I need to rub my legs together, overwhelmed by the desire his memories stir in me. It almost hurts to feel the moisture intensifying with every second I think about him.

Breathing heavily, I open the message Andrew sent.

Good evening, Kate. How are you?

I glance back at his bedroom window, wondering if the man is naked in bed or about to enter the bathroom for a shower.

Good evening, Andrew. What are you doing?

I can barely breathe when I click send. I know I'm being too bold, and maybe he'll think I'm impertinent, but it doesn't hurt to ask.

I bite my lips while waiting for a response, and what I long for soon arrives.

I'm dead tired, little fox. I'm going to take a shower now.

The thought of him possibly being naked leaves me breathless.

It's been an intense day, hasn't it?

A second later, he responds back.

Yes.

I stare at the screen for a few seconds. But Andrew doesn't say anything else. I begin typing, wondering if I should say exactly how I'm feeling, that I miss him and that I miss our daily activities, but I end up deleting it.

A few minutes later, my phone vibrates again with a message from him, and I feel the shock hit me.

I miss you, little fox.

I read and reread the messages a few times, unable to understand what's happening, why I feel this way. It's been a month, a long month, it should have passed by now, I shouldn't miss him this much, but the feeling I have is that the more time passes, the more I feel trapped by him, in our conversations, our laughter.

I miss you too.

I type back and send it along with a smiling emoji, completely the opposite of what I'm feeling.

Come over tomorrow, and bring Spot. We can have some wine together.

I open and close my eyes when I think about meeting him after work, having a nice wine, and talking like we used to. I think it could be good for both of us, and maybe this feeling of loneliness will lessen.

Let me know when you arrive. I'll be there.

Sleep well, Kate.

Sleep well, Andrew.

I turn off the phone screen and return to the bed. I lie down with my back to the ceiling, staring at it for a while, eager for the morning to come soon.

The seconds pass, the minutes. The memories of the days we spent under the same roof come strongly, and I close my eyes. I remember every detail of his smile, his distinctive voice sinking into my ears, the scent of a man. Finally, once again, that feeling of loneliness overwhelms me. The hours pass, and I stay awake, feeling so alone even though I'm surrounded by people I love.

I turn off the laptop and the lights and return to lie down in bed. I try to fall asleep, but I can't. I miss something I've never lived. I miss having a baby with me, a child that's only mine. But when I close my eyes and picture the little face in my head, all I can think of is a toothless smile with eyes identical to Andrew's.

I confess that I'm overwhelmed by all these sensations rushing at me like a tornado, from every direction, but my heart asks for it so strongly that it's hard to say it's madness. It feels so right, so beautiful, that I feel my eyes burn, and my throat goes dry.

After a while, I finally manage to sleep. It's a peaceful night, no nightmares.

When the day breaks, I wake up to Spot and Caleb jumping on my bed and getting tangled in the sheets. I open my eyes, a bit disoriented, but as soon as I see the two little rascals playing, I can't help but smile.

"Good morning, my loves," I pull Caleb into my arms and squeeze his chubby cheeks.

The little boy laughs and squirms to get out of the tight hug I'm giving him. He lies down on the bed and places his face on the pillow, sighing.

"It's time to wake up, Aunt Kate," I almost die from affection when he opens his little mouth and calls me Aunt Kate.

"Auntie is already up, my love."

Spot starts barking at me, and I hold him in my arms as well. I hug the little dog and cover his head with kisses.

"Calm down, Spot, I'm getting out of bed."

It doesn't take long before I gather the strength to get up, and Angelina appears at the door adjusting an apron over her body.

"Oh Kate, I'm so sorry. Did they wake you up?"

I open my mouth to say that I was already awake when the two of them climbed onto the bed and started jumping, but a yawn throws all the argument I had in the air.

"It's fine. I should have gotten up anyway."

"Try to sleep a bit more, it's still very early." My friend enters the room and picks up the little boy in her arms. "Come on, little guy, let's go have pancakes."

"Don't worry," I argue. "I'll be downstairs in a second to help you with the kids."

My friend smiles and nods in agreement as Caleb squirms, trying to get free.

I smile watching the two of them, pick up Spot, who is still on the bed, and put him on the floor. The little dog follows Angelina with his tail wagging, knowing he's also going to have his breakfast.

Another yawn takes over me, and I look toward the direction of my window covered by the curtains, wondering if Andrew is already awake and if he's still lying down.

I get out of bed and do my morning tasks. I change clothes, brush my teeth, and use the bathroom. A few minutes later, I go downstairs to help Angelina change the boys and prepare breakfast while Hattie, the family helper, finishes organizing the rooms and gathering the toys.

Around noon, I help Angelina with lunch and then tidy up the kitchen while she gets the kids ready to go out. My friend invites me to go shopping with the family, as she needs to renew some things at home, especially the boys' wardrobe. She says she'll take the opportunity to have dinner with the family later at a nice Italian restaurant, but I decline her invitation, telling her I need to write and that I'll make good use of the rest of the day organizing my things.

In a way, I'm not lying to her, just withholding some information about my schedule. Although going to Andrew's house is expected after we've lived together, I can't act nonchalantly in front of him with Angel, Alex, and the boys as an audience. I would give myself away, my gestures and gaze would reveal everything we've shared.

After everyone leaves, I turn my attention to my book and write all afternoon. I end up finishing the last chapter with tears in my eyes. I leave the epilogue for the next day, when my mind will be less overwhelmed, and adjust the final details for the marketing of the launch.

Before I know it, the afternoon is over. I make a quick sandwich for a snack, rush back to my room, and take a long, hot bath in the tub.

Since it's very cold, I opt to wear a snug, lined pair of tights and a warm wool-lined overcoat. I put on boots, gloves, and a hat.

Ten minutes later, Andrew sends a message letting me know he's waiting for me. Feeling anxious, I wait a few minutes, go look for Spot, and hold the little dog in my arms. I put a scarf around his neck and head out the front door.

The cold wind hits my face hard. My body shivers from head to toe due to the intense chill that has taken over New York in the past few days with the arrival of winter. I reach the street and walk slowly toward Andrew's house.

As I get closer, I notice an unfamiliar car parking right in front of his house, and then a blonde woman, well-dressed and very beautiful, in her thirties, gets out of the vehicle.

She's tall, and despite the elegant and cozy clothes, I can see her slim, well-defined body, perfectly matching her long blonde hair. The woman walks quickly toward the door and rings the doorbell.

I slow my pace but continue walking toward the house, wondering if Andrew might have forgotten he scheduled something with someone else.

Spot is anxious to see him. The little dog squirms in my arms, wanting to get down, but I don't allow him to go.

I continue walking, moving slowly to avoid looking like I'm intruding. I stop a few meters away from the garden path that leads to the house when I see Andrew open the door. I can't decipher his expression from where I stand. He doesn't look like he's dressed to go out as usual. He's wearing flannel pants and a white polo shirt, his hair seemingly damp. I blink, a little confused, but my heart stops for a beat when the woman steps forward and they embrace. And then she kisses him on the mouth, running her hands over his neck.

The world seems to spin around me. It's as if the solid ground disappears beneath my feet. I feel dizzy, the air leaving my lungs. I try to make sense of all the emotions I'm feeling, but nothing seems to add up. All I feel is an overwhelming urge to run away from there, to disappear without looking back. It's exactly what I'm about to do when Spot starts barking desperately to go to him. I realize when the woman pulls away from Andrew, and they both turn toward me. It's quick, but I catch the look on his face as he focuses on mine, completely alarmed, as if he's just been shocked. Andrew moves toward me, but I don't have the strength to talk to him right now. I simply turn my back and hurry to return to Angelina's house.

"Kate..." I hear his voice behind me, but I can't stop, I don't want to stop.

A cold sensation takes over my face, and I bring my hand to my face, realizing my cheeks are wet.

Damn, I'm crying, and I can't even understand why. I'm running away from him, even when there's no reason. Andrew isn't mine, we're nothing to each other. I'm being a fool, acting this way, but I can't help it. I just need to get out of here, I need to feel safe in my room. I just need this pain I'm feeling to stop.

CHAPTER 22

ANDREW

I finish setting the plates on the table and take the dinner out of the restaurant bags. I open the French wine I carefully selected to share with Kate and pour two glasses.

As I finish organizing everything, I hear the doorbell, and I imagine it's her, since it's been a few minutes since I sent the message.

It's been weeks since I've seen her up close, since Kate moved in with Angelina. I feel like she's been avoiding me in some way. At first, I concluded that the distance was the best choice for both of us. Things got a bit strange when we lived under the same roof. But then I really needed to keep my distance because of the FBI. Work has been consuming all my time these past few days. The leads are hot, and it's very likely that the serial killer will be caught soon. I've been working late lately, and I haven't even had time for Angelina and the kids.

However, when I get home and the silence reigns, Kate is the first person that comes to my mind. It's stronger than me, I can't avoid it. I know it's wrong, and I'm a fucked up person for thinking about all the ways I'd like to fuck her, but it's not just that. I miss the company, I miss having a woman with me, sleeping in my bed, in my arms. And she was the closest thing to that in the past few months.

Taking a deep breath, I leave the kitchen and head to the front door. When I open it, I'm struck by the biting cold, and the image of a certain person in front of me completely surprises me.

"Safira?"

"Andrew," I barely have time to process her presence here before the woman hugs me tightly. "I've missed you so much."

In the name of the friendship we once had, I return the hug in a restrained manner. Despite the discomfort it causes me, she was important in my life.

"What are you doing here?" I pull away slightly.

"I needed to see you." Her voice comes out almost like a plea, and her lips are firm on mine. Safira's hands slip around my neck, and she clings to me, closing all the space between us.

The kiss is demanding, I feel her breath on my mouth, I feel the desperation of her body. But I don't feel anything, it's as if all the kisses we shared were erased like footprints in the sand.

"Safira..." I move to pull away and put an end to this once and for all, I need to be harsher with her, I need her to understand it's over, I need her to move on, but the familiar bark of a dog completely derails me, and my blood freezes in my veins.

I curse silently as I realize the mess that just happened. Everything in me freezes.

Safira moves to look toward the noise made by Spot, and I do the same. I see the moment when Kate watches us with an alarmed look, completely pale, holding our dog in her arms. I feel a tightness in my chest, a kind of agony that crosses my body from one side to the other. A damn imaginary spear. I feel as though I've betrayed her, even when we have nothing between us. Even when the kiss Safira gave me meant absolutely nothing.

Agitated, I take a step toward her, but Safira grabs my arm, drawing my attention back to her. Upon realizing my intent, Kate seems to snap out of a trance. The girl turns around while pressing Spot against her chest and moves quickly to leave.

"Andrew, where are you going? Who is she?" Safira's voice echoes in my ears, demanding something that doesn't concern her.

I feel my nerves flare and clench my fists in anger, but I hold back.

"Not now, Safira. Please!" My tone is icy.

I notice the surprise in the woman's eyes, mixed with the distress of realizing that between us, it's definitely over.

"Andrew..."

I don't hear anything more she says. I follow my most primitive instincts, pass by her, and walk after Kate, quickening my pace.

"Kate!" I call her, but she doesn't listen to me or pretends not to hear.

Spot is agitated, trying desperately to come to me, but the girl doesn't allow it. I don't know what's happening between us, I don't know what the hell could be going through her mind right now. But the truth is, I feel obligated to explain everything, to tell her who Safira is and that she means nothing to me. It seems foolish of me to make Kate understand this, to make the girl realize that I don't have anyone else, even though we are free, even though we have nothing between us.

When she reaches the front door of Angelina's house, I speed up my pace and reach her before Kate can enter. Upon realizing my proximity, she still pulls away and tries to flee, but in a quick movement, I grab her arm by the elbow, preventing her from breaking free from me.

"Kate!" My voice comes out demanding, hoarse, stunned. "Listen to me!"

I feel the tremors in her skin, feel the agitation of her body when she turns to face me. I see a mix of confusion and pain in her eyes.

"Andrew, I... I need to go. Please." She tries once again to move away, but I don't let her.

"Listen to me," I ask again, and she continues to stare at me, her gaze wavering. "That woman, her name is Safira. We were more than friends, but it's all in the past. I broke up with her some time ago." I move closer to her, so close that I can feel the heat emanating from her body, contrasting with the freezing wind almost freezing me outside. "She showed up out of the blue, I wasn't expecting her. Safira has been trying to reconcile, but I've made it clear it's over. What you saw meant nothing to me, Kate. Do you understand that?"

She takes a deep breath and lowers her head, trying to hide a tear that rolls down her face. Seeing this makes me even more distressed. Realizing that I caused her any kind of pain makes me feel like the worst kind of jerk.

"You don't need to explain anything to me, Andrew, we don't..." Spot barks, squirming to get down, and this time Kate allows it.

"Yes, I do!" I interrupt her directly, making it clear that I would never lie to her. "Kate, I never lied when I said you could trust me in every way."

Her eyes shine, but she remains silent, analyzing my face as if looking for any signs of falsehood.

"We don't have anything between us, I..." She looks away, avoiding facing me. "I just got scared and ended up running away."

I lift my hand to her face and hold her small chin, forcing the girl to look at me again. She's lying, I can see it in the way her body trembles, I notice it in the suffering her expression shows.

"I know we don't have anything, Kate," repeating that out loud is more staggering than I thought it would be. It's like someone is forcing me to take acid. But there are no choices for us both. Thinking of Kate as my woman is at least terrifying. It's immoral, wrong, and dirty on every imaginable level. "But that doesn't matter. The truth is, I need you to always know the truth when it comes to me."

I slide my fingers across her face and wipe away a tear that insists on falling.

"Don't cry, little fox. It's okay, I'm here."

She nods at me, but remains silent, her gaze locked on mine, as clear as the waters of the Pacific.

"I don't know what's happening to me, Andrew," she confesses, her voice weak.

I close and open my eyes for just a second, and move closer to Kate.

"I don't know either," I answer sincerely, feeling dazed. Maybe I'll never know, and perhaps it's better that I never do.

I gaze at her lips, and my mouth salivates with the desire to taste them again, to have her body in my arms, under my touch. But she's so young, so forbidden. I can't be this stupid, I can't take advantage of her fragility.

She looks back at me, her gaze curious as it passes over my mouth. Her lips part slightly, and I know exactly what she wants. The truth is, we're both fucked by this shit that's happening with no explanation. I want to pull away, I can't get closer, but I can't help it. It's like she has a magnet that draws me to her, like a bug to light.

Before I know it, I'm leaning my face toward hers, pressing my lips against hers, desperate to take her innocence. I feel the softness, the touch, I feel her warm, quickened breath.

But then, I hear a voice behind me, and the enchantment I'm trapped in is broken. I hadn't even remembered Safira, but I could already imagine that she would come after me.

"Andrew."

I pull away from Kate, almost letting out a curse, but I search the girl's eyes for reassurance that she trusts me.

"You deal with her. It's okay," she murmurs softly.

I nod in agreement and wait for her to go inside before I turn to speak with Safira. When the door closes, I turn back and face the woman who was once so close to me.

"I didn't know you were with someone else." She seems embarrassed as she expresses it. Her tone is soft, almost regretful.

"I'm not." I affirm, because it's the truth, but that doesn't mean I'm open to anyone.

"But you're in love with her." I feel a pang in my chest when I hear what Safira says, and I breathe in sharply. I can't deny it, there's nothing to say. The truth is, I've never felt this way, not even when I was married, no one has ever made me feel what Kate does, no one's even come close to that.

"Maybe," I confess.

Saying it out loud makes me realize the mess I'm in, but I can't get out of it. I can't get close to Kate.

"I'm sorry for kissing you that way." I notice that her eyes are watery, and again, I hate myself for it. I never wanted Safira to fall for me or feel anything more than friendship.

"It's already been resolved."

She nods and turns her back to leave.

"Take care, Safira. You're a good person, and you were a loyal friend. Remember that."

"Goodbye, Andrew." Her voice cracks, but she continues walking without looking back.

"Goodbye..." I reply to the wind, knowing she didn't hear my last words, but I feel like I've taken a weight off my shoulders. In any case, I feel relief knowing she will move on, while I stay here, living day by day, watching and desiring Kate from afar.

KATE

YEARS AGO

TODAY I MET SOMEONE special. Her name is Angelina, and we will be sharing the same room at the convent. She's a shy and very obedient girl who follows all the monastery rules to the letter. I've been here for a few days now, and it's been calmer than I expected. Helping with the care of the children is a fun task, it helps pass the time and forget my problems.

After the last prayer, we retreat to our rooms in silence, and I remove the white habit covering my head. Angelina enters the room right behind me, still reserved and a bit unfamiliar with the convent's routines, but she will get used to it soon.

"I'm so happy to have someone my age to talk to," I express my contentment.

The girl smiles at me, but I see a trace of sadness in her greenish eyes.

"I like it here. I studied for a long time at a nun's school, so in a way I'm used to the rules and the prayers," she says.

She looks at me, and I see affection on her face, the same feeling I'm experiencing.

"You seem a bit sad. Did something happen, Angel?" I ask, acting as if I were the least problematic person in the world.

"I don't know, Kate. It's just that... I wanted to spend time with my dad, but he's so busy," she responds.

I nod at her and approach.

"I understand. But the important thing is that he loves you, right?"

Angelina smiles, but her smile doesn't reach her eyes.

"Yes, he loves me, and he said that I'll be going back home soon."

I also curve my lips into a smile, trying to share the same hope she has. But the truth is, there is no hope for me, I have no home and no one waiting to meet me outside of here. So I just live one day after the other, doing the best I can.

"I think we'll be good friends." I hold her hand, and this time Angelina truly smiles.

"I think so too, you're really nice, Kate. I'm so happy to meet you."

CHAPTER 23

KATE

1 YEAR AND A FEW MONTHS AGO

The years passed, and Angelina didn't return home as she always dreamed, nor did I.

Her father didn't come to get her, my sister moved to another country, and my mother never showed up.

However, we became best friends as we promised each other when we first met, and for a while, we decided that our lives would be dedicated to God. She became the perfect and obedient novice, and I became the rebel who constantly broke the rules and disrespected the great silence.

Everything was going well, and it was only a matter of time before both of us would say yes to God and become nuns. But once again, our plans changed when Angelina was kidnapped and disappeared for a while. After a few months, she returned to the convent, pregnant.

It was the worst moment of my life when I learned what had happened to her. No one knew her whereabouts, the local police didn't find any clues. It was as if she had gone to sleep and disappeared, and one fine day returned as if nothing had happened.

I admit I am still shocked by everything I heard. Just a few minutes ago, I clearly overheard the mother superior talking to Angelina and saying that my friend might be pregnant. Everything started to make sense because for a few days she had been feeling unwell, especially in the morning. Anyway, Angelina doesn't seem the same since she returned. I notice her sad gaze, the sorrowful expression. Only her body seems to be here, and her soul is somewhere else. She doesn't say anything about what happened, but I don't ask. She will talk about it when the time is right.

We do our daily tasks as usual, she always silent, thoughtful. We haven't talked much lately, and I give her space. I feel like something's wrong with her, but I don't want to be intrusive, more than I already was by overhearing the conversation. So, I stay quiet.

When night comes, I go to bed as soon as it's time. I try to sleep, but I can't stop worrying about Angelina, especially when she sits on the bed next to me and turns her full attention to the window, as if waiting for something or someone. She stays like that for a long time. She hugs her knees and murmurs some prayers. I can feel her distress from where I am, I can sense the exhaustion that has taken over her body. I know that this change in her behavior is likely related to the pregnancy, but there's more to it.

After some time, exhaustion finally takes over, and I fall asleep. My eyes slowly close, my senses dissipate, until everything fades away.

And suddenly, the calmness that had settled in my body is replaced by a scream of shock when I hear a loud noise coming from downstairs, probably from the entry hall. I jump out of bed, completely stunned and lost. The room is pitch dark, but I can hear Angelina's subtle movements on the bed beside me.

"Angel? What was that?"

After a few seconds, she replies, "I don't know, Kate."

Little by little, my vision adjusts to the darkness, and I follow Angelina's gaze toward the door. Some of the sisters have also woken up and turned on the lights in their rooms. I take advantage of the faint light coming from the hallway and run to Angelina's bed. I feel something strange in the air. A sense of danger, as if something very bad is about to happen, and I shiver to the bone.

I feel the fear invade me, and no matter how much I try to control the course of my thoughts, I clearly remember Garath and everything he did to me that night. The feeling is the same. The anguish that takes over me almost drags me back to the past. I hear another loud knock, as if someone is trying to break down the front door. My heart races, my body suddenly starts shaking, and I reach for Angelina's hand.

I hear the voices of the sisters, and suddenly a scream echoes through the air. It's the mother superior. It's her voice. Panicked, I stand up to go to her, but then the unimaginable happens, and I freeze where I am, petrified: men, I hear the voices of men approaching.

Angelina takes a few steps toward the door, but I don't let her continue. I'm terrified, my body frozen with fear, but I can still think clearly.

"Angel, where are you going?" I grab her arm, preventing her from moving forward.

"I need to know what's going on, Kate. I'm scared..."

She takes a few more steps toward the door, but the sharp sound of a gunshot stops her in her tracks. The shock takes over me, the trembling in my body increases, and I sob softly, sure I'm living a nightmare. More gunshots are heard, and the screams burrow deep into my mind.

Angelina is completely beside herself, the desperation for the sisters is so great that she doesn't even care about getting killed, and I need to hold her back so she doesn't throw herself into the crossfire.

"Angel, are you crazy?" I hold her tighter, sobbing. "We need to hide, get out of here."

"No, Kate, I need to help them," she murmurs, her body trembling.

"Don't go," I beg as I hold her tighter. "Think about your child, Angel. I heard when the Mother Superior said you might be pregnant. Think about that child, Angel, we need to get out of here."

"Kate... I'm the one to blame for all this," she says, but I shake my head in denial.

"Don't say nonsense." I embrace Angelina and pull her out of the room.

The sound of gunshots is deafening downstairs, but we run as fast as we can to the end of the hallway. We head straight for the attic.

My body doesn't react when we reach the top; it's like I've died. I feel inert, my breath erratic, my heart almost out of my chest. I feel like I'm having a panic attack, it's almost impossible to breathe. I move mechanically, and, trembling, lean against the single bed that's up there.

"Kate... Don't make a sound," Angelina murmurs, but I can't even move.

I muffle the sob that insists on escaping my throat, feeling the cold consume me. I barely notice when Angelina covers my body with a sheet.

She starts moving again, analyzing the door and the walls. I'm surprised by her ability to recover and start thinking rationally.

"Kate." She gestures toward me and whispers, "The window."

She tries to run to the window on the other side of the attic just as the sound of heavy footsteps grows louder.

I crawl to the window and crack it open to check the height. It's far too high; jumping from here to escape would be a death sentence.

"I can't do it," I murmur back.

Everything around me stops when the door is violently kicked open. Angelina freezes in the middle of the room, utterly terrified. And then I see them—the men who will decide our fates from now on.

What follows is a chaos of voices, violence, and threats. Angelina is strong; she doesn't give in and fights for her freedom, even though she's paralyzed with fear. I understand now: they're after her. She's their target, but they'll destroy anyone in their way without hesitation. I feel myself die inside as one of them advances toward me, his filthy gaze revealing exactly what he intends. There's no hope for me; I'm powerless.

The man grabs me by the neck, his disgusting hand sliding over my breasts through the fabric of my long nightgown. His lips curl into a revolting grin, and I smell the repugnant stench of alcohol and cigarettes. For a moment, I can almost see Garath in his features as he holds me tightly and throws me violently onto the bed.

The cold wraps around me like a freezing shroud, mingling with the fear that steals my breath and suffocates me, draining my strength and locking every joint in my body. My mind is frantic, and my body is frozen. A solitary tear rolls down my face, and it feels like the warm drop freezes upon touching my cold skin. I'm frozen—inside and out. The man's dirty hands grip my body roughly, and all I feel is disgust, nausea, and overwhelming terror. All I can do is cry in despair.

My nightgown is ripped apart, shredded from top to bottom. I let out a long murmur of pain as he resumes touching me intimately. My dignity crumbles under such degradation. I feel like nothing, like something disposable. But I still try to fight. I thrash, I scream, and I cry for help. That's when I see Angelina suddenly approach, holding a lamp in her hands.

I don't know how, but by some divine miracle, she manages to free herself from the man restraining her. With a single blow, she incapacitates the monster touching my body, using the lamp. The room plunges into darkness. The shadows terrify me, paralyzing me further. My senses blur. I feel like I'm losing control, haunted by bitter memories rushing back with force. I don't want to remember.

I don't want to remember. I shut my eyes tightly, panicked. My heart pounds, screaming for help. The painful memories strike, and I gasp, my chest aching as I've never felt before with memories I fought for years to bury.

Angelina's hands grip me firmly and swiftly, pulling me back to reality. Terrified, I get up and follow her, hearing the men's curses right behind us. Aimlessly, I rush down the stairs as fast as I can, screaming to myself that it's over, that I'll never allow this to happen again.

But what I see when I finally reach the living room fills me with an unimaginable dread. It consumes my soul. Our sisters... They're dead. I'm in shock. A panic attack overtakes me; all I want is to scream, to get out of here. I need to leave. To breathe!

Guided by the faint glow of the fireplace, I run desperately toward the door, drawing strength from the depths of my soul. But then I hear a familiar sound—something falling to the ground—and Angelina's voice calling for help. I stop just before reaching the doorway, hesitating for a second about helping her up. She seems hurt. But when I hear the men's footsteps descending the stairs, my heart races. Fear overtakes me, and I can't think straight anymore. I mutter something like an apology—I'm not even sure what I say—and I run as fast as I can.

My heart bleeds for being so weak, for leaving my best friend to her fate. But I keep running frantically, searching for safety, as images of the past play like a film in my mind.

I was a child... I was innocent... Why did they do this to me? I can't relive this. My past haunts and pursues me. It's like a tattoo that marks my heart indelibly. A terrible stain that drove me to seek refuge in the convent. I admit to myself that my smiles are nothing more than a façade I've worn for years to hide all traces of the pain I've lived and tried to erase from memory.

"Forgive me, Angel. Forgive me... Forgive me."

The sobs take over uncontrollably. Tears blur my vision, and the cold that bites through the rips in my nightgown makes me hug myself. When I realize it, I'm no longer running. I'm standing under the dark sky, holding myself for warmth, struggling desperately to catch my breath. I can't. I can't breathe. I'm suffocating.

And then the terrifying footsteps echo behind me. Rough, calloused hands grip my shoulders and force me backward, throwing me harshly to the ground. My body aches from the impact, my back throbbing. But I still scream in desperation, fighting back, though it's useless. The rest of my clothes are torn away, leaving me completely exposed on the cold ground.

I close my eyes and pray, begging God for it to end, to let me die, because I can't live through this again. I hear their voices, their obscene, filthy, vile words as their hands roam between my legs and touch me where I fear most. I let out a low groan as they do what I dreaded. One of them pins me to the ground, holding my arms, while the other brutally forces himself into me, choking me to the point where I can't breathe. He violates me mercilessly, hurting my body until he spills himself inside me. Then it starts again as they switch places. My mind retreats into a parallel universe; it's as if I no longer exist. I have nothing left. I just want to die.

"Please, God... Please."

When they finish, it feels like they've taken my soul with them. They leave behind nothing but a heap of garbage discarded on the ground. I feel disgusted with myself, with my own body. I hate myself for being a woman.

Then a heavy blow to the left side of my face scatters my senses, and I am grateful. The physical pain doesn't even come close to matching the unbearable torment and humiliation forever etched into my soul.

CHAPTER 24

KATE

1 YEAR AND A FEW MONTHS EARLIER

When I wake up, I am being carried away from there by someone I don't know. But I don't have the strength to say anything. The world is spinning, my body aches, my throat is choking.

At some point, my mind fades and I don't remember much. I hear Angelina's voice, but it feels like she is distant, in another dimension. My consciousness refuses to process what happened. My mind refuses to continue experiencing the pain, I refuse to keep feeling it, every second.

Everything goes blank again. The darkness clouds my mind, it feels like my brain is suffering a blackout. When I regain consciousness, I recognize Angelina as soon as I open my eyes. But that's not enough to make my brain understand that I am safe.

The uncomfortable bed, the shutters on the window, the smell of disinfectant, and the IV in my arm make me realize that once again, I'm in a hospital room. And once again, the memories come flooding back, along with a completely distorted crisis of reality. I scream desperately, asking for help, for someone, for something, anything that can take the demons out of my head.

I see Angelina crying, shouting for help, and soon the room fills with nurses and doctors. Experienced hands hold me down in bed while someone else works quickly on the IV in my arm. Soon, the calming substance takes effect, and I close my eyes again.

The same scene repeats countless times until they start giving me something that allows me to stay awake, but at the same time disoriented. I don't understand anything happening around me, I am just being manipulated from one side to the other.

After a few days, I am told that my mother came to New York to take me home and that everything will be fine. Despite Angelina's protests, my mother acts decisively and decides to take me back to California so I can be better cared for, according to her.

I make the journey back, practically drugged. I don't remember anything on the plane, not even the moment I return to that house. As the days go by, the medication is gradually reduced, until I begin to recognize the things and the place around me.

And then everything resurfaces again. The crying, the nightmares, my screams at night. All of this is too much for my mother to bear. Soon, I am being evaluated at a clinic specializing in psychological damage, and shortly after, I am admitted to the psychiatric hospital.

With the medication under control, I feel my body out of sync, and I hardly pay attention to what's happening around me. I remain quiet, nothing leaves my mouth, everything feels lost as if I'm not living. I just exist. The weeks go by, the months. I hardly see my mother, but it doesn't really matter much.

Then, after a while, I am sitting outside in the garden with my arms wrapped around my body, staring into nothingness. I feel my stomach in knots, but I say nothing to anyone. For some time now, I've been having stomach spasms and vomiting in the mornings, but I continue living one day after another as if nothing is out of place.

A butterfly flies in front of me and lands on a dry rosebush branch. I watch its wings flutter, its small movements, but I remain still.

Then I hear footsteps approaching, and I believe it's a nurse with another dose of medication. But no, it's my mother, accompanied by an elegant woman in a white lab coat whom I've never gotten close to or spoken to, and nurse Emma.

"Hello, Kate. I'm Dr. Sarina, how are you?" Sarina places her hand on my shoulder, giving a light massage, but I remain silent, with no energy to speak to any of them. I stay trapped in my lost world.

"Aren't you going to talk to your mom, dear?" My mother asks, holding my hand. But somehow, her touch also repulses me. I can't stand any contact, I don't tolerate being touched by anyone, not even her.

I pull away from her hands and Sarina's touch. I shrink away, trying to distance myself.

I hear her frustrated sigh, but I ignore it too.

The three women start talking, but I don't pay much attention to what they say. My head throbs, and the noise of voices around me makes me anxious.

But then, Emma approaches and starts speaking with her sweet voice. She is the only person I allow to get close to me, as she is the only one who also respects my space.

"Darling, my dear Kate. We have something very important to tell you."

Silence reigns, but I focus on what she has to say. I remain attentive to any sound.

"Darling, you're going to have a baby. That's why you've been so unwell these past few months."

At first, I can't process the information coherently. At first, I hear only empty words that make no sense. Then Emma's voice seems to repeat endlessly in my head, and I let out a deep sigh, understanding what she just said.

You're going to have a baby.

You're going to have a baby.

You're going to have a baby.

Slowly, I bring my trembling hand to my stomach, and it feels like the ground is returning to my feet. It's like being thrown forcefully back into reality, and the impact is so great that I feel dizzy.

I take a deep breath, hearing the people talking around me—Emma, Sarina, my mother—but it's like they are distant. My vision is blurry, the air feels far away. Everything in me hurts, everything comes rushing back.

KATE

PRESENT DAY

A FEW MORE WEEKS HAVE passed, and I've just returned from a visit to the house I had longed to rent. And to my happiness, I got exactly what I wanted. The house is a charm both inside and out. It's quite small, but with well-divided rooms, and it's already fully furnished. Plus, it's fairly close to Angelina's house, so I'll be able to visit my friend whenever I want.

I haven't told her about my move yet. I'm going to do that right now. First, I needed to be sure that my plans would work out and that I would have the necessary funds.

Finally, everything is falling into place. My new book performed well, and I'm already preparing to start the next one. It will be amazing to write in my own little corner, sipping a cup of tea while admiring the view through the window. Of course, I will miss Angelina and the kids' company; they are the family I never had, but I'm excited for this change of life and fresh air. It will do me good.

As soon as I enter the cozy, well-heated house, I hear the children's giggles coming from the kitchen, and my heart fills with joy. I take off the heavy coat I'm wearing because of the intense cold, and I do the same with my gloves and hat.

I walk slowly toward the kitchen and stop at the door before they see me. I look around, still enchanted by all the decorations we've done in the past weeks to celebrate Christmas. Everything is colorful and bright. The lights adorn every corner of the doors and windows, and the huge Christmas tree in the living room looks absolutely stunning with the ornaments the kids placed with Alex's help.

I smell gingerbread cookies baking in the oven, and once again, I smile, completely moved. Caleb and Kaleo are covered in flour, while Angelina doesn't look much different from the boys. Her cheeks are white, her apron is a complete mess, but the smile on my friend's face is simply priceless. There, while she prepares the cookie dough on the counter, I truly know that Angelina has found her purpose.

"Hello." I call the attention of the three of them, and their pairs of eyes turn in my direction.

Caleb comes running toward me, while the other baby, who still can't walk by himself, is stuck in his high chair.

"Aunt Tate!" I scoop Caleb up into my arms and hug him tightly, not caring that I'll be covered in flour too. "Hi, my love!"

Kaleb wriggles in his high chair, banging the spoon in his hand on the little bowl in front of him with a piece of cookie dough.

I walk over to him and gently caress his rosy, chubby cheeks.

"Hi, sweetheart. How are you?" The little baby opens a sweet smile, showing his two little teeth. I have the urge to squeeze him. "You're making quite a mess."

Angelina chuckles and leaves the bowl of flour on the counter.

"They're loving making Christmas cookies." She wipes her hands on her apron.

I curve my lips into a smile, still holding Caleb in my arms. I feel my heart warm, my soul at peace.

"They're looking like Christmas cookies themselves, with all that flour," I joke, and Angelina laughs out loud.

She leans in front of Kaleo and lifts the baby out of his high chair. She hugs his little body and turns back toward me.

"I think I should give the kids a bath. Can you check on the cookies in the oven?"

I nod in agreement, but before I do, I decide to say what I need to about my move. I don't want to prolong the subject any further, and besides, I'm so anxious and excited that I couldn't wait.

"Angel, I need to tell you something important. Do you have a minute?"

My friend rocks the baby in her arms, and I set Caleb down on the floor. The little boy runs off looking for Spot, and Angelina nods with a small gesture of her head.

"Sure, go ahead."

She stares at me expectantly, and for a moment, I hesitate, wondering if I'm making the right decision. They've been so good to me, and the last thing I want in the world is to leave Angelina upset or hurt by my departure. However, it's time for me to take control of my own life.

"Angel, today I went out to do something I've been thinking about for the past few days. I want you to know how grateful I am to you and Alex for everything you've done for me."

I notice when she furrows her brows, looking confused, but she doesn't interrupt me.

"The past few months have been the most amazing of my life, and being able to live with you again and your beautiful family has been an honor for me. But my time has come, the time to fully take control of my life, and that's why I decided to rent a little house nearby."

My friend stares at me, a bit stunned, but soon I see the curve of a smile forming on her lips.

"Oh, Kate," she steps closer. "If it were up to me, you'd live with us forever."

I hold her free hand and squeeze it in mine, feeling my throat go dry, my eyes welling up with emotion.

"I know, Angel. And I'm so grateful for that. But I also have another little secret to tell you."

My friend raises an eyebrow, visibly curious, yet surprised by all my nuances.

"Oh my God, what's the secret, Kate? What else are you hiding under seven locks?"

I smile softly, shaking my head, and focus my attention on Angelina's face. She looks back at me with anticipation, her irises sparkling.

"I recently published two books, and I'm getting great feedback. I think I've finally found what I want to do for the rest of my life. I think I've finally found a way to express myself and get all my anxieties out of my heart."

Angelina's eyes widen, and she remains silent for a few seconds. She puts her hand to her mouth, shocked by my declaration, and I give her a huge smile, completely proud of myself, of everything I've become, of the courage I've gained.

"Oh my God..." She whispers in disbelief, steps closer, and hugs me, placing the baby between us.

Kaleo, who had almost fallen asleep, is startled by the tightness around his little body and begins to complain with nervous little cries.

We both smile, but our smiles quickly turn into emotional tears, and my friend pulls away, wiping her eyes.

"I want you to tell me everything! Oh my God, I need to know everything!" She smiles while drying her eyes, emotion still dominating her face.

I also wipe a tear that has trickled down my face and clear my throat, feeling a huge lump in my throat, an overwhelming urge to express everything I'm feeling, the happiness I'm feeling, the gratitude.

"I'll tell you everything, don't worry."

After calming down a bit, I help Angelina with the kids and tell her about the books and everything that's happened since then. I show her my social media and the pseudonym I'm using, I also talk about the little house I rented and that I plan to move in the next few days.

Every now and then, I notice Angelina staring at me as if she has a question to ask, but she soon gives up. But deep down, I know exactly what's going through her mind. She wants to know about my daughter, she wants to know how I feel about everything that happened, but I don't feel ready to talk about it, and I silently thank her for respecting my wishes.

Maybe one day I'll talk about Hannah again, maybe one day the pain I feel will ease, and over time, I'll be able to say her name out loud without allowing myself to feel so much sadness.

CHAPTER 25

KATE

1 YEAR AND A FEW MONTHS EARLIER

"You don't have to keep this baby, Kate. We'll take care of it." Sarina, with her soft voice, tries to soften the shocking news that has been placed in my hands.

"It's going to be okay, Kate. You won't even remember that you're carrying... a bastard." This time it's my mother.

I close and open my eyes when I hear what she says. Somehow, I feel a lump forming in my throat, and a sense of anguish takes over me. I think about everything I've been through, I think about the pain I felt, I think about the crises I had every second I was sober. I wished I were dead, I wished my heart would stop beating so I wouldn't have to relive that again, and again.

But now, as I caress my belly and feel life growing inside me, it's as if my heart feels peace. It's not disgust I feel, nor anger, I feel peace, as if suddenly something began to make sense again. As if my life started to make sense again. For the first time in a long time, I let my words escape my mouth:

"How long?" I murmur softly, completely lost in time. Since everything happened, I no longer know the time, whether it's day or night, or how many weeks or months have passed.

"Three months, Kate." It's Emma who answers.

I feel like I'm going to collapse, but suddenly it's as if I am taken by a strength I didn't know existed. I am fully aware of how this child was conceived, I am fully aware that this baby is the child of a monster, and that is the worst thing that could ever happen to someone. But a soul like mine cannot be hurt more than it already is. And it's likely that I'll never be the same person I once was.

I'm stained, stained by suffering, stained by pain, stained by the evil of people, and that won't change, even if this child dies.

But contrary to that, I wouldn't feel better if I chose to follow Sarina's plan. I would die with it, because there's nothing inside me, no life running through my veins, except for her. And that is so painful that when I realize it, I'm fighting to keep a tear from falling.

"I'm going to have the baby," I say aloud, and maybe I'll regret it someday, but I decide to do what my heart is asking of me now. I will let this child live, maybe that way I'll start living again too.

KATE

PRESENT DAY

I FINISH SERVING DINNER and also place food for Spot near the kitchen counter. I grab the plate that was on the counter and start eating right there, enjoying the fullness and solitude of living alone.

Spot eats his food, wagging his tail, and I smile watching how happy the little dog is. I take a small piece of grilled meat and toss it to him.

After finishing dinner, I place the dishes in the dishwasher and continue walking through my new home, admiring how every detail is charming, like a little dollhouse. The kitchen is covered in light blue tiles with an old-fashioned design. The furniture follows the same vintage style.

The living room has light pink wallpaper, also vintage, and the sheer white curtains cover the glass windows that lead to the rose garden, now dormant under the snow.

I finish my quick tour in the bedroom. The double bed is covered with floral sheets, and on the nightstand rests a vase of artificial roses that I placed earlier for decoration. I look at the plastic flowers and can't wait to replace them with real rose bushes.

I lie on the bed, staring up at the white ceiling, and sigh softly. I close my eyes for a few seconds, and I almost see a movie playing in my head. I think about the whirlwind of emotions I've experienced in the past few months. How happy I was living with Angelina and the kids. I think about Andrew and how I miss every second I spent with him.

Since that strange night when Safira appeared, we haven't spoken face to face. Our contact has been solely through messages, but everything has been superficial. Our messages were reduced to "good morning" and "good night," I told him about my move and gave him my new address, but our conversations didn't go beyond that, and I didn't risk bringing up any other topic. I let life take its course, but the truth is, I miss him so much that my chest tightens.

Finally, I think of Hannah, her blue eyes like mine, her little rosy mouth, her dark hair. She looked so much like me that it felt as if she had been conceived by me alone. When I saw her face the moment she was born, it was love at first sight. I will never forget.

When I realize it, I'm lying on my side, my face pressed into the pillow, feeling tears wetting my face.

"Mommy loved you so much, Hannah," I murmur softly, overwhelmed by the anguish and the vivid memories that won't leave my mind.

I loved that child, from the moment I knew of her existence. It was something stronger than me. It was something I couldn't avoid. She was mine, my girl, my daughter. She had my blood, her little heart beat inside my body... and she was ripped away from me.

Losing Hannah was like being thrown into a precipice. I understood the purpose, but I will never come to terms with it. I was unwell, I was still having crises when Hannah was born, but she was my only light at the end of the tunnel, the only thing I could cling to.

Taking a deep breath, I try to push away the memories of my little girl and once again think of Andrew. And the first thing I remember is how incredible he is with the grandchildren. A smile escapes my lips, blending with my tears when I think of him as a grandfather. He would have been an amazing father to Angelina if he had met her earlier. He would have been an excellent father, in any situation.

And that phrase repeats countless times in my head.

Andrew would have been an excellent father.

Andrew would have been an excellent father.

And I trust him so much.

And suddenly, something unthinkable begins to creep into my mind, and I completely lose my reason and common sense. I jump out of bed and begin pacing back and forth, feeling anxious, my body trembling.

I want a baby, Andrew is a trustworthy man. Why not ask him?

Oh my God, could it be? What if he says no? What will I do?

Anxious, I place my hand on my chest and massage the spot. I feel my breath quicken at the mere possibility of having a baby, my heart feels like it's about to jump out of my chest. I can almost feel the anxious little cries for a bottle, the sweet smell after a bath, the toothless smiles.

I think about the direction my life has taken, thinking that now I'm self-sufficient and can support myself alone. I can also support a child. My heart fills with happiness, and I rush to the bed to grab my phone.

I don't think clearly, I'm not reasoning coherently, I just grab the phone and type Andrew's name. After the second ring, he answers the call.

"Kate? Is everything okay?" Hearing his voice on the other end of the line makes me close my eyes.

"Andrew... today I finally discovered what I've been longing for in my life and... Andrew, I want to have a baby." I'm filled with adrenaline and fear, but I tell him everything. "Andrew, I... I... Can we talk now?"

I remember that I didn't even ask if he was available, and I went straight to the point. However, the sound of cars and people moving around on the other end of the line brings me back to reality.

"I just parked the car, Kate." He says.

Taking a deep breath, I speak again: "Can you come to my house?" I cross my fingers for the answer to be yes.

The silence is almost deadly on the other end of the line as I wait for Andrew's response. I hear his heavy breathing, I close and open my eyes, as anxiety takes over me.

"Okay, give me a few minutes."

ANDREW

I'M STILL PROCESSING everything she said on the phone when the call ends. Maybe I misunderstood, or maybe Kate simply said what I heard.

She wants to have a baby? Damn it, is Kate seeing someone and I never knew about it?

I feel my blood boiling in my veins, and a bitter taste rises in my mouth. When I realize it, my hands are trembling, gripping the steering wheel with all the strength I have in me.

Everything is stirring inside me, all my senses go into full alert, and I have to breathe deeply to keep thinking coherently. My temples throb as I sit there, completely paralyzed by what I just heard.

After a few minutes, I throw my head back and close my eyes. The image of her with another man appears in my mind, and I feel the urge to do something reckless. I feel the urge to shoot someone, to wipe out the bastard until nothing is left of him.

Still, despite feeling completely destroyed inside, I turn the car back on and shift gears. I head toward Kate's new house, still not knowing how I'll be able to look her in the face without cornering her and telling her that she's mine. That every little part of her body belongs only to me.

What the hell am I feeling?

She's free, and if she's seeing someone else, I need to respect her decision, even if it tears me apart inside.

Controlling the direction of my thoughts, I drive to her new address, while I think about our almost nonexistent interaction over the last few weeks.

Since the night Safira showed up, I haven't spoken to Kate in person. I couldn't get close, I couldn't be alone with her when all I wanted was to kiss her mouth and feel her warm skin. Safira was completely right when she said I was in love with the girl. Yes, I'm fucking in love with her, and that's why it hurts so much. It's hard to breathe just thinking of her kissing another man, undressing for him, having sex. I'm losing my mind just thinking about it.

In a few minutes, I park the car in front of the small house, a few blocks away from mine. I wasn't far when Kate called me, I was coming back from another day of work to live my solitude, content with exchanging a few messages with her.

I get out of the car and walk toward the house, unable to take my eyes off the door that will open in a few moments. I ring the doorbell and wait for her.

In less than a minute, Kate opens the door, and I'm met with her sweet gaze and joyful expression. Her face looks alive, as if she just received some incredible news. Her cheeks are rosy, and her dark hair is loose, framing her beautiful face.

"Andrew." Her lips curve into a smile as she steps closer.

To my surprise, Kate throws herself into my arms and presses her face against my chest, her small hands wrapping around my torso.

"Kate..." I only feel pain as I bring my hand to the back of her neck, pulling her closer, returning the embrace, feeling the scent of her hair invading my senses.

"I'm so glad you came."

"I couldn't not come." The truth is, I can't say no to her, it's stronger than me.

Kate pulls away and walks through the small living room, turning her back to me. She's already ready for bed, dressed comfortably in pajama pants and a long-sleeve shirt. Still, I can see the silhouette of her small body through the clothes, and it excites me. I feel desire, I feel anger at not being able to have her for myself. I feel like I'm about to collapse at any moment.

"Andrew, about what I said on the phone..." She looks at me again, the smile that was on her face now replaced by tension, perhaps doubt.

I clench my jaw while I wait for her to drop the bombshell, for her to tell me that she's seeing another man and wants to have a child. I feel my neck sweat, but I remain silent, completely still, waiting for her to continue.

"Andrew, I had a daughter, and I think you should hear this from me." She starts talking about what happened in the past, but I remain quiet, focused on Kate's face. No movement shows on my face, because besides knowing about the child, I'm not sure I can stay indifferent when she talks about another man. Realizing I'm not going to say anything, she continues. "My daughter was ripped from my arms as soon as she was born, but I've never forgotten her, Andrew. She was my light, my hope... and..."

I swallow with difficulty, for the first time unable to think coherently or act as I should. I just look at her, thinking about how much Kate must have suffered when this happened. Still, I don't stop her from speaking, staying focused on her face, listening to everything she says.

"She was beautiful." The girl smiles at me, and I see her eyes glisten, stirring something in my stomach. She takes a step toward me and places her hand on my chest. "I can't forget her little face, but I know she's in good hands. But I feel the lack of something I've never had. I miss it so much that my heart hurts every day."

"What do you mean?" I finally ask.

Kate's eyes search mine, her expression resolute.

"You're the only man I trust." Hearing what she says feels like air filling my lungs after a long time without breathing.

Her hand moves to my chin, and she caresses my beard, making my excitement rise with just having her near, feeling her warmth. I watch her mouth, her nose, everything about her. I'm in a trance, focused on every perfect detail. Kate's hand slides down my jaw, and I feel a shiver on my skin, the crazy desire to touch her body comes to the surface, and I feel like I'm burning. I'm about to lose it, the desire exacting its toll.

"Andrew, I'm ready. I want to have another baby." I take her hand and hold it, stopping the dangerous caress.

I feel anger at myself for feeling all this shit. I feel anger at Kate for playing with me like this, almost making me lose my mind. I feel insane hatred just thinking about what she's going to do with another man. I won't stand for it.

"Why are you telling me this?" I clench my jaw as I let go of her hand and force myself to stay where I am. Otherwise, I don't know what the hell I'll do.

She takes a few steps back, bringing her hands together in front of her, looking at the floor. When she lifts her head and looks at me again, I see doubt in her eyes, a mix of fear and hesitation that leaves me stunned. Kate sighs, seems to take a breath of courage, and when she speaks again, I feel the world stop around me. Everything inside me freezes, then turns into burning lava.

"Please, get me pregnant!"

What?! Did I hear that right?! Oh my God, I heard it!

Holy shit!

CHAPTER 26

KATE

"Please, get me pregnant!" For a second, I feel like my heart might jump out of my mouth. I had to use every ounce of courage to say that to him.

Andrew stares at me for a few moments, looking stunned, his expression alarmed. He's been acting distant and withdrawn since he arrived at my house, but I ignored the signs of his indifference because of my desire to have another baby. Maybe he thinks I'm being foolish now, and maybe I am, but the truth is, he's my only hope. There's no one else in the world I trust to be the father of this child. Yet, looking at him now, I'm not so sure about my instincts. It's very likely that Andrew doesn't want to risk bringing more complications into his already complicated and dangerous life.

Maybe he'll say no, and I'll understand. It's not an easy proposition to digest, and to be honest, he won't gain anything from it.

"Why are you doing this to me? We can't..." I feel my cheeks burning as I finally realize the misunderstanding I've just created and everything that must have gone through Andrew's mind. I lose my words and have to take several deep breaths to recover from the shock I caused myself. "No... I mean... we're not going to do it the way you're thinking..." I try to explain.

He raises an eyebrow and steps closer, taking a step forward.

I feel like the bones in my body are melting, and I have the urge to hide in a hole from the shame. I need to use all my strength to recover and clear up the misunderstanding.

"We don't need to..." My gaze shifts to the lower part of his body, exclusively to his groin, and I swallow hard when I see the bulge forming in the front of his pants. "You know. We don't need to do that..."

"What do you have in mind?" I notice his clenched fists, his jaw set, his brow furrowed. "Your proposal seemed pretty clear to me, and I haven't thought of another way to make a baby naturally without sex."

I feel the tension in his shoulders, I feel how agitated Andrew has been since he arrived. It's like he's on the verge of collapsing.

"You can take your... your..." I can't finish the sentence because of the anxiety.

"Be clear, Kate." He demands, and I lose my balance. Still, I try to keep my composure.

"You can take your... sperm... and I'll do the insemination with a syringe." When I finish speaking, I'm almost out of breath.

Andrew takes another step toward me, and I take a step back, almost out of air.

"Just like that?" He questions. "And then?"

I look into his intense gaze and almost faint. His closeness overwhelms me, and I feel the urge to feel his mouth on mine again, brushing my lips. I want to feel his beard on my skin, and just thinking about everything we've done makes my body shiver. Still, I need to stay grounded, I need to remember how broken I am, and how my shards could hurt him.

"If you don't want to, I'll understand." My voice almost doesn't come out, I feel a lump in my throat, but I don't look away.

"What do you mean, Kate? You want to raise the baby alone? I'll just be the sperm donor? Is that what you want?"

I inhale deeply, trying to find an answer to something I hadn't even thought about.

"I don't know, Andrew. I don't know what you want, I don't know how much you want to be a part of this. If you want to be just the donor, that's fine with me, having this baby is all I want. But if you want to be a part of its life, I won't stop you, as long as you promise me that you'll never take the child from me."

I search for conviction in his gaze, trying desperately to decipher what Andrew is feeling, what he thinks about all this.

"And what about Angelina, what will she think about this?"

His gaze remains fixed on my face, and he waits harshly for an answer.

"Maybe it'll be hard for her to understand at first, but in the end, nothing will be that difficult. We'll just tell the truth, that the baby was conceived through home insemination."

Andrew continues to approach, and the closer he gets, the more my body shivers. It's as if there's a magnetic field pulling us toward each other, but I am fully aware of how dangerous this is, so I step back, until I find myself pressed against the wall.

"I'm not going to stay away from the child, Kate. I want to be there for everything, from the pregnancy to the birth, the first steps, the growth. I want to be there for everything."

I nod in agreement, knowing exactly that this would be his stance on everything, if he accepts.

"So, is that a yes?" I ask, hopeful.

He narrows his eyes, analyzing me from head to toe, as if searching for the truth of my intentions deep in my soul.

"I think I'm crazier than you for agreeing to do something like this," my smile widens, and I have to hold myself back from jumping into his arms. "I can't say no to you, little fox. And if you want a baby, fine, we'll have one."

"You don't know how happy that makes me," I admit, still smiling.

"Let's make a contract. You can be sure I will never take the baby from you, but I insist on covering all the expenses of the pregnancy, the birth, and his life. I want to accompany you to the exams, I want to be present for every moment, do you understand?"

I swallow hard because, even though I know Andrew would want to be involved in the child's life, I never imagined he would want to take on all the responsibilities to this extent.

"That's not necessary, I... I don't mind taking care of that part, I'm the one who wants the baby, you're not obligated to any of this."

"There are no choices, Kate. Either this, or we don't have an agreement."

I take a deep breath and nod. Despite Andrew's demand, I'm so happy that he agreed that I don't want to dwell on it.

"Do I have any choices?"

He sighs, and I feel his body relax, as though he's lifted a huge weight off his shoulders: "No, you don't have any choices."

He slides his hand to my chin, not allowing me to lower my head. Andrew forces me to keep looking at him.

"I thought you were seeing someone, little fox." His words make my eyes widen, leaving me alarmed, and I shake my head in denial.

"That will never happen."

He takes a deep breath and his fingers slide to my jaw, as he caresses the area: "Why do you say that with so much conviction? You're so young, Kate."

I feel his touch on my neck, even on my nape. Andrew grabs a few strands of my hair in his hand, and I close my eyes, overwhelmed by the pleasurable sensation of having him near.

"Because I'm broken, Andrew. My soul is shattered into millions of pieces."

I open my eyes again and meet his. His expression is serious, his gaze intense, so imposing it sends chills through me.

"Something very serious happened at the convent, didn't it? Is that what I'm thinking?"

His question is precise, hitting every layer of my mind. The memories come flooding back, and with them, the wound in my soul opens again. Yet, I can't hide this from him, it's part of me, part of my past. Andrew needs to know, and I need to release everything that destroys me.

"There were two men..." I feel Andrew's hand tremble as he still holds my neck, yet his expression doesn't change, he remains impassive, his focus on my face. "They hurt me, and they did exactly what you're thinking. At some point, I passed out and vaguely remember being carried to a truck by Alex."

"And then, Kate?" I notice traces of pain in his voice, and that torments me even more. I need to control myself to stay strong. I can't break down now, not again and again like it's happened so many times.

"I started having panic attacks and anxiety. I completely lost touch with reality, and my mother had me admitted to a psychiatric hospital. During that time, I was told I was pregnant."

The pressure of his hand on my neck intensifies, and Andrew pulls my body to him, making me rest my face on his strong chest. I take a deep breath, inhaling the scent I love, feeling safe in his arms.

"But I couldn't take care of the baby. She was a beautiful little girl..." My voice breaks, I feel weak, but I continue: "She was taken from my arms the day she was born and placed for adoption."

"Oh, darling... I'm so sorry."

I try to hold back the tears that come rushing, but I can't. Every second I remember Hannah, it's like a knife being driven into my chest.

"I loved her, Andrew. No matter what. I wanted that baby for myself, she was mine."

"I know, little fox. I know..." He whispers softly and leans in to place a kiss on top of my head. "Do you plan to find your daughter? I can help you with that, Kate."

I close my fingers on his chest and pull back slightly, searching his eyes, seeking the certainty of what I need: "No. Don't do that, Andrew. Hannah doesn't belong to me anymore. She's being taken care of and loved by other people, I don't have the right to do that to her."

Andrew nods and uses his thumb to dry the tears under my eyes: "Now I understand why you want a baby so much."

"Don't you think I'm being crazy?"

"No, I don't think so. You have every right to love someone, and if that love is directed toward a child, that's fine with me. I'll give you what you need, Kate."

I nod at him, feeling my heart filled with gratitude. I admire him even more for this: "Thank you, that means so much to me."

"Have you eaten?" Andrew changes the subject.

"Yes. To be honest, I was already in bed when I called you."

"Then I'm going to take you back to your bed. Where's the bedroom?"

I smile when Andrew moves and leans to lift me in his arms, as if I were just a helpless little girl.

"For God's sake, I'm not a child anymore." He ignores my protests, slipping one arm behind my back and the other under my thighs.

"Trust me, Kate, I know exactly what kind of woman you are. Now tell me where the bedroom is."

I point down the hallway and show him the door to the room I'm using.

Andrew kicks the door open and steps in with me in his arms. A second later, he places me gently on the flowery bed and looks around, raising an eyebrow.

"Are you sure this isn't Barbie's house?" he asks, and I laugh. I grab a pillow and throw it at him.

"Yes, I'm sure. It's Kate's house now."

He smiles this time, and his smile makes my heart race uncontrollably in my chest.

"Where are the blankets?" I point to the closet and indicate the compartment where I keep the essential bedding and bath items.

Andrew walks over and grabs one of my new blankets. He drapes the fabric over me, creating a warm and cozy layer over my body. Then, he adjusts the heater and turns off the room light, leaving only the soft light from the lamp on my work desk.

I hold my breath as I watch him remove his jacket and unbutton his white shirt. One piece after another is removed from his body, including his gun, holster, and belt. Andrew takes off his shoes and socks, leaving only his dress pants on. He walks over to the bed and lies down beside me in silence, pulling the blanket to cover his body.

I turn toward him, lying on my side, our faces so close I can feel his breath.

"When are we going to... you know... do the insemination?"

Andrew raises his hand to my face and leans closer. I feel his warm chest against mine, his powerful legs pressed against mine. This is so intimate and so good at the same time, and the most amazing part is that I don't feel afraid because I know he won't overstep my boundaries.

"I'll arrange everything for tomorrow night, including the contract."

I nod and place my hand on his that's on my face, as we gaze at each other, lost in one another.

"I want you to rest now," he says huskily, and his touch slides down to my neck.

Andrew slowly pulls me toward him, his gaze focused on my mouth. I feel the anxiety building up inside me, I can almost taste him on my lips again, and the sensation of having him near is so good that I feel my skin warm.

Our lips meet slowly. His mouth is soft, sweet, and the feeling of his beard scratching my face sends shivers all the way to my soul. I feel his tongue trying to make its way into my mouth, and I allow it. I part my lips and let Andrew Thompson penetrate my mouth with his tongue.

The kiss isn't long, it's quick and intense, but enough for us both to be out of breath, and I crave more.

However, Andrew pulls away, and I notice a trace of agony on his face as he closes his eyes and groans softly.

"I missed you," I declare, but I feel an immense ache in my chest when Andrew doesn't say anything, not a single word.

I try my best not to look foolish in front of him, but the truth is, I don't know what I feel, I don't know what I think. Everything is perfect when we're together, he awakens all my senses, even the most intimate ones. I feel dizzy in his presence, I feel my sex pulse when he looks at me, I feel my skin burn under his touch. But I can't move forward, and I'm grateful he doesn't insist. However, it's agonizing to be so broken, I feel the urge to scream in anguish, I hate myself for being this way.

And that's why I turn my back to him, I can't look at Andrew's face without breaking down again, and again.

"Good night, little fox," I hear his murmured voice and the touch of his hand pulling me by the waist, drawing me closer to him. I shiver when I feel his body pressed against mine, but I remain still, unable to speak or pull away.

Andrew buries his face in the curve of my neck and takes a deep breath, keeping his protective arm around my body. Soon, I feel his deep breath and know he's fallen asleep.

Despite everything, my fears and frustrations, I curl my lips and allow myself to be held by him. Despite the anguish I feel, my heart is at peace, and in a few minutes, I fall asleep too.

CHAPTER 27

ANDREW

I confess I'm more nervous than usual as I drive to Kate's house with everything we'll need for a home insemination. All day long, I've been overthinking it. I've concluded that I've completely lost my mind and all sense of reason. I simply agreed to father a child, just to fulfill the wish of my daughter's friend.

Obviously, I wouldn't need to take responsibility for anything—I could just act as a donor. I'd give her the semen, Kate would have her long-dreamed-of baby, and I'd go on with my life. But I'd never be able to sleep knowing there was a child of mine in the world without my support. The moment I agreed to Kate's request, I knew my life was about to turn upside down. I'd be a father again, without even having a relationship with the child's mother.

The idea of being a father at this stage of my life scares me a little, but damn, I'll get to see the baby grow up. I'll have what I didn't have with Angelina, and as crazy and unconventional as this all is, I want it to work. I want to see Kate's belly grow with my child inside. I want...

So many things that I don't even know where to start thinking about them.

I stop the car in front of Kate's house, halting my conflicting thoughts, and stay there, quiet and pensive, for a few minutes. Excitement takes over just thinking about seeing her, smelling her, and knowing she'll be inserting my sperm into her vagina. I shouldn't let my mind wander there, but it's stronger than me. It's impossible to control my damn cock, which is now as hard as steel.

A bit more composed, I get out of the car and ring the doorbell. Kate answers a few seconds later. She looks nervous as she gazes at me. Her hair is tied back in a ponytail, and she's wearing a wool robe over her sleepwear.

"Hi," I murmur softly.

"Andrew..."

She steps aside to let me in, and I do. I walk in slowly, carrying everything we agreed upon the night before. The house is eerily quiet, our voices caught in our throats, with no words spoken for the next minute.

I turn my attention to Kate, noticing how nervous she is. Only then do I step closer.

"Are you okay?" I ask, holding back the urge to pull her into my arms and steal a kiss from her lips.

"I'm a little nervous, but I'm fine. And you?"

I nod at her and finally summon the courage to proceed with the plan.

"I brought the contract and the supplies. Would you like to read through it first?"

I hand her the envelope containing the document and wait for Kate to read it. The contract is straightforward, listing the items we discussed last night. Kate scans the lines quickly and nods. "I'll grab a pen to sign."

After signing, she places the pen on the coffee table over the paper and straightens up slowly, looking back at me. I can feel her nervousness from where I stand. Kate is edgy, her hands trembling. I know how difficult this is for her. She glances from me to the bag in my hands, her face turning a lovely shade of red. It's beautiful and sexy at the same time. I get aroused just thinking about what must be running through her mind right now.

"I imagine you'd like some privacy to..." She points a finger—unintentionally, I think—towards my crotch, and I almost groan as I feel myself grow harder, straining against my boxers. "You can use my bedroom if you want. The bathroom wouldn't really be suitable in this case."

"All right. Your bedroom works for me."

She folds her hands in front of her body, and I grab the sterilized glass jar I brought. I waste no time turning and heading to Kate's room. The space is dimly lit, and I prefer it that way.

I take off my shoes and lie down on her soft bed. Her scent hits me hard, and my balls ache with an intense desire to release. I place the jar on the nightstand and pull my cock out of my pants. It springs out, hard and thick. The head is so red and sensitive from the brief moments of arousal that I grunt as I run my hand over the tip, spreading the pre-cum that's already oozing out.

"Damn..."

I close my eyes and start the up-and-down motion on my shaft. It's not hard to stay as stiff as a rock. All I have to do is think about Kate and that seductive mouth of hers. I repeat the motion countless times. The pleasure is good, I'm soaked in excitement, but the release doesn't come. It's as if my body refuses to climax unless it's inside her, and it's maddeningly frustrating.

I imagine all the positions I'd love to take Kate in. I think about her mouth taking me in, swallowing me whole until she gags on my cock.

But even that isn't enough to make me cum. It's as if she's the only thing that could suffice—in the flesh, right here, being touched and fucked by me. Irritated, I run my hand through my hair and curse softly, desperate to finish. I glance at the jar on the side and feel my erection start to deflate at the thought of filling that damn container instead of her.

Frustration overwhelms me, and I get off the bed. Without thinking much, I cover myself back up, grab the jar, and head to the door.

I find Kate sitting on the couch, legs crossed, her anxious gaze meeting mine. She stands as soon as she sees me, but I notice the confusion on her face when she sees the empty jar. Without waiting or overthinking, I close the distance between us in quick strides and reach her.

I slide my free hand around her waist and pull Kate closer, my mouth landing squarely on hers. I pour all my desire into the kiss, showing her with my lips everything I've wanted to do with my body. I plunge my tongue into Kate's mouth, leaving her trembling and breathless, just like me.

"I need your help to finish, sweetheart," I murmur into her ear, feeling her body shudder. "Don't worry, I'm not going to do anything to you."

I take her mouth again, giving her deep, intense kisses, sucking her tongue and lower lip.

"What... what are you going to do?" she finally asks, her voice breaking through the whirlwind of kisses I'm stealing from her lips. She looks at me, confused, utterly lost in the storm of my desire to feel her skin against mine.

"I need more stimulation to finish," I explain between ragged breaths. "I'm going to take my cock out and touch myself while kissing you. It won't take long, I promise."

Her breath falters, and I feel her body tremble. Kate is on the brink of combusting. She places a hand on my chest, stepping back slightly to catch her breath.

"I'm nervous," she whispers. "Do I... will I need to touch you?"

I swallow hard at the thought of Kate touching my cock, her soft, delicate fingers holding the tip. Damn, I almost lose control and have to gather myself to not ruin everything.

"You don't have to touch me. Only if you want to," I whisper back.

She nods slightly, and I guide Kate to the sofa so we can be comfortable while I try to finish into that damned jar. Sitting her beside me, I seek her mouth again, plunging my tongue between the full lips that drive me insane.

I place the jar on the coffee table and pull down the waistband of my boxers, releasing my aching cock. It springs out, as hard as steel, and I pause the kiss briefly to lower my pants and boxers to mid-thigh. When I turn back to Kate, I catch her wide-eyed, staring at my exposed erection. Her expression is a mix of shock and curiosity, pushing me to the edge of arousal.

"Kate..." I call, but she doesn't look at me. She's analyzing every detail of my cock with careful fascination.

I place a hand on her face, gently tilting her head to meet my gaze. Kate snaps out of her trance, blinking a few times to regain her composure.

"Look at me, fox," I murmur. "Does this scare you?"

She gasps, taking in a sharp breath, and runs her tongue over her naturally red lips, making me groan softly.

"A little..." her voice wavers. "It's... big. And thick... Andrew, how does that even fit... inside a woman without hurting her?"

I confess I'd give anything to know what's running through her mind right now. I want to know if she's wondering what it would feel like to take me inside her.

"When a woman is really aroused by her partner, her body gets ready," I explain. "The vagina becomes lubricated. Penetration doesn't hurt, Kate. It only brings pleasure."

My answer seems to satisfy her curiosity about how consensual sex can be enjoyable.

Kate tilts her head again, her eyes fixed on my cock. She looks like a curious little animal encountering something new. But what really drives me wild is noticing her press her thighs together, as if seeking some relief. My eyes close as I imagine how wet she must be, longing to feel me inside her. I muster all my self-control not to cross the line and scare her with the primal instincts screaming in my head. Otherwise, I'd have her right here, on this sofa.

Unable to endure another moment of torture, I lean toward her again, capturing her lips. She responds so willingly, so eagerly. Kate melts in my arms, her breathing erratic, shifting restlessly on the sofa.

I start masturbating, moving my hand back and forth, completely desperate to cum. My most primal instincts scream at me to slide my hand under Kate's clothes and reach the waistband of her panties. I'm driven mad with the urge to feel her warm skin under my fingers, to find out if her pussy is as hot and wet as I imagine. Kate moans into my mouth, sliding one hand over my shoulder and neck, restless, agitated, as if searching for something. And I know exactly what she wants. She's aroused—I can feel it in her ragged breathing, in the desperation with which she touches me. Her body is consumed by desire, and the longing for pleasure is overwhelming her thoughts. Kate wants to cum just as much as I do.

I speed up my movements on my cock as I feel my balls tighten, knowing the moment is close. My hand is already slick with pre-cum, and the delicious sensation in my groin drives me insane.

I release Kate's mouth and pull away to grab the jar just as my body begins to tremble. Placing it near the head of my cock, I keep moving steadily. I see stars as I start to ejaculate, using all my self-control to keep the jar from slipping to the floor. With every spurt, a low groan escapes my lips, taking me to the peak of pleasure. My entire body trembles, my heart races, and sweat beads on my temples.

When the last drop falls into the jar, I practically collapse onto the sofa, panting and exhausted, trying to catch my breath.

I turn my attention back to Kate, and her expression is one of pure amazement. I notice how nervous she is, but at the same time, she's fascinated by everything she's witnessed.

The image of her climaxing in my mouth hits me with full force, and if I hadn't just ejaculated, I would probably be hard again. It's stronger than I can resist; it's maddening to have her so close and not act on my deepest desires.

It's like trying to escape from a tank filled with water while struggling not to drown in the process.

"Let me make you cum, little fox," I practically beg, the sexual tension between us pulling us closer together.

Kate opens and closes her mouth. I can see the doubt etched on her face, mingled with the arousal. I can feel the intensity of her excitement, almost tangible.

"Andrew... I..." She stands, adjusting her robe, and turns her back to me.

When she faces me again, panic fills her gaze—a mix of fear and hesitation so overwhelming it leaves me breathless.

"I can't..."

I set the jar of cum on the bedside table and straighten my clothes, tucking my cock back into my underwear. Kate watches from a distance, analyzing every move I make. I can feel how much she wants to touch me, how badly she wants to be touched, but fear holds her back.

The trauma of her past is the wall separating her from a normal life, the barrier keeping her from being loved and experiencing pleasure. Realizing this leaves me shaken. My blood boils with rage and frustration at everything she's endured. I want to go to her, to kiss her until she surrenders completely, but I know now is not the time. And maybe that moment will never come because, despite everything I feel, I can't forget who she is. I can't forget that Kate is my daughter's friend—a woman utterly forbidden, someone I shouldn't even think about touching.

"I think we should stop this," she says, and I nod, though I'm fighting every urge not to take her in my arms.

I hand her the jar and the syringe I had brought. Kate accepts the items with trembling hands, her cheeks flushed, but she doesn't hesitate as she heads toward the bedroom.

Then I sit back down and wait for her, feeling the tension build within me. The agony of desiring something I can't have consumes me. I feel myself dying inside as my brain finally accepts the truth: Kate is forbidden.

CHAPTER 28

KATE

I look at the pregnancy test in my hands, feeling as though the ground has just collapsed beneath my feet. Several weeks have passed since I did the home insemination using Andrew's semen. Weeks have gone by as I've waited anxiously to find out if I will finally be holding a baby in my arms.

During this time, Andrew and I have drifted apart again. Every day we communicate by phone, he asks how I'm feeling, and I ask how his day was. But our conversations are limited to just that. We happened to meet once, at Angelina's house. He was polite, and I greeted him as if nothing had happened. His distance hurts, but we both know it's for the best. I can't give him what he wants, I can't have what I want. Our only connection was the baby I so desperately wanted, but even in that, I've failed again.

A tear slips down my cheek as I read the instructions on the test and realize it's negative. I'm not pregnant, the insemination failed, and the most likely reason my period hasn't arrived is stress and anxiety.

I've been so nervous these past few weeks. I thought about Andrew, I thought about that night, about how fascinating it was to see his desire and his body releasing pleasure. I thought about everything I felt, the longing to be his, to be touched and penetrated by him. But I was so scared, the memories of the past haunt me like a cold shadow that freezes me to the bone.

I sob quietly for a few minutes, feeling as though something of inestimable value has just shattered. Anguish hits me hard, and I lie down on the bed, exhausted, feeling like a walking failure.

Hours pass as I remain still, lost in my own pain. Spot barks, trying to get my attention, but I can't muster the energy to play with him. Eventually, the little animal gives up and curls up in a corner of the room. Animals have a gift for knowing when their owners aren't doing well.

My phone rings, and when I pick it up, I feel my chest tighten even more when I realize it's a call from Andrew. I had left him a message earlier, telling him I was going to take the test since my period hadn't arrived. However, since he was out of service and hadn't returned my call until just a few minutes ago, I decided to do it on my own.

"Hi, Andrew," I answer, bringing my hand to my face to wipe away the traces of tears, hoping he won't hear it in my voice that I've been crying.

"Kate, hey. Sorry for the delay, I had to leave town today."

"It's okay, it doesn't matter."

"Is everything alright?" He asks, and I feel the urge to burst into tears again when I hear the hope in his voice.

"Yeah, everything's fine." I sniffle quietly, pulling the phone away so he won't hear. I just don't understand why it's so hard to talk about something that never even happened.

"And the test, have you taken it? If not, can you wait for me? I'll be there in a few minutes."

"Andrew, I'm sorry, I... I already took the test. I was anxious and..." I try to explain, but the truth is, what's tormenting me the most is having to tell him that our attempt failed.

"It's okay. I understand."

"Andrew..." My voice cracks when I say his name. "The test was negative." He sighs deeply on the other end of the line, and we both fall silent, only hearing each other's breath.

"We can try again, if you want," he suggests.

I close my eyes, recalling every detail of that night, remembering everything I felt when I was with him. I don't know if I could go through all of that again without breaking down, without feeling less of a woman for simply not being able to receive pleasure from a man.

Taking a deep breath, I decide I won't give up on having a baby with Andrew, but maybe it's time to take the next step. Maybe it's time for me to go further, even if it's just once, for something bigger and more important than anything else. I can do it.

I repeat to myself over and over that I can do it, until I truly begin to believe it. But... will I...? I don't dare think about the future.

When I feel a little calmer, I hear his voice calling me from the other end of the line, and I finally make a decision. Something that will change my life forever.

"Can you come here, please?" I ask, even though I'm aware of how much I'm bothering him with my issues.

"Now?"

"Yes!" I confirm without hesitation.

"Alright."

When Andrew rings the doorbell, I'm already waiting for him in the living room. He's still dressed as he usually is for work, which indicates that he just left the investigation department and was heading home. I notice his tired expression, as though he hasn't slept in days. His beard is a little longer, but it doesn't lessen how charming he is, making my legs weak. His serious expression is a clear indication of the same disappointment I'm feeling. It was obvious that Andrew had already become attached to the idea of being a father, it was obvious how deeply he got involved in this madness with me, and I let him down.

"Hey. Come in." I step aside, and Andrew takes a step into the house.

"I'm so sorry, Kate." He begins as soon as I lock the door behind me.

I can't look at him. Everything we've been through is still vivid in my mind, and I know it is in his as well. However, I can't keep acting like a scared little fox all the time. Just like he sometimes calls me. I am a scared little fox.

"Andrew... Please, I need you to listen to me calmly." I turn to face him and stare into his eyes.

"Did something happen?" He narrows his eyes, watching me from head to toe as if searching for something out of place.

I shake my head in denial, and take a deep breath, gathering the courage to say what I need: "I want to try again... but in a different way this time."

The man steps closer, taking a step toward me, searching for sincerity in my eyes.

"Be more specific." His voice is deep. Andrew is smart enough to understand where I'm heading.

Nervous, I swallow hard, but I don't back down. Even though I'm embarrassed and scared, even though I have the urge to run away, I move forward.

"We can try... the natural way." I try to control my heavy breathing, but it's almost impossible to manage.

I see him clench his jaw as he stares at me intensely, analyzing every detail of my face. When he speaks again, I feel every particle of my body shudder.

"Do you realize what you're asking me?" I take a step back, and Andrew takes another step toward me. I try to move away from him slowly until I find the wall behind me. And now there's nowhere to escape. Andrew corners me, and I gasp. He places his hand on the wall behind my head, and I feel like I'm going to pass out at any moment. But I don't look away. I don't run from him, I meet his gaze, making it clear that I've never been more serious.

"Yes, I know what I'm asking. I want you to get me pregnant, even if it takes both of us... You know."

I see him blink a few times, as if what I just said caused him pain.

"Kate..., don't joke with this." He practically pleads.

I feel his quickened breath on my face, I feel the tension in his body, and I know that he's aroused now as he looks at me.

"I'm not... joking..." I pant.

"Fuck... Why don't you understand?" He runs a hand over my face and grips my chin, forcing me to pay attention to everything he says. "We can't do this, you're off-limits to me, you're an ex-novice, you're my daughter's best friend." His gaze drops to my mouth, and I see desire there, a flame so intense that his eyes shine. "And you're so young. You're so young, Kate, and I feel like a fucking bastard when I touch you, it's like I'm corrupting you."

"You just need to say no, Andrew." I lift my chin, feeling fear take over me, the fear of being rejected. Suddenly, it's like the air is thinning. I can't breathe, it feels like a prelude to death.

He watches me closely, his fierce eyes drifting down to my neck.

"I can't say no." When he looks back at me, he seems lost, confused, facing such great anguish that his expression morphs into pure agony.

My cheeks heat up as I realize this is real, that Andrew is agreeing to get me pregnant the natural way, and I release the breath I was holding.

"When can we do it?" I ask, determined to go all the way. To have the baby I so desperately want.

He pulls his hand away from my face. "Maybe it's wise to consult a gynecologist to know when the best time is."

I choke after hearing what he says, but I conclude that Andrew is right. Nothing can go wrong this time.

"Alright. I'll arrange that tomorrow," I agree.

"I'll have my assistant schedule an appointment for you."

I nod, and the man continues to stare at me closely, as if he wants to decipher my thoughts.

"You want this baby as much as I do, don't you?" I'm direct, realizing that for him, this isn't something he's indifferent to.

Andrew seems to share the same desire as I do, as I noticed it in the disappointment on his face when he arrived at my house after learning the pregnancy test was negative.

"Yes, Kate. I want this baby, I really do."

"Alright," I pant softly. "I just need to say that our involvement will be purely an agreement. You want the baby, so do I. We'll make it happen and then go on with our lives."

He tilts his head, so close that I feel the warmth of his breath on my skin.

"Is that what you want?" he asks in a whisper.

"Yes," I answer, panting.

"Alright."

We still spend a few minutes staring at each other, our mouths aching to touch. But Andrew doesn't do what I want. He simply steps back slowly and takes his hand to his neck to loosen the knot of his tie.

He checks the time on his watch and turns his attention back to me.

"I'll let you know about the appointment." His gaze slides down my body, covered by a simple and comfortable pajama. "Take care, Kate."

"Goodnight, Andrew." Then he leaves, and I stay there, trying to breathe, hardly believing what I did, or rather, what we're about to do.

I feel a fear of everything, but I know that Andrew will respect all of my wishes. I repeat to myself that the decision I've made will be for a greater good, everything will be fine, everything will work out. Andrew won't hurt me, and I won't be forced to do anything I don't want to do.

I RECEIVE A MESSAGE from Andrew early the next morning, providing the details about the clinic and the obstetric gynecologist I will be consulting with. The appointment is scheduled for three hours from now at a hospital specializing in pregnancy and childbirth in New York.

I reply to the message with an "ok" and head to the wardrobe to pick out something presentable to leave the house. I haven't had breakfast yet, so I decide to take a quick shower and wash my hair before eating.

I go to the bathroom and start removing my clothes. That's when I notice that my delayed period has finally arrived, leaving a small stain of blood on my underwear. Still, I go ahead with my plan and take a quick shower.

I head to the kitchen, fill Spot's bowl with water and food, and prepare something light for myself. I feel nervous, and the slight cramps beginning to appear don't help much. I finish eating and return to my room to get ready. I choose to wear warm pants, thick socks, boots, a long-sleeved wool sweater, and a winter coat. I complete the look with a hat and scarf.

Half an hour later, I'm in a taxi heading to my destination. I'm on my way to find an answer that will change the course of my life.

I arrive at the clinic much earlier than I should have. But I don't mind; I take the opportunity to walk around the streets and browse some perfume and makeup stores. I end up buying a light vanilla-scented cologne and a nude-colored lip gloss that I thought was very pretty and subtle. It matches my skin perfectly.

With just a few minutes to spare before my appointment, I go to the hospital's reception and complete the registration process. I fill out the necessary information and am informed about the doctor who will attend to me.

When I'm called in for the consultation, despite the intense cold, I feel my hands sweating from nervousness. Despite everything, I take a deep breath and move forward. I enter the consultation room and am warmly greeted by the doctor.

"Hello, Kate, how are you?" He reviews my records. "Please, have a seat."

"Hello." I force a smile and run my hand through my hair, trying not to seem too anxious.

I sit in the chair the doctor indicated and wait while he finishes reading the information. After a few seconds, the doctor looks back at me, folding his hands over the desk.

"Alright, Kate. How can I help you?" he asks.

I bite my lower lip, feeling shaky and too nervous. I think to myself that it's still not too late to back out of all of this, and almost give in to fear, but I take another deep breath and push forward.

"I really want to get pregnant, and that's why I decided to consult with a specialist to know the best time to try."

The doctor listens carefully to everything I say and asks some questions about my menstrual cycle, which, ironically, started today.

In just a few minutes, I leave the consultation room with the certainty that this time everything will go right. And before I even think about calling a taxi to head home, I pull out my phone and send a text message to Andrew.

From today, in 9 to 14 days, I will be in my fertile window.

I read and reread the message a million times before I finally click send.

A second later, the phone rings again with his response.

Do you trust me?

His question is unexpected, but there's no doubt that he is the only man I trust.

Yes.

As soon as I reply, I anxiously wait to see what he'll say next. Andrew's message takes a few minutes to arrive, but when it does, it leaves me completely anxious.

Then be ready in 10 days. I'll pick you up in the morning, and we'll go to a quiet place to spend a few days together. Everything will happen according to your timing, Kate.

I inhale and exhale. My body trembles, and my heart races to alarming levels just thinking about the days I will spend with him, alone, just the two of us.

Alright.

CHAPTER 29

KATE

"Oh Kate, of course Spot can stay with us." Angelina pours a little more juice for me and cuts another slice of lemon pie. "He's adorable, and the kids love him."

I feel like a traitor, not a shred of shame in my heart as I ask Angelina to keep Spot while I plan to spend an entire weekend with her father, doing things that leave me breathless just thinking about them.

"I'm really grateful, Angel." I watch Kaleo and Caleb playing with Spot in the living room. The little dog wags his tail and barks as the kids laugh. Caleb gets up from the floor and hugs Spot while Kaleo crawls to touch the animal's shiny, soft fur.

I sigh with happiness watching the scene, imagining that it will be my own baby doing all of that soon. My heart even races as I think about everything I'm going to experience from now on.

"When do you plan to leave?" she asks between bites.

I turn my attention back to my friend, curving my lips into an eager smile. If my cheeks weren't already so flushed from the cold, Angelina would probably think something very strange was going on with me.

"Tomorrow morning, it'll be just a few days."

She smiles warmly, her grin stretching from ear to ear.

"I'm so happy for you, Kate. You're living, you're doing your own things, you're traveling. You even live on your own now. I can only feel proud."

My cheeks heat up again, and images of Andrew completely naked flash in my mind. I push away the intrusive thoughts that leave me breathless and force a smile.

"Yeah, I think it will be good for me to rest a bit before starting to think about the next book."

Angelina nearly jumps out of her chair, ready to do a little happy dance. We talk a bit more about the kids, and I give her all the information about Spot. We laugh and have a great time while the kids play and we practically devour the entire lemon pie.

Before it gets dark, I decide to head back home, as I don't think it's safe to walk around alone after the sun sets.

I say goodbye to Angelina, the kids, and Spot. I hand her everything the little dog will need for the next few days and head home, knowing I'm making the right choice.

THE MORNING SUN SHINES timidly through the thick clouds. It's a cold winter morning, and the snow fell heavily overnight. I thought it might be impossible to leave the house this morning, but by some twist of fate, the sun appeared at dawn, and the snow stopped.

I didn't sleep very well last night. I couldn't relax while thinking about what would happen from today onwards. I couldn't stop thinking about Andrew, and even less about what we were going to do together.

When I hear the doorbell, my heart races. I know it's him, and a deep nervousness runs through my body. I take a deep breath and rush to the mirror to check if I look alright. Only then do I head to the living room and open the door.

There he is, with a deep and intense expression, holding a bouquet of flowers in his hand. He's elegant, as always, wearing a thick overcoat. His careful gaze calms me a little, but I can't avoid the flutter in my stomach.

"Hi." I try to smile, but my smile dies on my lips when our eyes meet, and images of us kissing and doing intimate things flash through my mind. I try not to think too much about it, but it's stronger than me. "Come in."

"Hi, Kate." His voice comes out in a whisper, and Andrew watches me intensely before handing me the flowers. I take them somewhat awkwardly, feeling more anxious than usual. He's serious, I'm nervous, and we're both a dangerous mix, with one being the complete opposite of the other.

"Thank you... they're beautiful." The bouquet is a mix of red roses and lilies.

"I thought you might like them." I bring the flowers to my nose and inhale deeply, taking in their fresh scent.

"I love them, thank you. I'll put them in my room." Andrew nods, and I gesture toward the couch. "You can sit down, I'll be just a minute."

I don't expect him to say anything. I walk back to the bedroom with the flowers and sit on the bed as I try to stay calm. I breathe in and out several times, closing and opening my eyes. When I feel less anxious, I remove the artificial flowers from the vase and replace them with Andrew's.

I grab the coat I left on the bed and put it on. I look at the small suitcase I packed with some clothes and toiletries, deciding that it's time to go. It's time to face my fears and move forward with what he and I have agreed upon. I return to the living room with everything I'll need in hand, and Andrew stands up as soon as he sees me.

"I left Spot with Angel yesterday. I told her I'd be traveling for a few days, to relax and clear my head. She'll take care of Spot for me," I inform him. "I hope you don't... mind."

"It's fine." He nods. "I had thought about bringing him with us, but this way is great."

I nod in agreement, and we stand there staring at each other, as if we were two strangers who had just met. He furrows his brow, studying me, and I have the urge to run away from his intense gaze.

"Shall we?" Andrew finally breaks the silence.

"Yes, let's go."

IN THE CAR, THE PATH we take becomes a mix of anxiety and excitement. Andrew tries to make conversation, talking about the snow and the cold weather, but I'm so lost in my thoughts that I only respond with smiles and soft murmurs. The urban landscape of New York slowly gives way to roads lined with snow-covered trees, and I feel my body relax, though the expectation of spending the weekend alone with him keeps me alert.

After a few hours on the road, we arrive at the place we'll be staying. I get out of the car completely surprised when I see a rustic wooden cabin. It's like something straight out of a romance movie. It's cozy, with large glass windows and a porch that overlooks a frozen lake surrounded by tall pine trees, all covered in a white blanket. Snow falls gently, making the scene even more breathtaking.

When we enter, the warmth of the fire in the fireplace welcomes me, but my mind is still racing. Andrew is beside me, completely serious, but there's a gleam in his eyes that makes me even more restless. I try to hide my anxiety, but he seems to sense the turmoil in my mind, as he takes my hand and reassures me with a gentle touch.

"Welcome to my lake house, Kate," he comments, tightening his grip on my hand covered by thick gloves.

"It's beautiful here." I still feel dazed, taking in everything around me, as if I'm living in a fairy tale.

The scent of burning wood mixed with the aroma of herbs creates an atmosphere that engages all the senses.

"I asked the caretaker to stock up the pantry and light the fire before we came. I want you to feel comfortable and safe here, Kate."

I turn my attention to Andrew and nod, knowing that nothing could be more perfect than this. I feel special that he thought of this place when we decided to spend time together. The air here calms me, and the close connection with the wild nature gives me a sense of freedom.

"I'll go get the bags. Feel free to explore the cabin."

Andrew turns his back to leave, and I do as he says. I walk through the room, observing the details, feeling at home. The stone fireplace dominates one corner of the main room, with flames warming the space and casting shadows over the wooden floorboards.

Around the fireplace, there's a fluffy sheepskin rug, with two large, soft armchairs upholstered in woolen fabric. There's also a sturdy wooden coffee table, marked with signs of use, and an old wooden bookshelf filled with books.

At the back, the bed is covered with a warm quilt and woolen pillows. A thick blanket is folded at the foot of the bed, ready for the cold nights. The large windows, protected by linen curtains, reveal the white world outside, while snowflakes accumulate on the sills.

When he returns, Andrew sets the bags on the floor near the fireplace and moves closer to the fire to warm his hands. When he comes back to me, his eyes are sparkling just like the flames.

He takes a step toward me, and I feel my breath quicken with his proximity, my heart beating irregularly, everything inside me destabilizes.

"Kate..." I close my eyes when his raspy voice reaches my ears, and I shiver from head to toe. "I've waited a long time for this, you know?"

I swallow hard and reopen my eyes. He looks fascinated as he watches me, and I know he's holding himself back, struggling not to move closer.

"I'm a little nervous." I'm honest. I don't hide what I'm feeling, let alone how much this is taking all my strength.

"I know." Andrew pulls me toward him and takes my body in a strong hug that makes me weak. "All in your time, little fox." His beard brushes against my ear, and he places a soft kiss on my earlobe, followed by a nibble. "I won't be a hypocrite and say I want to wait, Kate. I'm dying to do everything with you, damn, I'm so excited. But I give you my word that I won't cross the line until you're ready for me."

I feel the air leave my lungs, and Andrew pulls away briefly to look me in the eyes.

"Alright." My voice comes out breathless, nervous, almost inaudible. "Do you want to try now?" I know that the sooner we do this, the sooner it will be over.

I see his eyes widen for just a few seconds before being consumed by a wild fire that sends chills down my spine: "You want to?"

I open and close my mouth a few times. I can't find the words to answer Andrew's question. I wish I could say yes, I want to do this with him, but I would be lying to myself. I'm scared, almost terrified. I close my eyes and quickly open them again, taking a deep breath to respond firmly:

"Let's do this."

Andrew slides a hand over my face, down my jaw, and chin. He starts kissing me slowly. His experienced mouth takes mine in a passionate kiss that demands all of me. I gasp softly, trying not to get more involved than I already am, but it's stronger than I can bear.

I allow him to kiss me slowly, and I open my mouth to welcome his tongue. Andrew sucks on my lips, doing the same with his tongue. He disorients me with just a kiss, leaving me dizzy and clouded. I feel like I'm going to faint in his arms any second when he stops the kiss and takes my hand.

"I need to introduce you to the bed first," he murmurs softly, his voice heavy with desire. "There are so many things I want to do with you, Kate."

I follow him toward the large wooden bed, looking comfortable. I notice the bulge in Andrew's pants, but I try not to think too much about it. I'll just do what I'm supposed to do, no more beating around the bush.

When we get closer to the bed, Andrew sits down and pulls me onto his lap, holding my face with both of his hands.

I try to remain as calm as possible, so I control my breathing to avoid showing too much anxiety. Our gazes meet, and he tilts his head to place a soft kiss on my lips.

"I wish I knew everything that's going through that little head of yours, Kate," he comments, and I swallow hard.

"I think the light is making me a little too shy."

He smiles, and his smile warms me from the inside out.

"You're perfect, every detail."

"Andrew," I place my hand on his shoulder to get his attention, feeling like I'm about to suffocate any moment. "Please, be quick."

I feel him tremble, and the euphoria I saw on his face suddenly disappears. Andrew continues to look at me, but his gaze is no longer filled with desire, it's something more like anguish, suffering. He strokes my face and leans in more. A kiss is placed on my forehead, and then he pulls away.

"I think it's time for something to eat, Kate. I'm starving."

It feels like a bucket of cold water has been thrown over my head. I have the urge to beg him not to leave, to scream until I understand exactly what he wants from me. But I can't. I just get up and wrap my arms around myself, feeling empty inside, hurt, and rejected. I don't understand why he's pulling away like this. My brain can't comprehend why Andrew isn't moving forward. It shouldn't be this difficult. Another man would take what he wants without a second thought and finish it quickly.

I see Andrew move from the bed to leave. He doesn't look at me, or at least I don't notice it. I don't know how long I stay there as he moves away and walks to another room I haven't seen yet.

CHAPTER 30

ANDREW

I try my best to keep my composure and not lose control, but I can see the fear in Kate's eyes and hear it in her voice. She's scared. She's not ready yet, and she thinks being with me will feel the same as it did with the bastards who hurt her.

Kate doesn't understand that sex can be good and pleasurable for both of us, but that takes time. Time I'm more than willing to give her. That's why I've decided to step back a little, to let her come to me of her own free will. When that happens, I'll give her the best of me in every possible way until she's too exhausted from pleasure to do anything but sleep in my arms.

I leave her in the room, still staring at me with a confused expression, and head to the kitchen. I try not to look at her too much, but damn, I'm at my limit. I've been aroused since the moment I laid eyes on her this morning. I can't stop imagining her naked, legs open as I bury myself inside her. I can't stop thinking about how delicious it will be to slide my tongue along her folds and taste her arousal. I'm sweating despite the cold, and it's driving me insane.

My balls ache as I walk, and I curse under my breath, almost regretting stepping away. Still, I press on.

The kitchen matches the rustic feel of the cabin. The table, chairs, cabinets, and counters are all made of wood, crafted to complement the wild nature surrounding the place. I usually use the cabin for vacations and a bit of fishing. The lake is full of perch and trout, just what I need to escape the stress of city life. Out here, I reconnect with nature and recharge.

I grab a few cans of food from the pantry and set them on the counter. Then I head to the cold storage, stocked with two freezers full of meat, and take out a good cut of sirloin for grilled steaks.

The cabin is well-equipped with modern appliances for when they're needed. A high-performance generator powers the electricity and hot water. Most of the time, though, the fireplace keeps the cabin warm enough, thanks to the insulated walls that trap the heat inside.

Still, I decide to turn on the heater to make Kate more comfortable before I start preparing lunch. I take off some of my layers, leaving only my pants on and going barefoot.

Some time later, she shows up in the kitchen. Her expression is serious, and she focuses on anything but me. She's also shed her heavy clothes and is wearing a tank top and pants. Her hair is loose, with a few strands tucked behind her ear. It only takes one look at her for me to feel my cock harden.

"Are you hungry?" I ask, trying to distract myself from the overwhelming urge to grab her. Her eyes finally meet mine.

Kate tries to smile, but it fades quickly. Her face shows a mix of uncertainty and unanswered questions. I know her mind is a mess right now.

"A little," she finally replies. "It smells amazing."

I nod at her and grab two plates from the cabinet. I serve her a portion of corn, peas, and potatoes alongside a thick slice of steak. I make the same plate for myself and bring them both to the table.

Kate sits down to eat, and I watch her closely. She eats slowly, struggling to swallow her food. She's anxious, maybe a little restless, unsure of what to do. But in a way, that's good. She needs to trust me completely for this to work.

"I was thinking about doing some fishing and then taking the snowmobile out for a ride. What do you think?" I suggest, even though my shoulders feel tense. Controlling myself like this is torture when all I really want is to stay inside with her.

She nibbles on her bottom lip, hesitant, but eventually nods.

After lunch, Kate seems more relaxed and even smiles a little. We chat about the cabin and how I fish on the frozen lake. She seems fascinated as I explain everything.

When I stand up to clear the table, she does the same. Several times, I catch her stealing glances at me, her eyes lingering on my bare chest. I'm fully aware that I'm not a young man anymore, but I take care of myself. I'm in good shape, my body conditioned by intense training.

I notice her gaze drifting to my stomach and then to my groin. She doesn't even realize what she's doing. My jaw tightens as I feel control, reason, and all sense slipping away. I try to keep my distance, to stop thinking about burying myself inside her, but it's impossible. I've already lost the battle with myself. Resisting everything Kate stirs in me with her veiled innocence is utterly impossible.

"Kate..." I call her, and she seems to snap out of a trance, her eyes meeting mine again. "You're not making this easy for me, little fox."

She blushes as the meaning of my words sinks in, and her gaze follows mine as I tilt my head to gesture at the noticeable bulge in my pants.

"Shit," I groan softly.

"Andrew... I..." She stammers, and I think she's about to run. Yet, her eyes remain glued to the obvious outline beneath the fabric. Then, she looks back up at me, her expression hesitant but gradually resolute as she clenches her teeth. "Why did you leave me in the room? I thought... I don't understand."

I take a deep breath and close the distance between us.

I touch her chin gently, tilting her face upward. I don't let her look away. I want her to hear every word I'm about to say.

"Because I was at my limit, Kate. I was desperate to see you naked, to kiss every inch of your body from head to toe. I was burning to fuck you, but you were afraid."

She shivers at my words and instinctively tries to step back, but I don't let her move an inch.

"What do you mean?" she asks, stunned.

"You need to want this, Kate. Not just because of the baby. Or because you've decided you want to get pregnant. I want you to enjoy it. I want to hear you moaning and screaming my name while I'm inside you." I release her chin and let my hand slide to her neck. I grasp the back of her neck and pull her closer, eliciting a gasp from her lips. "This can't be rushed, and it can't happen if you're still afraid. Your first time needs to be unforgettable, and the past needs to stay buried. Your life is so much more than those painful memories."

She tries to pull away from my touch, but I hold her by the waist. I feel the sweat on my body and the tremble in hers. We're both a tangle of unsatisfied desires, fears, and raw emotions.

"You know I'm not a virgin, Andrew. I've had a first time... and a second," she says, her voice tinged with bitterness and resentment, but it breaks slightly at the end.

I can feel her pain, her anger screaming to be released, but she doesn't realize how wrong she is.

"No, Kate. You didn't have a first time. That was stolen from you."

Her eyes widen, and she gasps sharply. She no longer tries to pull away, her gaze fixed on my face as if still processing my words.

"They stole your innocence, little fox. They did things to you that you didn't want. But your first time will be with me. The man you chose to touch you willingly. There's no such thing as a first time without both people agreeing."

Her eyes fill with tears, but she fights to hold them back. She raises a hand to touch my face, her soft touch sending shivers through me, driving me mad.

"Oh, Andrew," she murmurs my name, and I pull her into a tight embrace, burying my face in the curve of her neck.

"I'll be ready when you're ready for me," I murmur.

I press a kiss to her neck, letting my tongue glide over her soft skin until I reach her delicate chin. I capture her lips with mine, pouring all the desire, all the pent-up need, and all the madness consuming me into the kiss. Then I pull back, feeling her breath against my face, heavy and uneven.

"Just give me a little more time, please," she whispers, and I nod.

"Take all the time you need."

CHAPTER 31

KATE

I try not to think too much about what Andrew and I will do after all this is over. I just focus on the moment when he drills a hole in the ice and pulls out a frozen tablet in the shape of a round disk.

We are bundled up to the bone in layers of warm, waterproof clothes. A wool hat and scarf protect my face from the cold wind. While Andrew handles the drilling equipment and prepares the hook, I watch him from a close distance—not too close to the thinner part of the ice, but not too far to miss any details.

It's simply fascinating to watch his expertise and how he does everything with mastery and speed. The cold intensifies, but Andrew doesn't seem to care as he casts the hook into the hole he just made. It doesn't take long for him to catch the first fish, which he says is a trout with excellent size and great appearance. Then it's my turn to try, but for some twist of fate, no fish bites the bait.

At the end of the fishing session, Andrew's tally is three trout and two perch, while mine is below zero. So, we leave the fish in the kitchen and return to a counter located on the other side of the cabin, across the lake, which I hadn't seen before due to the snow.

The place isn't large, but it houses top-of-the-line equipment, including a tractor with a snowplow to clear the usual paths and two snowmobiles.

Our ride starts around the lake. Obviously, I don't have the courage to go in a vehicle alone, so we only use one of the snowmobiles. I wrap my arms around Andrew, feeling the wind hit me hard, but it's all so incredible that the cold is one of my last concerns.

The ride continues along the snow-covered road until we approach the mountain, which looks endless amid the white sea. Andrew and I dismount briefly to take in the view. The late afternoon sun shines timidly through the pines, and the smell of nature seeps into every pore of my body. I feel light, free. I feel as happy as I haven't felt in a long time.

Life flows through my veins like running water, and so I allow myself to spin around in the middle of nowhere. When I turn my attention back to Andrew, he's smiling, but his smile carries a cynical air, as if he's up to something. It's too late when I realize his intentions. He crouches down and grabs a snowball, and in the next second, the snowball hits me squarely on the head.

I laugh in surprise, and also lean over the snow to return the favor. I miss the target with every attempt, but he manages to hit me with two snowballs.

Finally, I give up trying to hit him from a distance, fill my hands with snow, and run towards Andrew with the intent of filling his hair with ice flakes. Realizing my intentions, the man simply wraps an arm around my waist, and with his other hand, grabs one of my wrists, making me drop everything I was holding onto the ground.

"Andrew, that's not fair!" I try to protest, but the next moment, I'm thrown along with him into the tangled snow. I fall on top of him, letting out a startled scream, and Andrew laughs along with me.

We both turn into a true mess of entangled limbs and snow everywhere, especially in my hair.

"You don't stand a chance against me, little fox," he jokes as he holds me at the waist on top of his body.

"So that's why you threw yourself into the snow and dragged me with you?" I raise an eyebrow as I try to brush my hair from my face.

His fingers help me with the task, and I search for my hat that fell to the side. After putting the hat back on, I face Andrew again. His eyes are sparkling as he looks at me, and his gloved hands slide down my back over the layers of clothes.

"Give me a kiss, Kate," he asks, and I bite my lower lip, feeling capable of anything, even daring to kiss him.

I don't wait long to do what he asks; carefully, I contort and slide over him until my head is next to his. Andrew brings one hand to my neck and waits for me to do exactly what he asked.

I feel my breath quicken as I look at his experienced mouth. His attention also falls on mine, and he moistens his lips with his tongue. Breathing heavily, I slowly tilt my head, placing both hands on the snowy ground and lightly touch his lips with mine.

Andrew moans softly, and somehow, that drives me even more into ecstasy. I intensify the kiss, doing what I've learned from him. I part his lips with mine and introduce my tongue. I feel his grip tighten, and one of his hands slides to my thigh, squeezing the flesh. Andrew starts sucking my tongue, and soon after, takes control of everything. He holds me, sucks my air, intoxicates me. He devours me as if I were a juicy fruit. The kiss intensifies, and I'm breathless, completely trapped in him, our bodies so close they almost stick together.

He sucks my lower lip, nibbles it, then dives back in with his tongue, making such lustful movements that leave me dizzy, for I completely understand what he wants.

Breathing heavily, I pull away from Andrew a bit to catch my breath. I notice his feverish gaze, and an overwhelming hunger takes over his expression.

"We'd better go, Kate..." he suggests, and I agree, feeling my legs tremble and the tension rise to extreme levels, knowing exactly that there's no way to escape anymore.

Tonight, I will be his, in every way. It's decided.

CHAPTER 32

KATE

When we enter the cabin, the welcome warmth from the fireplace comforts me, and I sigh softly. Andrew removes part of his outer clothing, and I do the same while I watch every movement of his body.

I glance at the bed in the back, with a privileged view of the snow outside, then look back at Andrew, gathering my courage.

"I think I need a bath now," I walk toward the compartment he showed me earlier.

"Alright. Are you hungry? I can prepare something while you bathe."

I look at him cautiously; I can't be that direct with my intentions, especially when it comes to sex.

"Actually, I'm not hungry." I swallow hard, catching my breath. "Andrew..., I... I think I'm ready."

He narrows his eyes and clenches his jaw as he watches me closely. These are traits I've learned to decipher over the months when Andrew is excited. And now I know he's at his limit. Every pore of his body seems to scream for sex. His expression changes, and I feel myself shiver from head to toe.

He doesn't say anything as I turn my back and walk toward the suitcase near the bed, but I can feel his intense gaze on every step I take. I pick a white bathrobe and a set of pants and long-sleeve shirt to sleep in. I place the clothes on the bed and head toward the bathroom.

Before entering, I turn to Andrew, and I see him still in the same spot, watching me closely. His gaze is fixed on me, like a hungry animal stalking its prey. I feel my skin burn as I'm the target of his study. I open the bathroom door and enter, feeling my breath catch, my heart racing. When I calm down a little, I allow myself to do what I need. I remove my clothes and fold them neatly on the sink. Then I approach the huge bathtub and turn on the hot water compartment.

When I step into the water, the warm liquid envelops me in such a pleasurable way that I close my eyes and relax as much as I can. The bath isn't long, but I take enough time to calm my nerves and surrender to every sensation awakening on my skin.

When I finish, I dry my body and wrap myself in the soft bathrobe. I find Andrew crouched, feeding the fire in the fireplace, completely bare from the waist up. The temperature is a little higher because of the electric heater that amplifies the warmth from the flickering flames devouring the wood.

When he sees me wrapped in the robe, Andrew stands and walks slowly toward me, his attention focused on my face.

My eyes land on his chest and strong biceps. I can't even pretend to hide the mix of sensations I'm feeling; I just watch all of him, imagining what it would feel like to touch his naked skin, to feel the temperature of his abdomen in my hand, his... penis.

"Do you want me to turn off the heater?" He leans in to take my mouth in a quick kiss. His hand slides across my cheek, gently caressing my skin.

"No need. This is fine."

Andrew nods and steps away, heading toward the bathroom. Only then do I exhale the breath I was holding.

I start combing my hair, untangling it strand by strand until the wet strands are neatly aligned along my back. I glance at the sleepwear on the bed, but decide to go further. I put away the clothes I had chosen and replace them with a cotton thong that fits well on my body and accentuates my backside. I finish by moisturizing my skin and closing the bathrobe again.

I wait for him in one of the armchairs facing the stone fireplace. I grab a book from the shelf and begin flipping through the pages, though I can't actually read. I can't focus on anything, my instincts are heightened, waiting for the moment when Andrew will come out of the bathroom and come to me. When it happens, I leave the book on the chair and stand up, trembling, breathing heavily.

He exits the bathroom, drying his hair with a white towel. He's dressed only in comfortable flannel pants, and the bulge of his excitement shows through the fabric. Andrew runs his fingers through his hair, making it messy, and turns his attention to me. I've never seen him so casual, with his hair unkempt. But I confess that this more relaxed version of him makes my stomach churn with anticipation. Andrew is simply gorgeous, and I don't care if he's much older, I don't care if he's old enough to be my father. His gaze destabilizes me, his touch leaves me breathless, and I long to feel his mouth on mine.

Slowly, he walks toward me, and I take a breath, summoning the courage to do what I've planned. I close my eyes and move my hand to the tie holding the bathrobe to my body. I undo the knot and slide the piece off my shoulders, allowing the fabric to pile at my feet.

When I open my eyes again, Andrew is standing just a short distance away, observing me almost completely naked. The only thing I'm wearing is the cotton thong. My breasts and stomach are exposed.

I take a deep breath while he analyzes me and steps forward, closing the gap between us. His eyes fall on my exposed breasts, and I feel my face flush with embarrassment. I try to cover part of my nudity with my hands, but Andrew stops me.

"Don't do that, Kate," he asks as he touches my arms lightly, encouraging me to uncover my breasts again. "You're perfect in every detail."

Andrew slides one hand around my waist, pulling a soft gasp from my throat, bringing me closer to him. Our moans escape as soon as our skin touches. He's warm from the bath, and I'm warm from the fire. The sensation is incredibly delicious.

"I want to do so many things with you, Kate," he whispers in my ear, and I have to hold on to his shoulder to keep my balance. "I want to kiss every part of you, little fox, every curve of your body."

"I don't really know what to do," I reply, my voice faltering.

Andrew buries his face in the curve of my neck and begins to nibble there, planting soft kisses that send shivers through my entire body. His movements are subtle, the touch gentle; I can tell he's doing everything to calm me down.

"Just feel. Enjoy every second and surrender to me. I will never hurt you."

I close my eyes briefly and nod. Despite the nervousness consuming me, I know it will be perfect; I feel it in every nuance.

Andrew pulls away and I look at him again. I see in profile the crazy, burning desire in his eyes. I shiver from head to toe but don't move when he raises both hands and takes hold of my breasts. Andrew makes circular motions with his thumb on my swollen nipples, and my eyes widen when I feel a jolt in my groin. It's as if that part of my body is directly connected to my sex. It's different, and it feels so good, I'm completely stunned.

A curve of a smile appears on his lips, and I gasp.

"It's good, isn't it?" he asks, sliding one hand from my breasts to my neck.

"Yes... it's good," I gasp.

His warm mouth descends on mine as Andrew keeps one hand on my left breast and the other on my nape. He parts my lips, and

I feel his tongue invading my mouth, exploring and savoring before devouring me in a kiss filled with desire.

"Every time I slide my tongue into your mouth like this, I'm thinking about doing the same to your pussy—with my tongue and my cock."

I choke on his words, feeling my heart race so hard I can almost hear its frantic beats.

"Don't be scared, Kate. You'll get used to it over time. You'll learn to love all the sensations, all the stimuli I'll bring to your body."

Trembling, I cling to him as if my life depends on it. I'm still dizzy from everything Andrew said, and my whole body is a whirlwind of fear, shame, and ecstasy.

"Are you really going to do that... down there?" I ask, a little incredulous, shock and excitement spreading through my body.

"Yes, and you can do it to me too, if you want," he whispers softly. "But if you say no, I'll respect your decision."

I shut my eyes, feeling overwhelmed beyond reason. The image of Andrew's fully erect cock flashes in my mind, and I imagine it in my mouth. I'm breathless, strange sensations pooling low in my belly, and a warm liquid trickles through me, dampening my panties. The same thing happens when I imagine him licking me between my legs. It's terrifying how my body melts like this.

Andrew tilts my body back, placing me seated on the armchair. And I go, without protest, completely guided by his command.

"With you, I want everything," I whisper back, giving him total freedom to teach me how to feel pleasure. I hear him groan.

He sits beside me and begins kissing me slowly. Our kisses deepen, his fingers trailing down my neck, my breasts, until they reach my stomach. My hands explore every inch of his shoulders and chest.

"Are you feeling wet?" he asks in a whisper, and I feel painful throbs between my legs, but my nervousness is overwhelming.

"Andrew... please..." I protest, blushing furiously. He captures my mouth again, and I feel a hand sliding down my abdomen, pressing and caressing my skin slowly until it reaches the waistband of my panties. "Andrew..." I place my hand over his but don't stop him from continuing.

"Answer me," he insists, but his touch doesn't advance.

I take a deep breath, summoning all my courage to give him an answer.

"Yes..." I gasp. "I need you... please." I don't even understand why I'm pleading.

A groan escapes his mouth, and Andrew resumes the movements of his hand on my stomach. A finger slips beneath my panties, and I feel my blood pressure spike, my heart racing. The touch is slow and torturous, and I try to stop him from continuing. Andrew gently holds my wrist and moves his mouth from mine, looking directly into my eyes: "I want you to get comfortable in the chair, close your eyes, and just feel, Kate."

I open and close my mouth, unable to form a single word, my voice caught in my throat. The world seems like a metallic globe, thousands of colors swirling around me.

I feel his fingers hook into the waistband of my panties, and I almost faint from the intense sensation that causes deep inside me. It's not just fear; it's also desire, a yearning to feel everything without reservation, a longing to forget the past and focus solely on the present. This internal conflict drives me insane.

"Andrew, no..." I try to protest, but I don't have the strength to push him away because my body wants him beyond reason, beyond what I can control. My mouth says no, but my body screams yes, and I just need one more plea from him to give in completely.

"Close your eyes, Kate," he asks again, his voice carrying a demanding tone that makes me weak, making resistance nearly impossible.

I do as Andrew says: reclining in the chair as comfortably as possible and closing my eyes. All I have access to are the sensations his fingers evoke in me.

I hear him move in front of me and feel his hands on my thighs. Then, once again, his fingers hook into the waistband of my panties. Andrew begins to pull them down slowly along my legs, torturing me in the process. I squirm, gasping, dazed, unsure of what to do.

I hear his ragged breathing and feel his hands gripping my calves. Then, he slowly spreads my legs apart, and the warmth of the fireplace combined with the chill brushes against my core, making me tremble.

"Fuck!" Andrew curses, and I open my eyes to look at him. I feel like a puddle as I meet his face, transformed with desire. His expression is pure ecstasy. His brow is furrowed, and his jaw is tight.

Andrew is kneeling on the floor between my open thighs, staring directly at my exposed sex as if he's gazing at the eighth wonder of the world.

Panting, I can't even move.

Then he raises his gaze and licks his lips.

"You're so beautiful," he breathes. "And you're soaking wet."

I feel like my face is on fire. I let out a quiet gasp when Andrew's gaze returns between my legs, and he slides a finger along the inside of my thigh, nearing the lips of my sex. I shrink back, too overwhelmed, but he holds me more firmly.

"I need you to trust me, Kate. Surrender to me," he groans, and I feel his finger glide over the folds of my intimacy so lightly that intense shivers raise goosebumps all over my skin.

"Andrew..." I feel like I'm being tortured. I want him to touch me, yet I want him to stop.

"Hush, little fox," I breathe a sigh of relief when he pulls his finger away, but I moan softly when Andrew slides both hands along my thighs again, spreading them even wider, leaving me utterly exposed and vulnerable to him.

I brace myself against the backrest of the chair as he pulls my body to the edge, and without asking for permission, he lowers his face toward my core. A shocked cry escapes my throat as I feel his firm tongue slide directly onto my clit. The bundle of nerves throbs intensely, and Andrew captures it in his mouth, sucking and licking simultaneously.

"What are you...?!" I can't think coherently.

Before I realize it, my hands are in his hair, moaning and writhing, practically rubbing my sex against his face, driven by my body's instincts. I lose reason and all sense, gasping softly as I hold back from screaming. The sensation is intense, something I've never experienced before. Everything seems to shatter into a million particles within me. In that moment, I am a universe of wonder after eons of disillusionment.

"Andrew, what is this? What...?!" I cry out his name, completely beside myself, lost in the unknown, delicious sensation. My body is overwhelmed by the shock of his mouth on such an intimate part of me, even as pleasure consumes me from the inside out.

I feel his fingers caressing my folds, parting me as he sucks my clit into his mouth. His tongue slides over my folds, licking and sucking the delicate lips. He tortures me with his mouth, taking me to heaven and hell in seconds. I'm groggy, caught between reality and unreality, desiring something I can't even name.

I thrust my hips toward his face, yearning to be filled beyond my limits. Andrew seems to sense what I want as he slowly slides his tongue into my core just as he described. I gasp, moaning softly. My hands release his hair and move to knead my breasts, intensifying the violent sensation threatening to explode inside me.

"Andrew!" I scream his name as his sucking intensifies.

His firm tongue flicks my clit from side to side before sliding down to the entrance of my sex. He licks me there, sucks slowly, rubs his mouth and nose against my folds, then returns to suck my clit again.

I scream, trembling uncontrollably. Dazed, surrendered. His tongue plunges into my vulva again, and I lose all control. My legs begin to fail, and a pressure in my belly forces my hips against his face. My sex pulses, and the liquid of my arousal trickles down my already slick folds. Waves of pure ecstasy wash over me, and I open my mouth in a silent scream caught in my throat.

"Fuck, you're so delicious," he curses, losing control himself, and gives my sex one last lick.

Little by little, my breathing returns to normal, and life floods back into my body. I stare at him, confused, still not understanding what just happened. My body feels so weak I could pass out at any moment.

Andrew releases my thighs and rises to sit beside me. He pulls me into his arms, his panting mouth reclaiming mine, hungry like an animal.

"You came so beautifully," he whispers against my mouth, and I feel his finger slide between my legs. The romance and slowness of earlier are gradually giving way to his desperation and need. "You're so wet, Kate."

I flinch slightly when he touches my sensitive clit, and Andrew withdraws his hand, halting his caress. With care, he explores my breasts again, pinching the nipples between his fingers.

"You're sensitive, aren't you? Your clit is swollen. You were perfect." His voice is a raspy tangle of emotions.

When I look at his face again, I can almost feel the strain in his expression, the desperate need to reach his climax. Andrew is controlling himself as much as possible to help me adjust to each new movement, each sensation, each touch.

"This has never happened to me before... this sensation... I can't explain it."

"You came," he explains, cupping my chin again, his eyes locked on mine. "And now you're ready to be entered. This is how it should be."

Our mouths meet again, hungry, and I respond with equal voracity. Despite my sensitive clit, the desire to be completely filled by him is overwhelming, as if all my emotions are at their breaking point. My feminine instincts scream for him, my body craves his, and it's stronger than any pain or trauma. Andrew releases my mouth and begins to nibble my neck, leaving a trail of kisses and shivers.

I moan under his touch, bringing my hand to his chest, feeling the sparse hair there. I continue exploring his body, pressing into his flesh slowly, caressing his stomach. It's exhilarating to watch him unravel in the midst of the groans of desire I evoke in him.

His mouth reaches the lobe of my ear, and he sucks on it, drawing another groan from me. My breasts are kneaded in his hands, my thighs, my ass. He explores everything, leaving me dizzy and breathless, each second making me need him more.

"Now it's time for you to explore me a little, Kate," he murmurs, and I know exactly what he means.

Andrew pulls back, and I look at him, panting, completely dazed.

"I want you to touch my cock. Caress it, feel its texture. You need to get familiar with my body, okay?"

I bite my lower lip, feeling nervous, but I nod.

"You looking at me like that, with that innocent little face, drives me even crazier. I'm at my limit, you know?" Andrew holds my chin and leans in, our mouths barely touching. "You don't even seem like the same person who was grinding her little pussy against my mouth a few minutes ago."

I gasp at his teasing, still stunned by my lack of control.

"Did I do something wrong?" I ask, almost breathless.

His lips curl into a wicked grin, and his mouth brushes lightly against mine.

"No, little fox. You almost made me come in my pants."

And once again, we're kissing like lunatics, lost in the desire consuming us, completely surrendering to each other.

When Andrew pulls away this time, I realize he's at the edge of what any man can endure. I feel delicious throbs in my clit with every groan that escapes his lips, just from kissing and touching me.

His hands deftly work the waistband of his flannel pants, sliding the fabric down his muscular legs, making me hold my breath. I never cease to be amazed at how big and thick he is. I notice a clear, viscous liquid dripping from the tip, coating the entire length. The broad head is red and swollen, and I can almost imagine how soft it would feel—I can almost feel its texture in my mouth...

My intrusive thoughts are interrupted when Andrew grabs my hand and guides it to his impressive length. My heart races at the sticky texture of his precum on my hand, but when I hear the satisfied groan that escapes his lips, I begin to calm down bit by bit.

I constantly remind myself that this is Andrew here with me, and he would never force me to do anything I don't want to do.

"Like this, Kate, hold it tighter." He closes his fingers over mine, making me grip his cock, and lets out a deep groan, throwing his head back.

My hand trembles as I begin to explore his length, but I gradually get the hang of it.

Andrew digs his fingers into the armrest of the chair as I slide my hand along the prominent veins. I start making subtle up-and-down movements with both hands, fascinated as I cover and uncover the glans with the skin. Every touch of my fingers on the slick head makes him groan, and the more confident I become in exploring his body, the more I feel the need to have his thick length inside me.

"I need to be inside you, little fox, or I'll lose my mind."

He pants, grabbing my hand to stop my ministrations on his cock. Andrew pulls me to him in a gentle motion, crushing me against his chest and capturing my mouth.

He leans me back onto the chair and spreads my legs with his, positioning himself between them. My breathing quickens as Andrew lowers his body over mine, and I feel his cock nudging the entrance of my sex. An old fear begins to stir as anguishing memories surface, and I squeeze my eyes shut, terrified by the direction of my thoughts.

I barely notice as I turn my face away, denying him another kiss, once again swallowed by the darkness. My chest feels tight, my head dizzy...

"Fuck!" Andrew's voice pulls me back to reality as he holds my face. "Kate, look at me."

I open my eyes, meeting his gaze, and feel the calm gradually returning to my body as our eyes lock.

"It's me, darling. It's me." His expression is pained. He's as scared as I am. My heart pounds wildly, but I cling to him, refusing to let the painful memories stop me from having this moment.

I kiss him passionately, and he responds. Andrew claims my body, enveloping me in a warm, tight embrace, comforting me in every way.

"I want to continue... please," I nearly beg between the kisses we share, desperate for him. "I want you, Andrew. Inside me."

He groans softly, still holding me tightly, but nods in agreement. "I want you to sit on my cock—it'll be more comfortable for you."

I feel his hard length twitch against my thigh and swallow hard.

"I don't know what to do," I confess, though I feel less anxious about his suggestion.

"I need you to take control, Kate," he pants, his eyes boring into mine. "You'll feel less nervous in this position. You'll be able to control how far you go."

Andrew adjusts himself on the chair, sitting with his legs slightly apart, and instructs me on what to do.

"Hold onto my shoulders and straddle me. When you're ready, lower yourself onto my cock." He grips his length with one hand, taking a deep breath as he waits for me.

With shaky legs, I force myself to do as he says. Kneeling on the chair, I hold onto Andrew's shoulders and swing a leg around his hips as he steadies me by the waist. I glance down at his hard cock waiting for me and nervously bite my lip.

"Do it, Kate," his voice comes out hoarse, commanding.

Still gripping his shoulders, I guide his thick head toward my entrance with my free hand. We both moan as the glans touches my sensitive clit, and Andrew slides a hand between my legs to part the lips of my sex, making penetration easier.

"Lower yourself, darling." I glance down at the space between us, my cheeks heating with the immoral, dirty position. I'm completely exposed to him, my bundle of nerves swollen and aching, flushed red.

I look at Andrew, and he seems as mesmerized as I am. His mouth is set in a tight line, his shoulders tense. Involuntarily, I rub his soft glans against my entrance and nearly climax again from the simple motion. I feel so wet, so slick with my own arousal, it's almost embarrassing how much I've surrendered.

I position his head at my entrance and begin to lower myself slowly. At first, my canal resists, too tight for his thickness, and his cock slips to the side.

"Fuck!" he curses under his breath, and I bite my lip.

More slickness drips from my core, and Andrew's fingers glide over my ass, stroking every inch of my flesh. I try again, positioning his broad tip at my entrance and making subtle, deliberate movements, gently rocking up and down until I feel the pressure of his head stretching me to enter.

"Andrew..." I moan as his hard cock slides a little deeper, stretching me beyond my limit. My eyes widen as I feel his thick shaft filling me.

The pressure is intense, but there's no pain. The lubrication of my arousal makes it easier for him to slip inside, inch by inch.

"Kate," he murmurs, biting his lip. I brace myself on his shoulder, lifting slightly before lowering onto him again. This time, he slides in more easily, making me bite my lip to stifle a scream from the depth of the sensation. I keep lowering myself gradually, taking all of him in, to the last inch, until a dull ache presses against my cervix.

"You're so thick," I whimper, and he pulls me to him, holding me tightly as if to stop me from moving.

"Your pussy is squeezing my cock, and I'm holding back from coming, Kate."

Andrew seeks my mouth again, and I give him everything. I offer him my lips, welcome his tongue against mine. We become a delicious tangle of entwined bodies and locked mouths. His warm skin against mine intoxicates me, and I moan softly, eager to move in his lap and feel his cock sliding inside me.

"I'm taking you to bed now, and I'll slide into your pussy slowly until you come again," he whispers against my mouth. I try to squirm in his arms, desperate to feel more of him. "And you'll keep your eyes on me, Kate. I want your attention focused on me while I fuck you, so you'll never forget that it's me. I want to embed myself in your body and your mind, little fox."

As if I weigh nothing, Andrew grabs me by the ass and lifts me from the chair, still impaled on his hard cock, forcing me to wrap my arms around his neck. He walks slowly across the wooden floor, and with each step, I feel his thick glans pressing against my cervix, driving me insane and drawing moans from my lips.

Andrew lays me down on the bed without pulling out of me. He spreads my legs and places my ankles on his shoulders, leaving me completely open to him and his desires. I moan softly as his hands slide down my abdomen to my breasts. He squeezes both before slowly withdrawing his cock from my vagina, leaving me empty, craving to be filled again.

Only then does he thrust back into me fully, and I cry out, overwhelmed by the pleasure his movement brings. I bring my hand to my mouth and bite my wrist, delirious, squeezing my eyes shut. Andrew doesn't wait a second before sliding his fingers along my face and demanding that I look at him again:

"Here, Kate." He pulls his length out of me and thrusts back in, wrenching gasps from me. "Look at me."

I open my eyes again, propping myself up slightly on my elbows. It's the most deliciously obscene sight I've ever witnessed in my life. I feel as if I'm being split in two as Andrew thrusts in and out of me. My sex grips his entire shaft, and with each movement, he does exactly as he promised. He penetrates me slowly, pushing in to the hilt, making me feel every inch of his arousal, then pulls his cock out of my entrance.

I gasp, scream, feeling my body begin to tremble. Everything intensifies as he fills me again and increases the pace of his thrusts. His large body looms over mine, and the penetration reaches its peak. I feel all of him, deep inside.

"Ah... Andrew! God!" My entire body shakes from the invasion of his impressive cock. He doesn't stop, dominating me with his large hands gripping my thighs, holding them wide open for him.

He swivels his hips and thrusts deeply, filling me completely, to the hilt. I scream again and again, moans of pure pleasure spilling from my mouth. His shaft stretches me beyond my limit, almost to discomfort, almost too much to bear, but the intense sensation growing in waves in my belly tells me I'm on the brink of climaxing again.

His grip on my thighs tightens as Andrew rotates his hips repeatedly. He grinds against my slick canal, burying himself completely inside me. I feel his balls slapping against my ass.

Our eyes lock, completely connected, and then he pulls his cock entirely out of my vulva, replacing it with the touch of his thumb on my clit. I recoil as he begins to rub the swollen nerve, trying to pull away, but his strong arms hold me in place. Jolts of pure pleasure hit me as he intensifies the movements, and I throw my head back.

I thrust my hips upward, wanting to feel everything again, driven mad by the approaching orgasm.

"Andrew!" I scream his name as I lose all control of my body. My legs tremble, and waves of intense pleasure crash over me, sending me out of orbit. And then he penetrates me again, plunging all the way in with a single thrust.

"That's it, little fox, come hard on my cock!" I throw my head back, feeling as though I'll explode.

The penetration intensifies the orgasm, and I dig my nails into the mattress. My sex contracts around his shaft, and I hear Andrew's groans. One of his hands grips my chin, and I lose my breath, overcome by pleasure, madness, and the complete lack of control over my body.

Andrew thrusts once... twice... three times more and digs his fingers into my thighs. I feel his cock pulse inside me and know he's filling my canal with his release. Then he leans further over me, forcing me to look into his face.

"You're mine, Kate. All mine!" I gasp, still trembling, my mind hazy, my thoughts scattered.

His mouth descends on mine, and Andrew kisses me slowly, still buried inside me. I run my hands over his shoulders and neck, almost unable to believe everything I've experienced, everything I've felt. My fingers tangle in his hair as I take a deep breath, embracing this man who gave me everything and asked for nothing in return.

I feel tears welling in my eyes as I struggle to catch my breath.

When Andrew pulls back, I curve my lips into a smile and open my eyes again. He's staring at me with that intense look that always unravels me. His eyes shine, and I feel as though he's worshipping me. I lift a hand and gently touch his face, stroking his beard, his skin... feeling so alive, so much like a woman. A woman capable of anything, of achieving anything in the world.

"Thank you, Andrew. Thank you for everything. You saved my life in every way."

He kisses me again, and the kiss transforms into soft, slow caresses that send shivers down to my soul.

"I'm completely crazy about you, Kate," he declares, and I hold him tighter, feeling the intensity of my emotions bubbling to the surface with all the strength inside me.

And finally, I understand what makes me feel so safe around him, so surrendered and calm. It's because I love him. Realizing this is like being overtaken by an avalanche of emotions.

I love him! I'm completely in love with my best friend's father.

CHAPTER 33

ANDREW

I move to pull out of her after ending the deep kiss. Kate is still crying, but she's smiling too, and her smile stirs something in my chest because I know she's happy. My little fox has finally overcome her greatest fear and given herself to me completely.

Nothing in the world compares to what we've just done here. Feeling Kate climax while calling my name pushed me over the edge.

She lets out a soft moan as my cock slides out of her body, biting her lip as she keeps her gaze locked on mine. I glance down at her flushed, swollen sex, red from our passion and my teasing licks on her sensitive spot. I almost lose my mind when I see my cum dripping out of her, smearing her delicate folds. Kate is beautiful in every way, in every detail.

Her pussy is shaved, her clit redder than usual from the excitement. That small, swollen bud glistens, slick from her arousal. It's intoxicating.

I grip her thighs and press them together, trying to keep my seed from leaking out because, after all, the goal here is for her to conceive. Driven by my own desire, I reach down and push my cum back into her with my fingers. Kate clenches at my touch, and I groan at the feeling of her tight entrance gripping my finger.

"Stay like this, Kate. You need to keep your legs up for a while." She bites her lip and nods as I prop her thighs up.

I stack pillows on the bed to support her and keep her legs elevated. Then I lie down beside her, pulling her into my arms. I position her slightly on top of me, her head resting on my arm.

With my free hand, I caress one of her breasts.

"What do you want to have? A boy or a girl?" I'm curious to know what's on her mind since we've never discussed it.

She looks at me thoughtfully, moistening her lips with her tongue.

"I've never really thought about it, but I don't care about the gender. What about you?"

I take one of Kate's hands and bring it to my lips, kissing her fingers before resting her hand on my chest.

"I don't care either. Boy or girl, I'll love them so much, little fox."

She smiles at me, and I see her eyes glisten with tears.

"I've always wanted a family, Andrew. This baby will be the fulfillment of a lost dream. I never thought I'd have this chance again..." Her voice falters, but her smile widens. "I feel in my heart that it's going to work."

I nod at her, desperate to kiss her again. Desperate to bury myself inside her once more. But I hold back, my eyes scanning her petite frame.

"Now you do, Kate." I touch her lips lightly, and she parts them. "And even if you don't get pregnant now, you still have me."

She takes a deep breath, her hand beginning to trace circles on my chest.

"Andrew... we... I... I don't know what to think. I was so anxious and desperate to have the baby that now I have no idea how I'm going to explain all this to Angelina."

I can't help but laugh, seeing Kate turn completely red at the predicament she's found herself in.

"There's no turning back now," I tease her. "You're going to get pregnant, and sooner or later, your friend will know who the father is." I cup her chin, my smile fading as I continue seriously, "And even if you don't get pregnant, I'm not letting you go, Kate."

Her stunned expression is evident as her mouth falls open.

"I don't understand. What do you mean?"

"I mean that after today, I can't be without you, little fox." Her eyes widen, and Kate tilts her head to look at me directly. I take the opportunity to lean closer to her, our mouths almost touching. "I want you to be mine, Kate. My woman, my girlfriend, my wife. I was a fool to think I could just be the father of your baby. I've never been so wrong. I want the whole package—you and the child."

She opens and closes her mouth a few times, her eyes fixed on my face. Words fail her, but her shocked expression makes it clear she understood every single word.

"Andrew... I... I can't do this." I close my eyes at her rejection, but I decide I'm not giving up.

"What's stopping you?" I ask as she moves to get out of bed.

Kate places her feet on the floor, her back to me, wrapping her arms around herself.

"You don't understand..." Her voice is a broken murmur, and I know she's holding back tears.

I also get up, walking over to her. I stand behind her, close enough to hear her breathing, but I don't touch her.

"What don't I understand?"

She takes a deep breath but doesn't turn to face me.

"I'm a broken woman, Andrew. I can't make you happy. I'm not good for that..."

I lift my hand, intending to touch her shoulder and promise to mend every broken piece of her, but I stop. I don't want to scare her more, so I hold back, even though my chest aches with pain.

"It's okay. Don't think about it now."

She turns to me, her eyes brimming with tears, but I don't wait a second to pull her into my arms. I hold her tightly, knowing it's pointless to fight her demons at this moment.

"Let's take a bath?" She nods silently, and I lead her to the bathroom.

I fill the tub and step in with her, the warm water relaxing us both. I position her between my legs, her back against my chest, and we stay like that for a while. Her head rests on my chest, my hand caressing her breasts and stomach as we simply enjoy each other's touch. I feel her relax against me and pull her closer. My cock stirs at her proximity and her bare skin, but I control myself. After a few minutes, Kate turns her face to me, her hand reaching for my beard.

Her eyes search mine, but her expression is sad, lifeless, and it fills me with a deep sense of anguish.

"What is it, little fox?" I ask, intensifying the caress on her skin, moving my hand to her neck.

"I don't know." She blinks, withdrawing slightly. "Suddenly, I felt this strange sensation in my chest." Kate takes a deep breath, her voice faltering. "I don't want this to end, Andrew. I don't want to wake up tomorrow and have to say goodbye to you, to this place."

"It doesn't have to end, you know that," I say, and she gives me a faint smile, but the curve of her lips is so subtle that the sadness in her eyes overwhelms any trace of happiness.

"But it will end, even if I don't want it to."

I see the pain she carries in her soul, reflected in her ocean-blue irises. My whole body tenses with anguish, my blood boiling at the thought of everything she's endured to reach this state. My little Kate, the girl who owns my heart, is shattered into a million pieces. Maybe not even time can mend the fragments that remain, but I'm willing to try, no matter how much it hurts, no matter if I break myself in the process. After all, what's one more scar for someone who's already been so wounded?

"Please, kiss me," she pleads, and I don't hesitate for a second to grant her wish.

I lean down and claim Kate's lips with mine. My touch is gentle, demanding nothing from her. I only give her the comfort and affection she needs. I hold her tightly in my arms, cherishing her.

After a few minutes, we leave the bathtub, and I wrap Kate in a towel.

I give her a few minutes to get dressed, leaving her alone as I head to the cold storage to grab some cuts of meat for dinner, still wearing nothing but a towel around my waist.

It doesn't take long before Kate joins me, now dressed warmly in pajama pants and a long-sleeved shirt. Together, we prepare dinner and talk a little about the cabin and the places I'd like to show her the next day.

Little by little, the sadness I'd seen in her eyes earlier gives way to joy, and she starts to smile with me. Occasionally, I catch her sneaking glances at my abdomen, and I notice Kate biting her lip when she thinks I'm not looking.

My body heats up, my cock hardens, and the desire surges within me once more.

When I lead her to bed, her bright smile lights up her face. I can barely hide my excitement, as my arousal is all too obvious, tenting the towel wrapped around me. Her gaze falls to my groin as I lie on the bed and grab a pillow to prop my head, angling my body slightly. I gesture for her to come closer, eager to have her again.

"Come here." Kate lets out a mischievous grin, her eyes lingering on the bulge in my towel.

I grin back, placing both arms behind my head. I relax, watching her closely.

She approaches, climbing onto the bed. She crawls toward me until her face is level with mine, lying on her stomach beside me.

"And now? What do I do?" she asks playfully, and I reach out to touch her neck.

"Now, you can take off your clothes." She gasps, the sparkle in her eyes growing. "I want you to sleep with me naked, little fox."

"Why?" She bites her lip, her gaze shifting to the tented towel over my erection.

My cock twitches under her scrutiny, and I bite my lower lip to stifle a groan.

"Because I want to feel your warm skin against mine, with nothing in between."

Kate looks back at me, her expression serious now. Her breathing quickens, but she does exactly as I ask. Without breaking eye contact, she kneels and pulls her shirt over her head, letting the fabric fall onto the bed beside her. Her small, perky breasts are revealed, the pink of her nipples contrasting beautifully against her pale skin, as white as the snow outside. She does the same with her pants. Her tiny fingers hook into the elastic waistband, and she takes a deep breath as she starts to slide the fabric down.

I notice she's not wearing panties as the fabric slips below her hips, exposing her gorgeous pussy. It forms a delicate triangle between her legs. I swallow hard, unable to look away, committing every detail of her body to memory.

Slowly, she sheds the last piece of clothing and kneels before me, waiting, entirely mine.

I rise as well, pulling at the towel covering my arousal until I'm in the same position as her. The two of us are face-to-face, naked and ravenous for each other.

"Touch me, sweetheart." She gasps, her gaze shy as it drifts down to my cock.

Kate raises a trembling hand to my abdomen, caressing the skin, exploring its texture. I close my eyes and tilt my head back, surrendering to the pleasure of her touch. When her small hands finally reach my length, I'm already on the edge, completely overcome with lust for her. I open my eyes again, nearly losing my sanity as I watch Kate tentatively stroke my cock, as though she's studying her movements.

"Does this feel good?" she asks, and I hold back the urge to push her onto the bed and thrust into her in one swift motion.

"Yes, Kate, it feels so good."

Her grip tightens, and I clench my jaw. I begin to move my hips in time with her hand, and she slides a finger up to the sensitive tip. Kate starts applying gentle pressure to the head of my cock, her motions clumsy but delicate, driving me to the brink. Her touch is inexperienced, uncertain, but it doesn't matter. Every look, every movement she makes sets my blood on fire.

"Andrew?" she calls my name, and I let out a moan.

"Humm."

"Can I put it in my mouth?" I feel my lungs losing air, my heart racing. Everything inside me boils when I hear what she says.

"You can do whatever you want, little fox." My voice barely comes out.

Kate nods and studies my cock again, as if she's still deciding how to proceed. She uses my abdomen for support and leans on the bed to keep her head close to my cock.

She grabs my shaft, squeezes it, and brings it closer to her face. The slow, delicious torment leaves me in ecstasy, trembling. I'm desperate to feel the heat of her mouth around my length.

"Suck it, Kate." I urge her to continue, and she moves closer. I feel her warm breath on the tip, and my abdomen tightens as a moan escapes my throat.

She does as I say. Her tongue glides over her lips, moistening the soft flesh, torturing me in the process, before opening her mouth and closing her plump lips around the head of my cock. My entire body trembles, and I gasp, letting out a guttural groan. My hands find their way to Kate's hair, and I have to summon every ounce of self-control not to thrust my entire length into her throat.

"Fuck, Kate!" I grab a handful of her dark hair and tug lightly.

She starts timidly, curious, exploring the terrain. Her tongue slides over the soft tip, tasting me. Little by little, she takes more, her awkward and subtle movements driving me insane. A wet sound escapes her mouth as she sucks, and the faint noise of her working my cock almost makes me lose it.

I tighten my grip on her hair and pull her head back, sliding my cock out of her mouth before I spill everything inside her. Kate looks up at me, confused, her lips glistening with the evidence of my arousal.

"My turn to taste you."

Her eyes widen, and she opens her mouth to say something, but no words come out. I notice the blush on her cheeks and curl my lips into a smile of amusement and excitement. It still surprises me how shy she gets, even after everything we've done. Even after I've almost turned her inside out with how hard I've taken her. Her startled expression sends shivers through my cock; her delicate, innocent demeanor leaves me breathless as I pant for her.

Kate resumes her previous position, kneeling, and I move closer to her. I place my hand on her face, caressing her cheek. My fingers trace over her soft lips, sliding my thumb across the flesh that just sucked my cock. My exploration continues to her breasts. I pinch her hardened nipples between my fingers, and she gasps, staring at me with that intense look that leaves me breathless.

Bit by bit, I begin to explore her skin, sliding my fingers down her abdomen and to her inner thighs. Kate flinches when I reach the folds of her pussy, but she doesn't pull away, even though she's clearly nervous. I start exploring her sex, my eyes never leaving hers. I part her delicate folds with my fingers, exposing the sensitive bundle of nerves, and caress her clit. She moans softly, biting her lips, and my skin heats as her arousal coats my fingers.

I lower my mouth to hers, sliding my tongue over her lips while my fingers continue to play with her pussy. I taste myself on her saliva, going wild at the memory of her taking me so innocently.

"Lie on your stomach for me," I say, and she gasps against my mouth.

"Andrew, what are you going to do?" she asks hoarsely.

"Make you feel good."

Her chest rises and falls with her quickened breaths, but she complies without protest. I see the curiosity in her eyes, eager to learn everything I have to teach her—every way to feel pleasure. She lies on her stomach, and I grab a pillow to place under her pelvis, lifting her hips. I guide her through the process, and Kate raises her body so I can adjust the pillow beneath her.

I go crazy seeing her like this, practically on all fours. By the time she settles back over the pillow, my blood is already boiling with the need to ravish her with my tongue.

Slowly, I cover Kate's body with mine and start by kissing her ear, nibbling on her neck. She lets out soft moans, her skin covered in goosebumps, delicious gasps escaping her throat. I trail kisses down her shoulder, moving her dark hair aside, and continue exploring her skin with my tongue. I move slowly, savoring every inch of her, licking and sucking as I go.

Kate writhes beneath my touch, but I don't stop. The more she moans, the crazier I get. When I reach her ass, though, I completely lose my mind with desire. The view of her tight pussy in this position drives me wild.

Moaning, I grip her ass cheeks and spread them apart, revealing her tight little asshole and the slick opening of her pussy. She squirms and I hear her hoarse protests, but I pay them no mind.

"Andrew!" she squirms, reaching back to grab my hand, trying to push me away. "What are you doing?"

Her whiny tone only makes me more intoxicated, and I lower my face to Kate's ass. I start biting the soft flesh, savoring the little yelps escaping her mouth, and then bury my face between her delicious cheeks, driving my tongue into her tight hole.

"Andrew!" Kate cries softly, writhing and moaning, completely overwhelmed.

I start sucking and licking this private part of her body before trailing down to her pussy, taking the swollen bundle of nerves into my mouth.

Kate whimpers, her body twitching, but she no longer tries to escape my touch. She's consumed by desire and pleasure.

I spread her ass wider, leaving Kate's sex completely exposed to me. My tongue glides over her swollen clit before plunging into her channel. She screams, trembling, but I don't let her come. When her body starts shaking and she's babbling incoherently, I flip Kate onto her back, positioning her face-up, and cover her body with mine.

My mouth seeks hers, my hands gripping her thighs and spreading them wide, and only then do I guide my cock to the entrance of her pussy.

I start to push in slowly, and she lets out a soft gasp, her nails digging into my back, scratching the skin. I deepen the kiss, sliding my tongue into her mouth, moving it in and out in sync with the way I begin to move at her entrance.

I penetrate her slowly, inch by inch. I make her feel every bit of my length, leaving Kate breathless, gasping, and trembling as I give her everything I have.

"Andrew... I..." Her voice falters, and Kate throws her head back, her mouth falling open.

"Come for me, little fox," I demand, my voice nearly gone, as I feel her body begin to shake.

I lift my torso and start to thrust harder. My hands grip Kate's thighs as I drive deep into her, making her take every last inch of me. There's not a single part of my cock left outside her.

Her body writhes, and I feel her tight walls clamp down on my shaft. Her pussy contracts, her legs tremble, and Kate bucks her hips against mine, coming hard on my cock, crying out in a mix of pleasure and desperation as her orgasm takes over.

It's too much for me to handle. My fingers dig into her thighs, and I shut my eyes tightly as my own climax hits me hard. I start coming inside her, my balls tightening, my legs faltering, and sweat breaking out on my forehead. Wave after wave, I spill myself deep into her, her slick walls milking me as they contract around my shaft.

CHAPTER 34

KATE

I wake up a bit disoriented and far too early. The day isn't fully bright yet, but through the glass window, I can see the calmness outside. Judging by the level of the snowflakes, it didn't snow last night.

I shift in bed, careful not to wake Andrew from his deep sleep, and slowly begin crawling out of the heap of blankets.

Accidentally, I uncover his back, and Andrew stirs, turning onto his back. I stay still, watching to see if he'll wake up, but his sleep is so deep that he only takes a deep breath and continues sleeping.

Wrapped in a sheet, I can't help but admire how strong and masculine he is. Every pore of Andrew's body screams virility, and I end up biting my lip, imagining everything we did in this bed. I never thought a man and a woman could find so much pleasure together, and just thinking about it takes my breath away.

Everything we've experienced will forever be etched in my memory. It will be impossible to forget our kisses, the caresses we exchanged, everything he made me feel in his arms.

Andrew made me feel truly like a woman. And when I had him inside me for the first time, it wasn't revulsion I felt. It was love. I loved him even more at that moment; I connected with him completely, and now, when I think about all of this ending, it feels like my life has lost its meaning.

However, I try not to dwell on it now. I don't want to tarnish the time we've spent together with sad thoughts, even though I'm restless inside.

Slowly, I move closer to him again and lightly touch his chest. I feel his skin shiver under my fingers, but I keep going, exploring his torso. Then I go further, allowing boldness to consume me entirely as I remove part of the blanket covering his pelvis. I'm surprised to find his hard member, even as Andrew sleeps.

My core throbs with want for him again, and I let out a quiet gasp. Carefully, I reach out and wrap my hand around Andrew's shaft, holding it between my fingers. I feel it twitch, and a deep sigh escapes his mouth. I'm fascinated as I observe every detail. The thick head is a reddish hue, shaped like a juicy strawberry that makes my mouth water. He's magnificent—thick, large, veined. My fingers can't even close around his massive girth. My mouth waters at the thought of tasting him again, and my body shudders with desire.

I slide my finger along the soft glans and hear a moan escape Andrew's lips. Then I pull back, hesitant to continue and risk getting caught by him. A smile spreads across my face at the thought—he'd definitely enjoy it, but I'd be mortified if he caught me holding him like this while he slept.

I cover his hips again and start to leave the bed when I hear his husky voice calling my name.

My heart races, but I don't wait even a second. Holding back a laugh, I get to my feet and tighten the sheet around my body. I head toward the kitchen without looking back.

"Kate, come back here!"

I grab the kettle and turn on the stove, intending to make tea. While I'm working with the stove, I hear Andrew's footsteps behind me, and my heart picks up pace. A mix of desire and nervousness floods me, and I bite my lip because I know he won't let this opportunity slip away. I feel his presence close behind me as he places his hand on my waist over the sheet. I shiver from head to toe.

"Why did you run away from me?" he asks huskily, his mouth brushing the curve of my neck.

"I didn't know you were awake," I reply breathlessly, losing my composure just from his proximity.

Andrew's hands begin exploring my body as he searches for an opening in the sheet.

"I woke up when you let go of my cock and covered me up again. It felt so good, little fox."

I smile softly and try to stop his hand as he manages to slip it under the warm sheet. My attempt to stop him is futile.

"No, Andrew, not now!" I push him away, laughing, and turn to face him while holding the sheet to hide my nudity.

With his strong arms, he grabs me by the waist and moves me away from the stove. Andrew looks unbelievably handsome now, a relaxed smile on his face and his hair tousled. He's wearing pajama pants, but the fabric does nothing to hide the bulge that has formed in his pelvis. With a single tug, he removes the sheet covering my body, leaving me completely naked.

I bite my lip again, covering my breasts with my hands, feeling both shocked by his boldness and intensely aroused. Andrew doesn't need to say a word for me to understand what's on his mind. I take a step back, seeing the fiery determination in his eyes, and he takes a step toward me. We keep this playful chase going—me retreating, him advancing—until I'm trapped between his strong body and the rustic wooden table.

Breathing heavily, I let out a small squeal when he grabs me by the waist again and lifts me to sit on the table. His hands grip my thighs, spreading them apart as he leans them outward.

I inhale sharply, feeling utterly exposed and vulnerable to him. Propping myself up on my elbows to maintain balance, I gasp and moan. Without a word, he leans down, his tongue delving between my legs, licking my intimacy from entrance to the sensitive bundle of nerves.

I cry out, tangling a hand in his hair while instinctively trying to pull away. He shows no mercy, licking and teasing my clit, making me see stars. He uses two fingers to spread my lips and licks my clit with unrelenting intensity, flicking and teasing the sensitive flesh, biting and licking until I can't take it anymore and shatter into a million pieces under his tongue.

My core is still throbbing when he pulls his cock free from his pants and aligns himself at my entrance. Andrew fills me in one firm, powerful thrust, drawing a scream from my throat.

I take him fully inside me, even as I feel him pushing my walls beyond their limit. The pressure is intense, my cries are loud, but the pleasure his cock gives me leaves me weak. With one hand, he pulls me to the edge of the table, and I wrap my legs around his hips, while the other hand grips my waist. I feel his deep intrusion, his strength surrounding my body. An explosion of emotions overtakes me, and I cling to his neck as if my life depends on it.

He presses our foreheads together and slows the intensity of his thrusts. He pushes in and pulls out so slowly, giving me everything he has. And suddenly, I no longer know who I am, or what I'm becoming. I can't imagine a life without Andrew; I can't imagine waking up in the morning to find the bed empty.

Tears of anguish well up in my eyes, but I hold them back with all my strength, refusing to let them fall while I'm in his arms.

Then I lean back and surrender completely, allowing myself to feel pleasure one last time before it all ends and our lives return to normal.

"WHY DID YOU WAKE UP so early? Couldn't sleep?" he asks a few hours later while I finish packing the suitcase. The two days we spent together were unforgettable, but the time has come to go home, and it's tearing me apart.

After our lovemaking on the table, I turned off the stove and we cleaned up before going back to bed. We stayed curled up together, just enjoying each other's company, savoring the cold and the tranquility of the snowy cabin. At some point, we fell asleep.

"To be honest, not really. I'm a bit anxious," I reply, continuing the task.

I glance at Andrew and see him staring at me with an unusually serious expression. He seems lost in thought but doesn't comment further. I remain silent as well, just waiting for the moment to leave.

I know I shouldn't close myself off like this, but it's inevitable. I can't help but dwell on the fact that in a few hours we'll part ways, and these are our last moments together.

I think about what Andrew said, about me being his girlfriend, and my heart shatters into a million pieces because I know I'm not the woman for a man like him. My body feels tainted, my soul stained. Everything in me is broken, and I can't let him drown in my darkness. I can't let Andrew carry my demons with me. Sooner or later, he would break too.

We finish packing in silence. When everything is ready, Andrew turns to me and moves closer: "What's wrong, Kate? You're so quiet, so lost in thought."

"It's nothing. I think I'm just a little tired." I hate lying to him, but I don't know how to explain how I feel.

How could I tell him that we can't be together because I'm a coward? Because I don't know if I have the strength to fight my demons? That every time I imagine myself living with a man, I remember my mother and Garath?

His fingers graze my face, stroking my skin gently. I close my eyes, feeling my heart ache and my chest tighten unbearably.

"Shall we?" he asks, and I nod, opening my eyes again.

The drive back is quiet. My focus is on the white landscape covering the pines, but my thoughts are all about him.

As we approach Queens, I ask Andrew to drop me off at home so I can unpack, change clothes, and pick up Spot before nightfall. He does as I ask, but when he parks the car, he doesn't unlock the doors right away.

He turns to me, sliding his hand to the back of my neck and pulling me in for a kiss. His mouth claims mine slowly, his firm tongue parting my lips and slipping into my mouth. But the kiss is brief. I hear his heavy breathing as he rests his forehead against mine.

"Come home, Kate," he pleads almost desperately.

"I can't," I reply softly.

He nods after a few moments, pulling back.

I step out of the car, and Andrew circles around to grab my suitcase from the trunk before returning to the vehicle. I wave goodbye and attempt a smile, but it falters as soon as he drives off, disappearing from view. Tears well up in my eyes instead.

I enter my house, but I don't bother unpacking. The sun is nearly setting, so I hurry to pick up Spot.

I arrive at Angelina's house a few minutes later.

My friend greets me with a warm smile. Caleb and Spot race toward me, and I crouch to scoop up the little boy and pet the dog's head. Kaleo, who's playing on the floor, also crawls toward me. I'm welcomed with so much joy that I feel like the most important person in the world.

The conversation is brief since I need to head home. However, I promise Angelina that we'll go out for coffee the next day, and I'll tell her everything about the trip.

On the way back, I pass Andrew's house and notice that his car isn't in the driveway, and there's no movement inside. Apparently, he hasn't returned home, and somehow, that stirs a storm in my stomach. Jealousy begins to creep in, knowing I have no idea where he is.

I get home and immediately pour some food for Spot before heading to my room for a shower and a change of clothes.

As night falls, I begin preparing dinner and decide on mac and cheese, a simple and comforting meal. I'm nearly finished setting the table when I hear Spot barking at the back door. I see the little dog grow agitated before darting toward the doggie door.

"Spot!" I shout after him, but the dog doesn't even pay attention.

He dashes through the doggie door and continues barking outside, but his barks grow fainter and fainter until I hear nothing at all.

I wait for him to return for a few minutes, but he doesn't come back, and I'm already starting to worry. I open the back door and call for Spot, but there's no sign of him. Maybe I'm overreacting, and he's just off chasing a cat or a squirrel, but there's something strange in the air, as if my sixth sense is screaming at me to stay alert.

I place a hand over my chest, massaging the area as an unsettling sensation washes over me. A chill runs down my spine, like something is out of place. Once more, I call for Spot, but the only response is the deafening, icy silence.

Fearfully, I head back to my room and grab my phone to call Andrew. Despite everything, he's the first person that comes to mind, and I know he wouldn't hesitate to help me in any way he can.

I dial his number as I step back outside, continuing to call for my little dog.

I walk through the yard and onto the snow-covered street, still calling for Spot while Andrew's phone rings.

After a few seconds, he picks up, and the first thing I hear is the loud sound of live music in the background.

"Andrew!" I call his name, desperation thick in my voice.

"Kate? Is everything okay?"

"Andrew, Spot... I don't know, he's gone!"

"What do you mean he's gone? Where are you?"

Then I hear a sound ahead—a whining, almost like a baby's cry. I quicken my pace, pulling the phone away from my ear, and find Spot lying on the ground a few meters away.

Panic grips me as I realize the snow around him is soaked with blood. Overwhelmed with fear, I kneel beside him and see the blood seeping from two deep cuts on his chest and ribs.

"Andrew, I found him! He's dying, oh my God!" I scream into the phone, completely overcome with panic.

"Kate, for God's sake, get back inside. I'm coming to you."

I can barely hear Andrew's words because I drop the phone on the ground and cradle Spot's trembling head, feeling like my world has collapsed in a matter of seconds.

"Kate!" I hear Andrew shouting through the phone and switch it to speaker mode.

"He's been stabbed!" I cry, tears streaming down my face as my voice cracks. "He's..."

But I can't finish the sentence. Everything within me freezes as I feel a large, gloved hand cover my mouth and grip me tightly from behind, pinning my body by the waist. Panic floods through me, but I have no chance to fight back or resist, as the next moment, a blow to my head knocks me completely unconscious.

CHAPTER 35

ANDREW

"Kate! Kate!" I get up from the chair and shout for her, but the girl doesn't respond again.

I hear footsteps on the other end of the line and the call ends without any explanation. All of my senses go on high alert, and panic takes over me. I feel like I'm losing control, everything in me destabilizes, and the anguish takes its toll too quickly.

Something very bad has happened, my sharpened instincts know that for sure. And the worst part is, I need to keep my damn calm until I find a solution and figure out what the hell is going on, but it's hard to act rationally when it's my Kate possibly in danger.

I rush out of the bar where I went to drink a little after she refused to come home with me. I leave a few dollars on the table and run outside to find my car. As I walk, I call Alexander, and he picks up on the second ring:

"Speak!"

The two of us never had a close relationship, and we don't even talk frequently, only when necessary. Alexander does what's needed when I ask, and I uphold the agreement of not putting my son-in-law behind bars. However, I know he loves my daughter, and because of her, I trust that he'll do whatever it takes to help me find Kate.

"Kate is in danger. Arm yourself as much as you can and head to her house. I'll be there in a few minutes with reinforcements, I'm a little far."

I hang up and get into my car, starting it right after. I pick up the phone again and call the agent I set up to watch over Kate's safety. His phone rings, but the call goes to voicemail.

"Damn it! Pick up! Damn it!"

I slap my hand on the steering wheel in front of me, completely trembling, out of my mind. I start blaming myself for not insisting more for Kate to come home with me; that way, she wouldn't be in danger. But what could I have done? As much as I wanted to tie her up and take her home, I didn't want to pressure her, especially after what happened at the cabin. It was necessary to let Kate breathe a little, think for herself, and make a decision. I just didn't imagine something bad could happen in the meantime.

I slam my foot on the accelerator and speed through the streets of New York. My chest feels suffocated, and a deep agony takes over me. Anger begins to grow inside me, and I swear to myself that I will destroy the life of any creature who dared to lay a finger on my Kate. Without wasting a second, I make a direct call to my most trusted agents, to make sure they'll get the message. I give them her address and issue specific orders to start the investigation, mapping, and tracking until they find her.

I arrive at the girl's house a few minutes later. I get out of the car, dazed, holding my weapon, and run towards the entrance, praying softly that she's okay and safe. However, when I see Alexander coming to meet me, his expression makes it clear something serious has happened.

"Where is she, Alex?" I ask, almost insane.

The man shakes his head in denial, closing his expression, and places his hand on my shoulder, as if trying to calm me down.

"No sign of her. When I arrived, I found Spot stabbed in the back alley and called for animal emergency." He slides a gloved hand into his jacket pocket and pulls out a cell phone. "I found this, I imagine it belongs to her."

Panic takes over me as the reality sinks in, and I have to control myself not to collapse to my knees. I inhale and exhale, feeling my heart race so fast I can almost hear the frantic beats. I look at Kate's phone and hold it carefully, feeling a suffocating lump in my throat that leaves me breathless. Everything seems to be crumbling around me, and for the first time in my life, I stand still, frozen by shock.

"And the dog?" I'm still staring at the phone.

"It's hard to say if he'll survive."

I notice the veterinary service is already attending to Spot, and I move to go there. However, the man stops me.

"There's something else you need to see before anyone else." He says, and I look at him seriously.

Alexander gestures for me to follow him, and walks toward the back of the house where Kate is living. He takes me straight to the spot where he found Spot stabbed. The lighting is poor here, but I can clearly see the volume of blood on the snow and the footprints. There's a real mess on the ground, as if something or someone had been dragged. Everything inside me boils as I think of my girl in danger now, in the hands of some lunatic.

"There." Then he points toward a bush, a few meters away, and we both walk in that direction.

I close my eyes when I find what I feared most.

The agent I assigned to watch Kate is lying there on the ground, lifeless, with his neck slit and his eyes still open. The blood that spilled from the wound forms red puddles on the snow, creating a terrifying scene.

I hear the sound of the agents' cars approaching, and I clench my fists, feeling my rage consume me from the inside out. The place turns into a full-on task force, as I have the most experienced trackers in the country under my command. And I swear to myself that if I have to bring New York to its knees, I will, until I find my woman and bring her home. This is a promise.

CHAPTER 36

KATE

I force my eyelids to open, but an excruciating pain in my head stops me from continuing. Everything is too confusing, it's like I'm not actually inside my body, but in another dimension. I feel my arms numb and try to move them, but I have no strength, or something is preventing me. I can't tell.

A painful moan escapes my throat, and once again I force myself to open my eyes, despite the pain. Everything is spinning around me, my vision is blurred, and the only thing I hear is the crackling of a fire a few meters away.

When I finally manage to focus on something in front of me, my heart freezes when I realize that I'm not where I should be: at my house. The place is unfamiliar, stuffy, and dirty, but the dim lighting doesn't allow me to analyze everything properly.

I quickly lock my eyes and strong memories rush into my head like a whirlwind. I remember Spot barking in the kitchen and then going outside through the pet door. I remember my call to Andrew and the moment I went after the little dog in the street. And when I found him...

Oh my God. I found Spot stabbed in the snow, bleeding... dying... and then everything goes blank.

A desperate sob escapes my throat, and I feel the urge to scream, but I can't make a sound. My mouth is gagged with some sort of tape. When I start to regain all my senses, my heart stops beating as

I realize my wrists are tied above my head and my feet are hanging, barely touching the ground.

I move to look around, feeling panic take over me completely, and I realize I'm in some sort of closed warehouse. There's an improvised fireplace burning a few meters away from me, and near it, there are some logs of wood.

I squirm more, trying with all my might to free myself, but all my movements are in vain. I try to make noise, call for help, anything, but nothing works.

The numbness in my arms intensifies, and I feel tears of fear streaming down my face. I close and open my eyes, trying to control the panic that threatens to take over me, and for a while, I succeed, but as seconds and minutes pass, the pain in my body from the uncomfortable position increases, and I sob quietly, consumed by desperation.

I think of Andrew, I think of Spot. None of this would be happening if I had gone home with him, and thinking about it brings such a huge regret to my heart that I feel my body tremble with anguish and fear, thinking that I may never see either of them again. The memory of Spot bloodied in the snow comes like a knife to my heart, tearing my flesh into little pieces. I want to scream in pain, but I can't even do that.

I grunt, I squirm, trying with all my might to break free. Nothing. The only thing I manage to do is run out of breath, and with each second, I get more terrified. Whoever put me here knew exactly what they were doing and...

God. No! No! Please, no!

My thoughts stop when I think about who could have done this to me. I put my head to work amidst the turmoil of emotions, and when the possibilities finally come together, my eyes widen, and I feel like I'm going to die of panic.

I think of Garath returning to my mother's house after years in prison, I think of that day in the park when I thought I saw the man, I think of my own mother showing up at Andrew's house, saying that I needed to go home at his request.

It can't be! It can't be!

I close my eyes, and it's like going back in time. I see Garath perfectly in my mind, on top of me, stealing my innocence and then leaving me bleeding in the bed to die from hemorrhaging.

Thick tears bathe my face, and the fear of seeing him again in front of me hits me hard. I force my thoughts to turn to Andrew, but all the futures I imagine from now on seem too dark. Then I cling to our moments in the cabin, trying to remember each of the sensations he made me feel, every detail of his touch on my skin. I can almost hear his voice calling my name, making me a woman, making me happy.

Another sob escapes my throat when I remember that I rejected him simply because I am too weak. But I refuse to continue being weak, I refuse to allow Garath to steal the golden years of my life again and separate me from Andrew. I refuse to let him destroy me again.

Minutes pass as I remain focused on keeping my sanity. I won't allow myself to lose focus, I won't allow myself to fall into despair. However, it's hard not to feel the dread swirling and sinking into my veins when I hear footsteps on the other side of the door. It's hard not to wish for death when I know I'm going through hell.

And suddenly, the door opens with a creaking sound, and what I feared the most happens. It's like seeing the shadows of a nightmare appear before me, in flesh and bone.

Garath stares at me with vacant eyes and lips curled into an ironic smile, loaded with malice. He walks slowly toward me, one foot after the other. I hear the clinking of his shoes on the beaten concrete floor, every second closer, more dangerous, more terrifying.

The man is dressed in black from head to toe. His body is covered by a thick black coat, and on his head, a hat of the same shade.

His eyes lock on mine in a fierce, so malevolent way that it sends chills through my soul, and I know deep down that Garath won't let what I did slide, because it was my testimony to the police, along with the exams, that put him in prison.

I see two more men approaching behind him. Both are smiling at me, both are strong and holding a weapon, both look at me as if I'm a piece of meat, and I know I have no chance of escaping from here. One of them is as tall as Garath, with dark hair and a large beard. The other is a little shorter and blonde.

I feel the fear invade me, but I control myself as much as I can, even though my body is trembling from head to toe. At every moment, I think of Andrew, clinging to the memory of him to keep myself from losing my mind.

"Hello, dear little daughter." Garath closes the distance between us, getting so close that I can smell the cigarette smoke on his breath. Instantly, my stomach churns.

I stare back at him, feeling the rage eat me from the inside, much more than the fear.

He raises a hand, sliding his dirty fingers across my face, leaving me even more dazed by his proximity, but I don't lower my head, I don't look away, I don't allow myself to be oppressed by the threat he represents, even though inside I'm about to explode.

"You still have such soft skin, Kate." He says in a provocative tone, and the two men near him laugh.

"So it's her. The little girl who made you lose your mind and your freedom." One of them, the tallest with dark hair, steps closer and also slides his hand across my face, holding my chin. "It's a shame that this pale skin will be so marked after we're done with you."

The blonde one also steps closer, but this time his touch is on my neck.

"So soft..." He tilts his head between my hair, and I close my eyes, letting out a sigh of pure terror. "So fragrant. Don't be so cruel with her, Garath. I want to feel life in her body when you're done, I don't like having sex with corpses."

The men laugh, and I notice the moment Garath crouches down and pulls a knife from the shaft of his boot.

"Don't be shy, boys." He brings the sharp object toward my eyes and slides it down, until it reaches my neck.

Garath doesn't wait a second to grab the collar of my coat and rip the fabric from top to bottom with the blade.

I grunt when I realize what he's doing, trying to protect myself from his touch and approach, squirming and using my feet to kick him, but none of my efforts matter much when I can barely touch the ground with my feet, and my arms are burning with pain.

Garath continues with the task he set out to do while being watched by the other men. He tears my clothes apart. He cuts the jackets I'm wearing and throws them on the floor in pieces, leaving me with only my pants and a bra, trembling from the cold.

I grunt softly, trying to fight, but it's in vain. The men laugh at my efforts, and one of them takes the knife from Garath's hands.

"Are you cold, Kate? You're all goosebumps." He moves towards my breasts, but Garath stops him with just a command.

"I'll do it, Travor!"

The man's eyes are locked on mine, as red as liquid fire.

Garath moves closer and grabs my hair, pulling the strands hard. I tilt my head back as pain radiates from my scalp, and I feel like I'm dying inside when he says:

"I just won't fuck you again, Kate, because I like little girls. You're too old now. But do you know my friends?" The grip on my hair tightens, and he forces me to look at the two men in front of me. "They're organ traffickers, and they're happy with the little gift I gave them. Isn't that beautiful, sweetheart? Now you're going to pay for ratting me out."

Then Garath's hand slides down to the tape covering my mouth, and he pulls it off in one quick move, making me scream in pain in the process.

"Bastard! Damn it!" I shout, spitting in Garath's direction.

In response, he laughs and slaps my face, making my head snap to the side. An excruciating pain fills my jaw, and my ears ring.

But Garath doesn't seem satisfied, because the next moment he uses the knife to cut my bra in half, exposing my breasts to everyone in the warehouse.

"You're a bitch, Kate, and bitches like to expose themselves."

The men laugh, getting closer, and Garath holds me by the waist from behind.

I just clench my teeth, feeling the resentment invade me like a black mass that corrodes from the inside and destroys everything.

"Look, boys, how beautiful this bitch's breasts are." The filthy hands slide across my ribs, and one of them advances, touching and squeezing until he grabs both of my breasts with his dirty hands.

"You're going to die, Garath." A tear slides down my face as I feel my dignity being thrown away once again.

I close my eyes and try to elevate my thoughts away, to Andrew, Angelina, and the children.

And then Garath brings me back to reality, delivering another punch to my face, this time on the left side.

"Coward!" I scream, but I refuse to cry, trying to be strong, trying to resist the pain. I can't bow my head to him, even if he kills me.

He lunges again, and the blow to my head disorients me. I feel my vision blur, I feel my arms lose strength, the world starts spinning around me, and the strong taste of rust fills my mouth.

I hear the men laughing, but it's like I'm losing consciousness. And I really think that's what's happening for a few seconds, until

I feel a pair of thick hands grab me by the neck and squeeze hard, cutting off my air.

"Right now, at this very moment, your little federal lover thinks he's dealing with a serial killer, when in reality, there are many of them out there. He'll never trace a single clue, they all lead to a dead end." I hear his laugh, full of scorn. "Yes, my love. Daddy researched everything about you. I've been watching you from a distance, Kate, even without leaving your mom's house. I knew everything you were doing, I have my contacts."

Garath spits the words out, but I don't even know what he means when he talks about a serial killer. Everything sounds confusing, distant, terrifying. However, I record every detail of what he says about having kept me under surveillance.

Then he loosens his grip on my neck, and I gasp, pulling air into my lungs, coughing.

"What do you want?" I murmur, breathless.

He caresses my face, running his hands over the bruises he himself caused.

"You're mine, sweetheart. Even though I don't feel aroused by you anymore, Kate, you belong to me, you're mine just like your mother. And I do what I want with what's mine. And because of that, I'll make good money off your organs, after the men use you like bitches in heat, and your body will be thrown on the street, just like the other girls."

"You're crazy, Garath. Andrew will find you and..."

I receive another slap in response, and once again the ringing in my ear returns with full force.

"Remember, Kate. This slap was because you let the bastard touch you." And another punch lands on my chin. "And this one is for being a bitch."

I feel my senses dissipate, and I no longer know if I have the strength to stay awake. Little by little, I feel consciousness slipping away, and the price of physical pain surfaces.

At some point, I wake up with a start, completely dazed. I think I've had a nightmare, but I nearly faint when I realize I'm in the same place, practically hanging from the ceiling.

I no longer feel my arms, I don't have the strength to act. The cold is intense, and the only reason I haven't gone into hypothermia is because I'm near the fire.

Then Garath's voice pulls me back to reality, and I tremble from head to toe. He's behind me, not very close, but close enough for me to hear his movements.

"Did you sleep well, sweetheart?"

I don't answer him, I remain silent, lost in the pain and discomfort that radiates throughout my body.

The weight of my injuries is taking its toll. I realize I can't open my eyes properly, and my whole face is throbbing.

However, what I hear next makes all my senses snap to attention, and I feel my heart freeze. The blood starts to boil in my veins, and I hold my breath. Tears of pure panic well up in my eyes.

"I'm scared! I want my mommy!" Oh my God, it's the voice of a little girl. Garath has a girl here.

I hear him chuckle, and my stomach churns again. The turmoil in my gut is so overwhelming that I have to use all my strength not to throw up my last meal.

"Garath... what are you doing?" Tears fall hard, and desperation takes over me. "Garath, let her go, please..."

He laughs, and his cowardly laughter sinks into my ears like a hammer.

I have the impulse to kill him with my own hands, I have the urge to exterminate this bastard from the face of the earth, so he never hurts another child again.

I hear the little girl's whimper, followed by another laugh from Garath, and I feel my heart break into millions of pieces. I sob quietly, reliving everything I've been through, feeling the pain and fear that she is feeling. For the first time in so long, I pray, I whisper in prayer, hoping that if there is a God, He helps this child. I don't mind dying, maybe my pain will finally end. But the little girl, she can't go through this. I can't go through this again, reliving everything through the suffering of a child.

"Please God. Please!" I sob. "I have no other resources, I have no one else to turn to. My only resource is You. So, if you really exist, if You really care for your own, please help this little girl. She's innocent and suffering at the hands of a monster."

The sobs prevent me from continuing my murmurs, but I search for faith, I search to believe, I beg for help, with all my heart, with all my soul.

"I want my mommy!" And she cries, and I want to die.

I hear Garath's footsteps on the concrete floor, and he appears in my line of sight, holding a beautiful little girl by the hand, around seven or eight years old.

"Let her go, Garath, please, I'll do anything." Another sob cuts through me. "Please."

"Don't be ridiculous, Kate. She's just a toy, and you can't give me anything in return. After all, she's already mine."

The brown irises are shining with tears. She stares at me, frightened, rubbing one of her eyes with her free hand.

Her hair is as blonde as her eyelashes, and it's messy, forming a tangled mess around her head. The little girl is wearing a long woolen men's shirt with long sleeves that reaches the floor. Her attention is focused on me, and she blinks several times.

"Did you also get lost from your mommy?" She asks, and her tearful voice goes straight to my heart.

"Oh, dear..." I can't finish the sentence.

Garath picks the little girl up in his arms and kisses her head, while looking at me.

"Beautiful, isn't she, Kate? So innocent. But it's a shame I need to separate from her now. I'll give her to one of my friends, and then I can calmly finish what I started with you."

And then he looks at me, curving his lips into a disgusting smile, full of cruelty, showing his teeth stained by cigarettes.

I close my eyes and once again, I quietly pray to God, pleading in the name of my life and the little girl's, reciting a passage from Psalm 142:

"I cry out to You, O God, O Lord, I ask for help; I beg You to assist me. I bring to You all my complaints and tell You all my problems. When I am about to give up, You know what I must do."

I believe in You, Lord!

And in the next instant, it's as if the world is about to be turned upside down. The deafening sound of gunshots shatters the silence that had overtaken the warehouse. Garath doesn't even get a chance to draw a weapon when the door is kicked in, and I see the man I love storming into the place armed, accompanied by Alex and a small army of FBI agents.

I can only gasp with relief and thank God for hearing my prayers, as tears of gratitude run down my face, and I no longer worry about the pain.

CHAPTER 37

ANDREW

"I already have access to all the street's security cameras, I just need a few more minutes to locate the suspect," says Hope, one of the agents specialized in image analysis.

"Okay, stay on the line," I tell her through the earpiece and refocus my attention on the trackers who are discussing among themselves while reconstructing the scene of what probably happened at the location where Kate was taken.

Everything is now cordoned off to prevent curious onlookers and preserve any potential evidence at the crime scene.

I feel my temples throbbing, and I bring my hand to the back of my neck. I pace back and forth, nervous and distressed, controlling myself as best as I can to keep my head. Staying calm now is crucial because I need to stay alert to any clue.

"You're going to find her. I've been where you are now. Nothing in the world can stop a man from finding his woman." My son-in-law's voice worms its way into my ears, and I take a deep breath, realizing he knows about my involvement with Kate.

And I don't deny it. There's no reason to when I never intend to let Kate slip from my sight again.

"How did you know?" I don't look at him when I ask, keeping my attention focused on the crime scene in front of me.

"No man would act this way for a woman who isn't his." I blink, my thoughts being carried away to her with all the strength I have.

I recall everything, every kiss, every touch. The smell, the voice. "Besides, you disappeared during the days Kate was traveling. I'm not an idiot, Andrew."

I stay silent for a few seconds, digesting it all, thinking about what my daughter must think of all this.

"Angelina. She..." I try to formulate a question, needing to understand if my daughter knows anything about her father sleeping with her best friend, but Alexander interrupts me: "No. She doesn't know yet."

I draw in a sharp breath, knowing what my next step will be after I recover Kate.

At that moment, Hope speaks again through the earpiece, and I focus all my attention on what she says: "Shit, all the street's cameras are down. I can't access the footage from the last two hours."

Damn it, I curse inwardly, almost losing my mind.

"Then check the cameras from the surrounding streets. Something will show up, Hope."

"Got it, boss."

Time passes, minutes, hours. Everything feels lost. The tension rises as we work to find evidence. Neighbors are interviewed, but it's as if the kidnapper and murderer passed unnoticed by everyone. No traces. No fingerprints. The murderer of my agent and kidnapper of Kate knew exactly what they were doing.

Everything seems too overwhelming, when one of the agents informs that a woman saw a minivan parked across the street from Kate's house the day before. No one got out of the vehicle, but they spent too much time in the same spot. I immediately contact Hope and ask her to map all the footage from the previous day.

Minutes later, she returns with what I need, including the license plate number and precise information about the vehicle. The van is registered to a renowned surgeon here in New York, which makes no sense since there are no records of the vehicle being stolen.

"And Andrew..." She calls me again after providing the information. "The cameras on the nearby streets recorded the moment the van moved toward this direction one hour before Kate's call to you, and ten minutes after the call ended, the vehicle returned the same way."

And bingo!

A spark of hope rises in my heart, and I inhale sharply, knowing I've finally found Kate. I cling to any chance, any opportunity to be right. I pray to God that the clues are accurate. I just need her to survive until I get there.

"Send a signal with all the monitoring data to the team, Hope."

I close and open my eyes, clenching my fists, knowing that every second counts to find the girl alive.

I don't need to look at Alex to make him understand the next steps. I head towards the car, and he follows me, armed to the teeth. Two of the best field trackers go ahead. We'll follow the data from the traffic and security cameras in case Kate was taken somewhere in the heart of New York City, but if she was taken outside the district, tracking may become slower and will need to be done manually with caution and speed.

Time is my worst enemy now, but I won't let it win.

I tear off at full speed while receiving monitoring alerts from Hope. The minutes pass, the hours, time doesn't stop, and with each passing second, I feel more desperate to find my little fox.

An hour later, we are leaving the city, heading north of New York along the Hudson River. The destination is still the Hudson Valley, a historic and rural region connecting New York to Albany. Everything is going smoothly until the monitoring is interrupted by a lack of images from the highway's security cameras, which means the van took an isolated route, probably a dirt road, and the tracking will now have to be done manually.

Hope sends the latest data showing a deviation from the main path, leading directly to a mountainous area. The tracking specialists take over, and I follow behind in silence. Alexander stays alert to every detail, showing his competence, which I admire despite his criminal history.

The minutes drag on, time flies as we head deeper into the forest until we approach the foot of the mountain. The path is winding, the snow is deep, and at one point it becomes narrower. Then the lead car stops, and the men get out to inspect the area. They signal that we should continue on foot from here and that we'll need to leave the road and enter the woods.

I follow the instructions, and the other agents join me, along with Alex. The darkness of the night makes it harder to see, so I equip myself with night vision goggles and a tactical flashlight with infrared light, invisible to the human eye. We enter the forest, following a rough trail, but wide enough for a minivan to pass.

The forest is silent, as if there are no birds or other animals nearby.

After a few minutes on the trail, we spot faint lights that seem to be coming from some kind of abandoned factory. There are other smaller buildings and some cars parked nearby, but my attention is focused on the lights.

Slowly, I approach the building, accompanied by the others.

Two of the men take the lead and test the entrance door, confirming that it's open.

I signal the other agents to spread out and check the surroundings, and I enter with Alex and the other two men.

Slowly, we pass through several metal shelves piled with what appears to be documents and hospital records. A deeper sense of unease takes over me, and I feel my body freeze as I advance. The place is well-lit, highly sanitized, and completely silent. With my gun in hand, I move a little to the left wing, passing by documents and even medical books.

And then I come across a room with glass walls, allowing me to see everything happening on the other side. I hide behind the shelves to avoid being noticed, and inside I see a man dressed in white, wearing a kind of lab coat and surgical cap. He's sanitizing a stretcher and some instruments.

What the hell is this?

It's like a direct shock to the brain. I'm breathless thinking about what he could have done to Kate. Everything inside me destabilizes, and suddenly a huge realization starts to make sense in my mind. I remember the girls found dead—each of them had Kate's features, the same build, the same age, the same characteristics. And they were found without their organs.

Shit! It can't be!

It feels like I'm living a never-ending nightmare, a vicious cycle that tortures me without mercy. I can't breathe properly, the price of loving a woman exacts its toll as I think about the slightest possibility of having lost her.

I analyze the situation carefully, noticing that everything is clean. I conclude that there hasn't been time to do whatever this madman does here; otherwise, she would still be on the stretcher, and there would be blood.

It's disturbing to realize that there's a counter near the wall, stacked with human organs, preserved in what looks like formaldehyde and stored in glass jars. There are hearts, lungs, brains, kidneys, a hand, and even a whole fetus. I regain control of my emotions and signal for the agents to set up an ambush.

I turn my attention back to the man, now separating scalpels and scissors on the counter beside him. He appears to be unarmed, as I don't see any weapons in my line of sight.

The federal agents use a simple tactic to capture the man. An object is dropped to the floor, making a discrete sound, but loud enough to grab the unknown man's attention, while all of them remain hidden in attack positions.

The man walks cautiously, scanning the area. I notice he's holding a knife and heading toward the documents room. As soon as he passes through the door, he's hit in the head by a blow from Alexander's gun.

"What the... fuck!" He falls to the ground, and the men rush to capture him. "Who are you? Let me go!"

His mouth is gagged, and his hands are handcuffed behind his back. Alexander holds him and forces him to stand up. He places him face-to-face with me.

Without waiting a single second, I press my gun to the man's forehead and stare into his eyes to extract the information I need, making it clear I won't hesitate:

"Don't make a sound or I'll shoot. I'll ask only once, and you have one second to answer, or your fate will be a fucking grave," I threaten, not giving a damn about the rules set by the law. "Where is the girl?"

The man's eyes widen, and I increase the pressure of the gun on his head. I grab the tape on his mouth and pull it off, freeing him to speak.

"Please don't shoot. I'll tell you where she is, but please..." He shuts his eyes, trembling with fear from head to toe. A real fucking coward. "She's in the third building after this one."

I signal to Alexander to hand the man over to the other agents, and I give one last order before heading out to find Kate.

"Interrogate him until you find out all the shit that's going on here."

And then I leave, followed by Alexander who walks right behind me, alert to any movement.

Outside, I meet up with another group of officers, and we head straight for a warehouse, the third building as the man had said. I lead the way, and the men follow me. Weapons ready, senses heightened. We're prepared for any confrontation that might occur.

"Shoot anything that moves," I order.

As we approach, we communicate with hand signals, and the officers surround the building. I hear voices and some laughter, followed by the sound of glass bottles clinking. Based on the tone of the voices and the shift in sound, I calculate that about seven men are gathered inside.

One of the agents returns to me and informs that there's a small window on the right side of the building, but Kate isn't visible. However, there's a door that leads to another room inside the warehouse.

I conclude that the best tactic now is to attack by surprise, not giving them a chance to arm themselves and retaliate. They won't expect an attack; they're probably confident that the evidence has been erased, like the last time when they murdered those girls. They've never been more wrong.

The men get ready, and I inform them that once we enter, my focus will be to break into the other room to get Kate.

Alexander prepares to enter. He counts to three and kicks down the wooden door with a precise strike, splitting the material in half with the force of the impact.

As planned, the men are caught off guard, with no time to even get up. And before they even think about reacting, the warehouse explodes in gunfire. The place turns into a real bloodbath, and several bodies hit the floor. Blood pours across the concrete, but I don't care about anything else. I run toward the second door and do the same as Alexander did with the first. I know I've crossed every line of power and broken all the laws of the United States, but the only thing that matters now is rescuing Kate alive.

The door bursts open with a crash, and I charge in. Everything happens too fast. In one second, I'm inside with my men, and in the next, I recognize Garath standing there, holding a girl in his arms. The son of a bitch practically throws the child to the floor and tries to pull a weapon, but Alexander moves toward him with impressive speed, not giving the man a chance to react, knocking him down with a punch. I hear Garath's screams and the girl's crying, but my attention is focused on Kate.

I scan the room until I lock eyes with her, completely alarmed and crying, looking in my direction.

"Kate!"

I feel like dying when I see her hanging and so badly hurt, her upper body bare, her arms tied above her head. Her eyes and mouth are swollen, and her beautiful face is smeared with blood. My little fox is so scared that her gaze reflects the pain and fear she felt in the last few hours.

"Andrew!" she screams.

As if my life depended on it, I close the distance between us while my men handle everything else. I take off my coat to cover her nakedness, grab a pocketknife from my holster, and cut the ropes that are holding her in the air while I hold her with my free arm.

Kate moans softly when her body practically collapses, and I catch her in my arms. She's limp from the injuries and the position she was bound in. Her face is drenched with thick tears as I wrap her in the warm fabric and kneel, holding her tight on the cold concrete floor.

It feels like my life is returning to my body as I feel her skin and hold her tightly in my arms. I bury my nose in her hair and inhale her scent, swearing to myself that I will never let her slip away from me again.

"Kate," I whisper her name, feeling my throat dry, my voice choked. "I'm so sorry, my love. I'm so sorry. I should have killed the bastard the moment I knew he existed."

"Andrew..." She hugs me back, trembling amidst her sobs. "I was so scared..." Her voice falters. "Thank you for coming."

"I would never leave you," I swallow hard.

Her hands slide to my shoulders, and Kate shivers from head to toe, clinging to me as if to make sure she's not dreaming.

"Please, Andrew, don't let him live. I couldn't bear it."

I close my eyes, knowing this is too difficult a request to fulfill, as it goes against every code of ethics in the FBI.

She leans her face against mine, and I feel her skin slide against mine—a touch so soft, so comforting that I close my eyes, feeling relief wash over me for finally having her with me.

"I love you, little fox," I declare, driven by the desperation of almost losing her.

She snuggles closer against my chest.

"I love you too," she says breathlessly, and I feel a tightness in my chest, a happiness so immense it consumes me and leaves me breathless. "Please forgive me. I didn't—"

"No, Kate, don't say anything." I kiss her face softly, careful not to hurt her skin any further.

"Take me home, Andrew." I caress her face with one hand and nod to her, but first, I need to do something that will end all this mess; otherwise, I'll never sleep again. I rise with her in my arms, and Kate clings to my neck, still trembling.

I look around the scene and take a deep breath, determined to do what needs to be done. Perhaps it's blasphemy to say this, but not always can God do the job alone.

The little girl who was in Garath's arms is now crying, clinging to an officer's neck, calling for her mother. As for Garath, he is officially handcuffed and kneeling on the ground, escorted by Alexander and two other agents.

"Officer Carter?" I call out, and Alexander looks in my direction, stepping forward, responding to the surname he adopted after leaving the mafia.

"Take care of her for me. I won't be long." I hand Kate over to him, signaling for the man to get my girl out of here, and walk towards Garath, rolling up my shirt sleeves.

The officers make way for me to pass, and the bastard lifts his head to look at me.

"You can't condemn me, little fed. You're not much different from me," he sneers, showing his yellow, taunting teeth. I clench my jaw as I stare him down. "She's so young, and you're old enough to be her father."

I crouch down, getting face-to-face with the bastard.

"How does it feel knowing you're going to rot in hell, Garath?"

The bastard's smile doesn't fade; he keeps looking at me with that cynical air, as if he couldn't care less about the end of his life.

"I'll break free, Fed, and I'll go after her again and again."

Taking a deep breath, I stand, and in response, land a kick directly to his mouth. The sound of teeth breaking is like music to my ears.

Garath lets out a grunt, falling backward. But I don't stop; I can't control the fury that has consumed me, making me want to kill him with my own hands.

I hit him with another kick to the face, again and again, as I hear him scream. I make sure not a single inch of his filthy face goes unscathed.

Panting, I step back for a moment to observe the damage. The man is sprawled on the ground, his face bloodied and bruised, but that infernal smile is still there.

"Let's see if you keep smiling when I'm done with you, Garath." I curl my lips into a smile filled with hatred.

None of the officers in the warehouse speak or protest. They know what I'm doing is against the law, but they also know that justice isn't always on the right side. I have full confidence in everyone here.

Without taking my eyes off Garath, I walk to the makeshift fireplace in the center of the structure and grab a burning piece of wood.

The man's eyes widen when he finally realizes the hell I'm about to unleash. Garath grunts and starts crawling on the floor like the true worm he is.

"You can't touch me, bastard. You know it's against the law!" He yells, but his screams don't stop me.

I feel my blood boiling in my veins, my entire body burning. It feels like I'm going to explode with rage.

"Strip him," I command, and two officers follow the order. They rip off Garath's clothes as the man screams for help, but no aid will come to him.

I look down at him, seeing him on the ground, beaten and handcuffed, as helpless as my Kate was.

"Hold him upright!" When the agents do so, I look deeply into Garath's eyes. "Don't be afraid. You're going to enjoy this."

Without waiting another second, I press the burning log against the bastard's groin. His screams echo, and the stench of burning flesh fills the air. The smell is vile, but I've never enjoyed something so foul so much.

"You bastard!" he grunts, and I press the wood harder, tearing through the flesh in the process. Blood drips from the wound as Garath gasps for air, struggling to breathe.

"I told you you'd like it!"

His eyes turn to me, furious, and I pull the wood from between his legs in one swift motion. The man groans, bleeding, humiliated, and naked in front of everyone.

"It's a shame I have to get my woman out of here, Garath, because I'd love to spend the entire night playing with you."

"You... will... pay for this." His voice falters, and his head falls back, almost losing consciousness.

But I don't let that happen before delivering the final blow. I draw the knife that had cut Kate's ropes and drive the sharp blade into the bastard's stomach.

His screams reverberate off the walls as I continue the task I set out to do.

Smiling, I keep slicing through the flesh with the cutting object, dragging the blade down to the gaping wound I made in his groin. Only then do I slit his throat.

"Release him!"

The man falls to the ground, his body convulsing. Blood spills from his mouth, his eyes widen as he struggles to breathe. I watch closely as every second of his final moments unfolds. I see him writhe and fight for air. I watch as his body gradually ceases to move and the life of the man who destroyed Kate drains away on the floor in the form of vital fluid, and he takes his last breath.

Garath is finally dead.

CHAPTER 38

ANDREW

Two of the men who were with Garath are still alive and handcuffed when I leave the compartment where Kate was held. Outside, Alexander is still holding the girl in his arms, keeping her protected from the cold. Both of them, along with a group of agents, are waiting for me.

One of them gives me precise information about what was happening here. I can hardly believe the web of crimes Garath was involved in. The dead girls had been chosen by him because they resembled Kate. They made it look like New York was being targeted by a serial killer to complicate the investigation, when in reality, it was a group of psychopaths involved in organ trafficking, and my Kate would be the next victim, purely out of revenge.

"It's time to go, darling. I'll take you to the hospital." I take her from his arms and press her face against my chest. "Thank you, Alex," I whisper, so only he can hear.

The man nods, and Kate clings to me, wrapping her arms around my neck.

"Where's the little girl?" she asks sleepily, her body paying the price for the injuries and terror she endured.

"She's fine. She'll be with her family soon and undergo some tests."

I walk with Kate towards the cars, leaving a few officers responsible for cleaning up this mess. The little girl is also taken, and Alexander follows me to take the driver's seat.

As soon as we get into the SUV, I place Kate in the back seat and fasten her seatbelt. I walk around and sit next to her, constantly holding her body against mine to keep her warm. After all, the cold is intense. The temperature drops to exorbitant levels as the night progresses.

"The Spot... He..." She asks about the dog, but I notice her voice faltering, unable to finish the sentence.

"He'll be fine, Kate," I lie to avoid tormenting the girl any further, even though I feel bad about it. But the truth is, I haven't heard anything about Spot yet. Maybe he will survive, maybe not. Thinking about it torments me, but all I can do is wait.

"Andrew..." She calls me again after a few minutes of silence.

I reach for her face and brush away some strands of hair that have fallen on her forehead.

"Yes, my love."

"Please, don't take me to the hospital. Take me home."

"Kate, you need to be examined."

"I'm fine." She inhales. "I just have some bruises on my face and my arms hurt a lot. But I'm fine. Please, take me home and stay with me. I just need you, Andrew."

After a few seconds, hesitant, I sigh and nod at her. I bring her body closer, being careful not to press on her sore wrists.

"Alright. I'll take you home and stay with you."

Hours later, Alexander stops the car in front of my house, and I see Angelina at the door, waiting for us, along with the children and John. I get out and walk around the SUV to pick Kate up in my arms, cradling her against me. Angelina comes towards us, her expression revealing the anxiety that has taken over her face.

"Daddy? Kate?" She touches Kate's face and strokes her skin. "Oh, dear, thank God you were found. When my husband told me what happened, I thought I was going to die from worry."

Tears slip from Angelina's eyes, and she sniffles quietly, sliding her fingers to reach Kate's hands, whose voice comes out strained: "I'll be fine, Angel," She is exhausted from the fatigue.

I enter the house with Kate, and my daughter follows me, along with her husband and children. As I approach the stairs, Angel stops me.

"Daddy, Alex sent a message asking me to fill the bathtub in his room." She raises an eyebrow when she looks at me, but says nothing more than necessary, and I thank her for that. "I've already prepared everything."

Then Alex himself holds Angelina by the waist and says something in her ear that I can't hear. She just nods and turns her attention back to me but makes no move to follow her friend upstairs.

"Thank you!" My daughter shakes her head in agreement, and I turn to go up the stairs. I carry Kate straight to my bedroom. I sit her down on the bed and remove the coat covering her small body. She's trembling, her eyes focused on every feature of my face. I notice her wrist is red, turning a purplish hue, and I gently caress it, feeling my heart ache for her. Tears run down her face, and I take both her hands to my lips and place a kiss on them.

In silence, I finish removing her clothes and examine every detail of her body for injuries. I sigh with relief when I find nothing but bruises on her face, neck, and arms. My little fox is frightened, and the fear will remain with her for a while, but she'll be fine. I know she will be.

Carefully, I pick Kate up again and carry her to the bathtub. I submerge her small body completely in the water.

"You're a brave little girl, you know?" I lean in to hold her chin.

"For a second, I really thought it was the end." She says quietly, without looking at me.

Kate looks at the white wall in front of her, thoughtful, as if remembering something.

"When I saw Garath with that little girl, it was like seeing myself right there in front of me. And I prayed so much. I called out to God with so much faith, like I hadn't done in so long." She looks back at me, her eyes spilling with tears. "And then you arrived. I knew that little girl would be saved. I've never felt such relief in my life."

My fingers brush against her skin as my gaze drifts down to her mouth. However, I need to hold back until Kate heals from her wounds.

"I'm dying to kiss you." She smiles through her tears and places her hand over mine.

"Get in the tub with me," she asks, almost pleading.

I do as she says, undressing while feeling the weight of her gaze. Kate doesn't flinch or shy away when I'm completely naked in front of her. On the contrary, she seems captivated, her eyes scanning my abdomen and lingering down to my growing arousal, as if my presence alone makes her forget the horrors she endured.

I step into the tub and pull her into my arms, positioning Kate so she's facing me, her head resting against my chest and her legs draped over mine. I bury my nose in her hair and breathe her in, feeling life pulse through my veins.

"After what happened today, I've come to the conclusion that I can't stay away, Kate." I hear her quiet sigh as she falls silent for a few minutes, her breathing unsteady.

My heart races, and my throat goes dry, fearing she'll reject me again. My shoulders tense with each passing second, not knowing what I'll do if she decides to pull away once more. The idea of having Kate out of my sight is entirely unbearable.

"I can't be without you either." I release the breath I didn't realize I was holding and gradually relax.

I place my hand on Kate's back and pull her onto my lap, her body settling against my pelvis. For a while, I ignore my arousal and focus only on the feel of her soft skin against mine. We remain entwined in the tub, savoring each other's warmth until the water begins to cool.

I carry Kate to the bed and lay down with her on top of me. Our bodies, still damp from the bath, press together, and my excitement grows with every delicious touch. I feel her entire body against mine, like a second skin.

Kate touches my chest and lifts her gaze to meet mine.

I feel anguish claw at me whenever I look at her beautiful face, marred by bruises. I have an overwhelming urge to hold her in my arms and never let go until she's healed. Though there's no more blood, the marks left by that bastard's hands are still there, staining her snow-white skin. I trail a finger along her mouth, gently brushing her swollen, bruised lip. My mouth waters with the desire to kiss her, so I lean in and graze my lips against hers lightly, careful not to hurt her.

"You're perfect. I'm the happiest man in the world to have you, Kate."

She plants another soft kiss on my lips, and I hear her breath hitch. Her hands slide down my abdomen and continue lower until they reach my hardened length. I let out a low moan as she closes her eyes, touching me gently.

"Kate, you're not making this easy for me."

I bring my hand to her neck, tangling my fingers in her dark hair.

"Please, make me forget everything, Andrew," she pleads, and I clench my jaw, consumed by the desire she ignites in me. "I want you inside me."

"Kate..." Damn, how do I explain that she's hurt and shouldn't strain herself?

"Please." She presses her lips to mine again, and I simply can't refuse her.

I sit up in bed, meeting her deep blue eyes that transport me to an endless ocean. "Tell me if I hurt you in any way."

I grip Kate's waist and pull her to me gently, careful with every touch. Leaning over her, I cover her body with mine, letting her feel me in every inch of her skin.

I begin kissing her neck, leaving wet kisses along her skin, and Kate gasps. She's restless, clutching my hair and squirming beneath me, always seeking my touch.

"Easy, little fox..." I nip at her neck and trail lower. I reach her breast and take it into my mouth, sucking and licking the sensitive peaks, leaving her gasping and shivering.

I continue downward, my hands caressing her thighs as I spread them apart. Leaning down, I let my tongue glide out and slowly lick her clit, making Kate groan.

"Andrew... please..." she murmurs, agitated and eager, wanting all of me.

Using two fingers, I part the soft folds of her sex and slip my tongue into her tight opening. Kate lets out a small cry and writhes more, tugging my hair with both hands. I take her into my mouth, my tongue exploring, licking, and kissing as if I'm desperate for her lips.

She bucks her hips, and I devour her like a man possessed.

After drenching her with my saliva, I position myself over her, sliding my length between her thighs. One hand cradles the back of her neck while the other strokes her face.

I begin to enter her while Kate keeps her eyes locked on mine. She lets out a soft cry, digging her nails into my chest, her brow furrowing as she bites her lower lip. I slide in all the way, moving slowly. I pull out and thrust back in without breaking eye contact, driven wild by her reactions and the moans escaping her throat. Kate gasps, completely surrendered to me. Her body moves in sync with mine as I rotate my hips, massaging every inch of her inner walls.

I rest my forehead against hers, my body still reeling from the fear of almost losing her. I look at this beautiful, perfect, and sweet woman and realize there's no life without Kate. From the moment she arrived in my home, I understood the meaning of having someone who completes you. Kate pulled me out of solitude without even realizing it. She was mine before either of us acknowledged it. She brought light to my empty days, even amidst the darkness surrounding her. I've loved her since the first time I held her in my arms and breathed in her scent. For the first time, I can say with certainty that I am happy.

"Marry me, Kate," I ask, and her eyes widen as she gasps.

I roll my hips again, massaging every nerve ending, pulling another moan from her lips.

"Andrew, I..."

"Say yes. Don't say no to me, little fox."

I pull out of her and thrust back in, going deep. Kate groans and throws her head back. I repeat the motion countless times, one after the other, until I feel her nails digging into my chest and her body starting to tremble.

I pause my movements and pull her close again, holding her neck.

"Marry me!" I demand, and she lifts her hips, seeking more friction.

"Andrew, don't stop!" she pleads, desperate for me to continue, but I'm determined to break through her hesitation.

"Kate!"

"Yes. I'll marry you," she practically shouts, writhing beneath me, desperate to climax.

I curve my lips into a victorious smile and thrust into her again, gripping her thighs tightly. Kate screams as the orgasm overtakes her. She clings to me as if her life depends on it, and I feel her tightening around me, her walls milking me with each contraction.

It's too much for me to hold back. I lean over her, burying my face in her neck, and release inside her. I give Kate every last drop of my seed, giving her all my love, my devotion, my body, and my soul.

KATE

I WAKE UP AT SOME POINT during the day after having slept in Andrew's arms throughout the night.

The sunlight streams through the window, but I am completely out of orbit. I have no idea what time it is, my body is sore, and my head is throbbing like never before. However, I have never been so happy to wake up alive.

I look around for Andrew, but I can't find him. I don't hear any sounds from the bathroom, which means he is probably downstairs. Everything is calm and quiet until I hear the first bark and the laughter of the children.

I jump out of bed, my heart racing so fast I can almost hear the frantic beats.

Spot!

Oh my God, my little dog is alive. Tears fill my eyes, but I don't let them fall. I don't want to cry anymore, not when all I can do is smile widely, my heart full of joy.

I rush to grab a robe, not even having time to use the bathroom or brush my teeth. I go downstairs like this, with messy hair, a wrinkled face, and probably completely bruised from all the marks on my skin.

I find everyone in the kitchen. Spot is in the arms of John, Angelina's eldest son, a handsome and well-mannered young man adopted by the couple, now sitting at the table. Caleb and Kaleo are next to John, petting Spot's little head. My heart tightens when I see the puppy bandaged up, but he looks so happy to be home that I end up smiling and sighing. Andrew, on the other hand, is making something on the stove while Angel and Alex are sitting at the table, chatting with him.

All faces turn toward me when they notice my presence. Caleb runs toward me, calling me Aunt Tate, and Kaleo starts crawling toward me as well. Spot becomes desperate, struggling to free himself and come to me, but John doesn't let him run, due to the injuries. Angelina and Alex get up, and I see the curve of a tearful smile appear on my friend's lips. And lastly, Andrew, my future husband.

Our gazes meet, and he breaks into an intense smile that destabilizes me from head to toe. After everything that happened yesterday, I could never have said no to him. The danger I faced at Garath's hands made me realize that being cowardly doesn't lead to happiness and doesn't bring peace. And my peace is by Andrew's side, the man I have learned to love with all my heart.

He takes a step toward me while removing the apron from his body. His smile widens, and Andrew pulls me by the waist, lifting me off the ground. I let out a squeal and laugh as he spins me around in the middle of the kitchen.

"Good morning, my love."

I feel my face flush with embarrassment when Andrew puts me back on the ground and hugs me tightly, his lips landing precisely on the curve of my neck, and I realize that we are both the center of everyone's gaze in the kitchen.

"Good morning, love," I reply, although I feel a little nervous about Angelina's presence. However, after yesterday, it's almost impossible for her not to suspect something. Andrew made everything very obvious when he took me to the bathtub in his room to give me a bath.

"Aunt Tate, are you my grandma now?" Caleb's question brings a smile to my face, and I nod in agreement to the little boy. "I guess so."

Then I turn my attention to Angelina. I notice a subtle smile appear on her lips, and she nods. Alexander does the same when I smile at him in thanks for everything he did for me. I walk toward John and take Spot from his arms, feeling my world finally getting back on track.

The little dog barks in my arms and starts licking my neck while wagging his tail, so happy to see me. It's too much for me to bear. Tears begin to fall from my eyes, and I hug my Spot, being careful not to hurt his injuries any further. I would probably earn the title of the world's most tearful woman if there was a competition, but these were tears of pure happiness.

When I calm down, I give Spot back to John and head back toward Angelina. My friend walks toward me with a subtle glow in her eyes and takes my hands in hers.

"I'm so happy that everything worked out," she says, and I nod. "Welcome to the family, Kate." My friend sighs, and I also notice that her eyes shine with unshed tears. "Dad deserves to be happy, and you're simply amazing." She wipes her eyes with the back of her hands without stopping to look at me. "I understand him, and I understand you. I admit I was caught by surprise, but now I only have to thank God that everything turned out well."

Then my friend hugs me tightly, and I return her affection, locking eyes with her.

"I love you, thank you," I murmur with a shaky voice.

"I love you too."

FINAL CHAPTER

ANDREW

TWO MONTHS LATER

I watch Kate finish getting ready while I sit on the bed, already dressed. She's wearing comfortable tailored pants and a fitted wool long-sleeve top. Her hair is loose, parted to the side, and light makeup enhances the natural beauty of her face. Facing the mirror, she puts on earrings and a bracelet on her right arm. She adjusts her hair one last time and turns her attention to me, smiling. She looks absolutely stunning.

I get up and walk toward Kate, pulling my fiancée into me. Her arms reach around my neck, and she places a quick kiss on my lips.

"Are you feeling okay?" I ask, concerned.

My wife has been experiencing constant nausea ever since we confirmed the pregnancy. Today she will have her first ultrasound to make sure everything is going well with her and the baby. And I'm just too nervous.

"I'm fine. The nausea passed."

"Are you sure?" I place my hand on her barely noticeable belly and gently caress it.

"Yes, I'm sure." Kate bites her lip and gazes at my mouth, making my cock stir with a simple movement.

"Don't look at me like that, Kate, we'll be late for the appointment." I sigh and slide a hand over her waist, squeezing her flesh over the top of her shirt.

"You look so good in a suit." She keeps teasing me, and I furrow my brows, more certain than ever that I've created a little sex-obsessed monster.

"And you're still all hot and bothered." I joke, reminding her that we just had sex a few minutes ago. However, my cock is already full of blood again, wanting her pussy around my shaft.

"You can't blame me, Andrew. It's the pregnancy hormones. You're the one who did this to me." She flashes a beautiful smile, and I raise an eyebrow.

"Me? Are you sure? I was quiet, babe. You're the one who asked to be fucked by me, remember?"

My mouth descends to Kate's lips, and she moans softly, responding to each of my movements.

"Do we need to go now?" she asks hoarsely.

"Yes, babe. I'm dying to see my baby inside your belly."

Kate pulls back just to look at me, and her smile widens.

"I'm so happy. I can't believe we're having a baby."

I take her left hand and bring it to my mouth to place a kiss on her engagement ring: "Believe me, darling, after all that making love, it would've been impossible for you not to be pregnant by now."

Kate tilts her head back and laughs, her cheeks turning a rosy shade: "You're such a fool, Andrew."

"And I love you."

HALF AN HOUR LATER, we arrive at the clinic where Kate will be seen. We fill out all the necessary paperwork, and in a few minutes, she is called in. The doctor, a cheerful, balding man, asks Kate a few questions, evaluating her health history. He requests some tests and directs her to the ultrasound room.

The room is a bit cold, but it's well-lit and equipped with high-tech, state-of-the-art machinery. The smell of alcohol and cleaning products fills the air. An assistant leads Kate to a private changing room, and within a few minutes, she returns wearing a gown, ready for the exam.

"Make yourselves comfortable. The doctor will be in shortly to perform the ultrasound." The woman gestures for Kate to lie down on the exam table and exits the room.

We are left alone, and I sit in the chair provided for companions. I hold her hand and gently stroke it.

"Are you nervous?" I hear her take a deep breath.

Kate nods at me and fixes her gaze on the empty ceiling, as if trying to avoid looking at the monitor beside her at all costs. "A little. I'm scared."

"What are you afraid of?" I try to sound confident, but I feel a knot in my stomach.

"I don't know. My life is so calm and... I'm so happy, Andrew. But what if something's wrong with the baby? What if the pregnancy isn't going well?"

"Everything will be fine, love. You'll see."

I don't tell her that I share the same fears, that the anxiety takes hold of me whenever I stop to think about it. But I know it's just worry. I want this child as much as Kate does, so it's natural to be afraid of losing something we haven't even seen yet but already love with all our hearts.

"You're right." She smiles. "Everything will be fine."

At that moment, the doctor enters the room and continues with the examination.

He applies the cold gel to Kate's belly to help transmit the sound waves, and she shudders slightly. The sound of the monitor fills the room, a faint buzzing that seems to intensify the tension in the air. The man starts moving the transducer over Kate's skin, his eyes fixed on the screen as grainy images begin to appear.

The silence lasts longer than expected. The doctor furrows his brow, concentrating, and Kate, sensing the change in the atmosphere, squeezes my hand tighter. I can feel the fear growing within me, and I know she's feeling the same. Everything inside me is in turmoil, my hands sweat from the tension, my throat feels dry.

"What's happening, doctor?" My voice comes out more anxious than I intend.

He doesn't respond immediately and continues examining the screen. Time seems to stretch on endlessly, the silence overwhelming. Kate starts breathing faster, and I can feel the apprehension taking over her body.

"Please, tell us something," she practically begs, her voice trembling.

The doctor takes a deep breath, and for a moment, I think he's about to give us the worst news of our lives. But then he looks at Kate and then at me, a slight smile on his lips, his eyes shining in a way I wasn't expecting.

"Congratulations," he says slowly, allowing us to process the information. "You're having twins."

I feel as if I've just been shocked.

"Twins... What?" I stammer, unable to believe what I've just heard.

"You're having twins," he repeats, now grinning widely.

Kate looks at me, her eyes wide, tears beginning to form.

"Are you serious?" she whispers, looking back at the doctor.

"Yes," he confirms, moving the transducer again to show us the two tiny shapes on the screen. Two hearts beating perfectly.

As I look at the tiny lives on the monitor, I feel Kate's hand loosen from mine. She doesn't even care about cleaning herself up. The girl gets off the table, and I do the same, ready to embrace her in my arms, completely overwhelmed by the love and emotion I'm feeling.

LATER IN OUR BED, I hear her sigh softly with an intense smile on her lips. Our bodies are sweaty after sex, and Kate is on top of me, my cock still buried inside her pussy.

Her beautiful eyes seek mine as she slides her fingers through the hair on my chest.

"If this is a dream, please don't wake me up," she says, smiling.

"I'll never wake you up, little fox."

She moves on top of me, and I slide my hands over her back and ass, pulling her body closer.

"I think I need a shower now," she says, and I shake my head.

"If you take a shower after every time we have sex, there won't be a drop of water left in this house."

Kate laughs and leans back, sitting up with one leg on either side of my hips.

My eyes trail down to her small breasts, starting to swell from pregnancy, and I wet my lips with my tongue. I continue my exploration, moving down to her flat stomach and then to her thighs. She notices when my gaze focuses between her legs and spreads them wider, teasing me, allowing me to see her swollen lips encasing my cock. Her clit is engorged and sensitive, all red after coming twice. My mouth waters.

I moan softly, feeling my cock harden again, and Kate grinds her hips.

I go crazy as she moves up and down on half of my length, our sexes still slick from the last orgasm.

But then, something completely unexpected happens. My phone rings on the nightstand. I hesitate to answer, and the call goes to voicemail, only to ring again a moment later.

Frustrated, I watch Kate get up, withdrawing my cock from her body. She picks up the phone and hands it to me.

"You better answer it. It could be important," she comments. "I'll take the chance to shower."

I bite my lip, feeling the frustration overwhelm me. But when I glance at the phone screen, I see it's an official call from the state of California.

I watch as Kate enters the bathroom and answer the call. What I hear next makes a suffocating lump form in my throat, and I swallow hard.

I end the call with a bitter taste in my mouth. A sense of relief and apprehension washes over me because I have no idea how Kate will react to the news. I place the phone on the bed, put on some boxers and comfortable pants, and wait for her.

A few minutes later, Kate returns to the room wrapped in a robe, her hair covered by a towel. As she looks at me, her expression changes, because I can't even begin to hide how troubled I feel.

"Did something happen?" she asks, approaching.

"Love, come here." I gesture for her to sit on the bed beside me, and Kate does.

Her worried expression gives me butterflies in my stomach, but there's no point in delaying or hiding the news I just received. She has the right to know as soon as possible and decide what to do.

"Andrew, please. You're scaring me," she whispers.

I place a hand on her face and lean in to kiss her forehead.

"I just got a call from California," I begin, and she continues to look at me, waiting for me to elaborate. I feel her breathing quicken, and I see the fear in her eyes. "Darling, Nellie was found dead this afternoon. She took her own life."

Kate gasps, pulling air into her lungs sharply, and averts her gaze from mine. I notice the change in her expression, the anguish that overtakes her as she remembers her mother.

"I hope she finds peace," she says without looking at me, her breathing uneven.

"Do you plan to attend the funeral?"

Her attention remains fixed on the void in front of her, and she shakes her head.

"No..." A single tear rolls down her cheek, and my wife sighs softly. "I can't go back to that place. Nor... give a second chance to someone who never gave me a first."

Without a second's hesitation, I pull Kate into my arms and hold her tightly, conveying all my love and protection. I make her understand that she will never be alone again, that she will always have me, Angelina, and our babies.

"Don't worry, love. I'll take care of everything."

KATE

FIVE MONTHS LATER

"YOU LOOK ABSOLUTELY stunning," Angelina says, emotional as she sees me dressed as a bride.

I look at myself in the mirror and can hardly believe how beautiful I am in a white dress that accentuates my seven-month-pregnant belly. The skirt flares gently at my feet, and the off-the-shoulder sleeves, adorned with lace details, leave my shoulders exposed. The makeup is subtle, perfect for an afternoon wedding at a countryside estate. My dark hair is styled in waves, and a crown of delicate blue flowers rests on my head, supporting the tulle veil cascading down my back.

"Oh, Kate, please don't cry, or you'll ruin the makeup."

I fan my face with both hands to keep the tears from falling, and Angelina steps closer, holding me by the shoulders.

"You are the most beautiful bride I've ever seen," she says with a wide smile. "How do you feel?"

"Aside from being hugely pregnant, extremely hormonal, and about to get married, I'm totally calm."

Angel laughs openly and brushes a strand of hair from her face, tucking it behind her ear. She looks stunning too, in a pastel-colored dress that perfectly hugs her figure and highlights her adorable five-month baby bump. Her hair is styled in a loose bun, with a few strands framing her face, and her eye makeup is striking.

"Don't forget, you still have the book signing tomorrow before your trip."

I blink slowly, trying not to panic as I think about how much my life has changed in the last five months. In that time, I stepped out of anonymity and claimed my titles under my real name. My latest book was a massive success, and I was even invited to join a prestigious publishing house in the United States.

To top it off, the signing event for the physical book release is scheduled for the day after my wedding to Andrew. And now I have to handle it all, because as soon as the last copy is signed tomorrow, my husband and I will head off on a quick honeymoon to rest a bit before the twins are born. We'll spend two weeks in Brazil.

"Are you ready?" my friend asks, and I nod. "Let's go; it's time."

Angelina strokes my belly, and I feel a little kick on the left side, which brings a huge smile to both of our faces.

"Oh my God, she can't wait to meet you," she says.

I do the same for her, placing my hand on Angelina's belly and gently caressing the barely noticeable bump that carries a baby girl, the niece of my twins.

Once again, I have to hold back tears to avoid ruining my makeup. I feel happy for her and for myself. I feel complete because now I have everything I ever dreamed of. A loving future husband, true friends, an amazing dog, a dream career, and two babies on the way. It's so much more than anyone could ever ask of God.

My friend places a bouquet of fresh flowers in my hands and holds my other hand. Together, we walk the stone path leading to the ceremony site.

The sky is painted in warm hues of orange and pink, and a gentle breeze sways the wildflowers adorning the wooden arch ahead of me. The few guests are silent and smiling in my direction, admiring the details. The soft music, played by a small string orchestra hidden among the trees, floats through the air, helping me relax a bit.

And standing there, beside the priest who will officiate the ceremony, is Andrew Thompson, my future husband and the father of my babies. The only man I've ever loved in my life.

He smiles at me, and I have to resist the urge to hurry my steps and throw myself into his arms. Angelina walks beside me, holding my hand, and I focus on not letting a single tear escape my eyes.

I hear Spot's bark as I pass by him. The little dog is sitting beside Alex and the kids. Everything is perfect. The setting, the people, the atmosphere.

As I approach the altar, Andrew walks toward me, and I feel his trembling hand take mine. Angelina steps aside, officially handing me over to her father. He takes control, offering me his arm, and together we walk to the altar. Before we kneel before the priest, Andrew cups my face with both hands and plants a tender kiss on my forehead as I stroke my belly.

"There's no turning back now, little fox. You'll be in my arms forever."

I smile, overcome with emotion, and gaze into the intense eyes I love so much. Andrew's irises glisten with unshed tears, just like mine.

Our hands intertwine, trembling slightly, and our hearts beat in sync. The weight of the words about to be spoken and the meaning of the commitment about to be made feels so intense and real that it's almost as if the universe is waiting alongside us. It's a moment filled with hope, love, and new beginnings. I know, and Andrew knows too, that no matter what the future holds, this moment will always be a beacon of light and truth in our lives.

EPILOGUE

KATE

FIVE YEARS LATER

Through the window of my room, I watch my children playing in the garden with their father and Spot as they wait for me. We planned a family trip to the park later this afternoon since it's Saturday and my husband worked tirelessly all week.

I can't stop smiling at the scene in front of me. It's simply magical to watch Henry and Royce running across the lawn, throwing the ball for Spot to fetch.

I finish getting ready, slipping on flats and tying my hair into a ponytail. My hair is much longer now, and I'm dying to cut it, but Andrew loves it this way. Whenever he comes home, finding me waiting for him in the living room, his fingers instinctively release my tied-up hair. He says I look like a goddess when I'm lying naked in bed, my hair spread across the sheets.

I grab my bag with essentials and a change of clothes for the boys because you never know what two almost-five-year-olds and a dog might get into outside. In just a month, Henry and Royce will turn five. Five years since my best decision ever.

As I lock the door to my room and descend the stairs, an odd sensation suddenly grips my chest. I place a hand over the spot, massaging it, trying to catch my breath. I can't explain what's happening. It feels like nostalgia for something I've never had or experienced. Strangely, the feeling fades as quickly as it came, but I can remember it vividly. It's like a tightness in my heart.

I take a deep breath and step outside. Walking toward the men in my life, I wave at them. The boys come running to me, Spot trailing behind them, and Andrew follows with a bright smile.

They both hug me at once, leaving dirt and grass stains on my clothes with their tiny, messy hands, but I don't mind. I pull out some wet wipes from my bag and clean the little hands I love so much.

"Mom, hurry up! We're late." I can't hide my smile when Royce speaks. They're so clever and sharp they've given me more than a few gray hairs in the last few years. Henry is crazy about cars and loves hot chocolate. He's slightly calmer than his brother. Royce, on the other hand, loves football and is always up to something. Sleeping is his least favorite activity in the world.

I stroke their hair, grinning like the proud mom I am. They're identical, with dark hair and fair skin like mine, but their eyes and facial expressions are carbon copies of their father's.

Even Spot comes over, wagging his tail against my legs.

Andrew laughs at the scene and joins us, pulling me close for a kiss.

"That's gross," Henry grimaces at the sight of my husband kissing me, and Andrew runs a hand along my neck. He presses our foreheads together, smiling and shaking his head lightly.

"Alright, kids. Let's go." My husband steps back and signals for the boys to head toward the car.

They obey without needing a second prompt, Spot always following close behind.

Then he turns back to me, sliding his hand around my waist. His experienced lips claim mine in a quick kiss that leaves me momentarily breathless, yearning for more.

"You look beautiful," he compliments me, as he does every day.

I smile against his lips, resting a hand on his firm chest, feeling his muscles tense under my touch.

"You too, Mr. Federal Agent. You're looking quite dashing, dressed like a businessman to play at the park with the kids."

Andrew grins, his hand sliding into mine as we walk toward the car together.

The drive to Central Park in the heart of Manhattan takes a while due to traffic. When we arrive, Andrew drops me off with the kids and Spot at *The Mall and Literary Walk*, a wide avenue lined with majestic elm trees that leads to an area with statues of famous writers, while he parks the car.

Holding Spot's leash, I walk with the boys among the trees. They squeal and laugh, chasing each other and using the thick trunks as hiding spots. Spot starts barking, eager to join the chase, leaving me no choice but to follow their steps and join in the fun.

When they finally tire of playing, I'm completely out of breath and drenched in sweat, feeling like my heart will burst out of my chest.

Spot is still full of energy, as are Henry and Royce. The game resumes, but I can't take another step without risking collapse. So I unclip Spot's leash and let him roam freely with the boys.

That's when I see something that completely derails me. I blink a few times, unsure if I'm dreaming or imagining things.

A little girl approaches the boys, also walking a dog, but hers is a tricolor beagle with large floppy ears—absolutely adorable. Her laughter fills my ears as her dog interacts with the boys, and soon the five of them are running among the trees.

Slowly, I walk closer until I get a better look at her.

Her dark hair falls loose to her waist, her skin as pale as snow. But what strikes me the most are her eyes. They are identical to mine—the same shade, the same intensity, the same impression they leave on people.

When Royce notices me watching the girl, he takes her hand and pulls her toward me.

"Mom, look! I made a new friend, and she looks just like you." I try to smile, but it fades as the girl approaches, and I take in the striking resemblance.

My God! Could it be her?

"Hi, sweetheart. How old are you?" I ask, my voice trembling. The little girl looks back at me as if something about me fascinates her.

"I'm six, and I live nearby." She extends her hand politely, as sharp and confident as the boys.

The same age as my daughter. Hannah would be exactly six years and six months now.

I feel like I can't breathe.

I curve my lips into a smile, shaking her tiny hand, though I'm crumbling inside. Agitation and desperation bubble within me, as if destiny has just dealt me a devastating blow. That's when I notice a woman, perhaps in her mid-thirties, approaching the girl. Her skin is a warm, caramel tone, and her long curly hair cascades just below her shoulders. Her almond-colored eyes are kind, strikingly beautiful.

"Sweetheart, I finally found you. Where did you go?" she asks, crouching to adjust the girl's dress collar.

I notice the little girl is wearing a pendant around her neck, but I can't make out if it's the locket that once belonged to my family. Perhaps I'm imagining things, and her age is just a coincidence.

"Sorry, Mommy. I met some new friends and then talked to their mom."

"Oh, my love, don't do that. I nearly lost my mind looking for you." The woman turns her attention to me and smiles, extending her hand. "Hello, how are you?"

I accept her handshake, forcing a polite smile. "I'm Lilian, and this is my lovely daughter, Hannah. We just moved here from California."

And it feels like my heart stops beating. The world spins around me, my vision blurs. Everything inside me falters when I hear the girl's name come from the woman's lips.

Hannah. My Hannah. There's no doubt anymore.

"Are you okay?" she asks, and I blink a few times, trying to regain my composure.

"Oh, I'm sorry. I think it's the heat. I feel a bit out of breath," I explain, smiling at her. Despite the ache in my chest, watching the little girl play happily with my boys brings me a strange sense of peace. "I'm Kate. It's a pleasure to meet you both."

The woman smiles again, signaling that she's about to leave.

"Well, Kate, we'll see you around." She waves goodbye and turns to walk away.

"See you," I respond, almost in a whisper.

Then I watch as she approaches the little girl again. She kneels to embrace Hannah, who kisses her cheek. They walk away hand in hand, chatting and laughing, oblivious to everything happening around them. Oblivious to me. But I could let myself break down now. I could cry and run after them, shouting that Hannah is mine and that I want her back. But it wouldn't be fair to either of them. They love each other, and Hannah is happy. Knowing that makes me happy, too.

And that's why, when I notice my husband approaching, I wipe away the tears threatening to spill from my eyes and run to Andrew. I embrace him and kiss him, pouring all my love into that moment. Just as I am happy with the family I chose for my life, I know that Hannah is happy with hers, and that is enough for me.

The End

Did you love *Her Desperate Request*? Then you should read *The Good Girl's Reckoning*[1] by Nora Kensington!

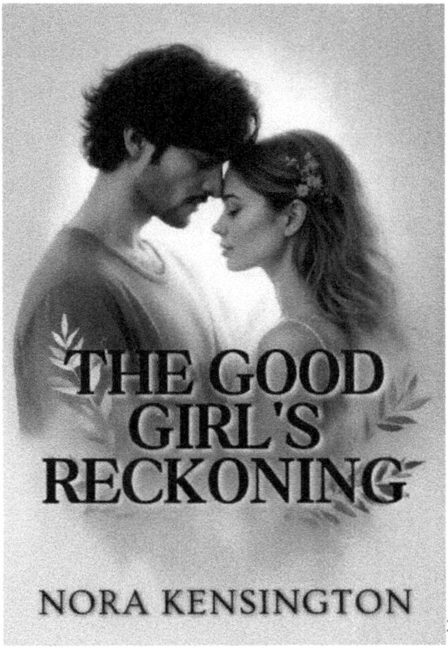

[2]

The Good Girl's Reckoning

Ana Luísa spent her life following the rules. She was the **"good girl"** who never stepped out of line, always striving to meet her parents' high expectations. But perfection comes at a price: a **suffocating job**, a **lifeless engagement**, and a crippling **anxiety diagnosis**.

When she discovers her fiancé cheating, Ana does the unthinkable—she walks away from everything and escapes to her hometown, seeking solace in her best friend's **empty apartment**. Except it's not so empty.

---

1. https://books2read.com/u/3yJ6pe

2. https://books2read.com/u/3yJ6pe

Enter Miguel: six-foot-three of pure, **infuriating charisma**. He's her first love, the older man who shattered her teenage heart, and the one person she swore never to forgive. Now, they're stuck under the **same roof**, forced into an uneasy truce.

Miguel is everything Ana should avoid—**arrogant**, maddening, and far too tempting. But as old feelings resurface and their shared past collides with an **undeniable spark**, Ana must confront the truth: breaking the rules might be exactly what sets her free.

Perfect for fans of steamy, second-chance romance with sizzling chemistry and emotional depth, *The Good Girl's Reckoning* will sweep you off your feet and leave you begging for more.

Also by Nora Kensington

Rogue Negotiations
Blame It on the Boss
Secrets Beneath the Vows
Faded Colors of Us
Waiting for You to See Me
Bound by Fire and Fuel
The Good Girl's Reckoning
Her Desperate Request

About the Author

Nora Kensington is an author known for her captivating blend of romance, suspense, and adventure. With a flair for crafting complex characters and heart-pounding plot twists, her novels transport readers into worlds filled with passion, danger, and emotional depth. Drawing inspiration from both everyday life and her love of classic literature, Nora weaves stories that explore the intricacies of love, courage, and resilience.

Milton Keynes UK
Ingram Content Group UK Ltd.
UKHW041949291124
451915UK00001B/68

9 798230 476108